THE MINDBENDING MINECRAFT
GRAPHIC NOVEL ADVENTURE!

GOING
VIRAL

Published in 2022 by Welbeck Editions
An Imprint of Welbeck Children's Limited,
part of Welbeck Publishing Group.
Based in London and Sydney.
www.welbeckpublishing.com

First published in 2019 and 2020 by Carlton Books Limited

ISBN 978 1 83935 188 4
Printed in Dongguan, China

MIX
Paper from responsible sources
FSC® C144853
FSC www.fsc.org

10 9 8 7 6 5 4 3 2 1

Creator: David Zoellner
Script: Eddie Robson
Special Consultant: Beau Chance
Design: Darren Jordan/Rockjaw Creative
Design Manager: Matt Drew
Editorial Manager: Joff Brown
Production: Melanie Robertson

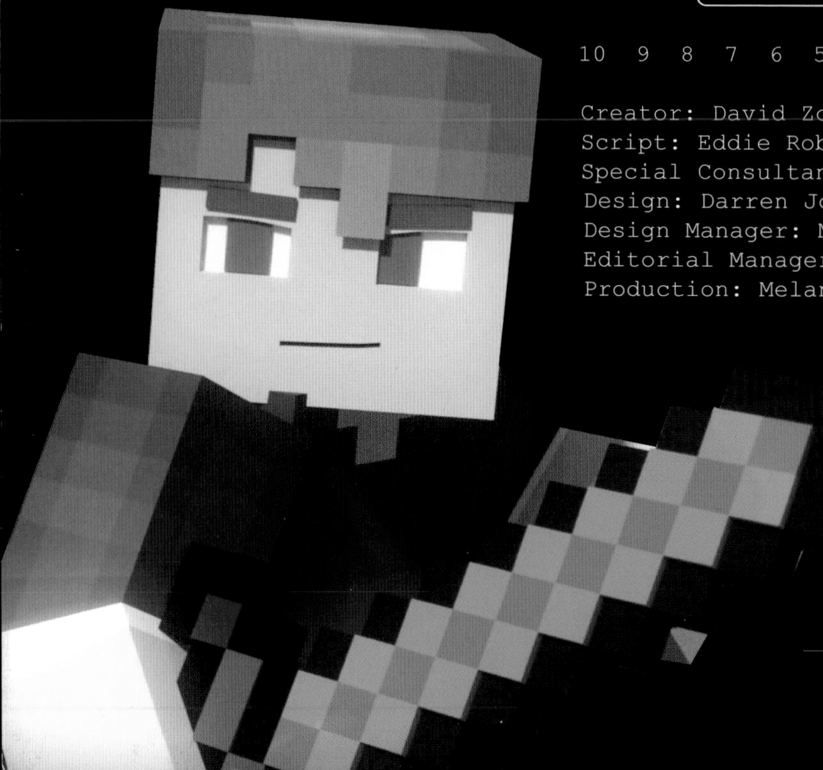

INDEPENDENT AND UNOFFICIAL

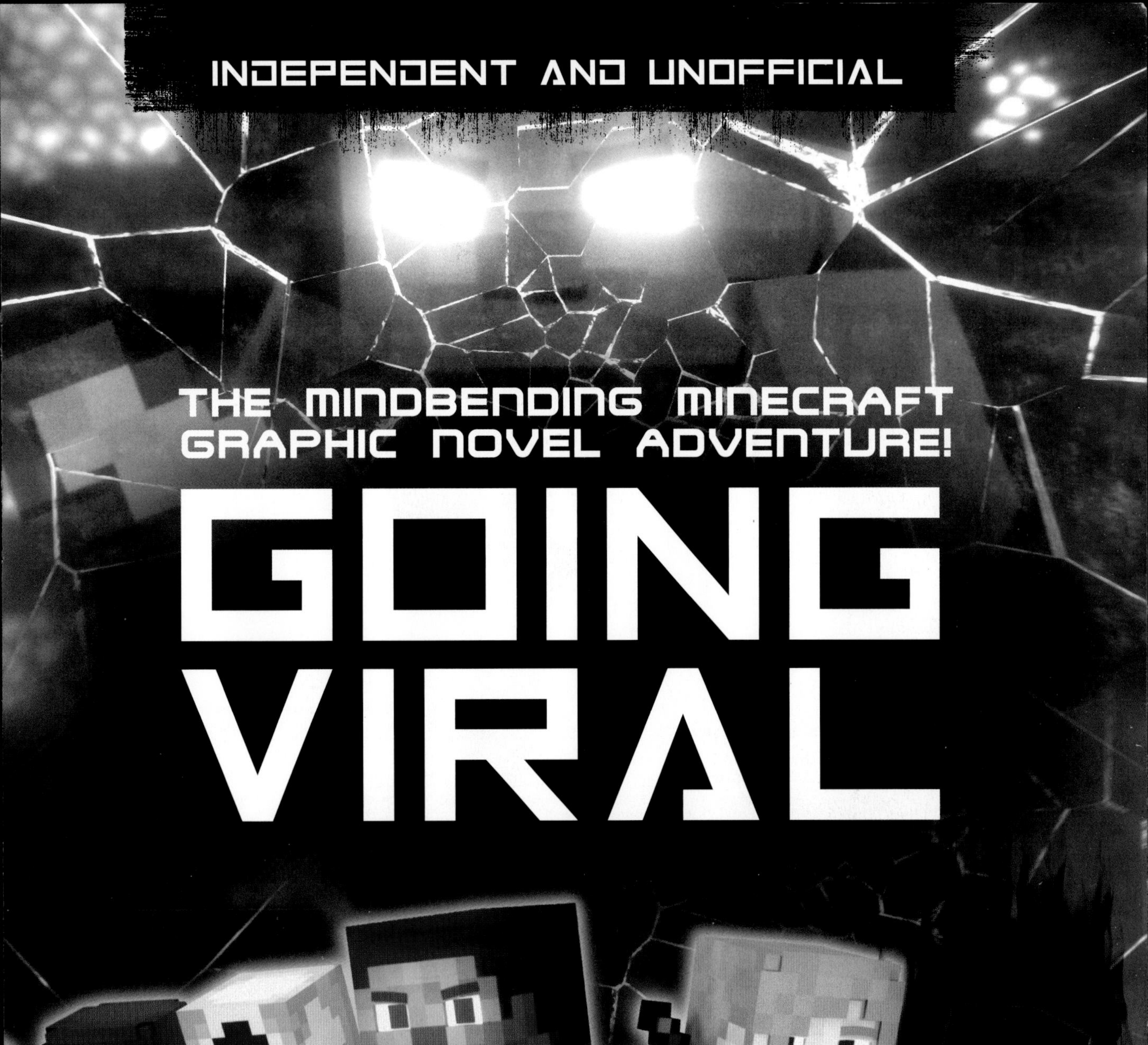

THE MINDBENDING MINECRAFT GRAPHIC NOVEL ADVENTURE!

GOING VIRAL

MORTIMER

ABOUT THE CREATOR

DAVID ZOELLNER, BETTER KNOWN AS ARBITER 617, IS THE DRIVING FORCE BEHIND BLACK PLASMA STUDIOS, THE BLOCKBUSTER INTERNET ANIMATION POWERHOUSE WHICH HAS CREATED VIDEOS WITH OVER 32 MILLION VIEWS. HE LIVES IN THE USA.

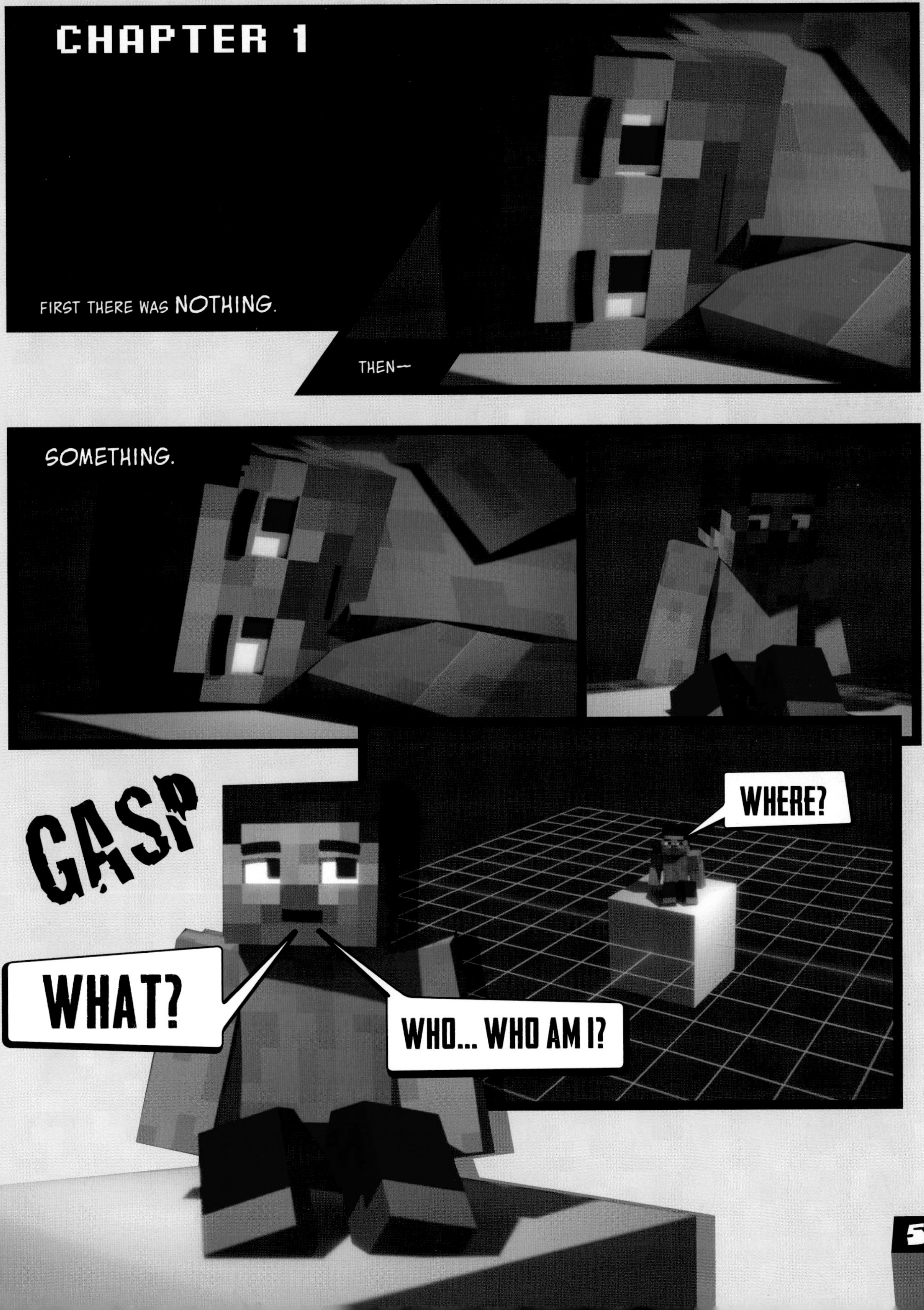
CHAPTER 1
FIRST THERE WAS NOTHING.
THEN—
SOMETHING.
GASP
WHAT?
WHO... WHO AM I?
WHERE?

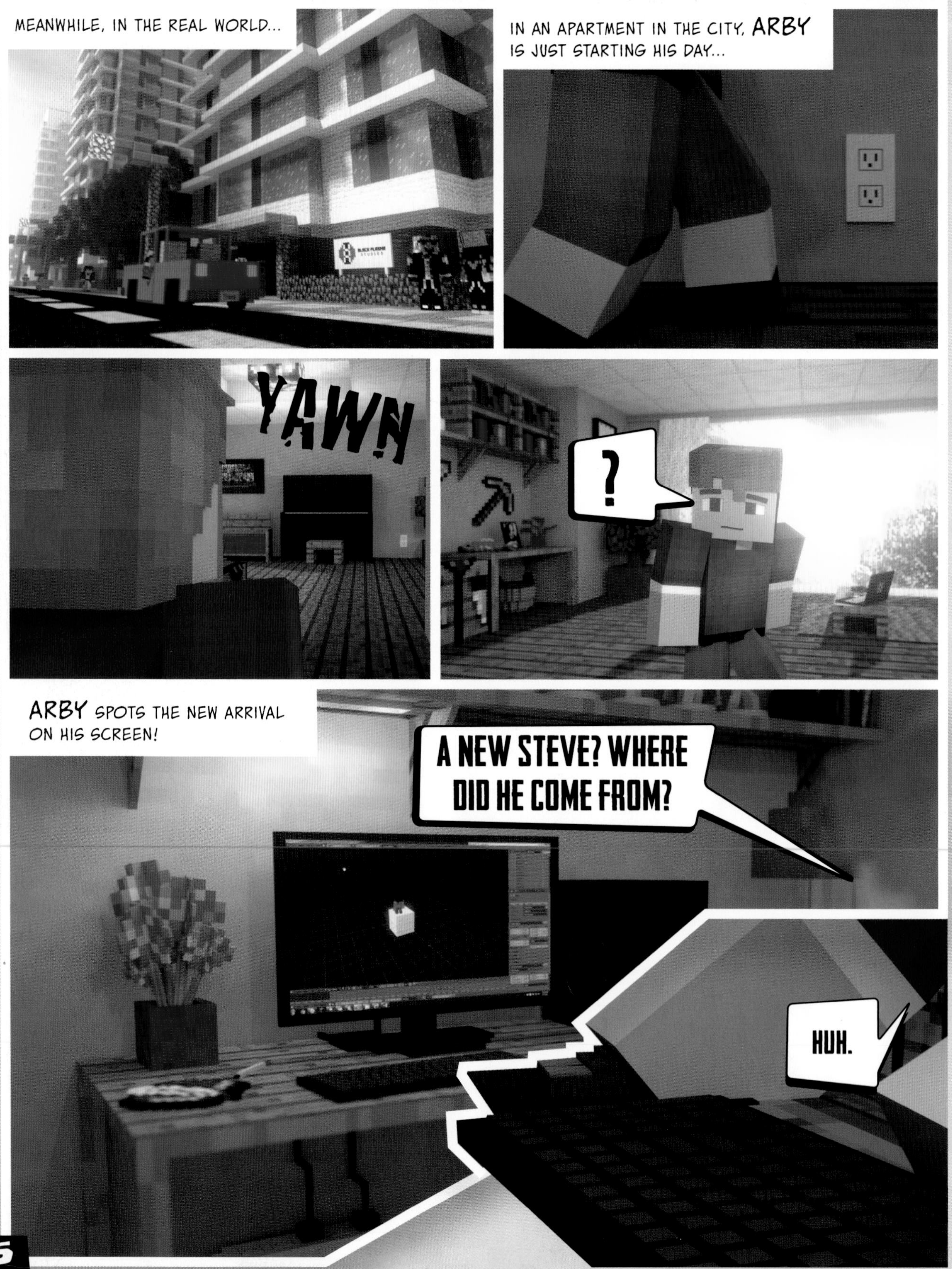
MEANWHILE, IN THE REAL WORLD...
IN AN APARTMENT IN THE CITY, ARBY IS JUST STARTING HIS DAY...
YAWN
?
ARBY SPOTS THE NEW ARRIVAL ON HIS SCREEN!
A NEW STEVE? WHERE DID HE COME FROM?
HUH.

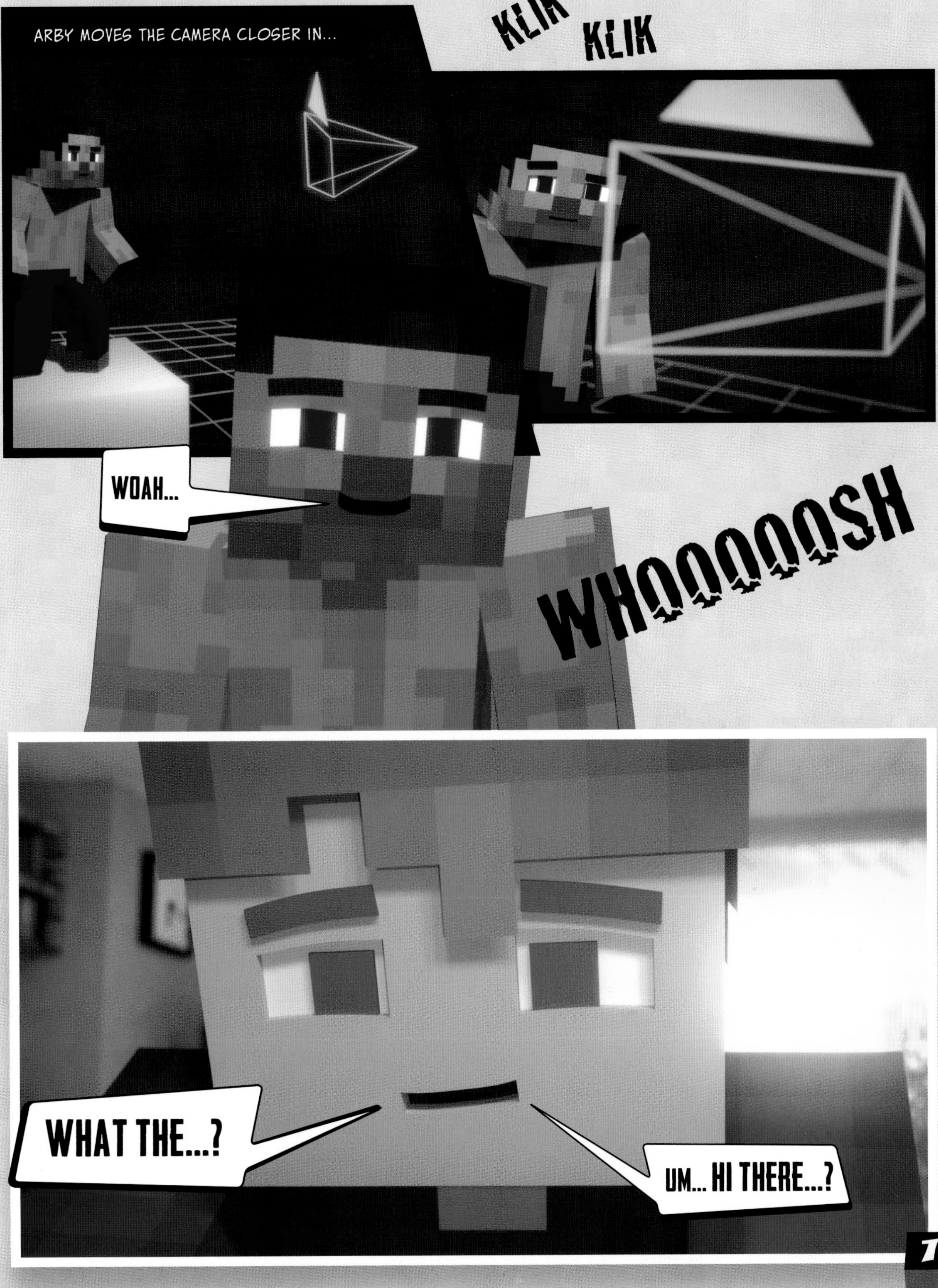
ARBY MOVES THE CAMERA CLOSER IN...
KLIK
KLIK
WOAH...
WHOOOOOOSH
WHAT THE...?
UM... HI THERE...?

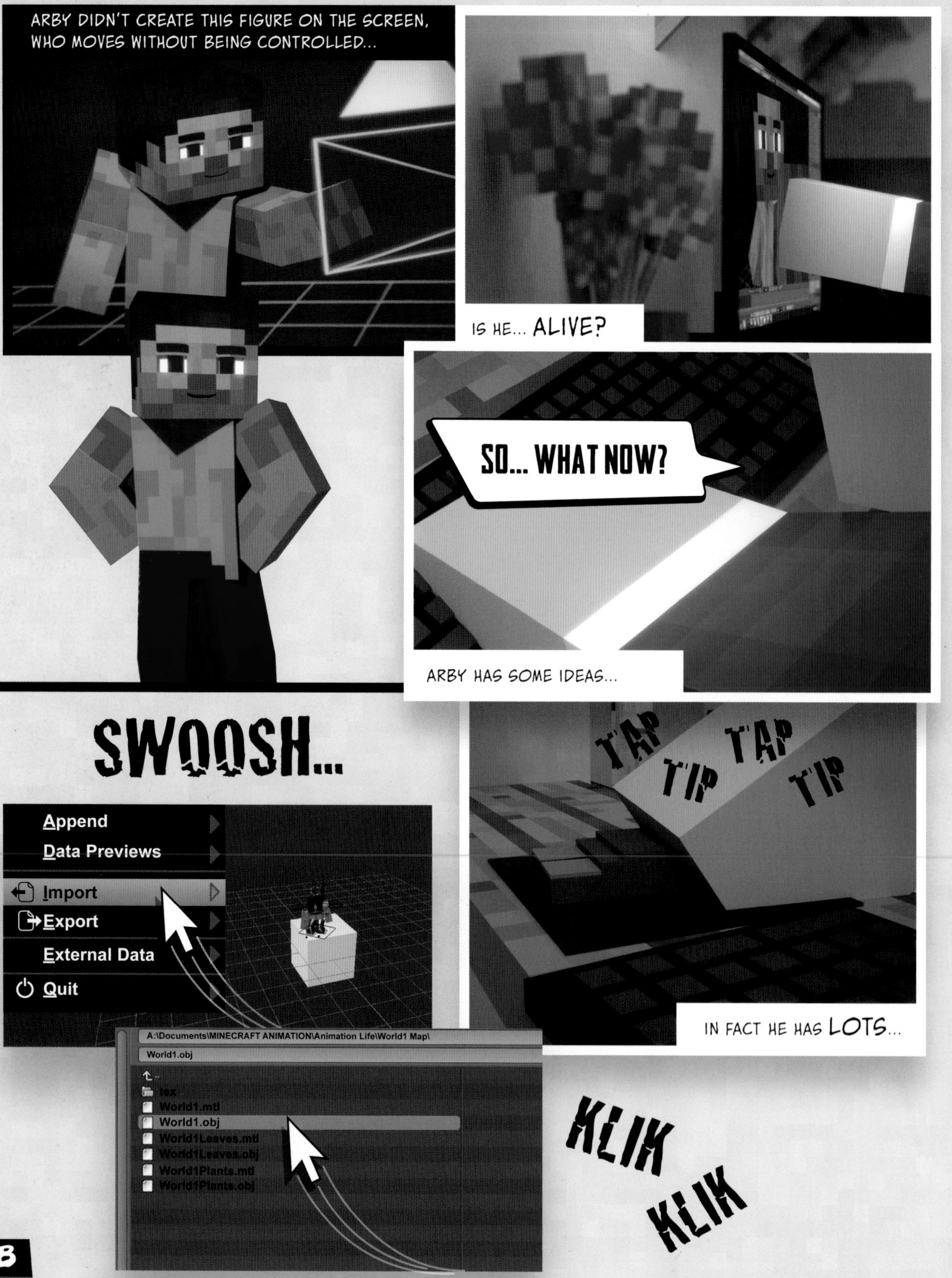
ARBY DIDN'T CREATE THIS FIGURE ON THE SCREEN, WHO MOVES WITHOUT BEING CONTROLLED...
IS HE... ALIVE?
SO... WHAT NOW?
ARBY HAS SOME IDEAS...
SWOOSH...
TAP TIP TAP TIP
IN FACT HE HAS LOTS...
Append
Data Previews
Import
Export
External Data
Quit
A:\Documents\MINECRAFT ANIMATION\Animation Life\World1 Map\
World1.obj
tex
World1.mtl
World1.obj
World1Leaves.mtl
World1Leaves.obj
World1Plants.mtl
World1Plants.obj
KLIK
KLIK

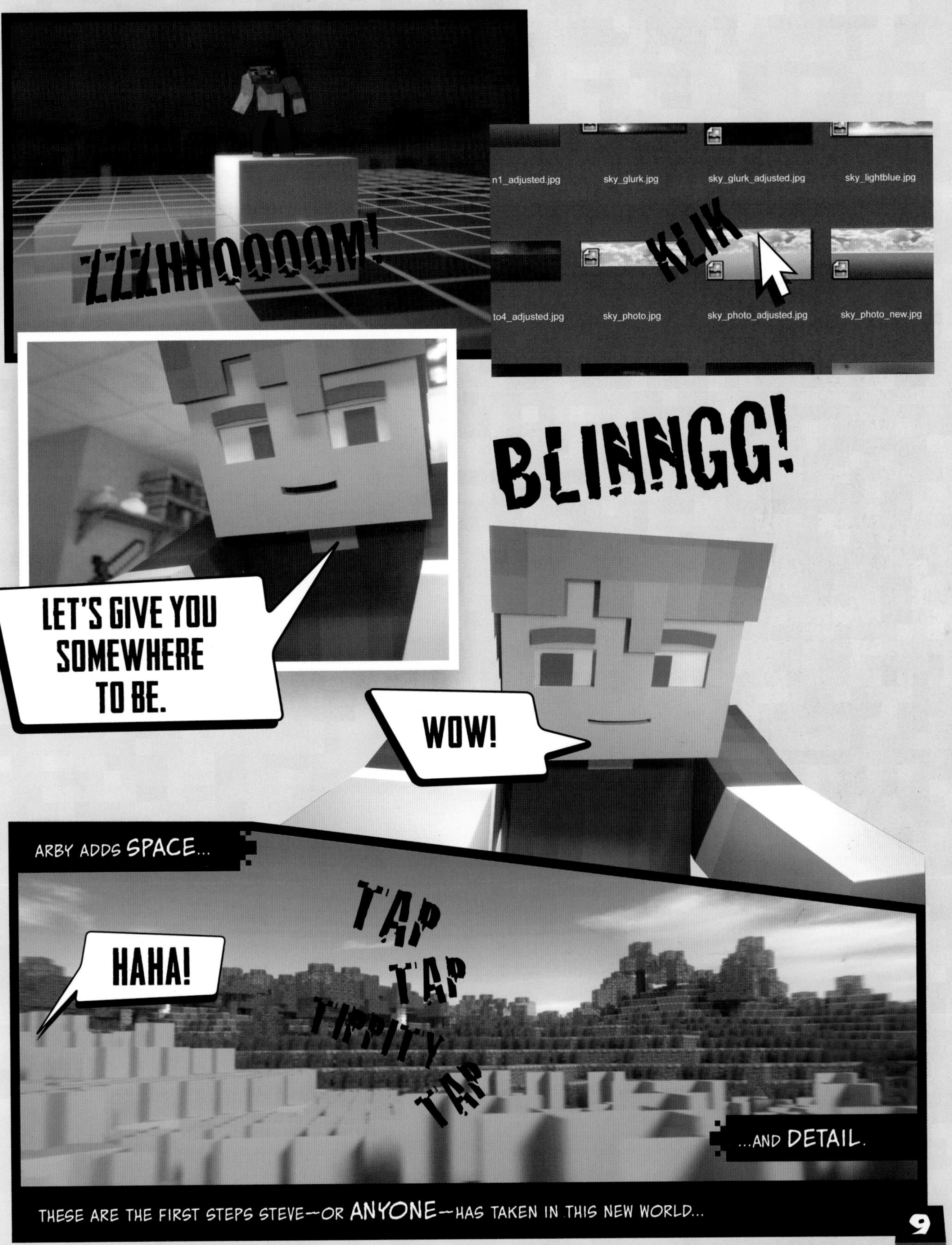

ZZZHHOOOOOM!
n1_adjusted.jpg
sky_glurk.jpg
sky_glurk_adjusted.jpg
sky_lightblue.jpg
KLIK
to4_adjusted.jpg
sky_photo.jpg
sky_photo_adjusted.jpg
sky_photo_new.jpg
BLINNGG!
LET'S GIVE YOU SOMEWHERE TO BE.
WOW!
ARBY ADDS SPACE...
HAHA!
TAP
TAP
TIPPITY
TAP
...AND DETAIL.
THESE ARE THE FIRST STEPS STEVE—OR ANYONE—HAS TAKEN IN THIS NEW WORLD...

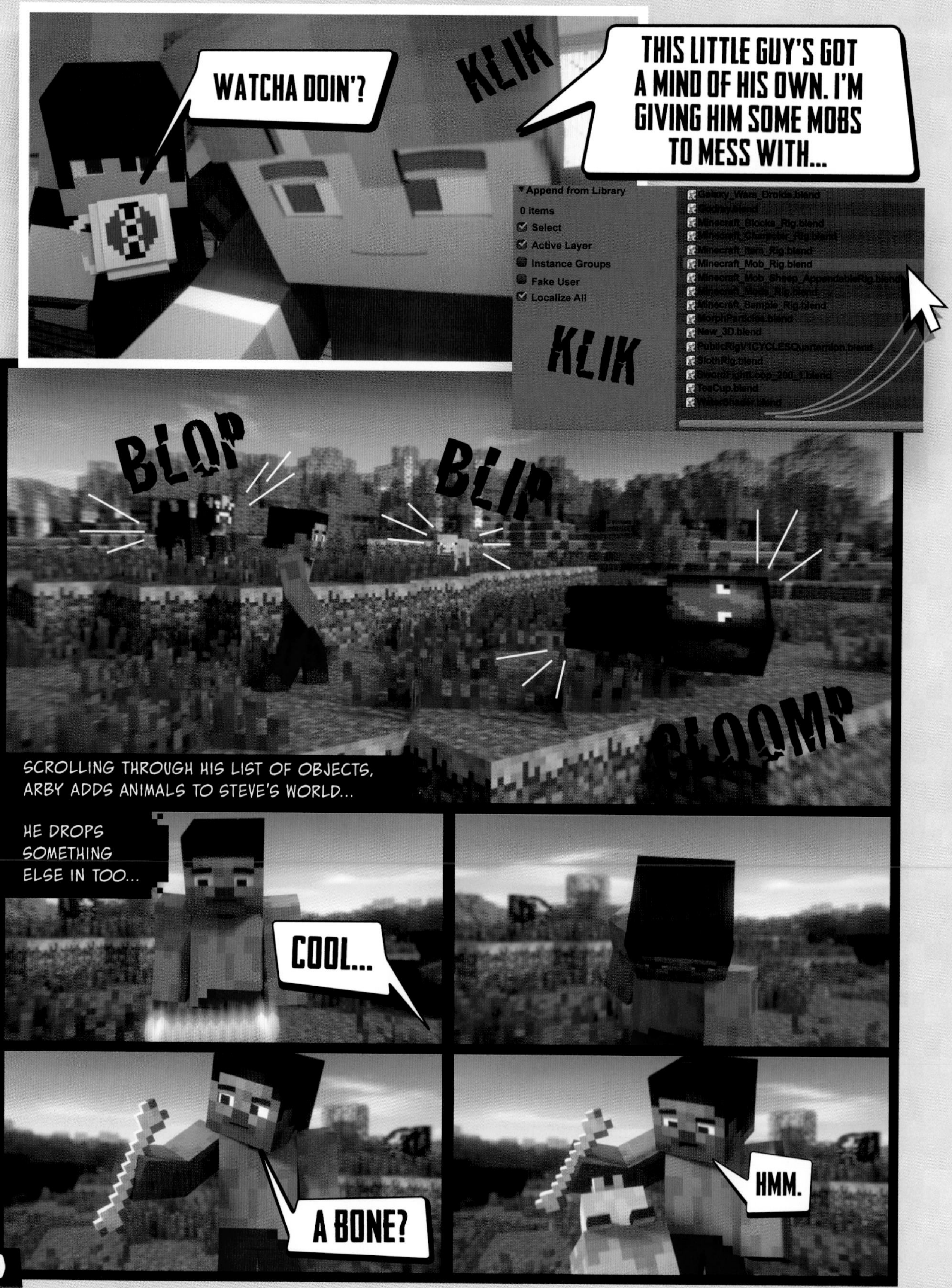
WATCHA DOIN'?
KLIK
THIS LITTLE GUY'S GOT A MIND OF HIS OWN. I'M GIVING HIM SOME MOBS TO MESS WITH...
Append from Library
0 items
Select
Active Layer
Instance Groups
Fake User
Localize All
Galaxy_Wars_Droids.blend
Minecraft_Blocks_Rig.blend
Minecraft_Character_Rig.blend
Minecraft_Item_Rig.blend
Minecraft_Mob_Rig.blend
Minecraft_Mob_Sheep_AppendableRig.blend
Minecraft_Sample_Rig.blend
MorphParticles.blend
New_3D.blend
PublicRigV1CYCLESQuarternion.blend
SlothRig.blend
SwordFightLoop_200_1.blend
TeaCup.blend
WaterShader.blend
KLIK
BLOP
BLIP
GLOOMP
SCROLLING THROUGH HIS LIST OF OBJECTS, ARBY ADDS ANIMALS TO STEVE'S WORLD...
HE DROPS SOMETHING ELSE IN TOO...
COOL...
A BONE?
HMM.

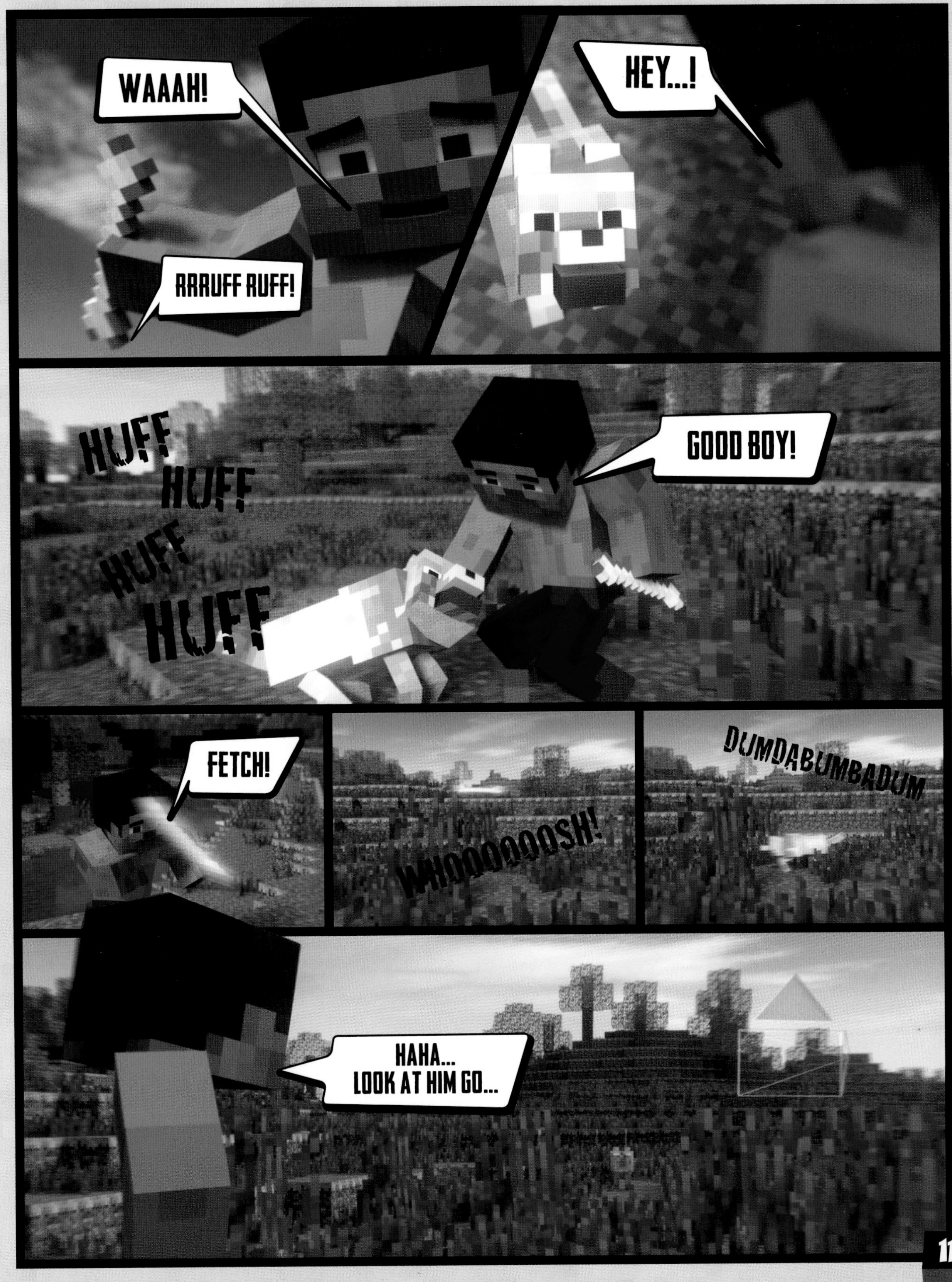
WAAAH!
RRRUFF RUFF!
HEY...!
HUFF
HUFF
HUFF
HUFF
GOOD BOY!
FETCH!
WHOOOOOOOSH!
DUMDABUMBADUM
HAHA...
LOOK AT HIM GO...

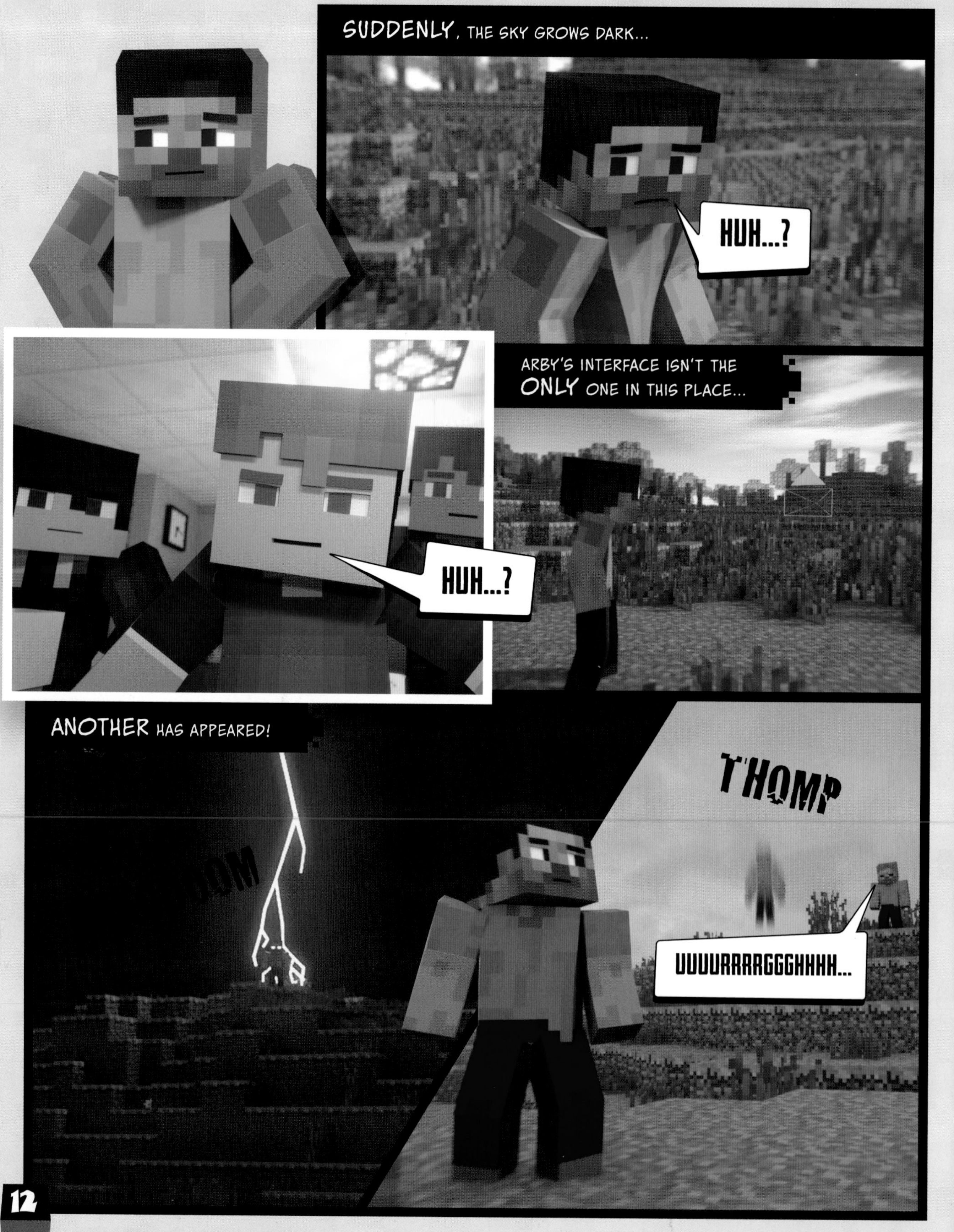
SUDDENLY, THE SKY GROWS DARK...
HUH...?
HUH...?
ARBY'S INTERFACE ISN'T THE ONLY ONE IN THIS PLACE...
ANOTHER HAS APPEARED!
THOMP
UUUURRRRGGGHHHH...

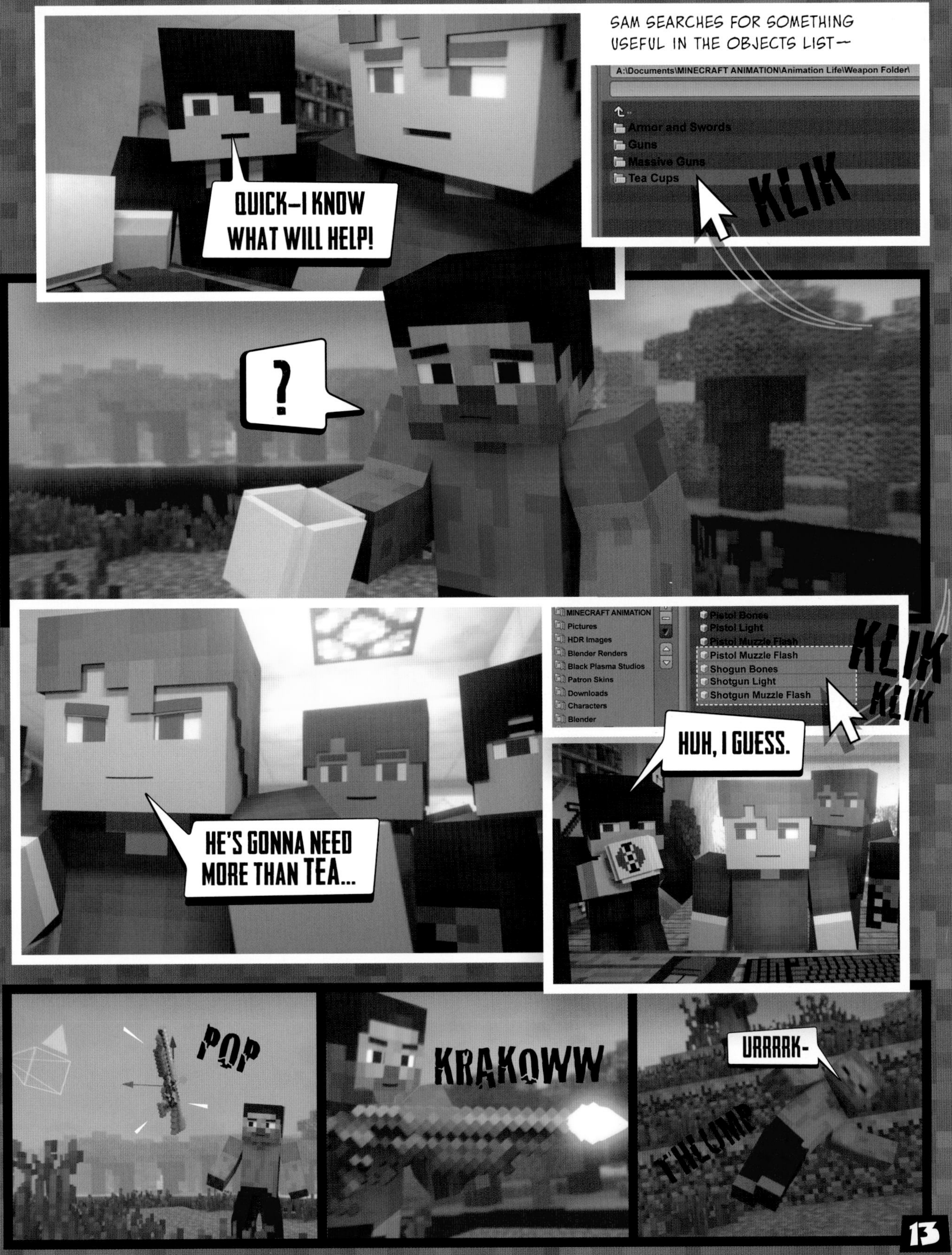
QUICK—I KNOW WHAT WILL HELP!
SAM SEARCHES FOR SOMETHING USEFUL IN THE OBJECTS LIST—
A:\Documents\MINECRAFT ANIMATION\Animation Life\Weapon Folder\
Armor and Swords
Guns
Massive Guns
Tea Cups
KLIK
?
HE'S GONNA NEED MORE THAN TEA...
MINECRAFT ANIMATION
Pictures
HDR Images
Blender Renders
Black Plasma Studios
Patron Skins
Downloads
Characters
Blender
Pistol Bones
Pistol Light
Pistol Muzzle Flash
Pistol Muzzle Flash
Shogun Bones
Shotgun Light
Shotgun Muzzle Flash
KLIK
KLIK
HUH, I GUESS.
POP
KRAKOWW
URRRRK-
THUMP

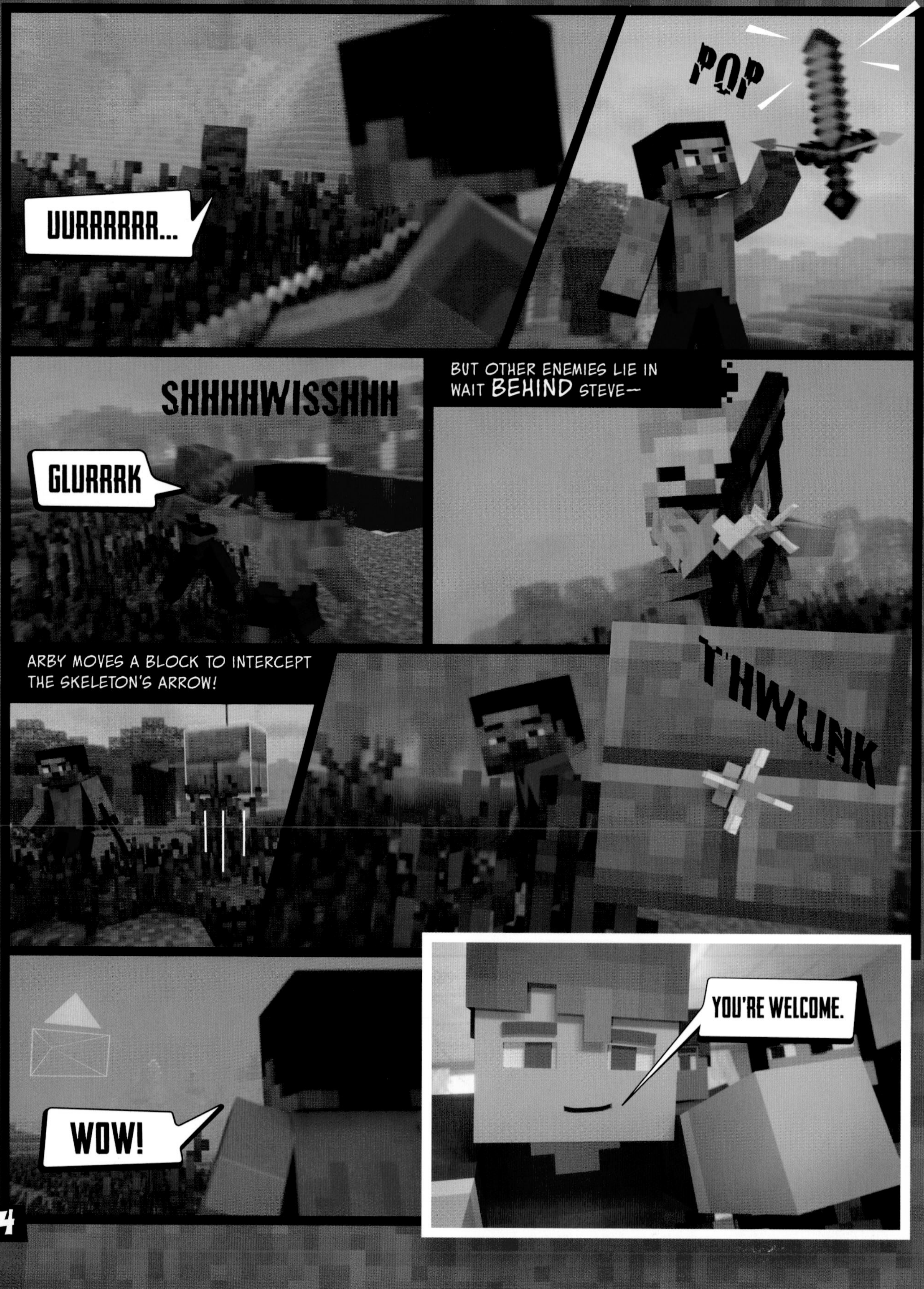
UURRRRRR...
POP
SHHHHWISSHHH
GLURRRK
BUT OTHER ENEMIES LIE IN WAIT BEHIND STEVE—
ARBY MOVES A BLOCK TO INTERCEPT THE SKELETON'S ARROW!
T'HWUNK
WOW!
YOU'RE WELCOME.

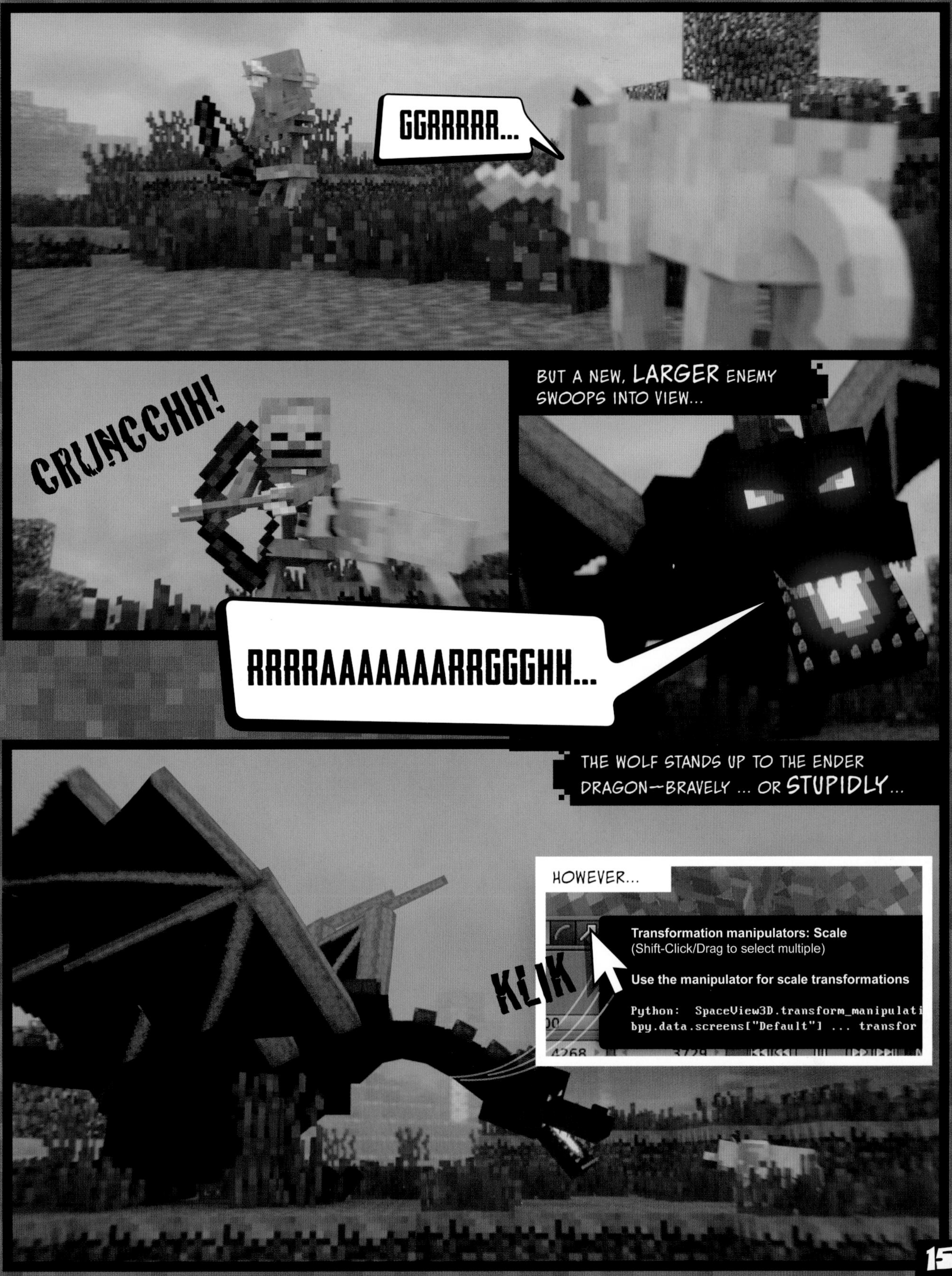
GGRRRRR...
CRUNCCHH!
BUT A NEW, LARGER ENEMY SWOOPS INTO VIEW...
RRRRAAAAAAARRGGGHH...
THE WOLF STANDS UP TO THE ENDER DRAGON—BRAVELY ... OR STUPIDLY...
HOWEVER...
KLIK
Transformation manipulators: Scale
(Shift-Click/Drag to select multiple)
Use the manipulator for scale transformations
Python: SpaceView3D.transform_manipulati
bpy.data.screens["Default"] ... transfor

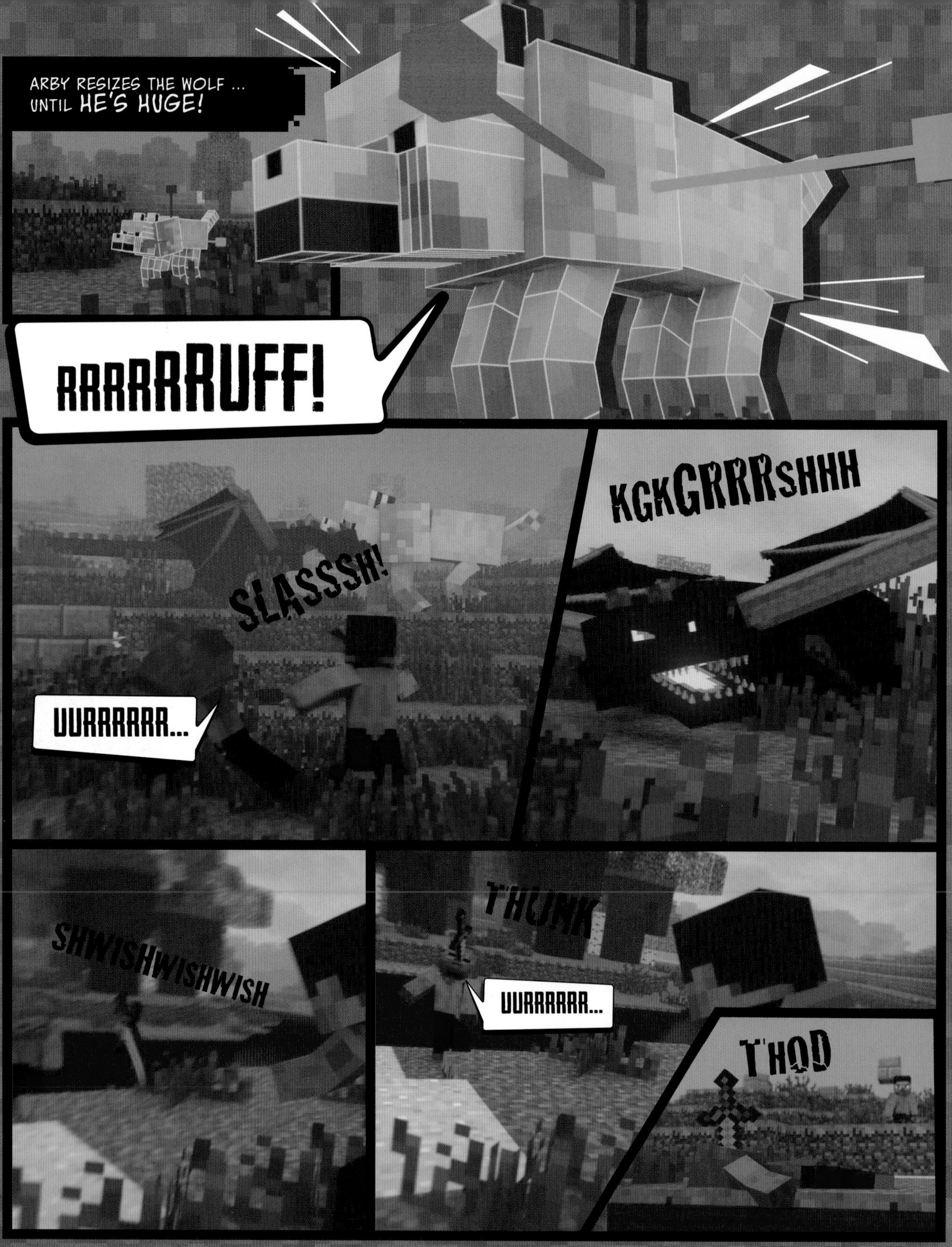
ARBY RESIZES THE WOLF ... UNTIL HE'S HUGE!
RRRRRRUFF!
SLASSSH!
UURRRRRR...
KGKGRRRSHHH
SHWISHWISHWISH
THUNK
UURRRRRR...
THOD

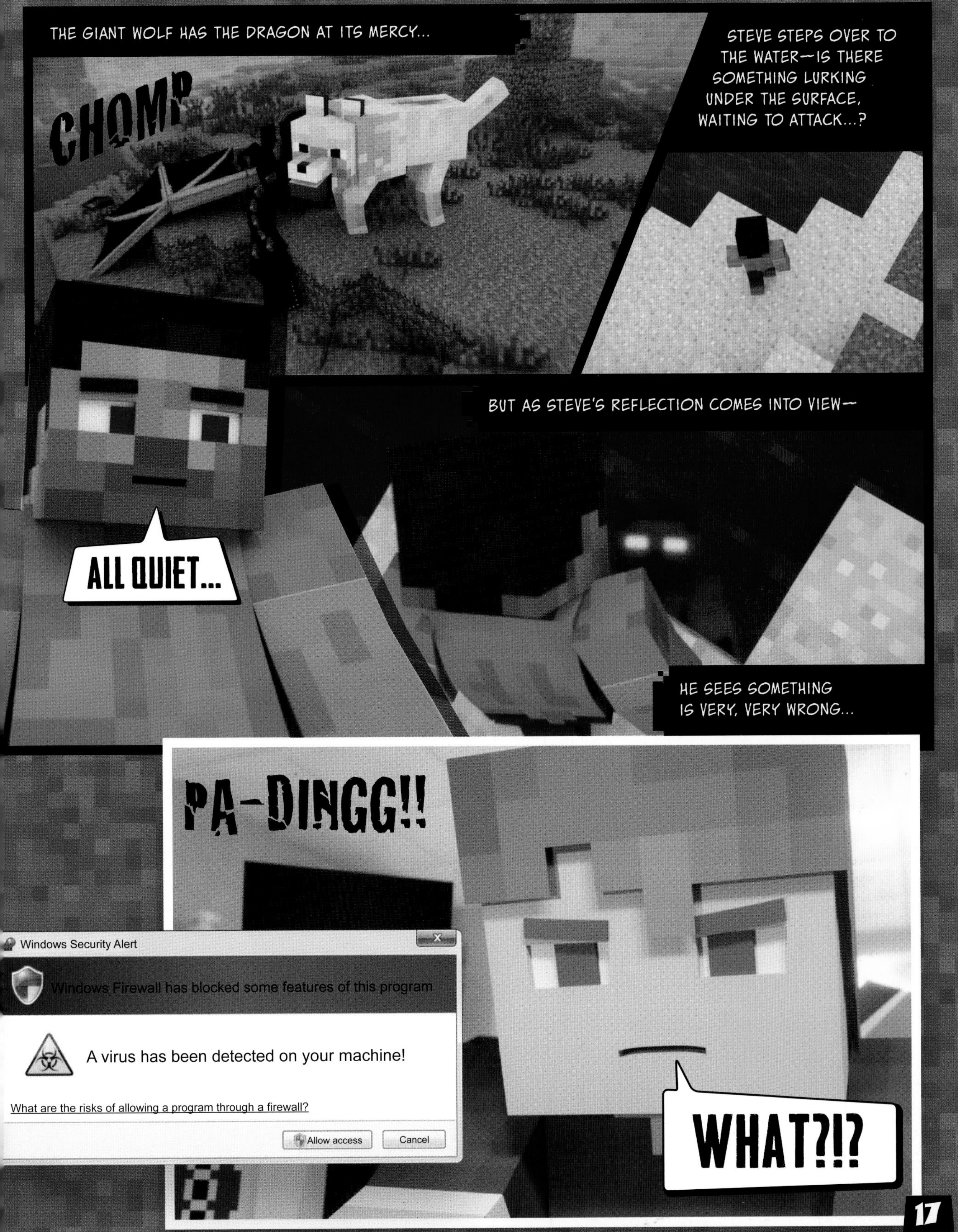
THE GIANT WOLF HAS THE DRAGON AT ITS MERCY...
CHOMP
STEVE STEPS OVER TO THE WATER—IS THERE SOMETHING LURKING UNDER THE SURFACE, WAITING TO ATTACK...?
ALL QUIET...
BUT AS STEVE'S REFLECTION COMES INTO VIEW—
HE SEES SOMETHING IS VERY, VERY WRONG...
PA-DINGG!!
Windows Security Alert
Windows Firewall has blocked some features of this program
A virus has been detected on your machine!
What are the risks of allowing a program through a firewall?
Allow access
Cancel
WHAT?!!?

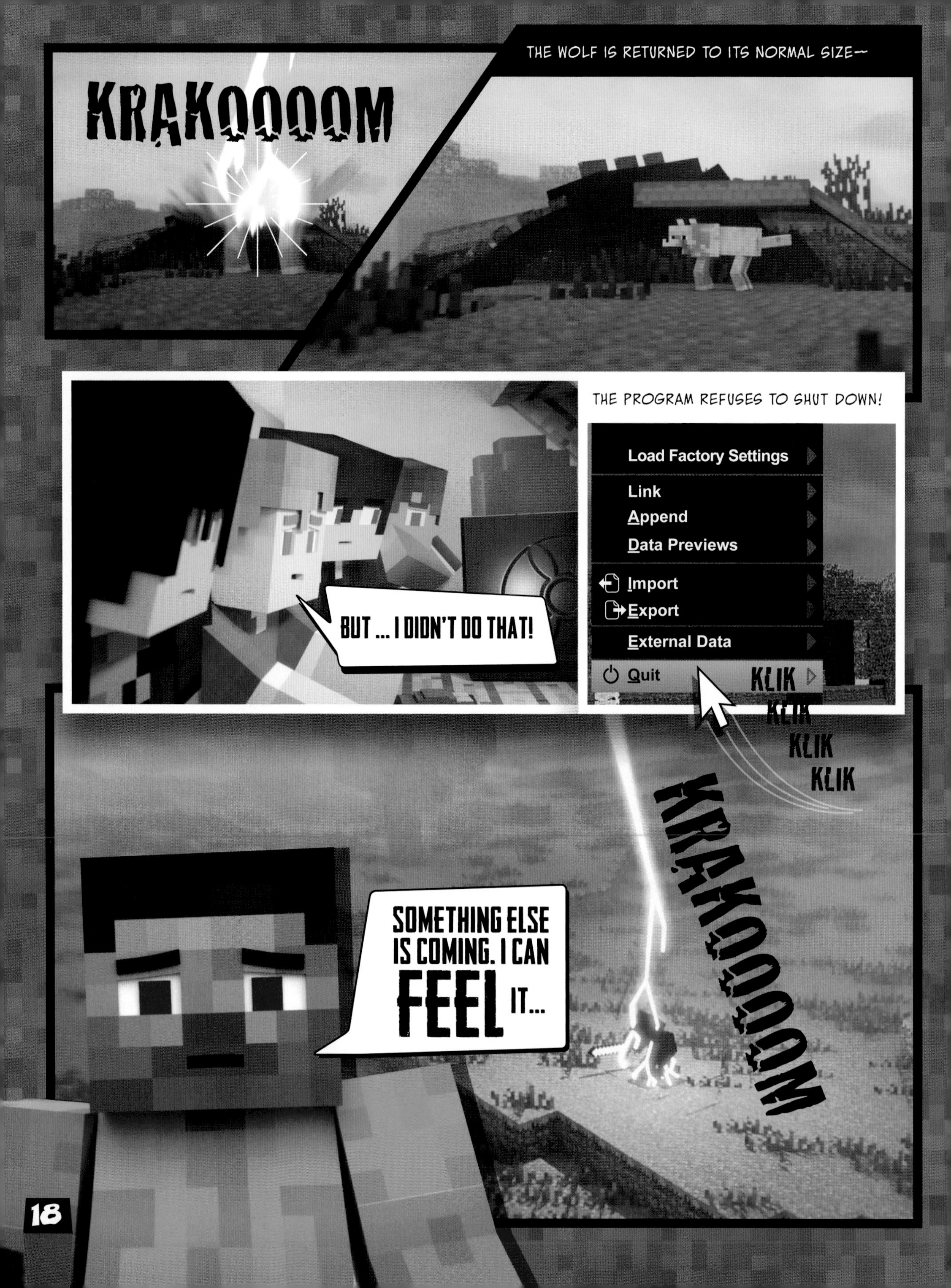

THE WOLF IS RETURNED TO ITS NORMAL SIZE—
KRAKOOOOM
THE PROGRAM REFUSES TO SHUT DOWN!
BUT ... I DIDN'T DO THAT!
Load Factory Settings
Link
Append
Data Previews
Import
Export
External Data
Quit
KLIK
KLIK
KLIK
KLIK
KRAKOOOOM
SOMETHING ELSE IS COMING. I CAN FEEL IT...

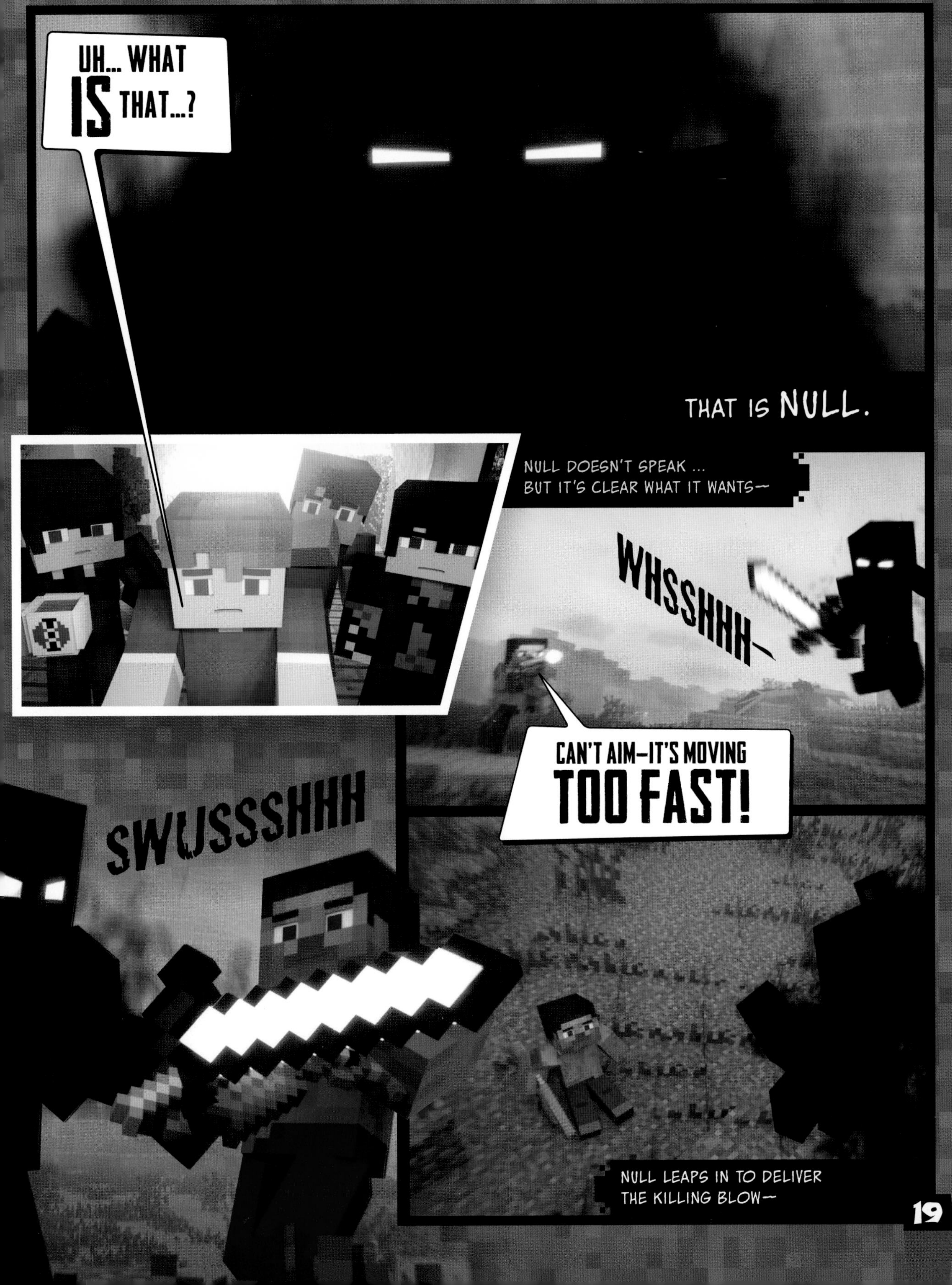
UH... WHAT IS THAT...?
THAT IS NULL.
NULL DOESN'T SPEAK ...
BUT IT'S CLEAR WHAT IT WANTS—
WHSSHHH—
CAN'T AIM—IT'S MOVING TOO FAST!
SWUSSSHHH
NULL LEAPS IN TO DELIVER
THE KILLING BLOW—

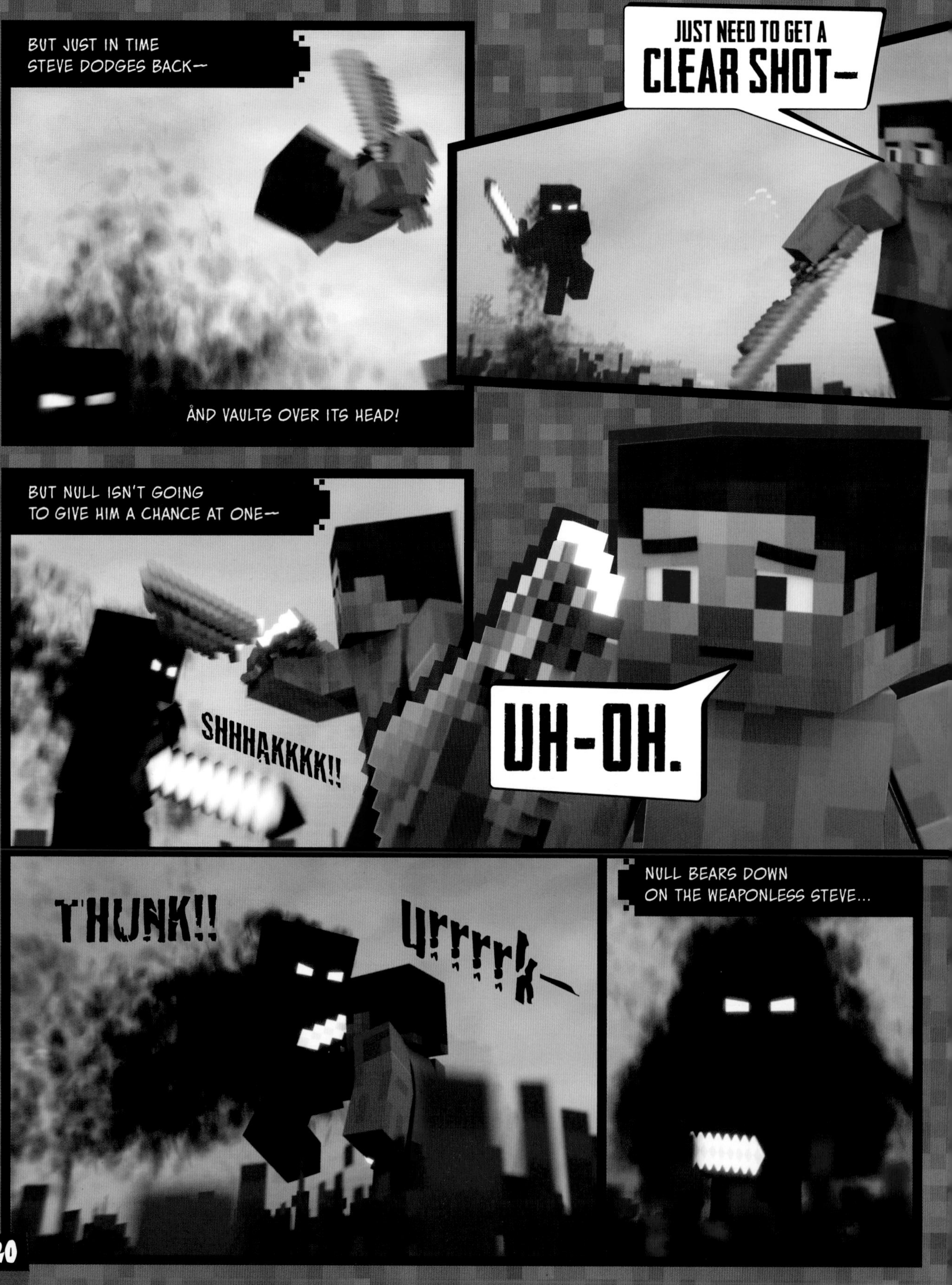
BUT JUST IN TIME
STEVE DODGES BACK—
AND VAULTS OVER ITS HEAD!
JUST NEED TO GET A
CLEAR SHOT—
BUT NULL ISN'T GOING
TO GIVE HIM A CHANCE AT ONE—
SHHHAKKKK!!
UH-OH.
THUNK!!
Urrrrk—
NULL BEARS DOWN
ON THE WEAPONLESS STEVE...

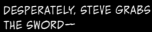
DESPERATELY, STEVE GRABS
THE SWORD~

CRUNCH
CRACK
CRUNCH

STEVE HIDES AND CATCHES HIS BREATH...

HUNFH *HUNFH*
HUNFH

21

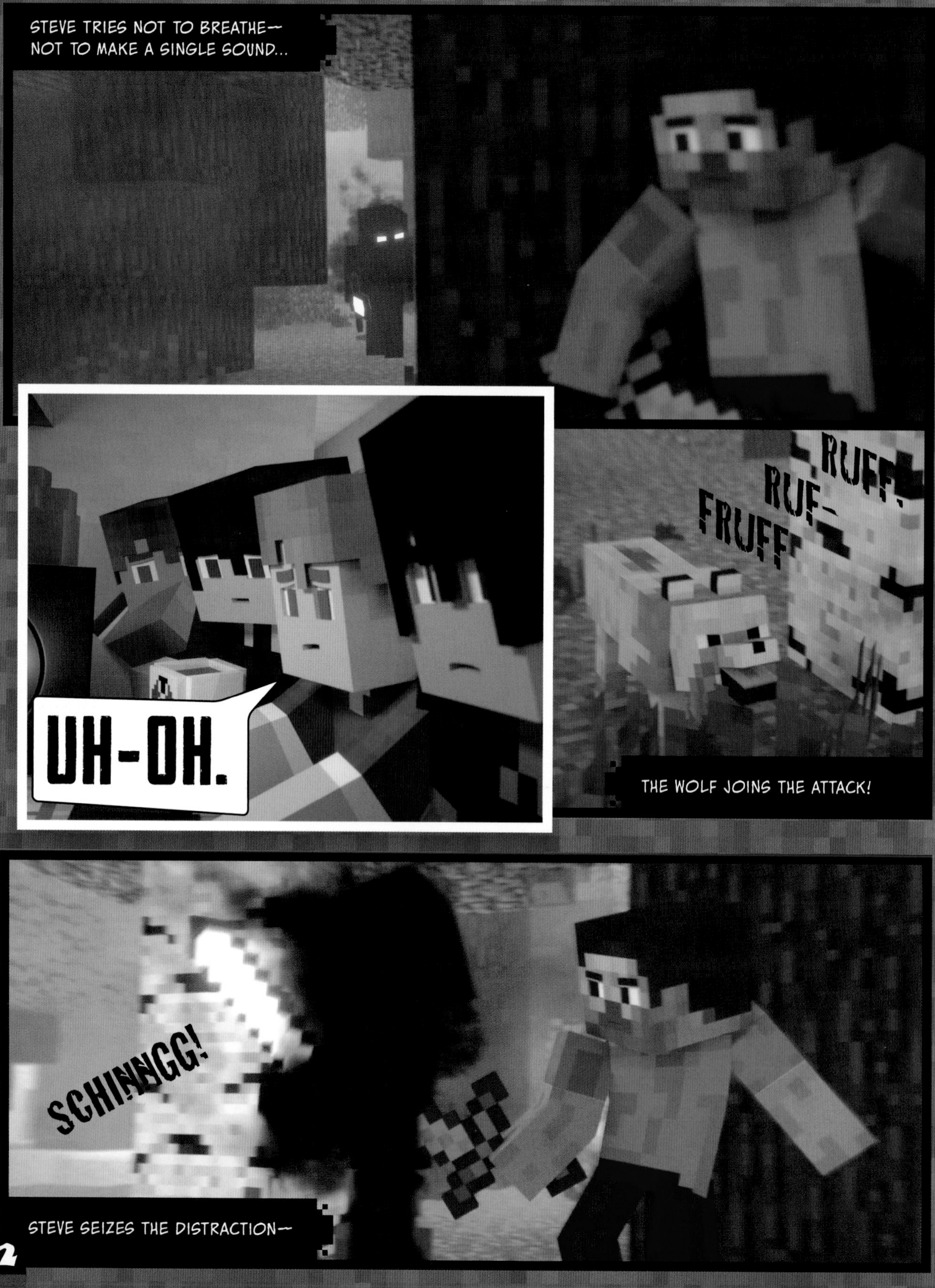
STEVE TRIES NOT TO BREATHE—
NOT TO MAKE A SINGLE SOUND...
UH-OH.
RUFF!
RUF-
FRUFF
THE WOLF JOINS THE ATTACK!
SCHINNGG!
STEVE SEIZES THE DISTRACTION—

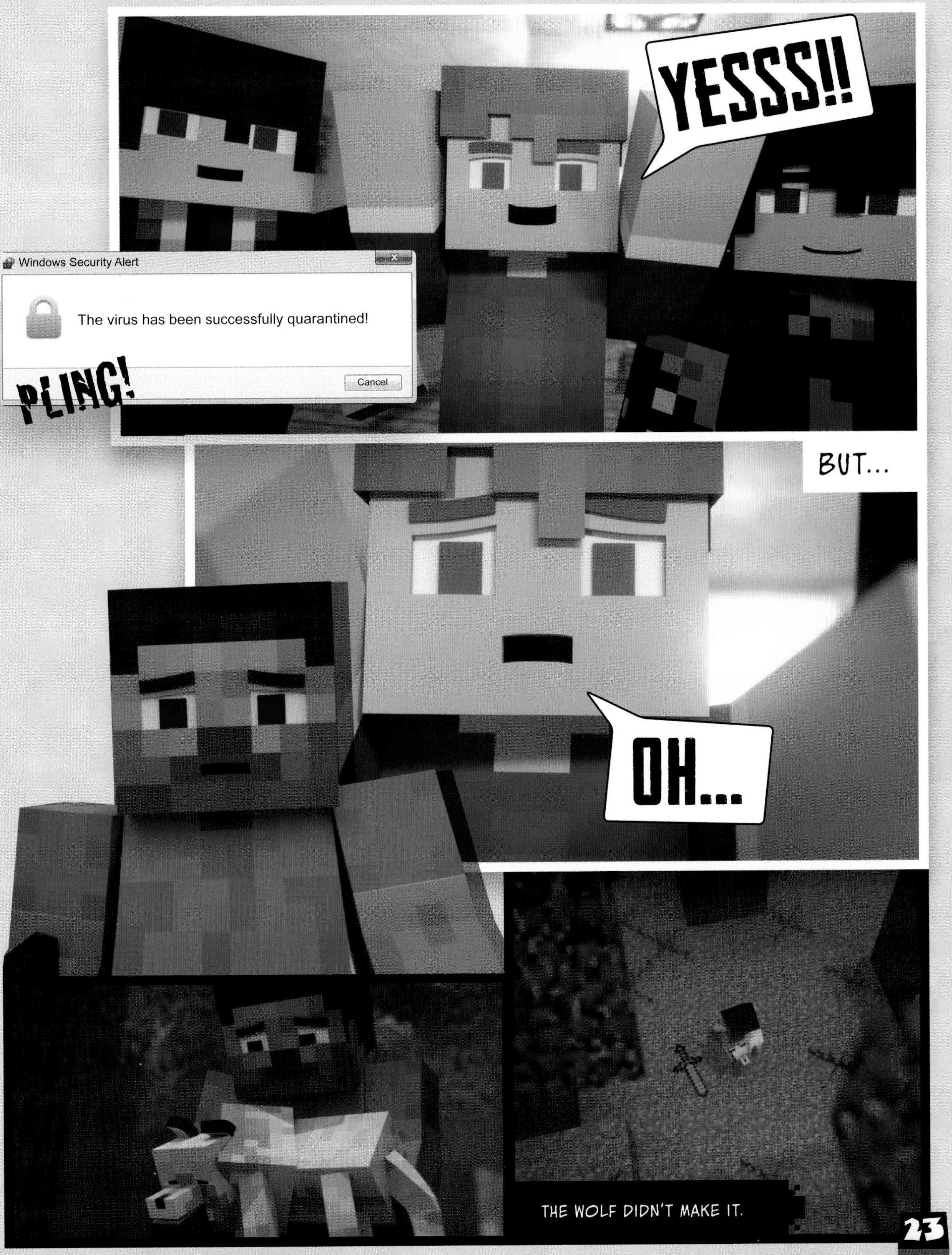
YESSS!!
Windows Security Alert
The virus has been successfully quarantined!
Cancel
PLING!
BUT...
OH...
THE WOLF DIDN'T MAKE IT.

CHAPTER 2

THE END OF THE FIRST DAY IN THIS NEW WORLD IS A **SAD** ONE...

AS STEVE SAYS FAREWELL TO A FAITHFUL FRIEND HE'D ONLY JUST MET—

BUT WHO SACRIFICED HIS LIFE TO SAVE HIS MASTER.

BEEP
BOOP
BIP

STEVE'S PAIN IS SHARED IN ANOTHER WORLD...

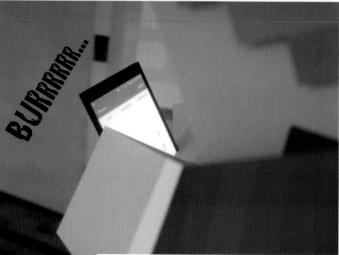

BURRRRRR...

BUT ARBY'S DETERMINED TO DO SOMETHING ABOUT IT.

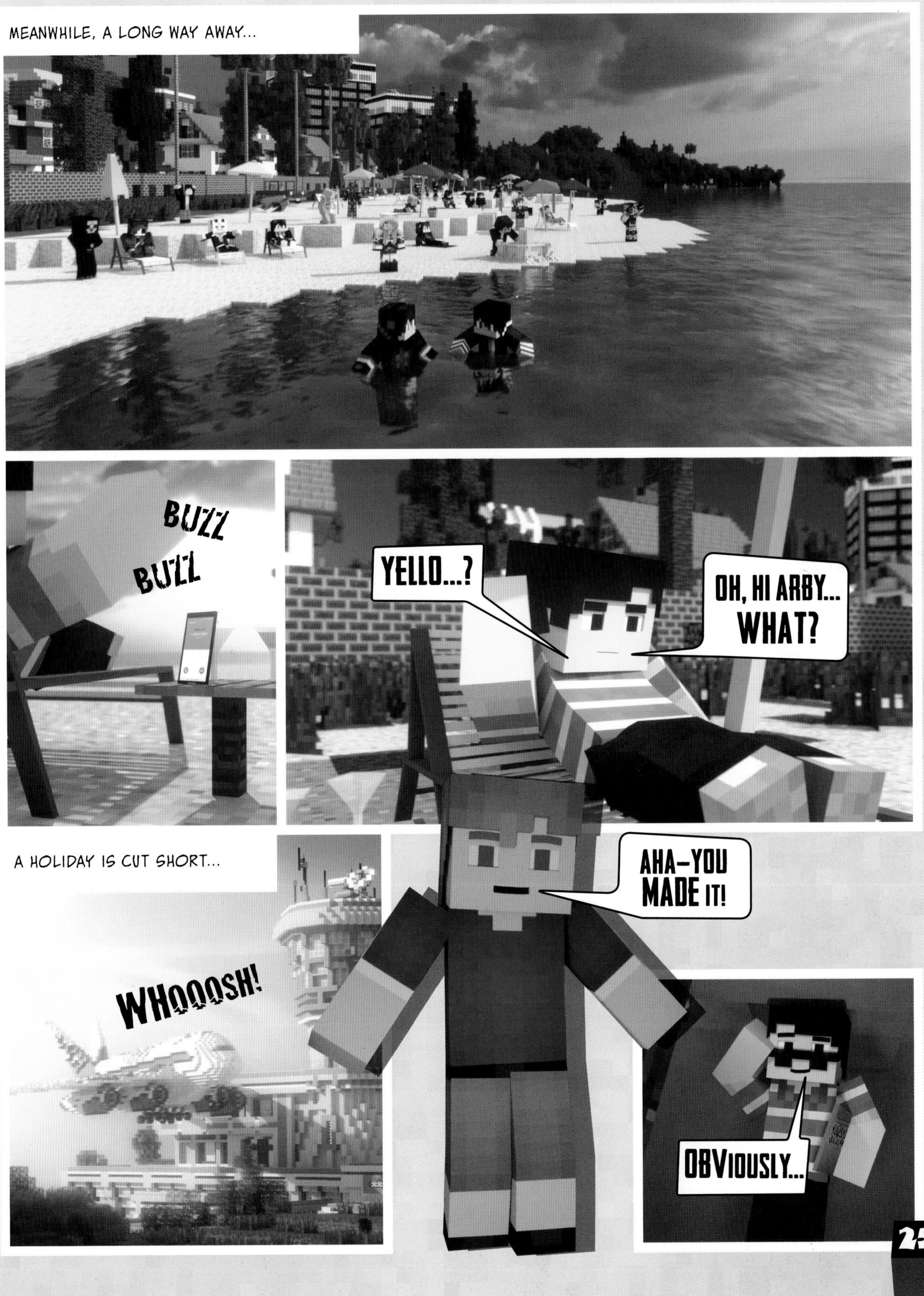

MEANWHILE, A LONG WAY AWAY...
BUZZ
BUZZ
YELLO...?
OH, HI ARBY... WHAT?
A HOLIDAY IS CUT SHORT...
WHOOOSH!
AHA–YOU MADE IT!
OBVIOUSLY...

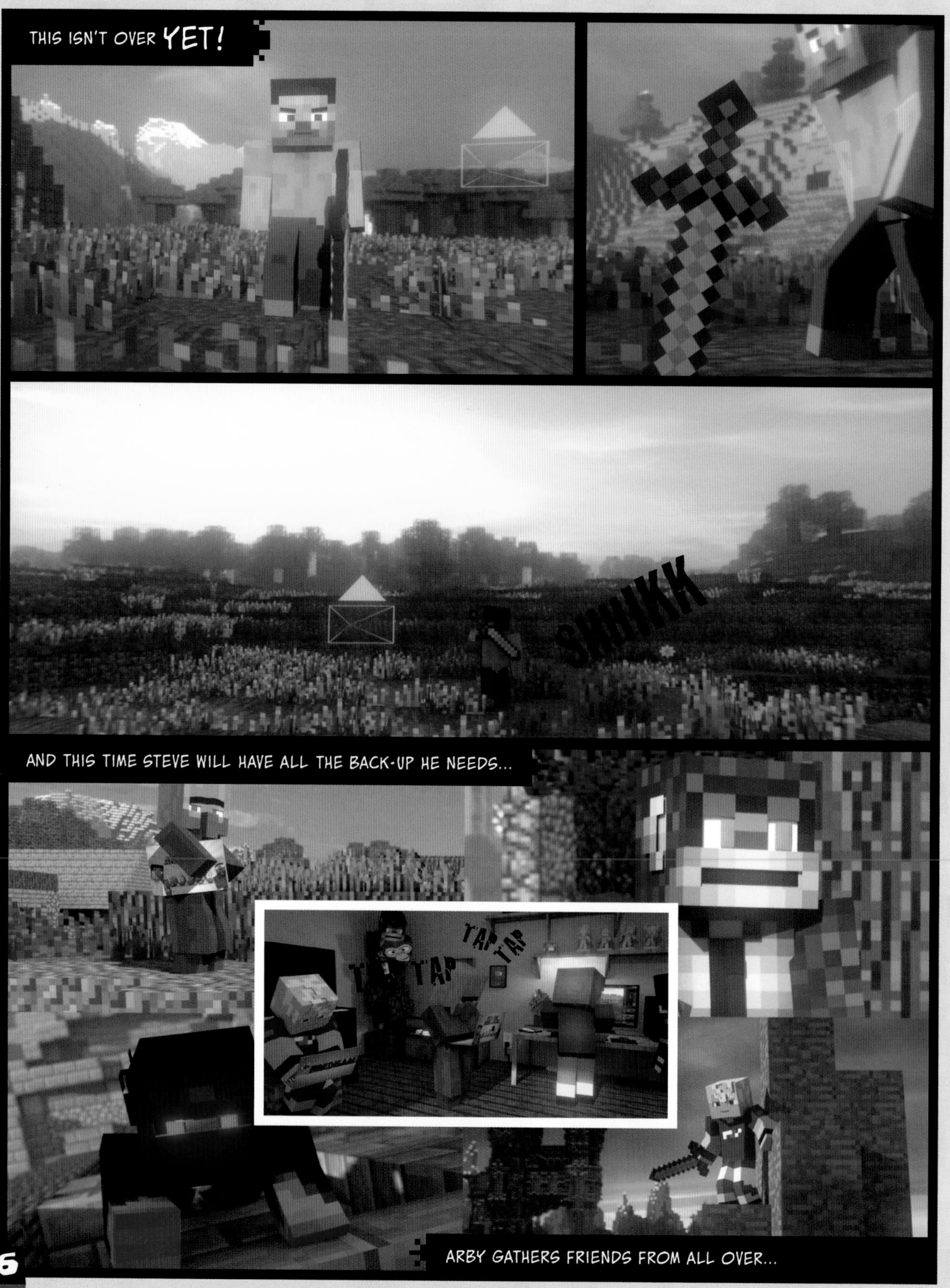
THIS ISN'T OVER YET!
SHUIKK
AND THIS TIME STEVE WILL HAVE ALL THE BACK-UP HE NEEDS...
TAP TAP TAP
ARBY GATHERS FRIENDS FROM ALL OVER...

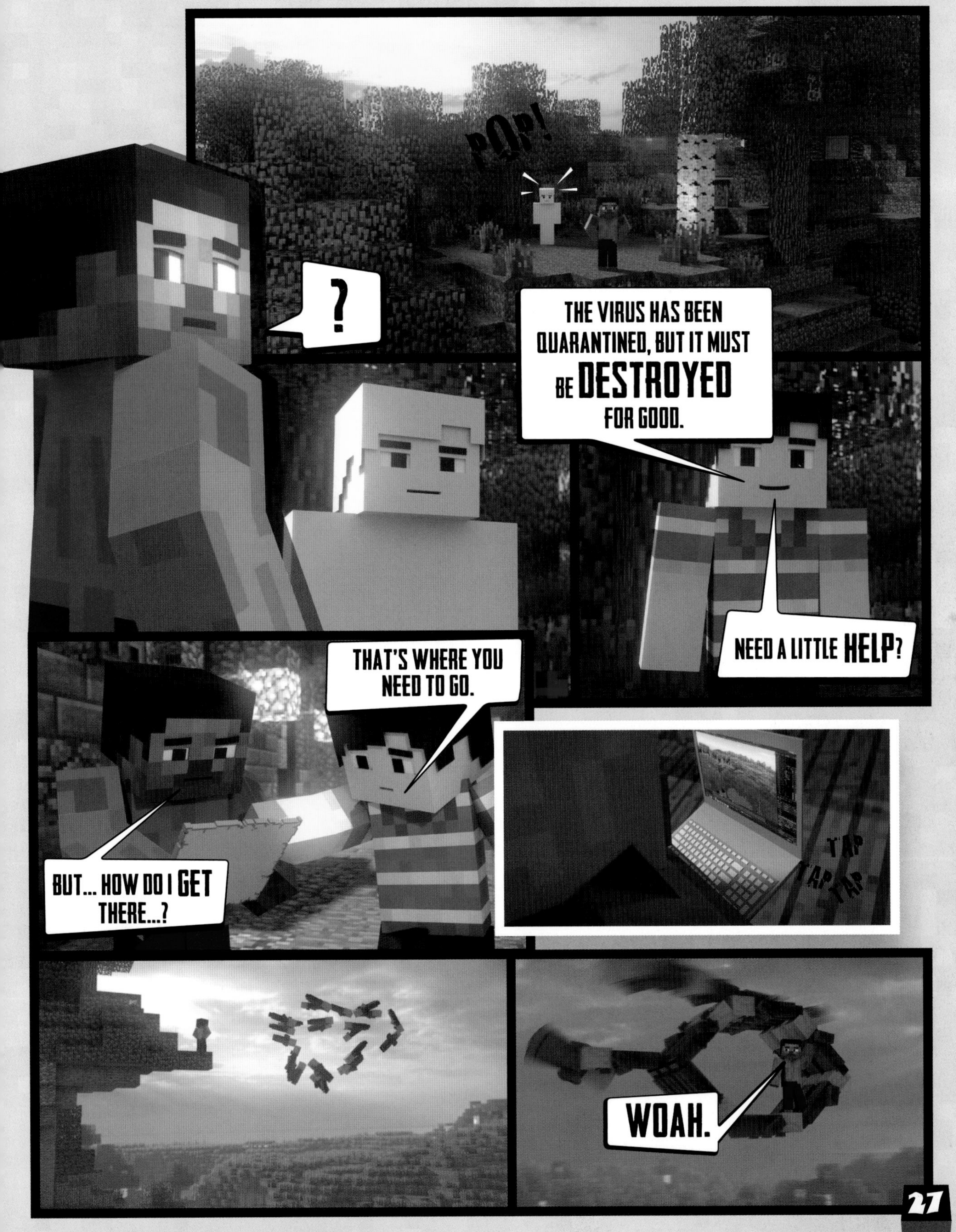
POP!
?
THE VIRUS HAS BEEN QUARANTINED, BUT IT MUST BE DESTROYED FOR GOOD.
NEED A LITTLE HELP?
THAT'S WHERE YOU NEED TO GO.
BUT... HOW DO I GET THERE...?
TAP TAP TAP
WOAH.

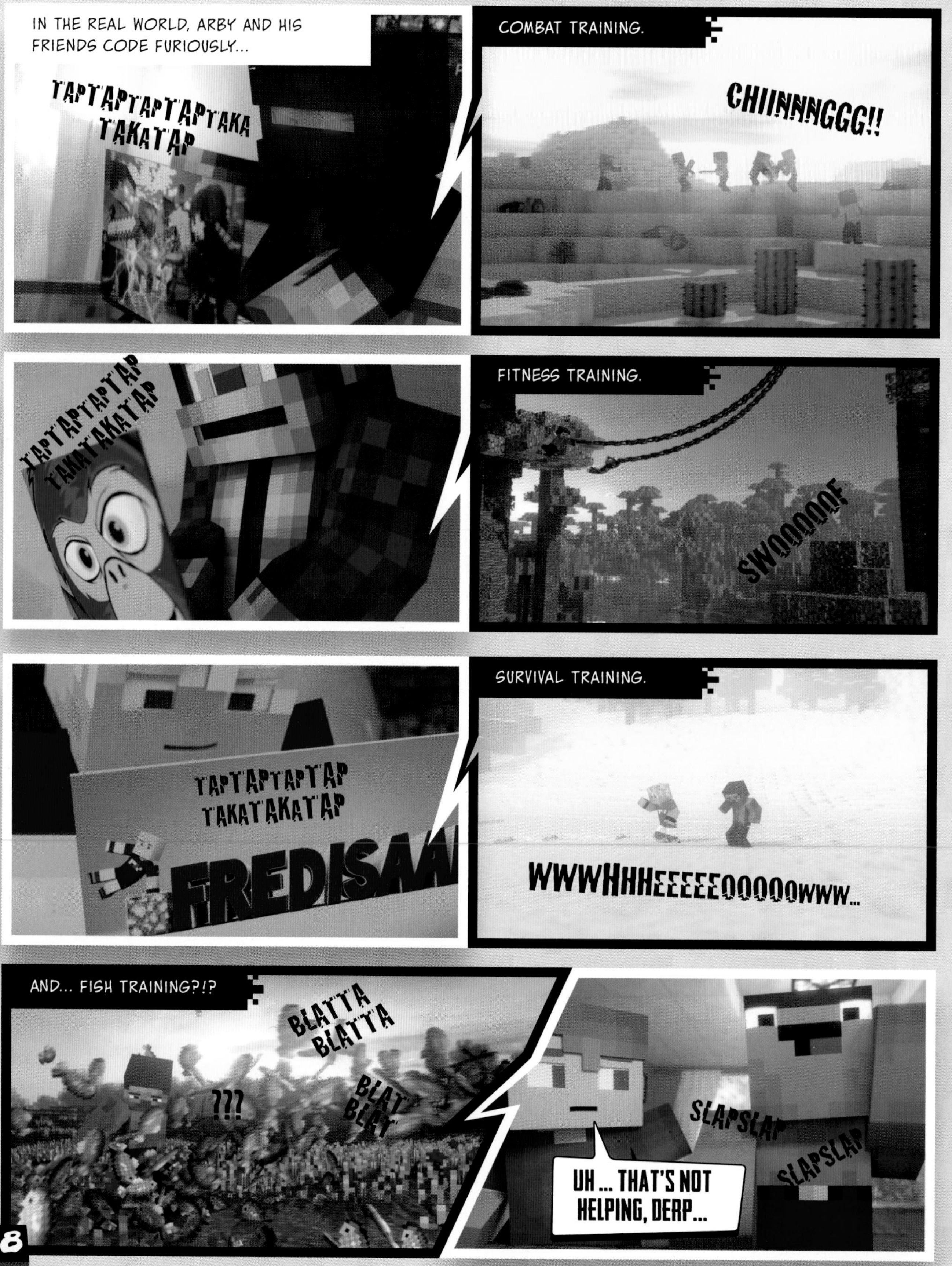
IN THE REAL WORLD, ARBY AND HIS FRIENDS CODE FURIOUSLY...
TAPTAPTAPTAPTAKA TAKATAP
COMBAT TRAINING.
CHIINNNGGG!!
TAPTAPTAPTAP TAKATAKATAP
FITNESS TRAINING.
SWOOOOOF
TAPTAPTAPTAP TAKATAKATAP
SURVIVAL TRAINING.
WWWHHHEEEEEOOOOOWWW...
AND... FISH TRAINING?!?
BLATTA BLATTA
???
BLAT BLAT
SLAPSLAP
SLAPSLAP
UH ... THAT'S NOT HELPING, DERP...

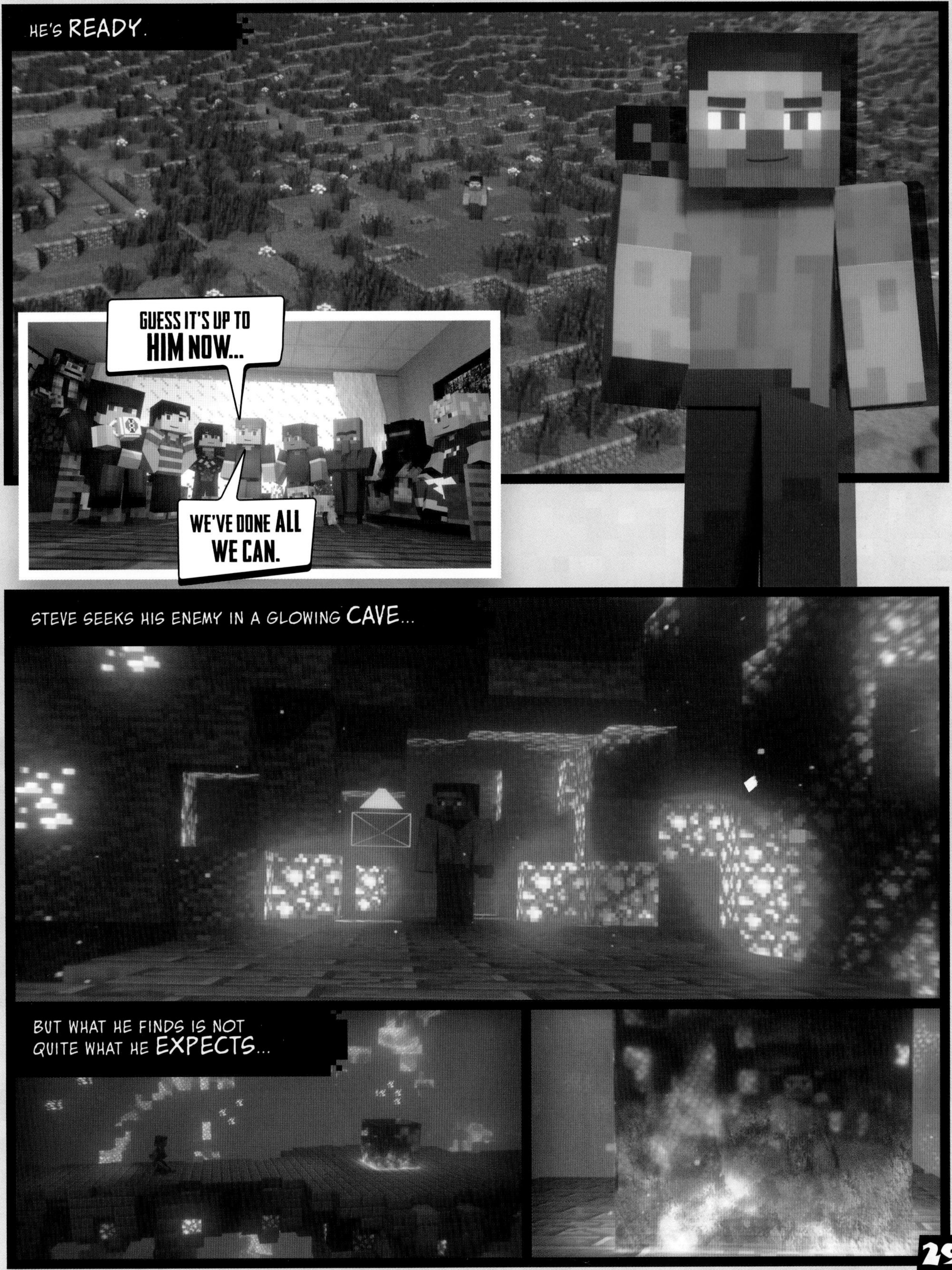
HE'S READY.
GUESS IT'S UP TO HIM NOW...
WE'VE DONE ALL WE CAN.
STEVE SEEKS HIS ENEMY IN A GLOWING CAVE...
BUT WHAT HE FINDS IS NOT QUITE WHAT HE EXPECTS...

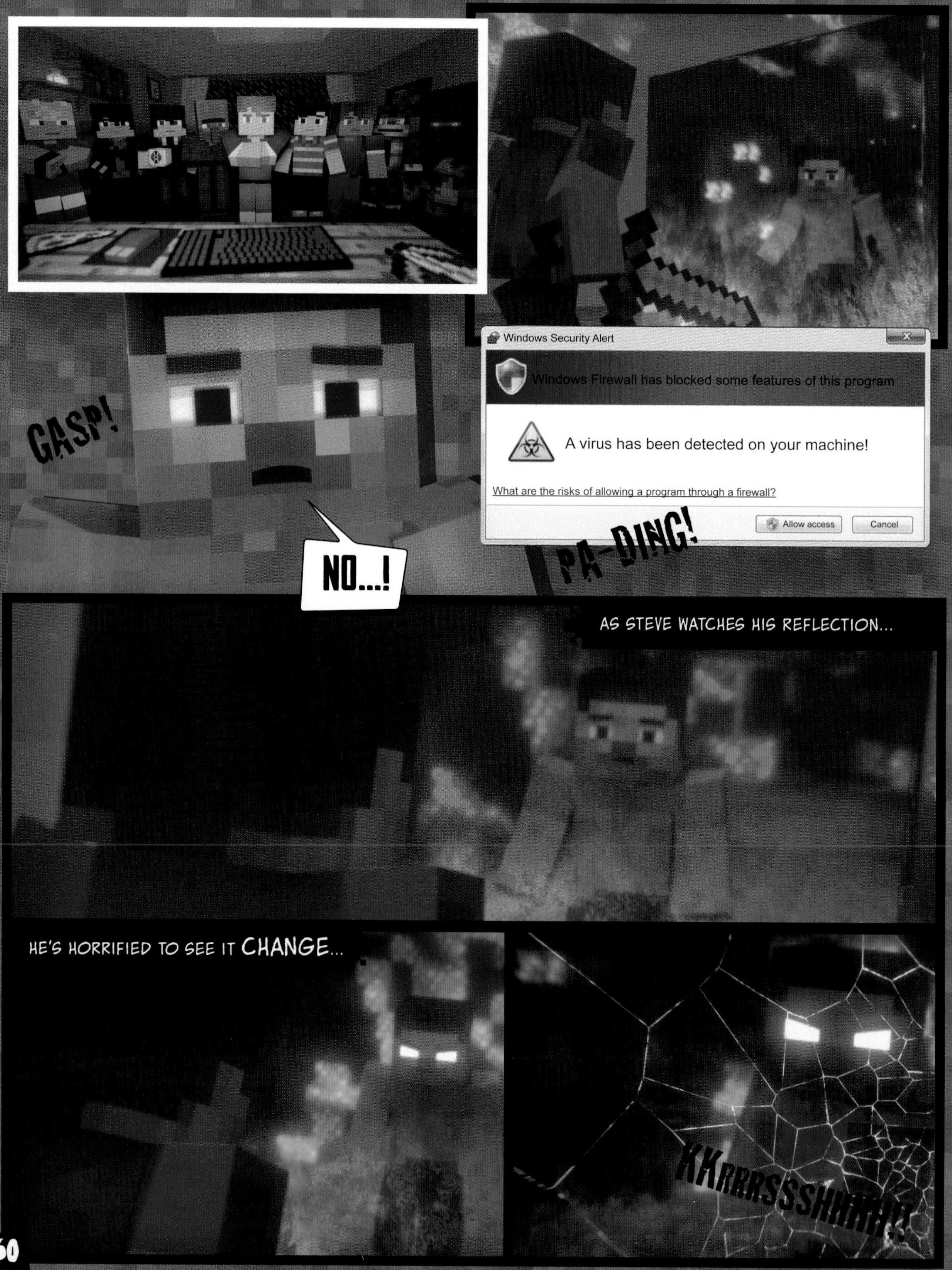
GASP!
NO...!
Windows Security Alert
Windows Firewall has blocked some features of this program
A virus has been detected on your machine!
What are the risks of allowing a program through a firewall?
Allow access
Cancel
PA-DING!
AS STEVE WATCHES HIS REFLECTION...
HE'S HORRIFIED TO SEE IT CHANGE...
KKRRRSSSHHHH!!

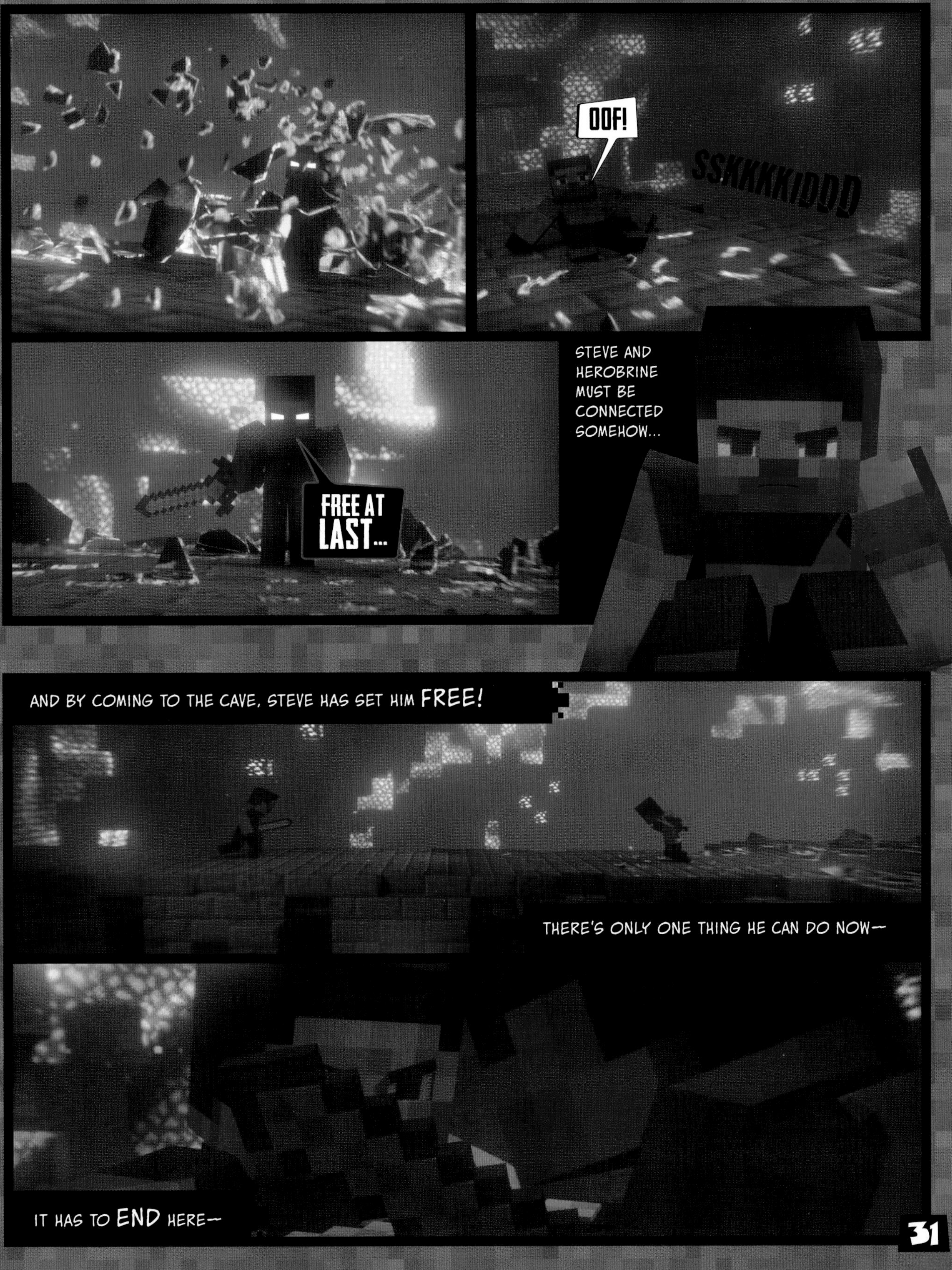
OOF!
SSKKKKIDDD
FREE AT LAST...
STEVE AND HEROBRINE MUST BE CONNECTED SOMEHOW...
AND BY COMING TO THE CAVE, STEVE HAS SET HIM FREE!
THERE'S ONLY ONE THING HE CAN DO NOW—
IT HAS TO END HERE—

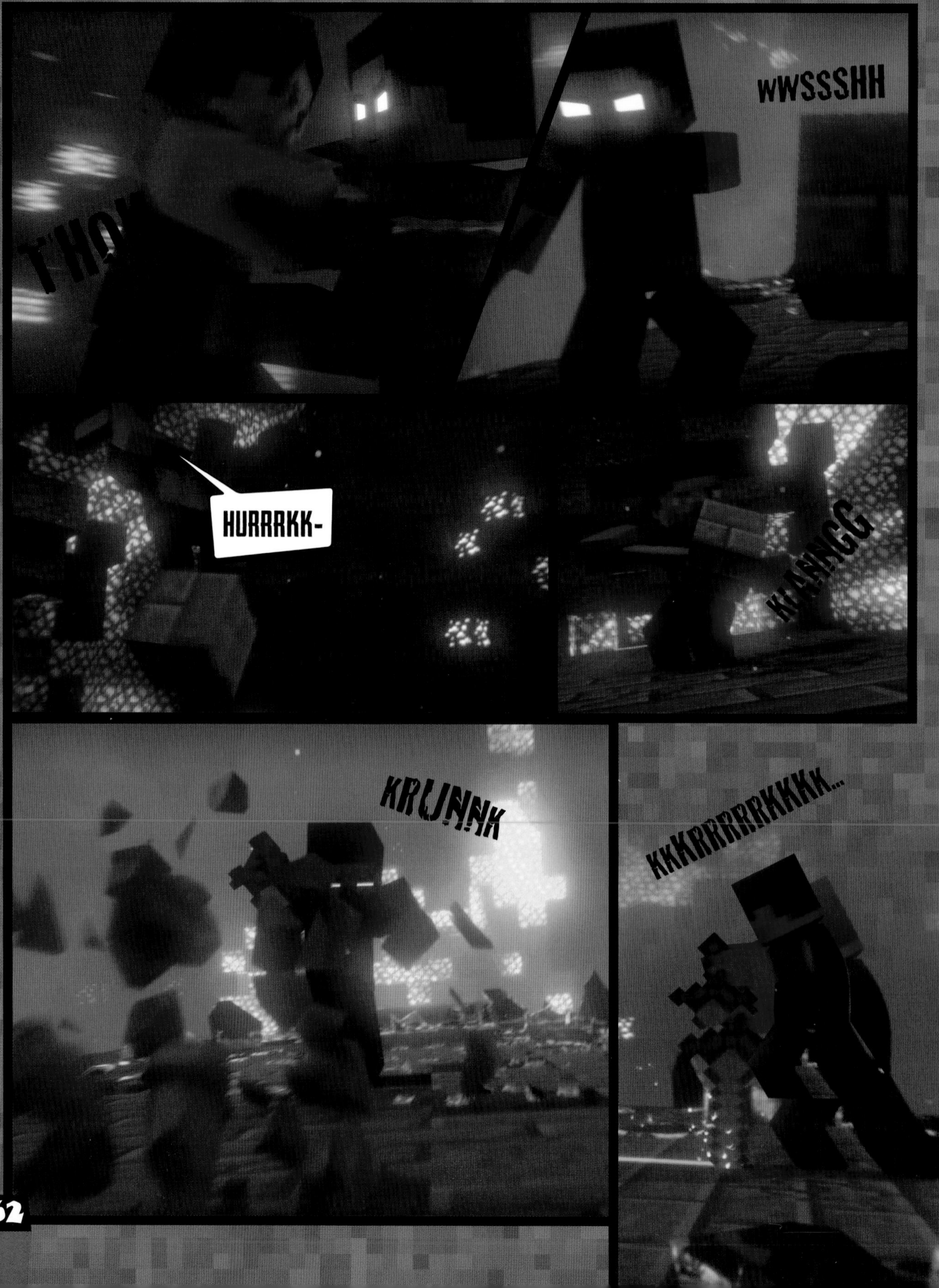
T'HO
WWSSSHH
HURRRKK-
KLANNGG
KRUNNK
KKKRRRRRKKKK...

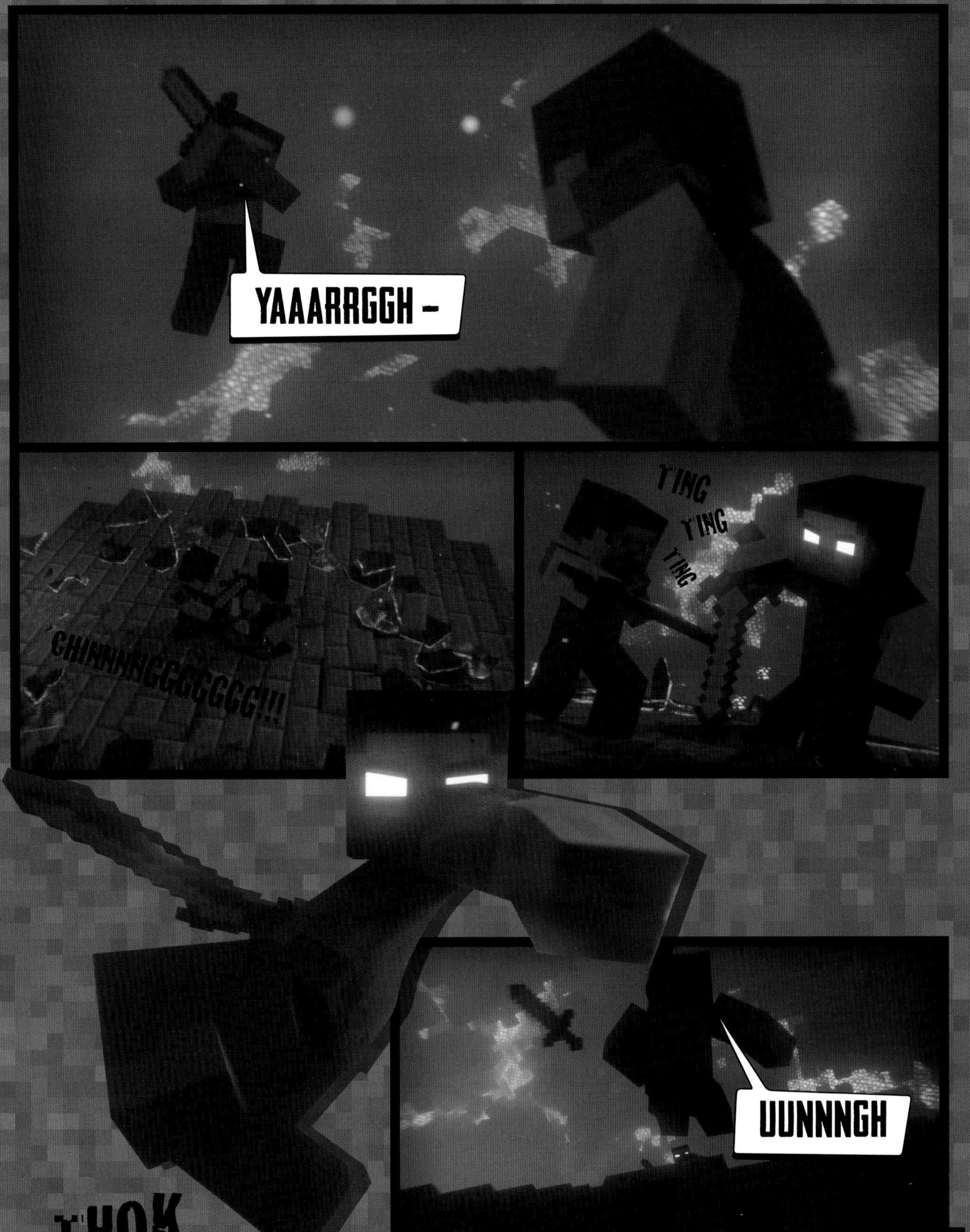
YAAARRGGH –
CHINNNNGGGGGGGG!!!
TING
TING
TING
UUNNNGH
THOK

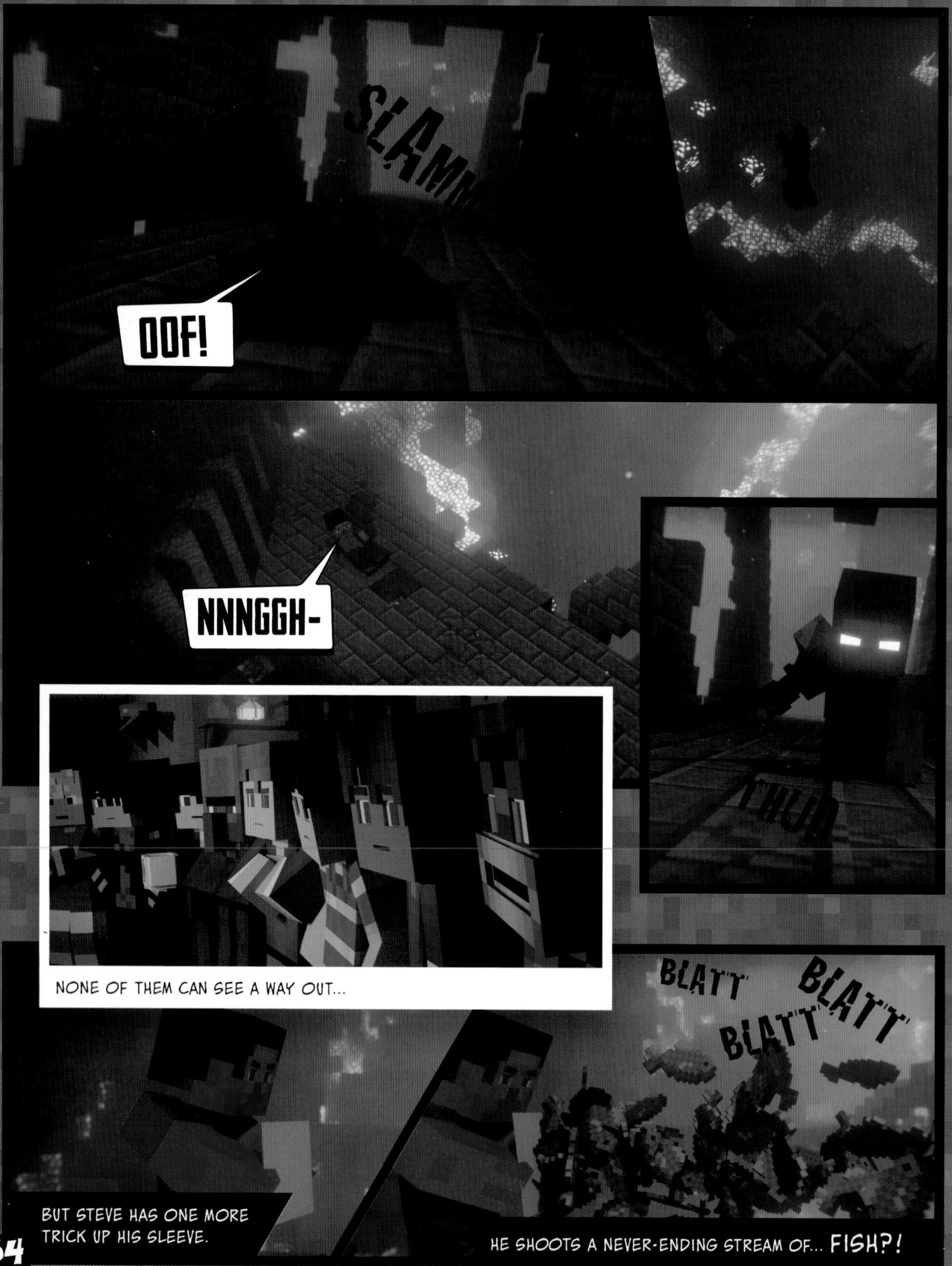
SLAMM
OOF!
NNNGGH-
THUD
NONE OF THEM CAN SEE A WAY OUT...
BUT STEVE HAS ONE MORE TRICK UP HIS SLEEVE.
BLATT
BLATT
BLATT
HE SHOOTS A NEVER-ENDING STREAM OF... FISH?!

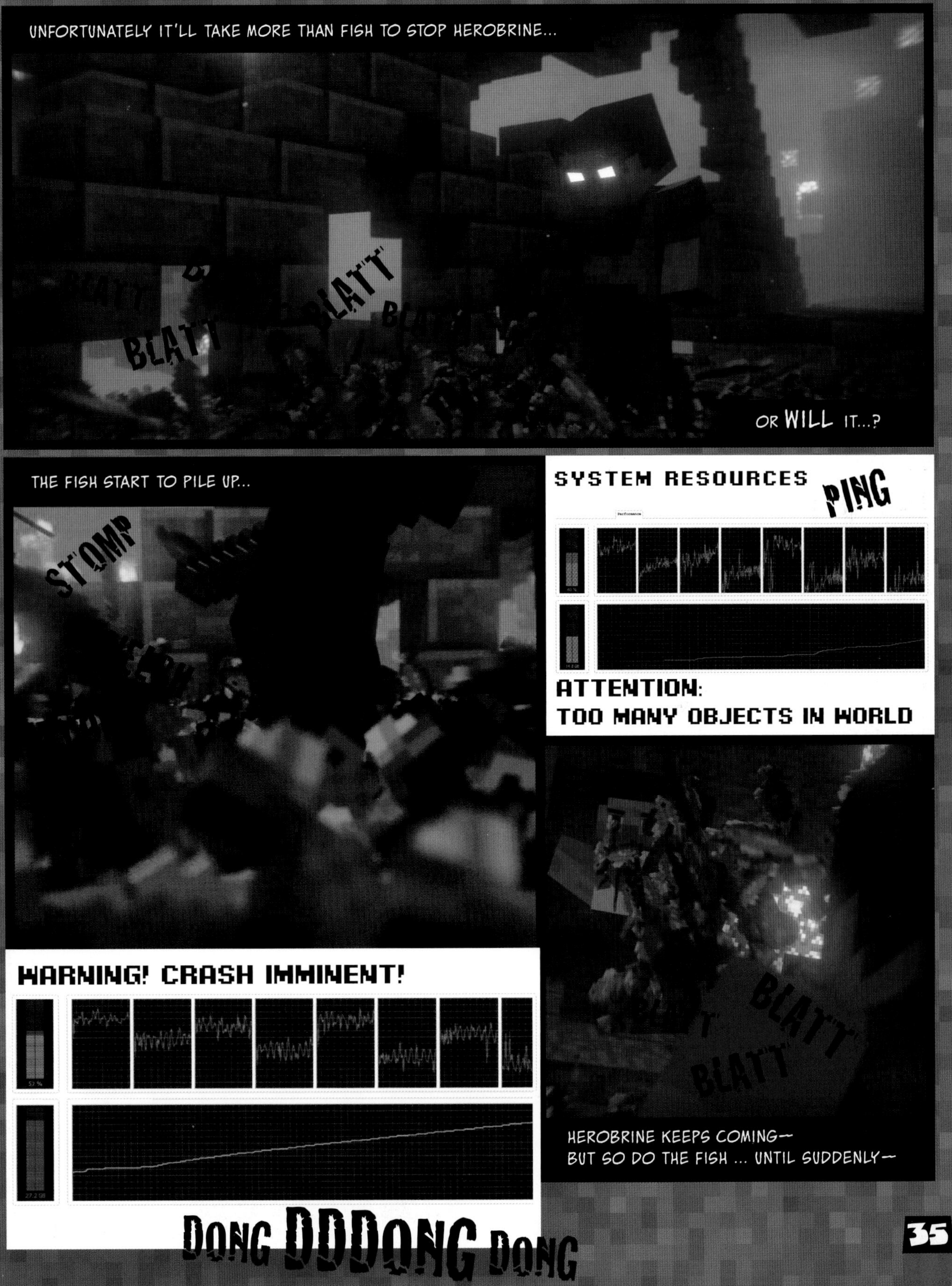
UNFORTUNATELY IT'LL TAKE MORE THAN FISH TO STOP HEROBRINE...
BLATT
BLATT
BLATT
OR WILL IT...?
THE FISH START TO PILE UP...
STOMP
SYSTEM RESOURCES
PING
ATTENTION:
TOO MANY OBJECTS IN WORLD
BLATT
BLATT
HEROBRINE KEEPS COMING—
BUT SO DO THE FISH ... UNTIL SUDDENLY—
WARNING! CRASH IMMINENT!
DONG DDDONG DONG

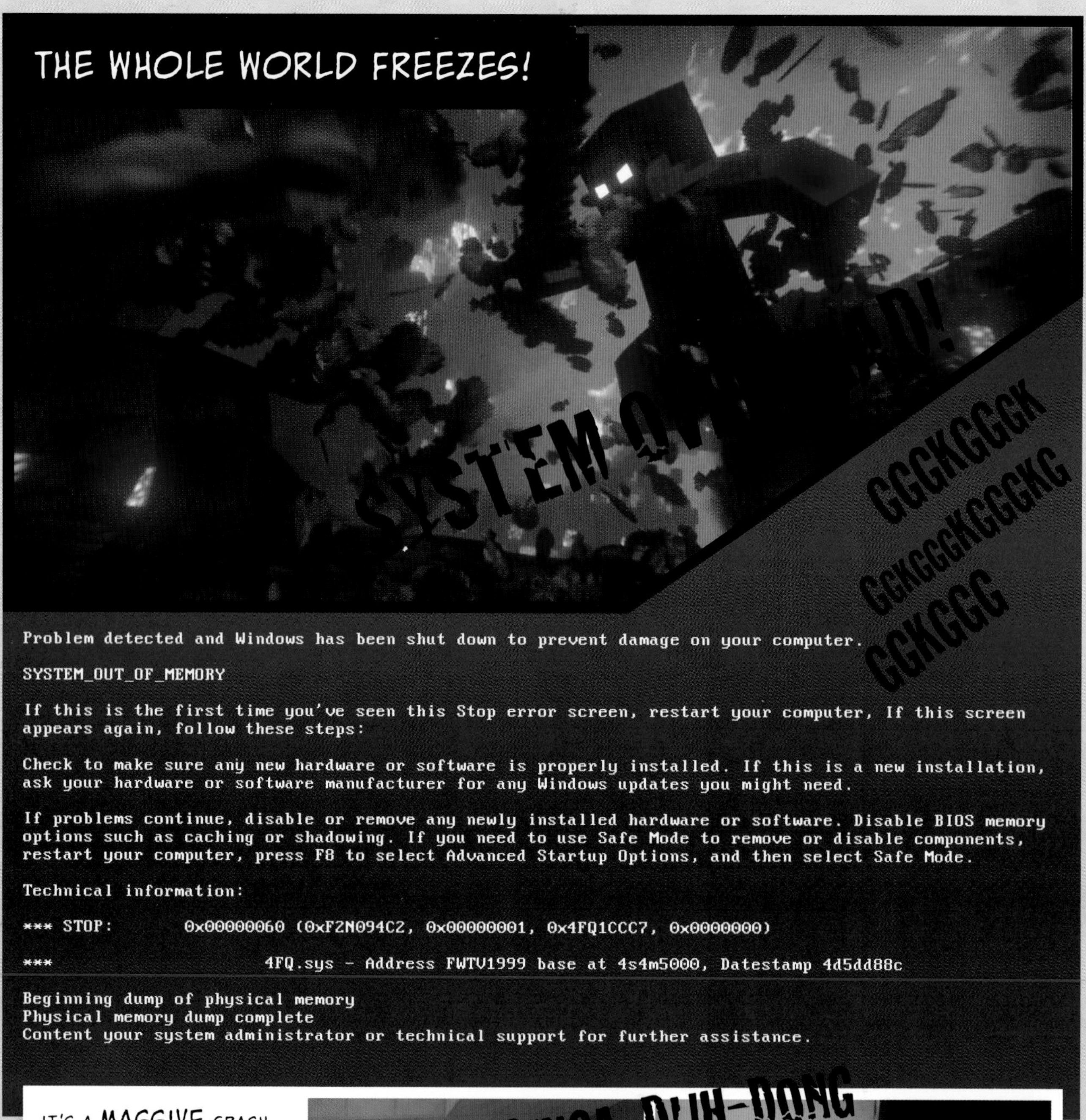
THE WHOLE WORLD FREEZES!
SYSTEM OV
GGGKGGGK
GGKGGGKGGGKG
GGKGGG
Problem detected and Windows has been shut down to prevent damage on your computer.
SYSTEM_OUT_OF_MEMORY
If this is the first time you've seen this Stop error screen, restart your computer, If this screen appears again, follow these steps:
Check to make sure any new hardware or software is properly installed. If this is a new installation, ask your hardware or software manufacturer for any Windows updates you might need.
If problems continue, disable or remove any newly installed hardware or software. Disable BIOS memory options such as caching or shadowing. If you need to use Safe Mode to remove or disable components, restart your computer, press F8 to select Advanced Startup Options, and then select Safe Mode.
Technical information:
*** STOP: 0x00000060 (0xF2N094C2, 0x00000001, 0x4FQ1CCC7, 0x0000000)
*** 4FQ.sys - Address FWTV1999 base at 4s4m5000, Datestamp 4d5dd88c
Beginning dump of physical memory
Physical memory dump complete
Content your system administrator or technical support for further assistance.

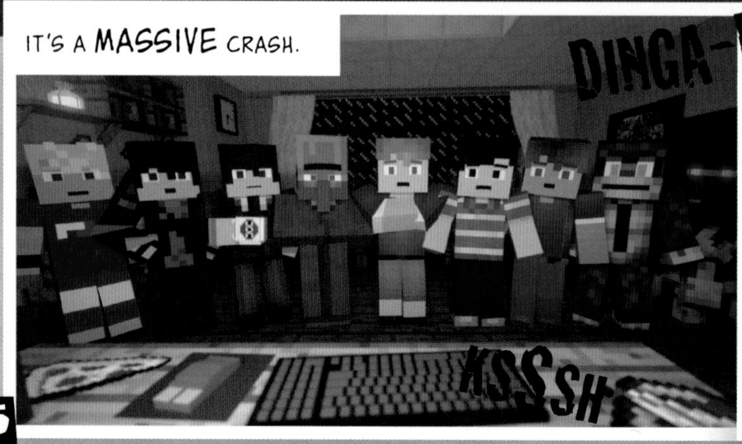
IT'S A MASSIVE CRASH.
DINGA-DUH-DONG
KSSSH

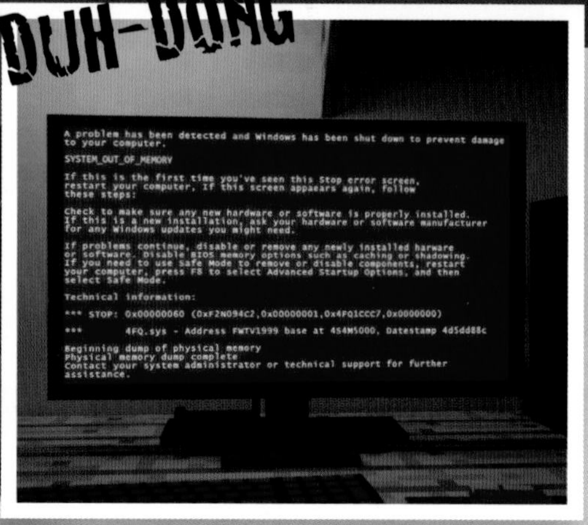

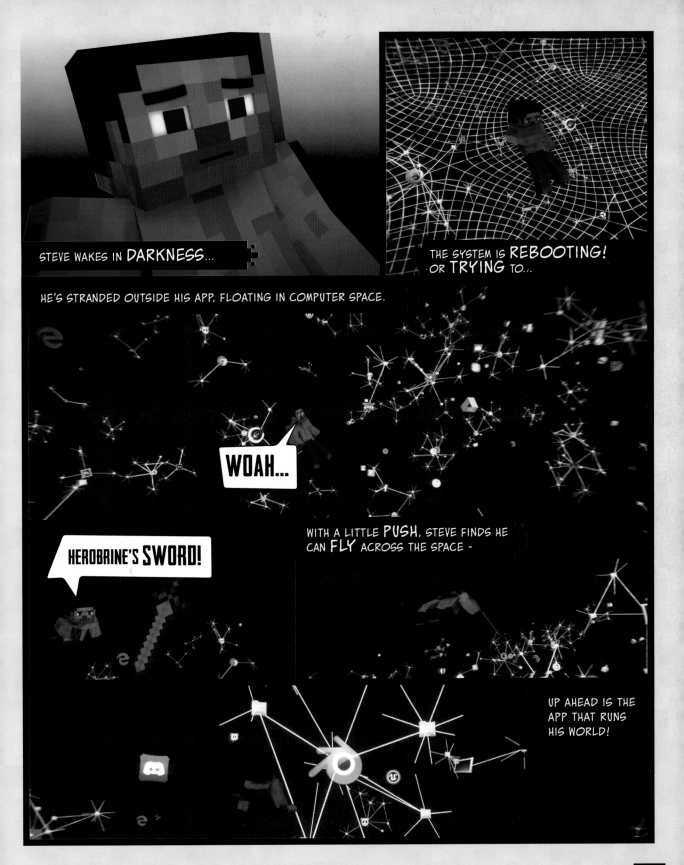

STEVE WAKES IN DARKNESS...

THE SYSTEM IS REBOOTING! OR TRYING TO...

HE'S STRANDED OUTSIDE HIS APP, FLOATING IN COMPUTER SPACE.

WOAH...

WITH A LITTLE PUSH, STEVE FINDS HE CAN FLY ACROSS THE SPACE -

HEROBRINE'S SWORD!

UP AHEAD IS THE APP THAT RUNS HIS WORLD!

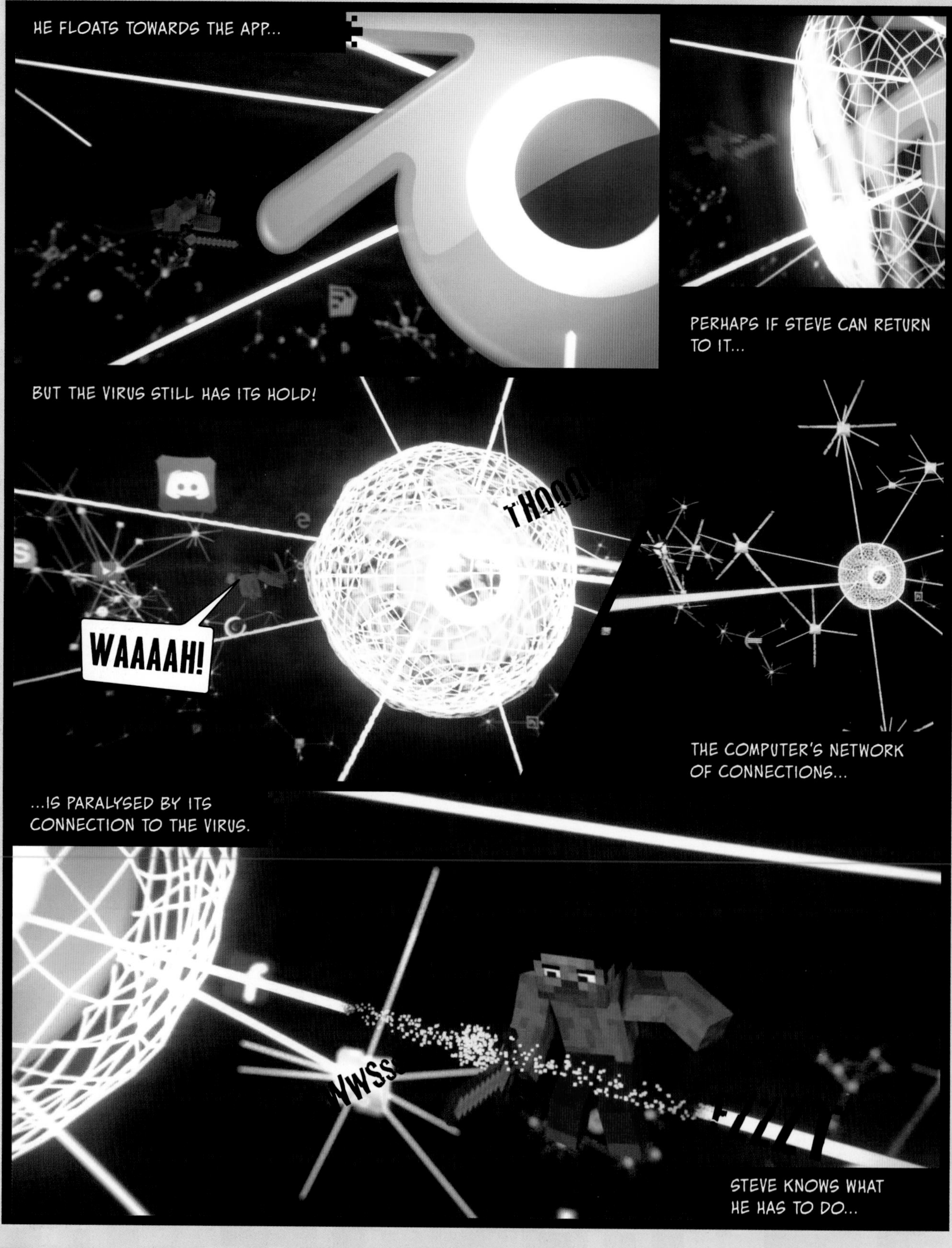

HE FLOATS TOWARDS THE APP...

PERHAPS IF STEVE CAN RETURN TO IT...

BUT THE VIRUS STILL HAS ITS HOLD!

THOOO

WAAAAH!

THE COMPUTER'S NETWORK OF CONNECTIONS...

...IS PARALYSED BY ITS CONNECTION TO THE VIRUS.

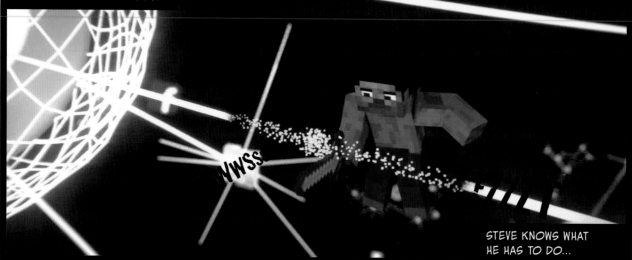

YWSS...

STEVE KNOWS WHAT HE HAS TO DO...

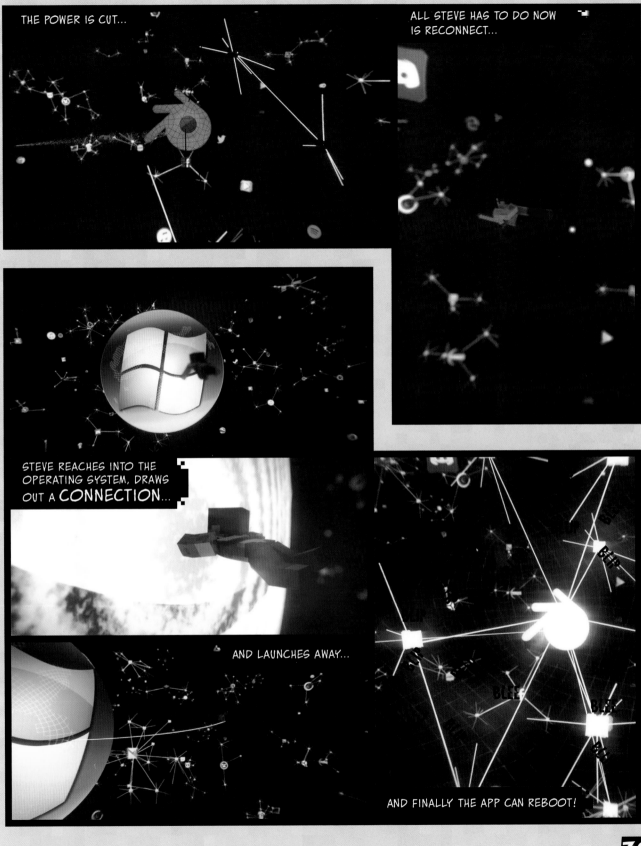

THE POWER IS CUT...

ALL STEVE HAS TO DO NOW IS RECONNECT...

STEVE REACHES INTO THE OPERATING SYSTEM, DRAWS OUT A **CONNECTION**...

AND LAUNCHES AWAY...

AND FINALLY THE APP CAN REBOOT!

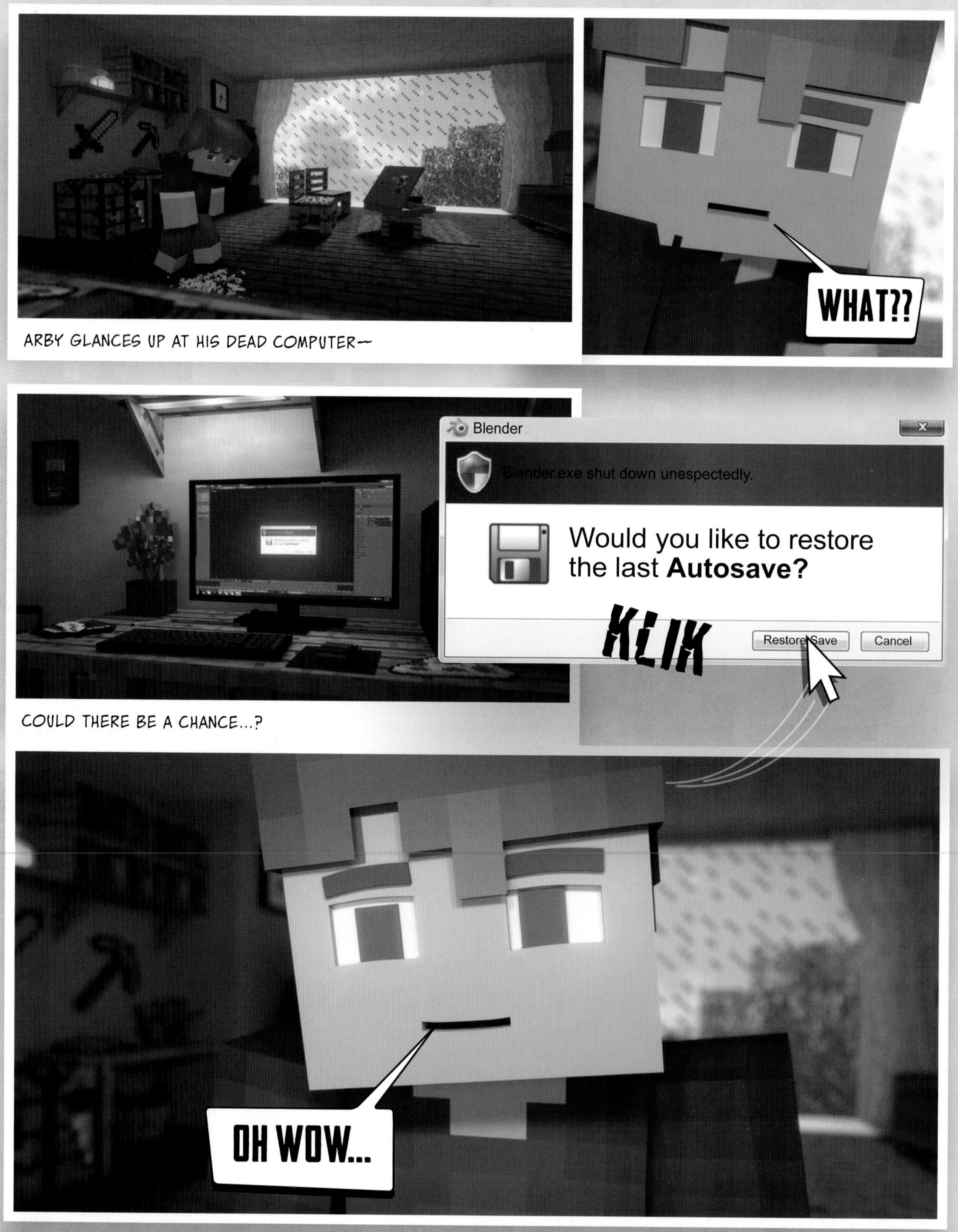
ARBY GLANCES UP AT HIS DEAD COMPUTER—
WHAT??
Blender
Blender.exe shut down unespectedly.
Would you like to restore the last **Autosave?**
KLIK
Restore Save
Cancel
COULD THERE BE A CHANCE...?
OH WOW...

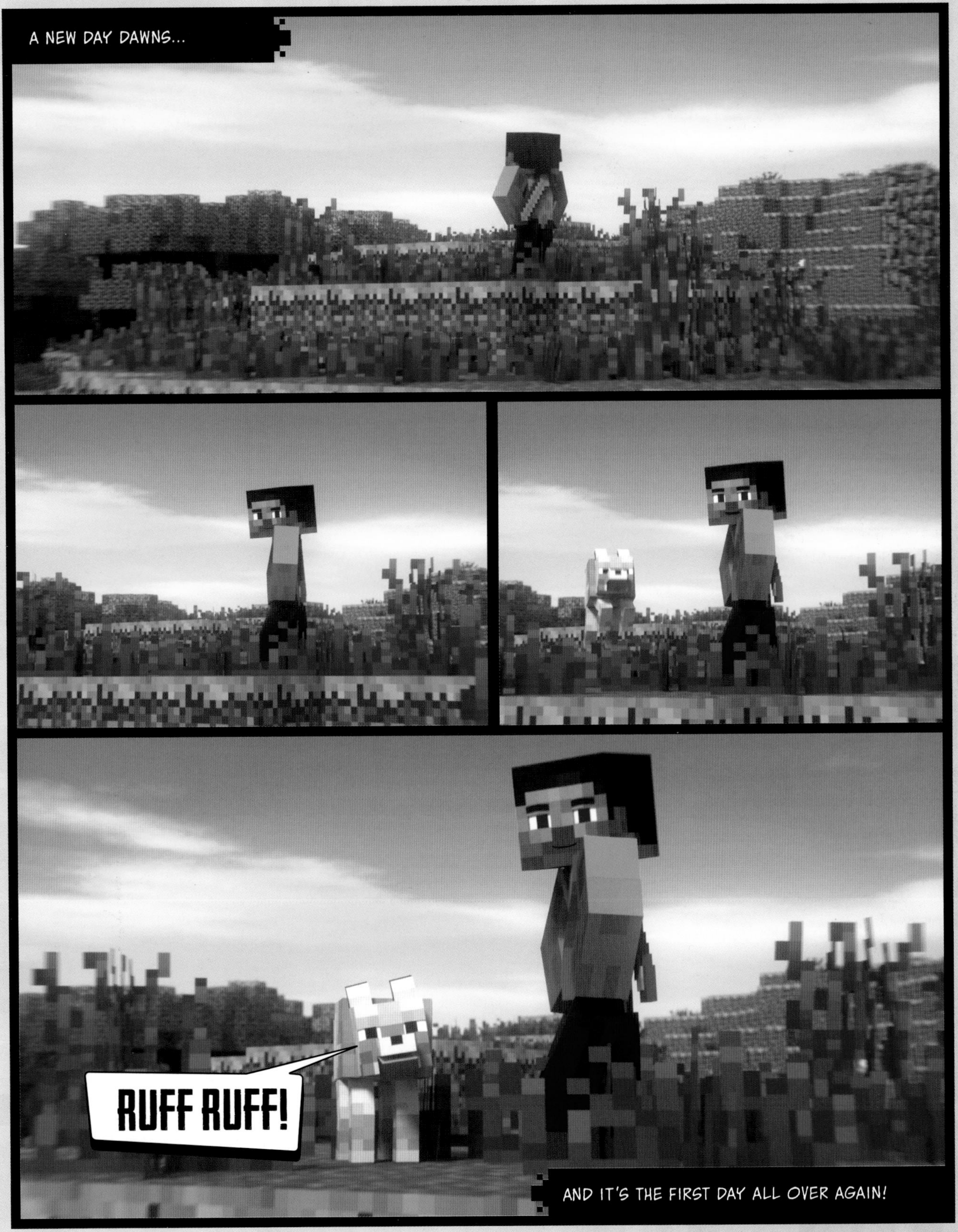
A NEW DAY DAWNS...
RUFF RUFF!
AND IT'S THE FIRST DAY ALL OVER AGAIN!

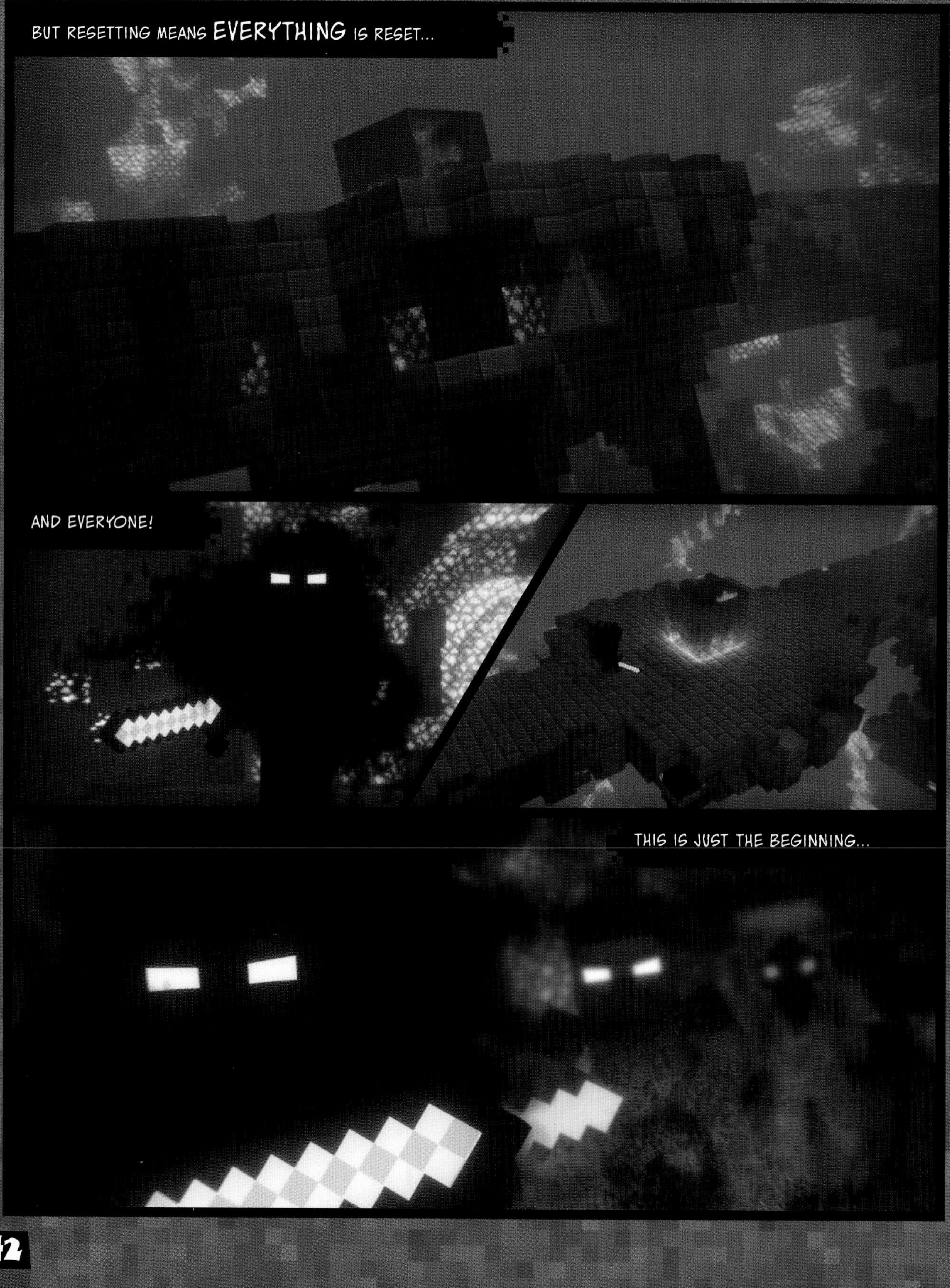

BUT RESETTING MEANS EVERYTHING IS RESET...
AND EVERYONE!
THIS IS JUST THE BEGINNING...

CHAPTER 3

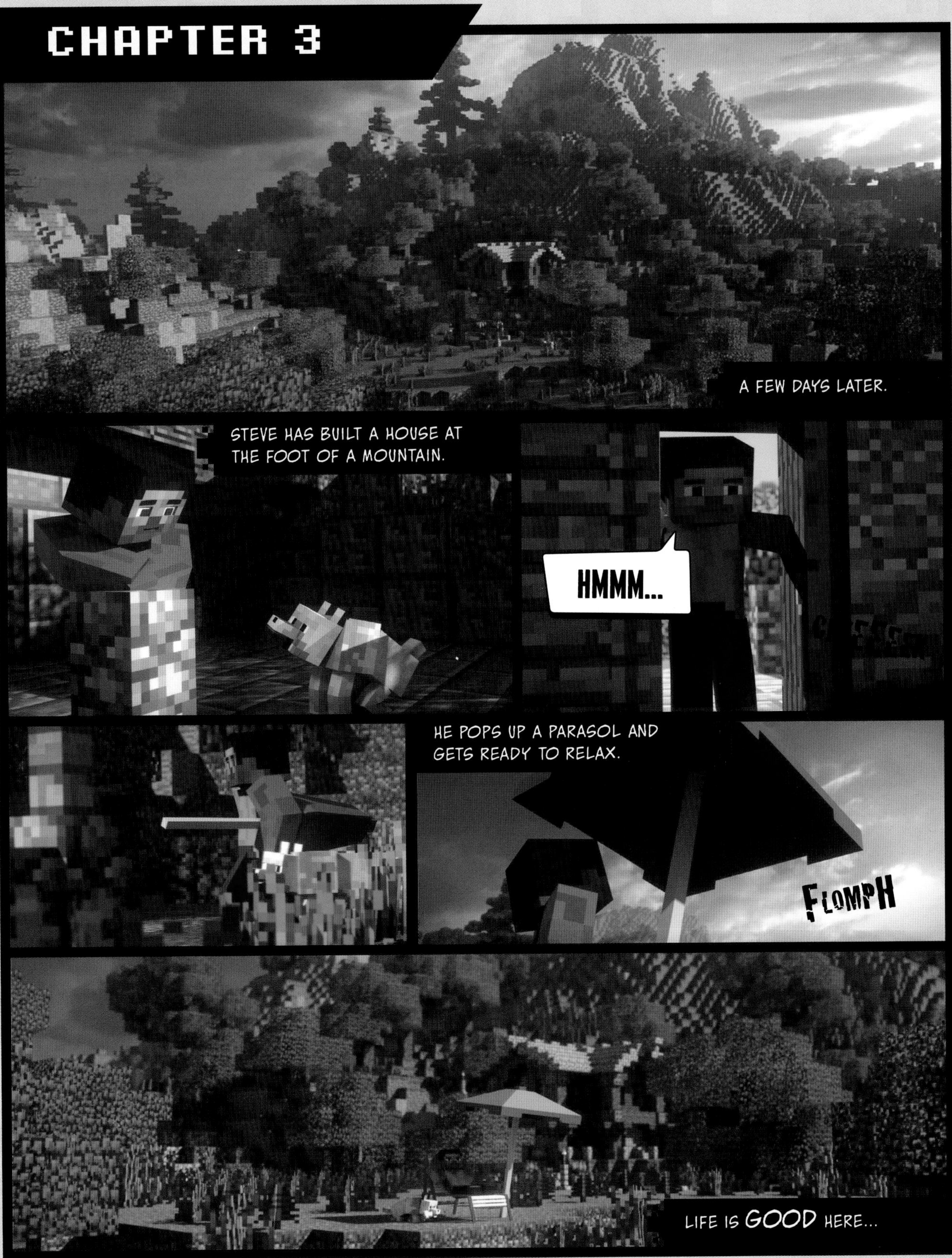
A FEW DAYS LATER.
STEVE HAS BUILT A HOUSE AT THE FOOT OF A MOUNTAIN.
HMMM...
HE POPS UP A PARASOL AND GETS READY TO RELAX.
FLOMPH
LIFE IS GOOD HERE...

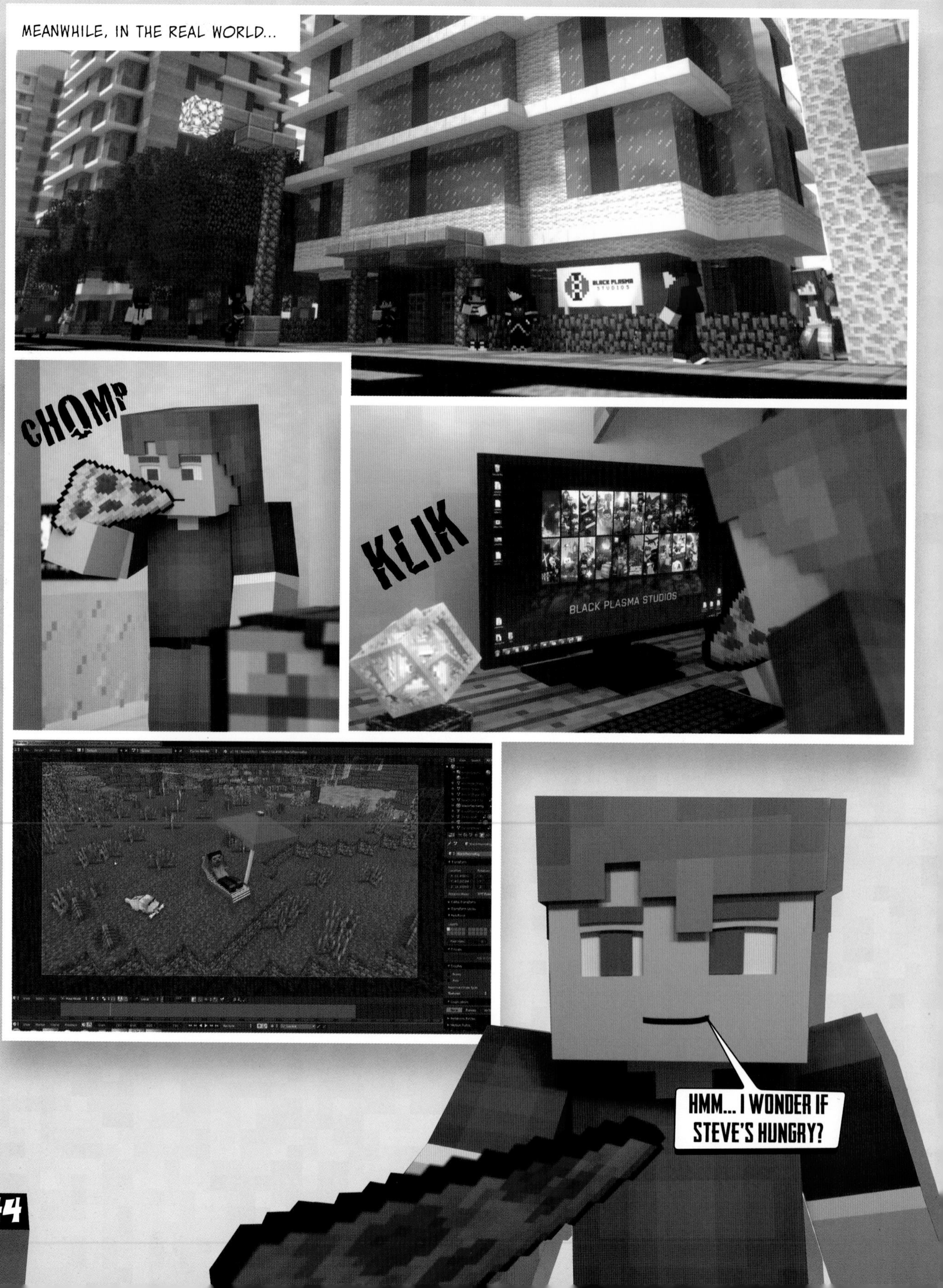
MEANWHILE, IN THE REAL WORLD...
BLACK PLASMA STUDIOS
CHOMP
KLIK
BLACK PLASMA STUDIOS
HMM... I WONDER IF STEVE'S HUNGRY?

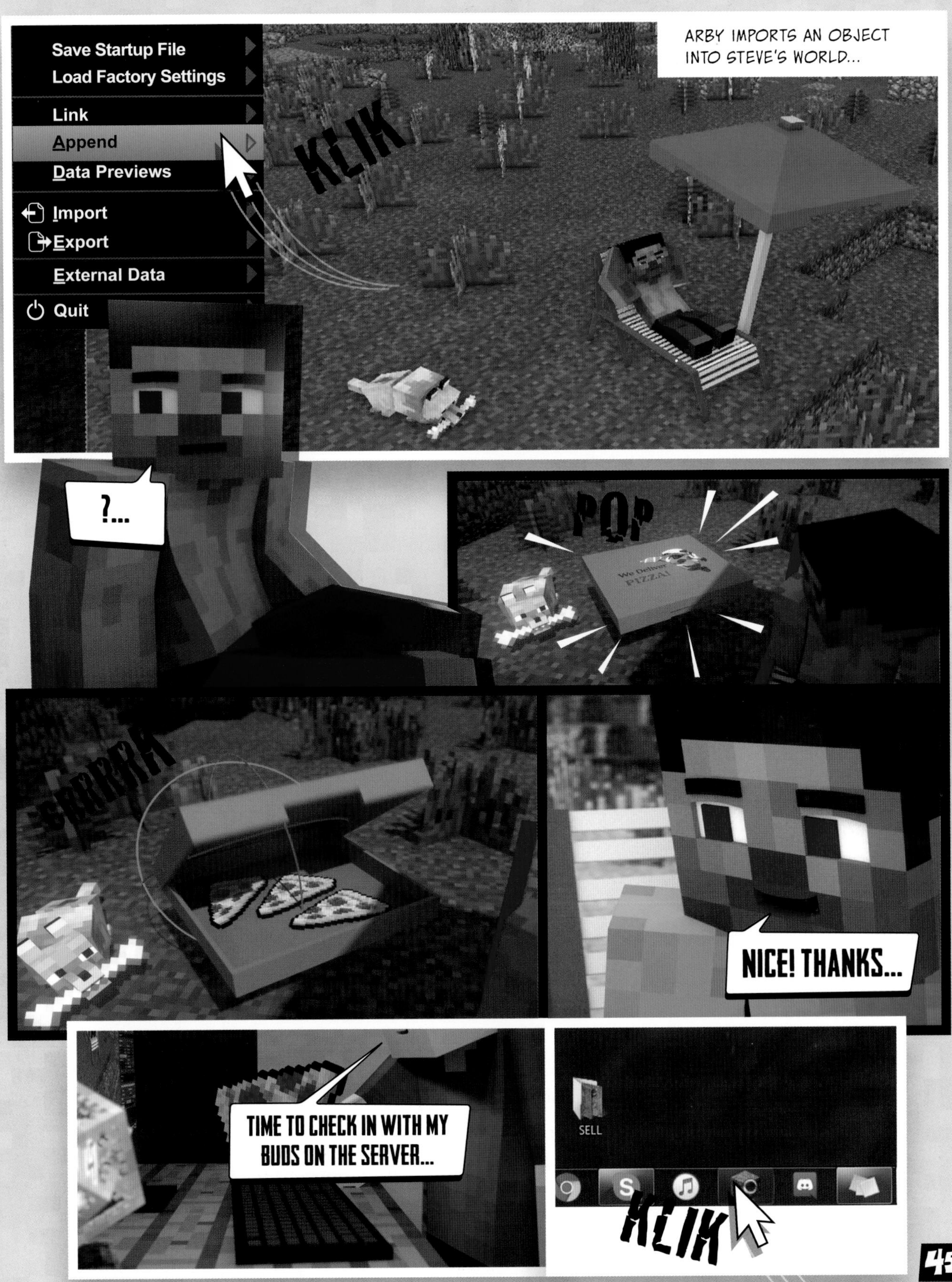

ARBY IMPORTS AN OBJECT INTO STEVE'S WORLD...
Save Startup File
Load Factory Settings
Link
Append
Data Previews
Import
Export
External Data
Quit
KLIK
?...
POP
We Deliver PIZZA!
CRRRRK
NICE! THANKS...
TIME TO CHECK IN WITH MY BUDS ON THE SERVER...
SELL
KLIK

ARBY SELECTS A SERVER TO JOIN...

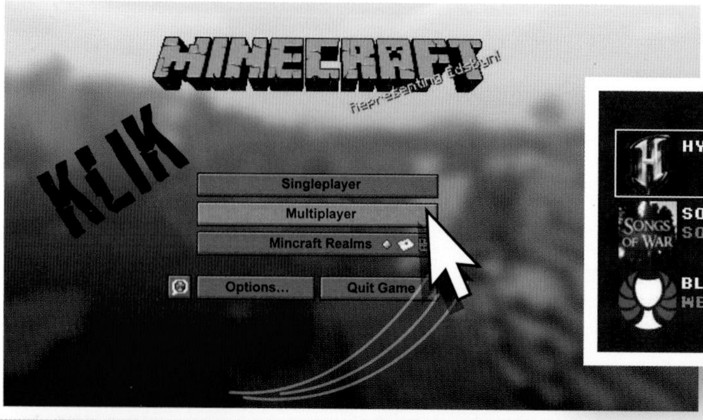
MINECRAFT
KLIK
Singleplayer
Multiplayer
Mincraft Realms
Options...
Quit Game

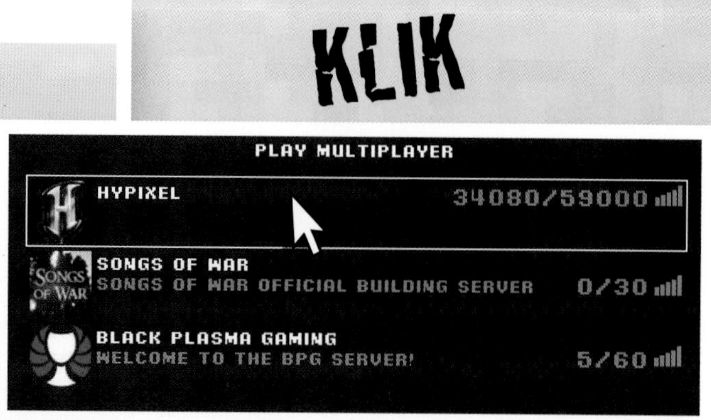
KLIK
PLAY MULTIPLAYER
HYPIXEL 34080/59000
SONGS OF WAR
SONGS OF WAR OFFICIAL BUILDING SERVER 0/30
BLACK PLASMA GAMING
WELCOME TO THE BPG SERVER! 5/60

THE HYPIXEL SERVER!

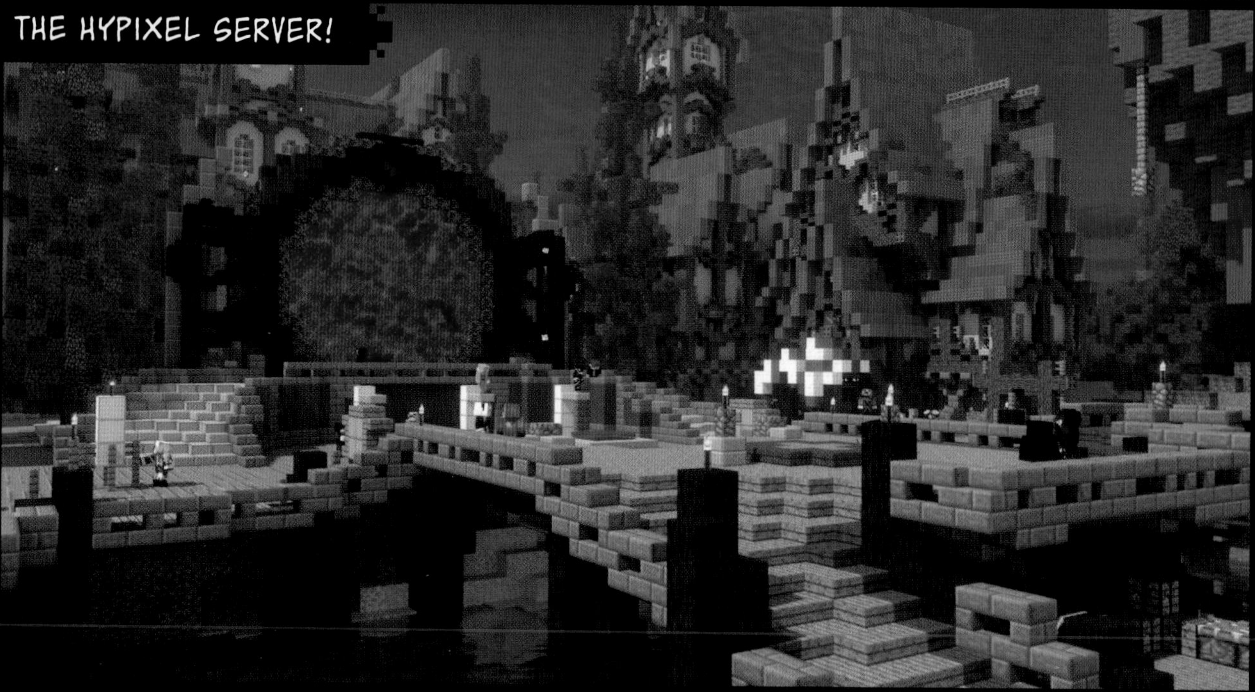

THIS LOOKS LIKE A FUN PLACE TO KICK BACK AND CHILL...

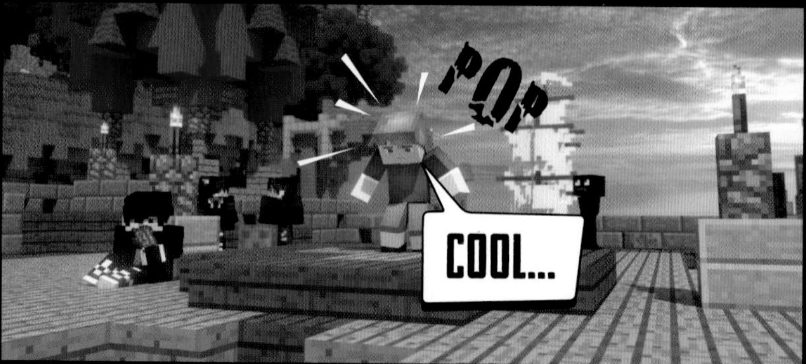
POP
COOL...

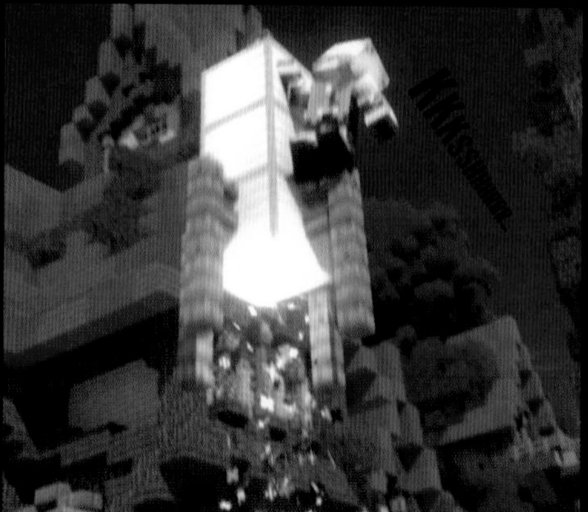

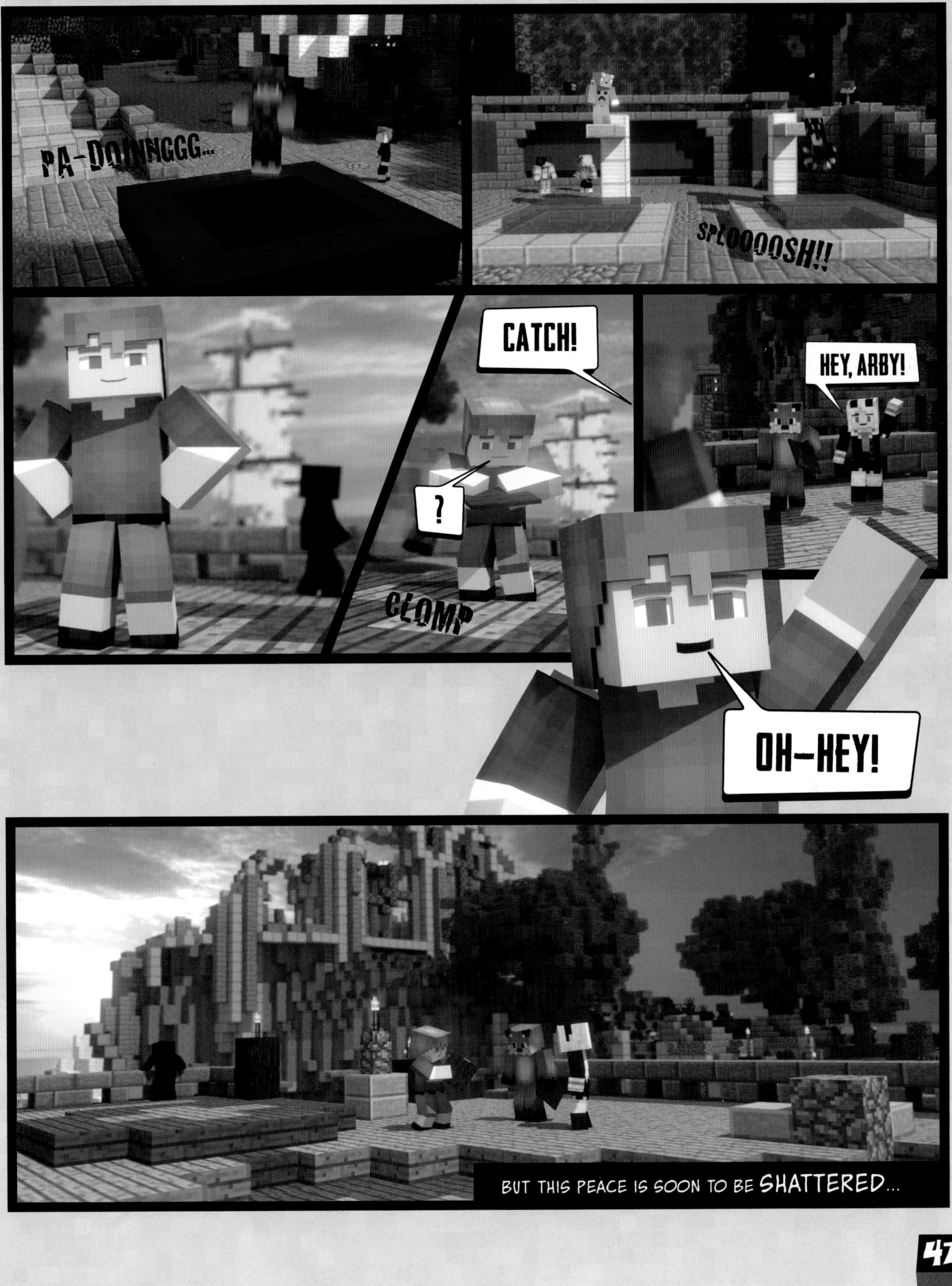
PA-DOINNGGG...
SPLOOOOOSH!!
CATCH!
?
CLOMP
HEY, ARBY!
OH—HEY!
BUT THIS PEACE IS SOON TO BE SHATTERED...

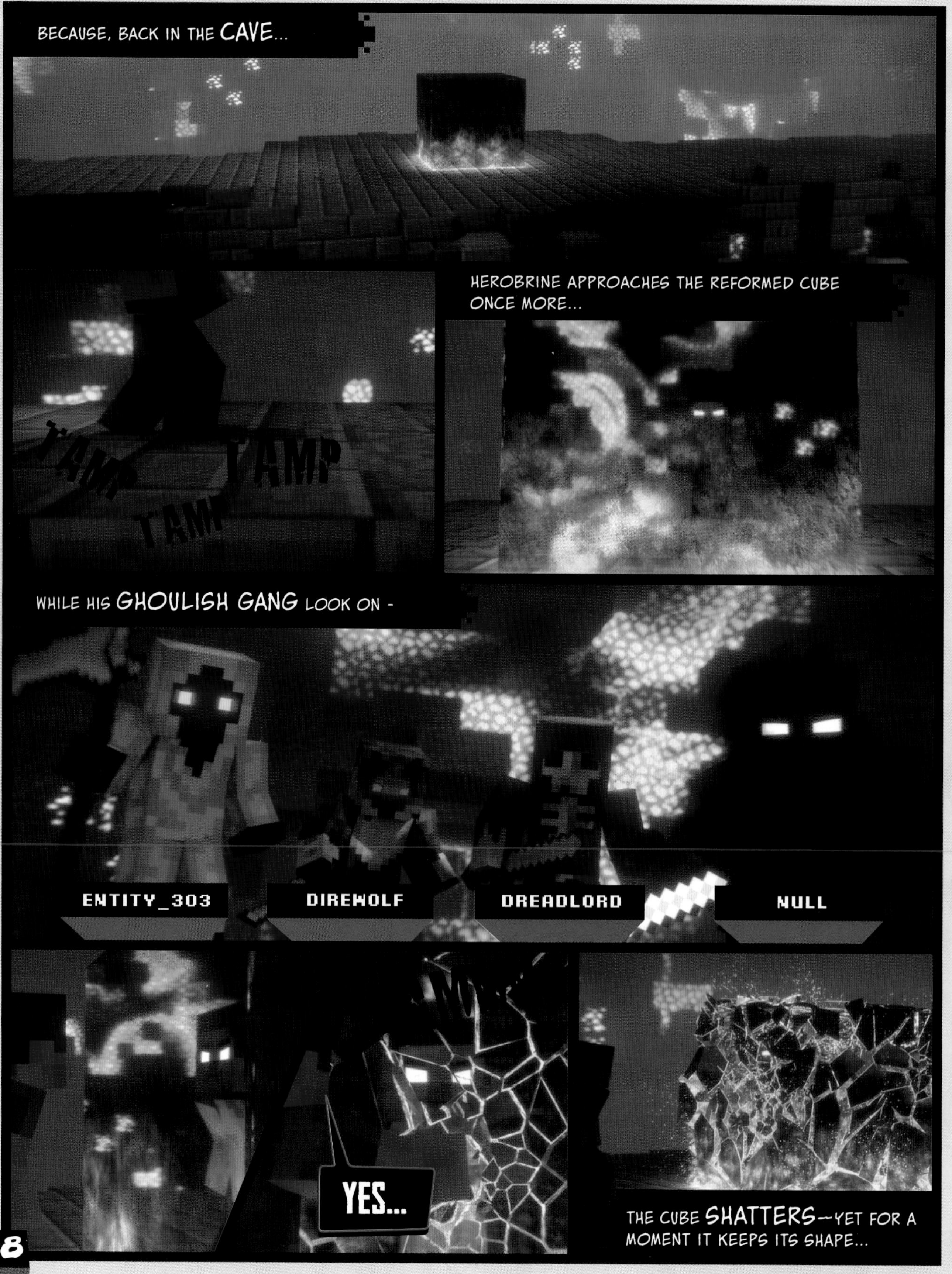
BECAUSE, BACK IN THE CAVE...
TAMP
TAMP
TAMP
HEROBRINE APPROACHES THE REFORMED CUBE ONCE MORE...
WHILE HIS GHOULISH GANG LOOK ON -
ENTITY_303
DIREWOLF
DREADLORD
NULL
YES...
THE CUBE SHATTERS—YET FOR A MOMENT IT KEEPS ITS SHAPE...

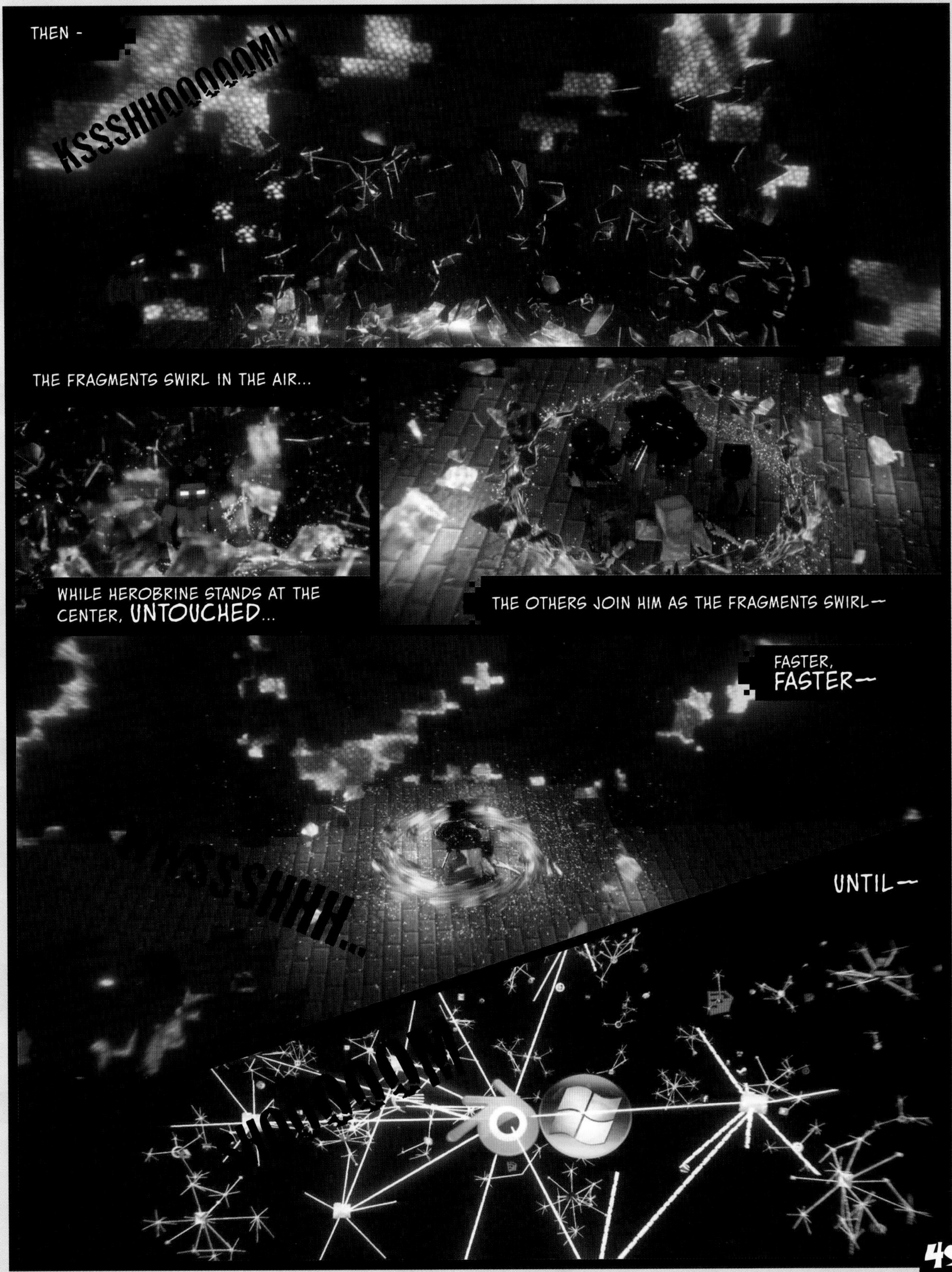
THEN -
KSSSHHOOOOOOM!!
THE FRAGMENTS SWIRL IN THE AIR...
WHILE HEROBRINE STANDS AT THE CENTER, UNTOUCHED...
THE OTHERS JOIN HIM AS THE FRAGMENTS SWIRL—
FASTER, FASTER—
UNTIL—

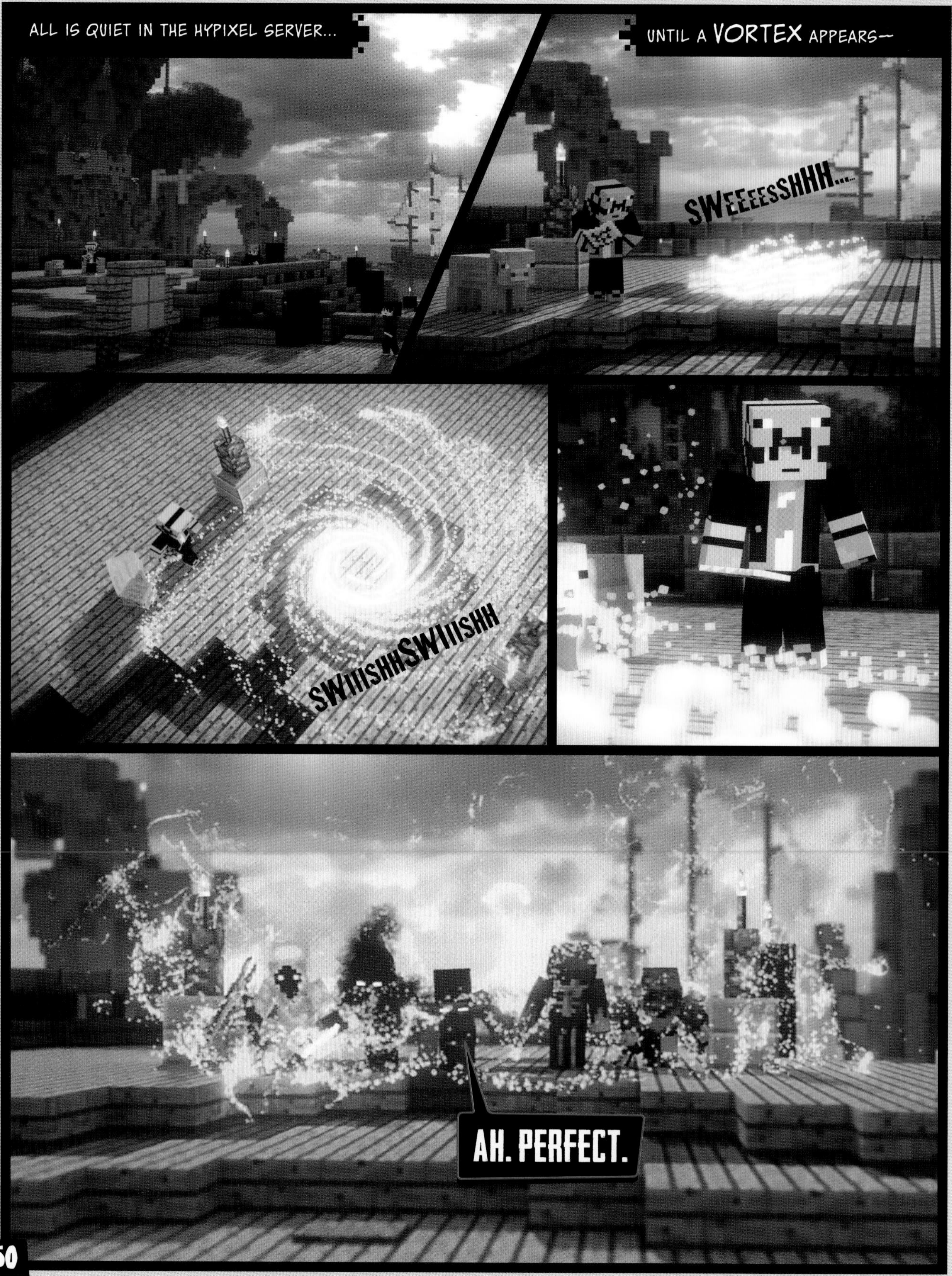
ALL IS QUIET IN THE HYPIXEL SERVER...
UNTIL A VORTEX APPEARS—
SWEEEEESSHHH....
SWIIIISHHSWIIIISHH
AH. PERFECT.

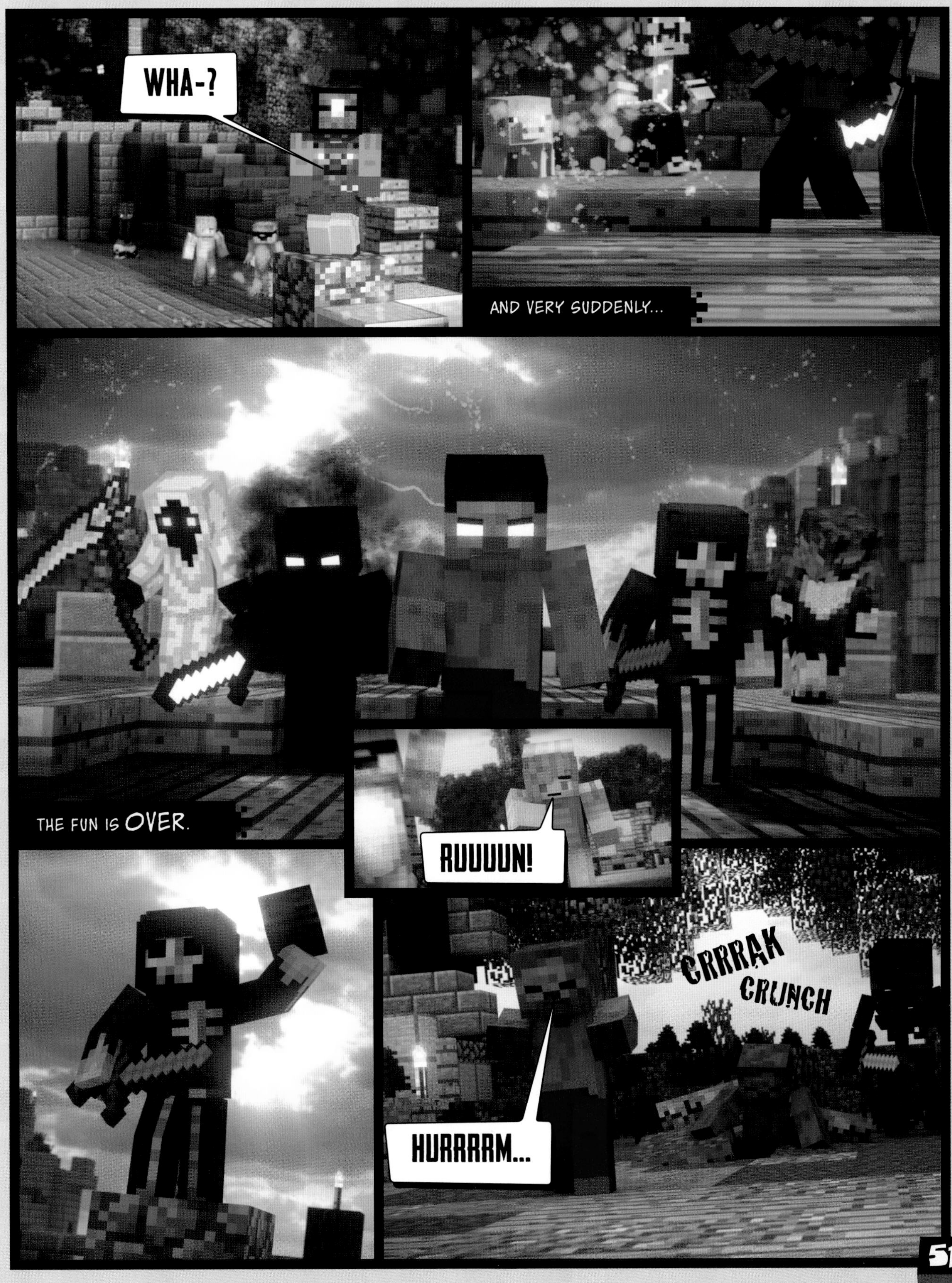

WHA-?
AND VERY SUDDENLY...
THE FUN IS OVER.
RUUUUN!
CRRRAK
CRUNCH
HURRRRM...

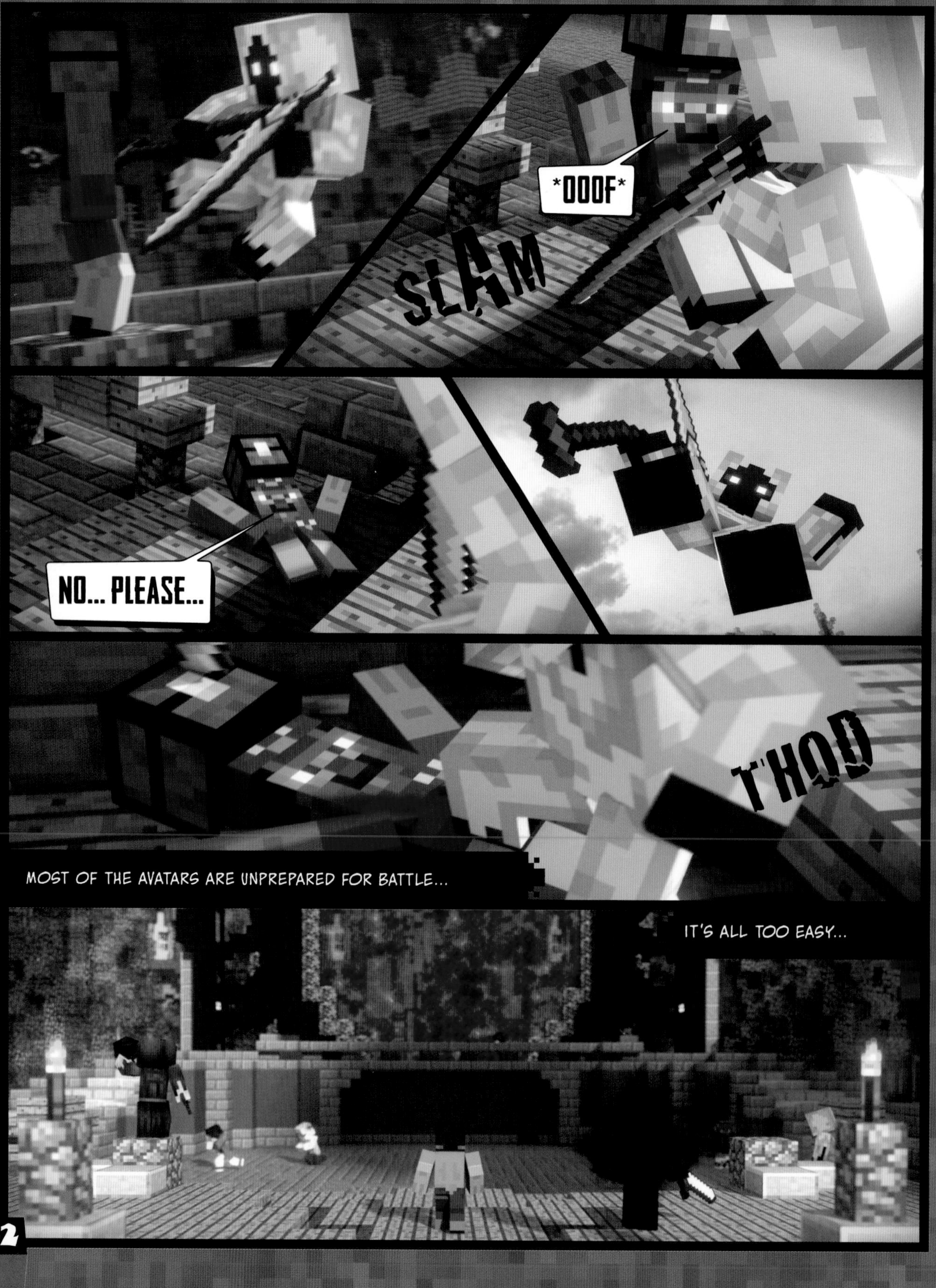
OOOF
SLAM
NO... PLEASE...
THOD
MOST OF THE AVATARS ARE UNPREPARED FOR BATTLE...
IT'S ALL TOO EASY...

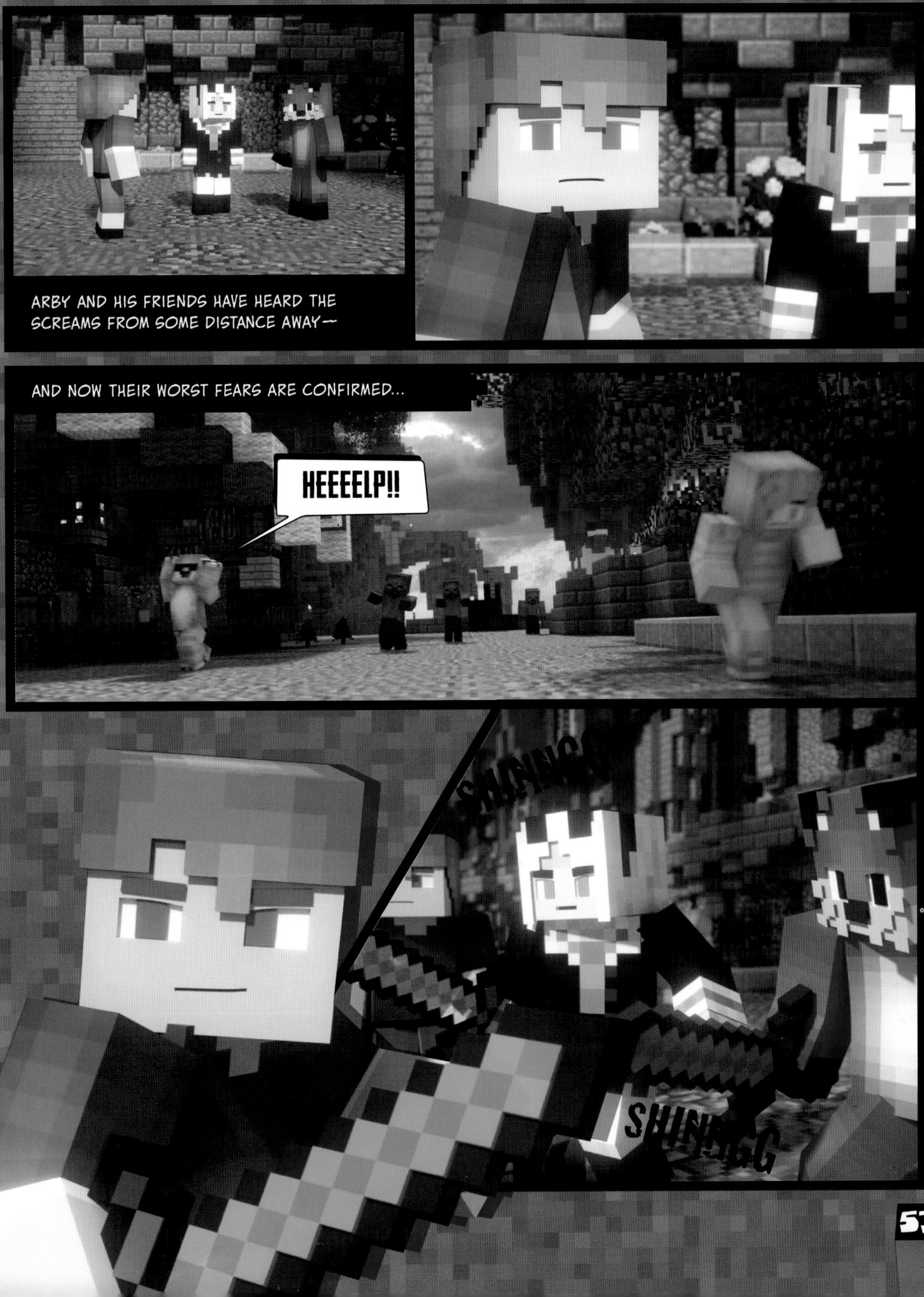
ARBY AND HIS FRIENDS HAVE HEARD THE SCREAMS FROM SOME DISTANCE AWAY—
AND NOW THEIR WORST FEARS ARE CONFIRMED...
HEEEELP!!

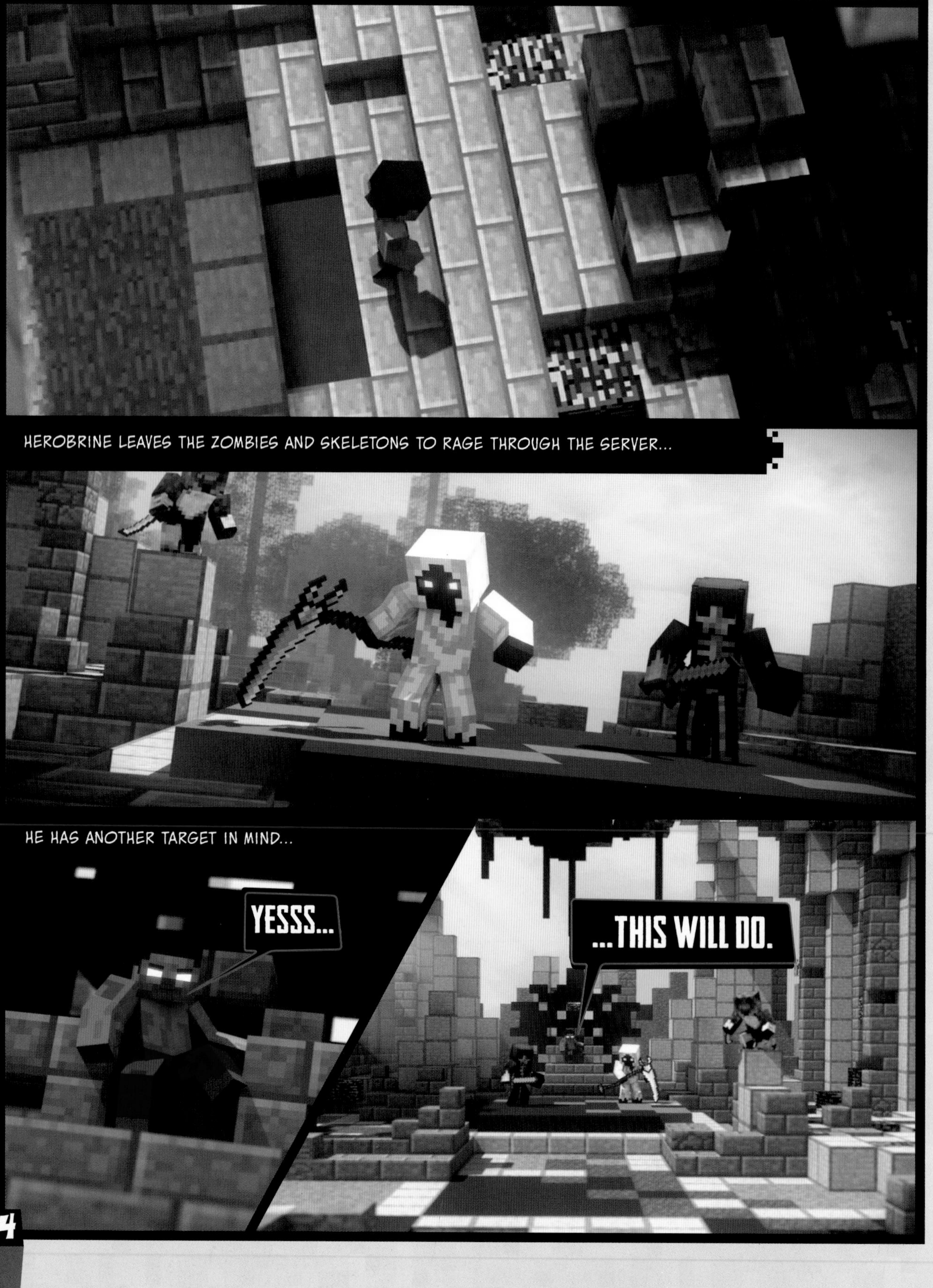
HEROBRINE LEAVES THE ZOMBIES AND SKELETONS TO RAGE THROUGH THE SERVER...
HE HAS ANOTHER TARGET IN MIND...
YESSS...
...THIS WILL DO.

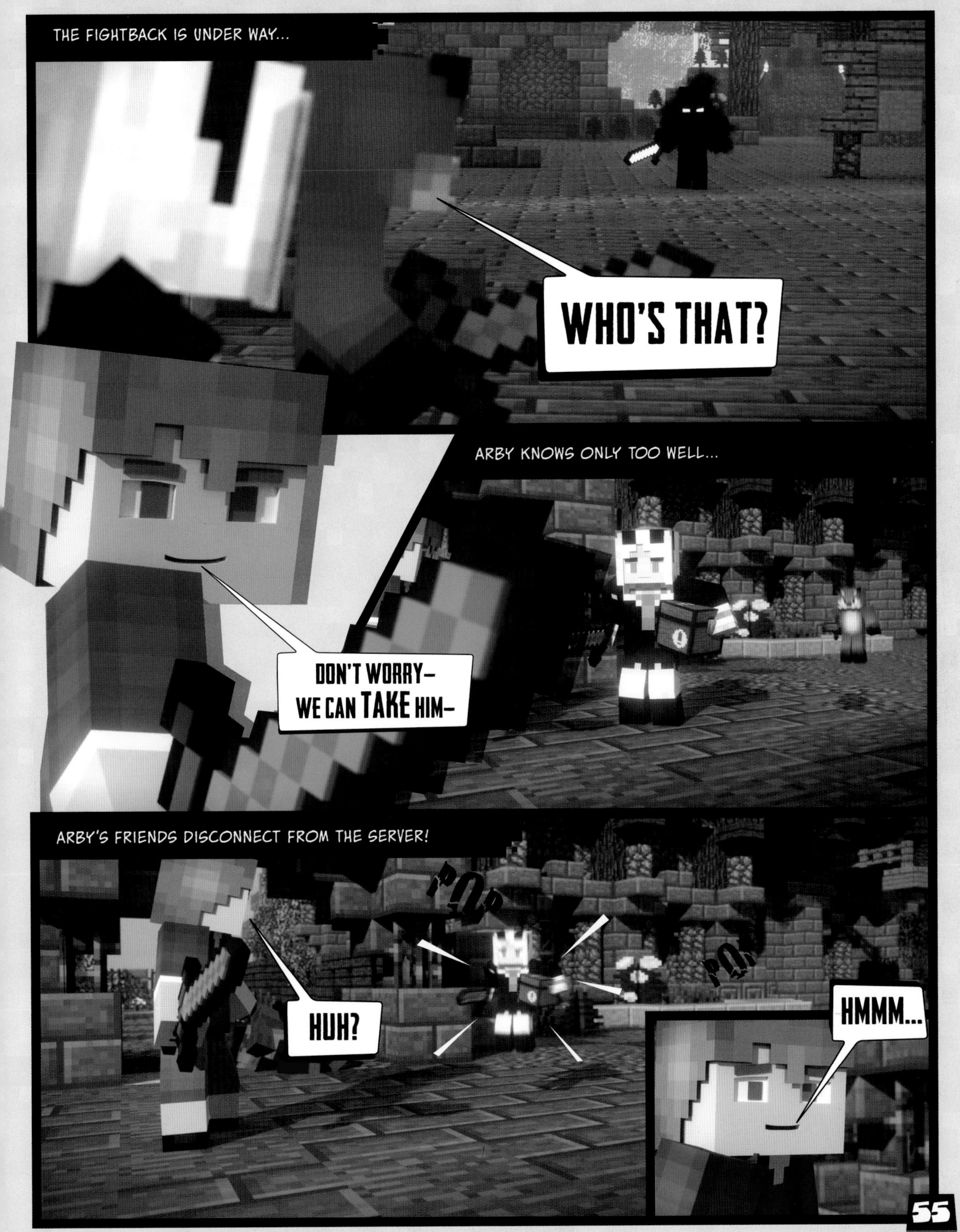
THE FIGHTBACK IS UNDER WAY...
WHO'S THAT?
ARBY KNOWS ONLY TOO WELL...
DON'T WORRY– WE CAN TAKE HIM–
ARBY'S FRIENDS DISCONNECT FROM THE SERVER!
HUH?
HMMM...

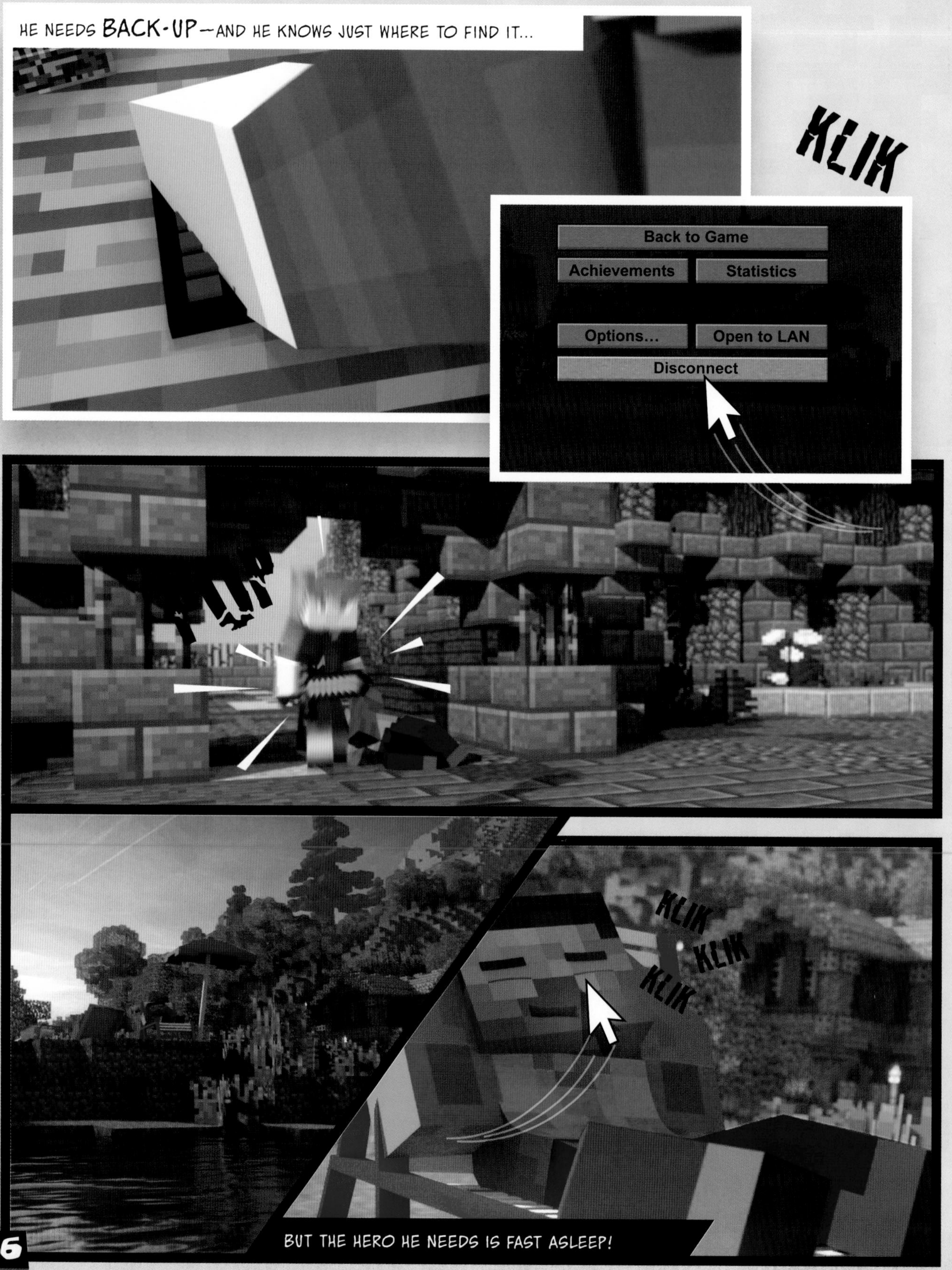
HE NEEDS BACK-UP—AND HE KNOWS JUST WHERE TO FIND IT...
KLIK
Back to Game
Achievements
Statistics
Options...
Open to LAN
Disconnect
KLIK
KLIK
KLIK
BUT THE HERO HE NEEDS IS FAST ASLEEP!

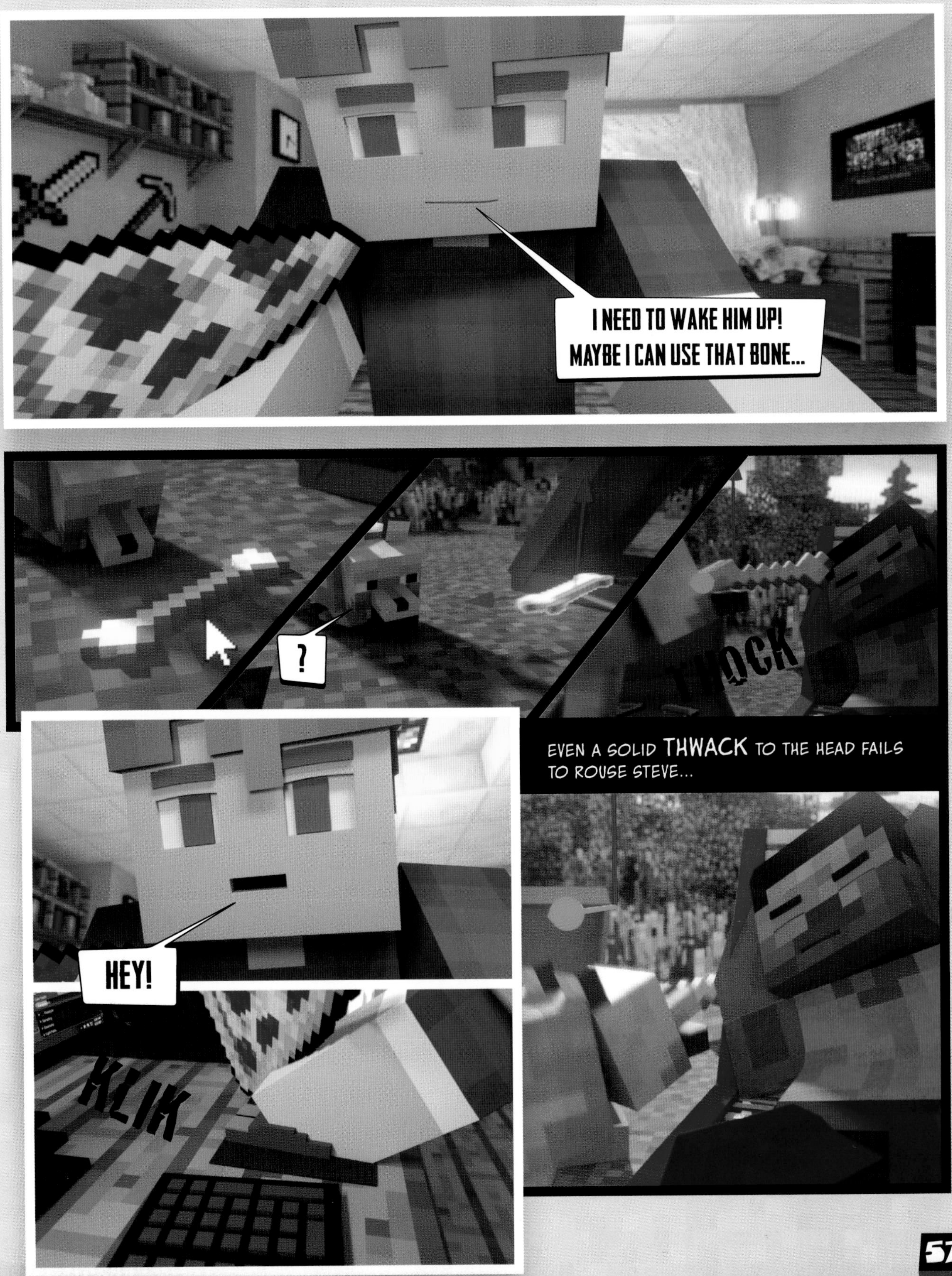
I NEED TO WAKE HIM UP!
MAYBE I CAN USE THAT BONE...
?
THOCK
EVEN A SOLID THWACK TO THE HEAD FAILS TO ROUSE STEVE...
HEY!
KLIK

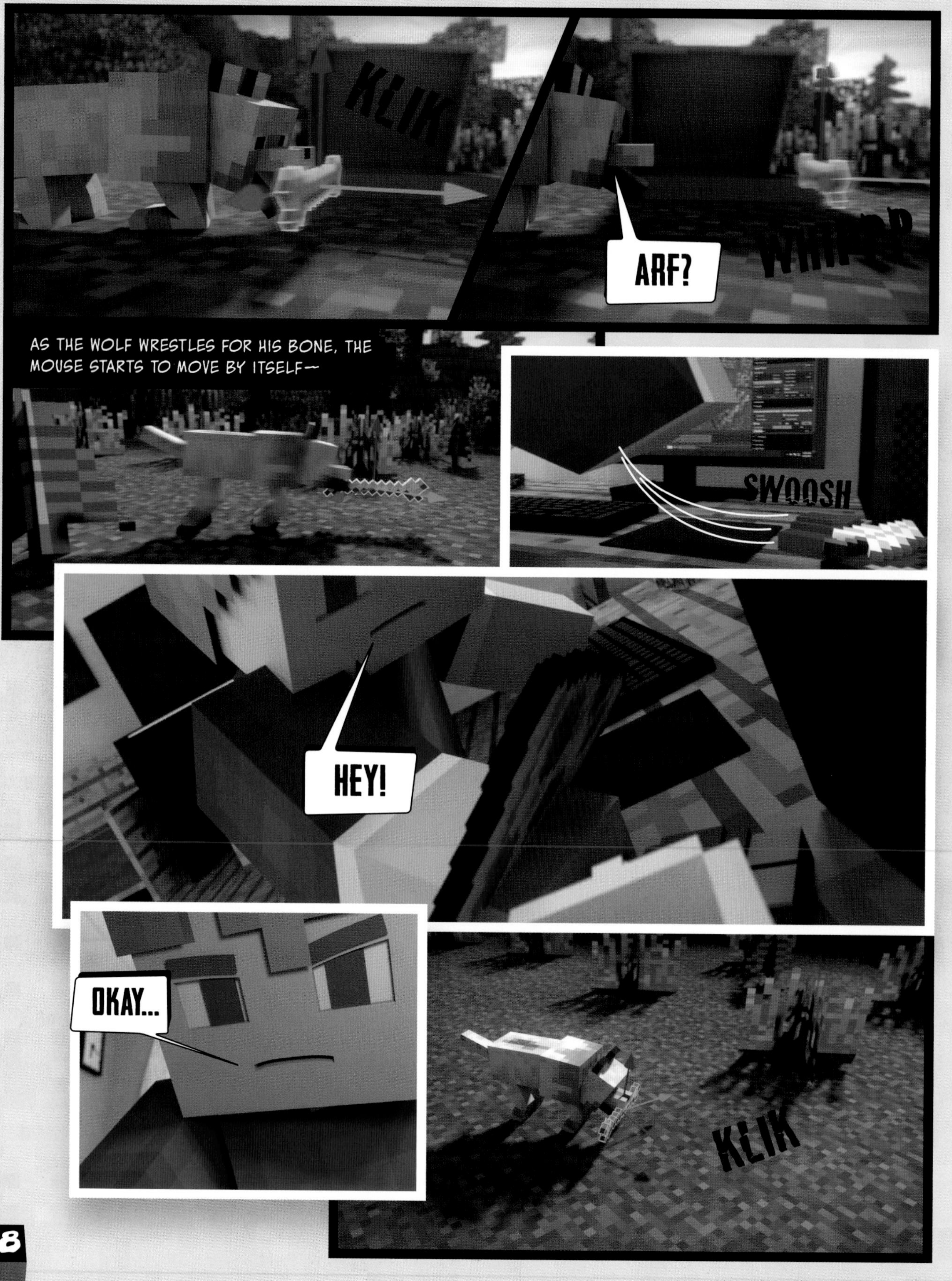
KLIK
ARF?
AS THE WOLF WRESTLES FOR HIS BONE, THE MOUSE STARTS TO MOVE BY ITSELF—
SWOOSH
HEY!
OKAY...
KLIK

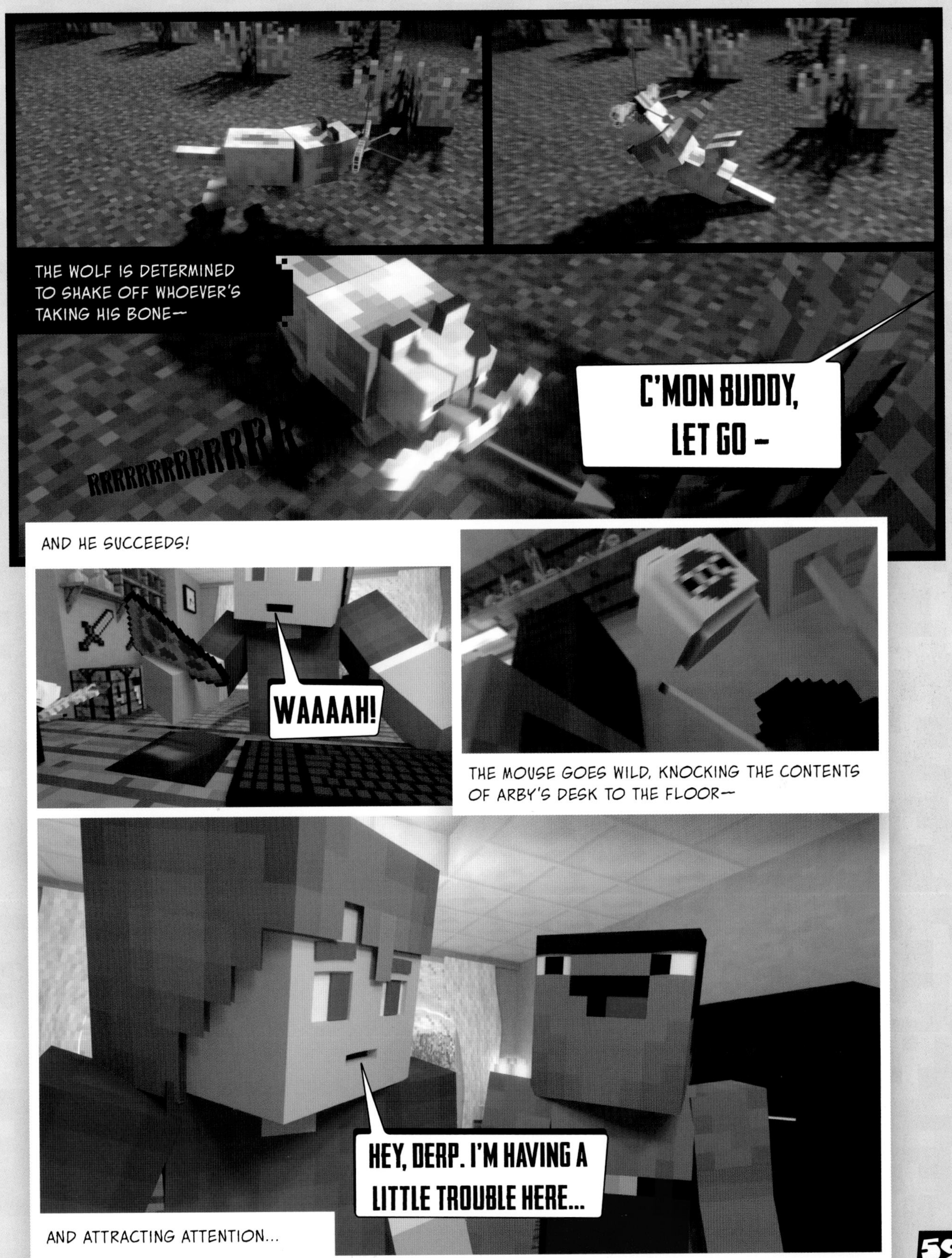
THE WOLF IS DETERMINED TO SHAKE OFF WHOEVER'S TAKING HIS BONE—
RRRRRRRRRRRRR
C'MON BUDDY, LET GO –
AND HE SUCCEEDS!
WAAAAH!
THE MOUSE GOES WILD, KNOCKING THE CONTENTS OF ARBY'S DESK TO THE FLOOR—
HEY, DERP. I'M HAVING A LITTLE TROUBLE HERE...
AND ATTRACTING ATTENTION...

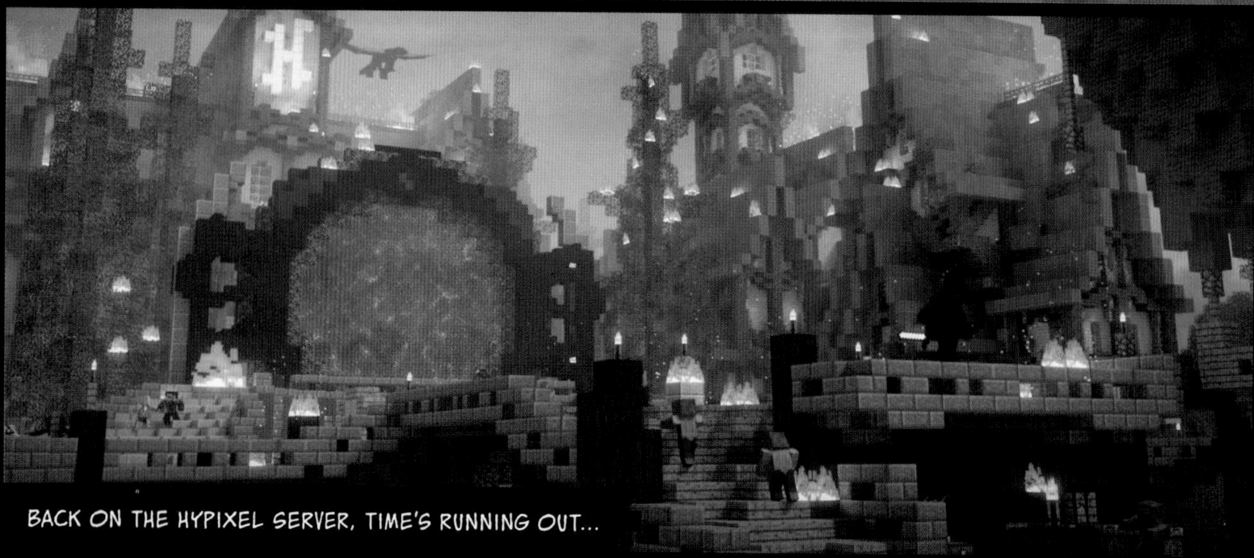
BACK ON THE HYPIXEL SERVER, TIME'S RUNNING OUT...

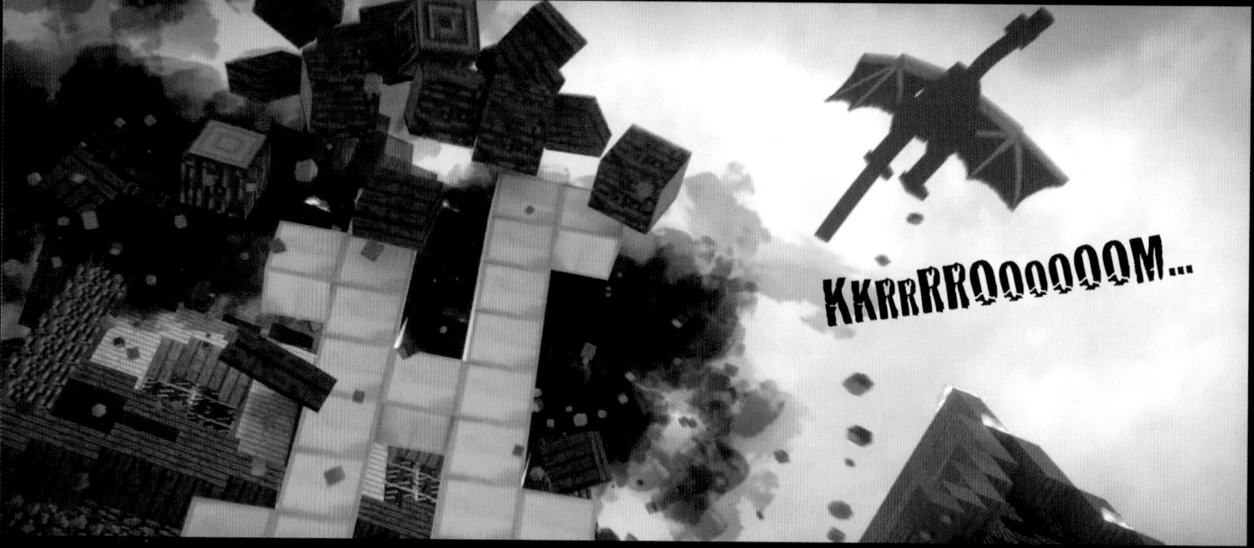
KKRRRROOOOOOM...

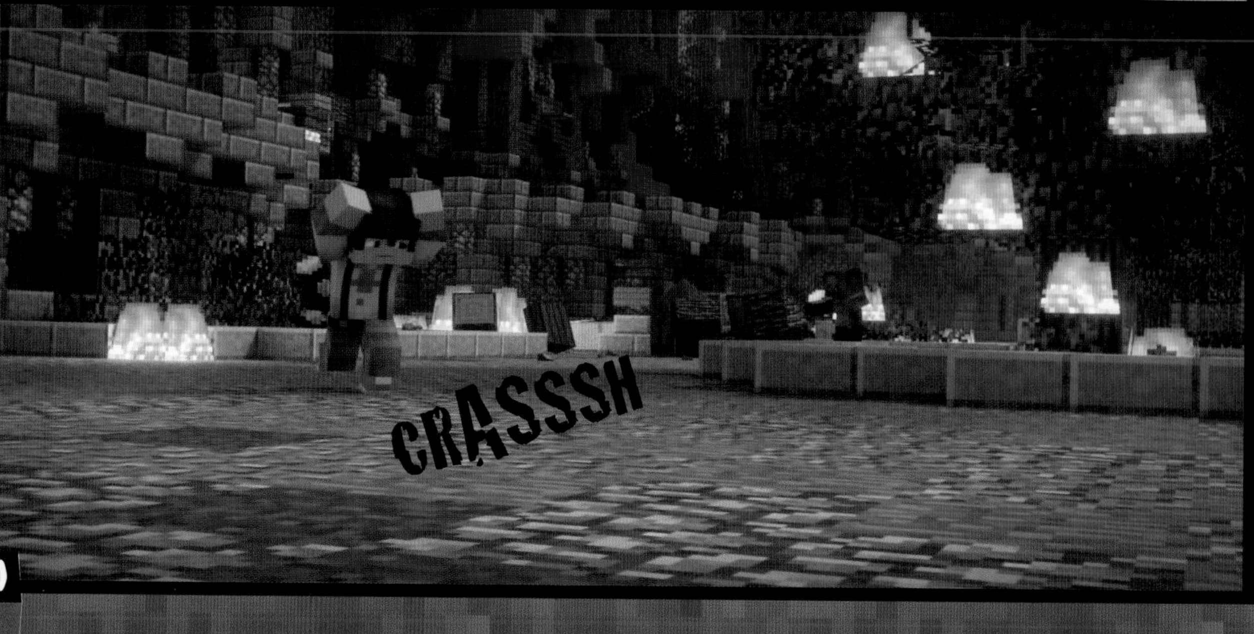
CRASSSH

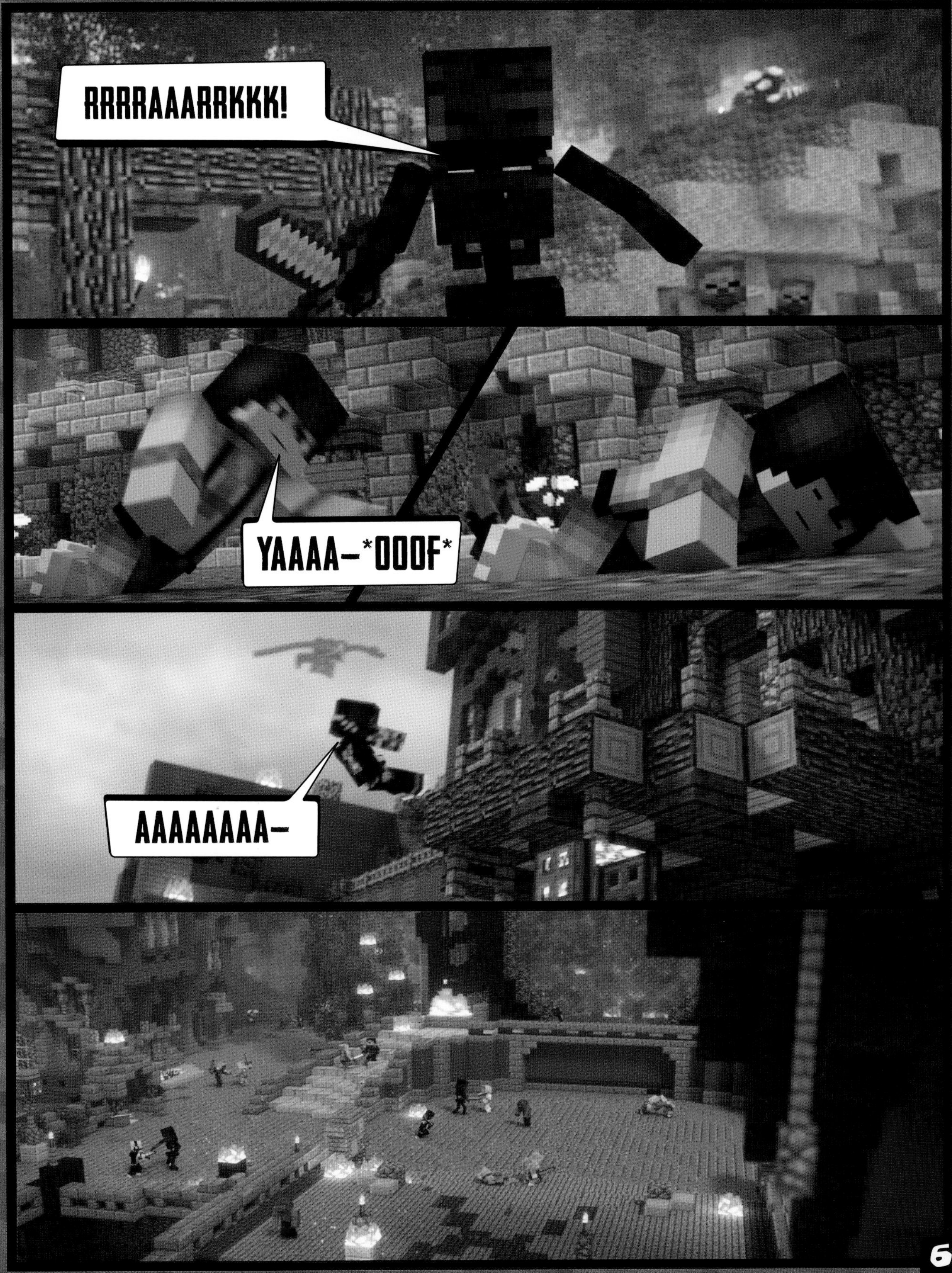
RRRRAAARRKKK!
YAAAA-*OOOF*
AAAAAAAA-

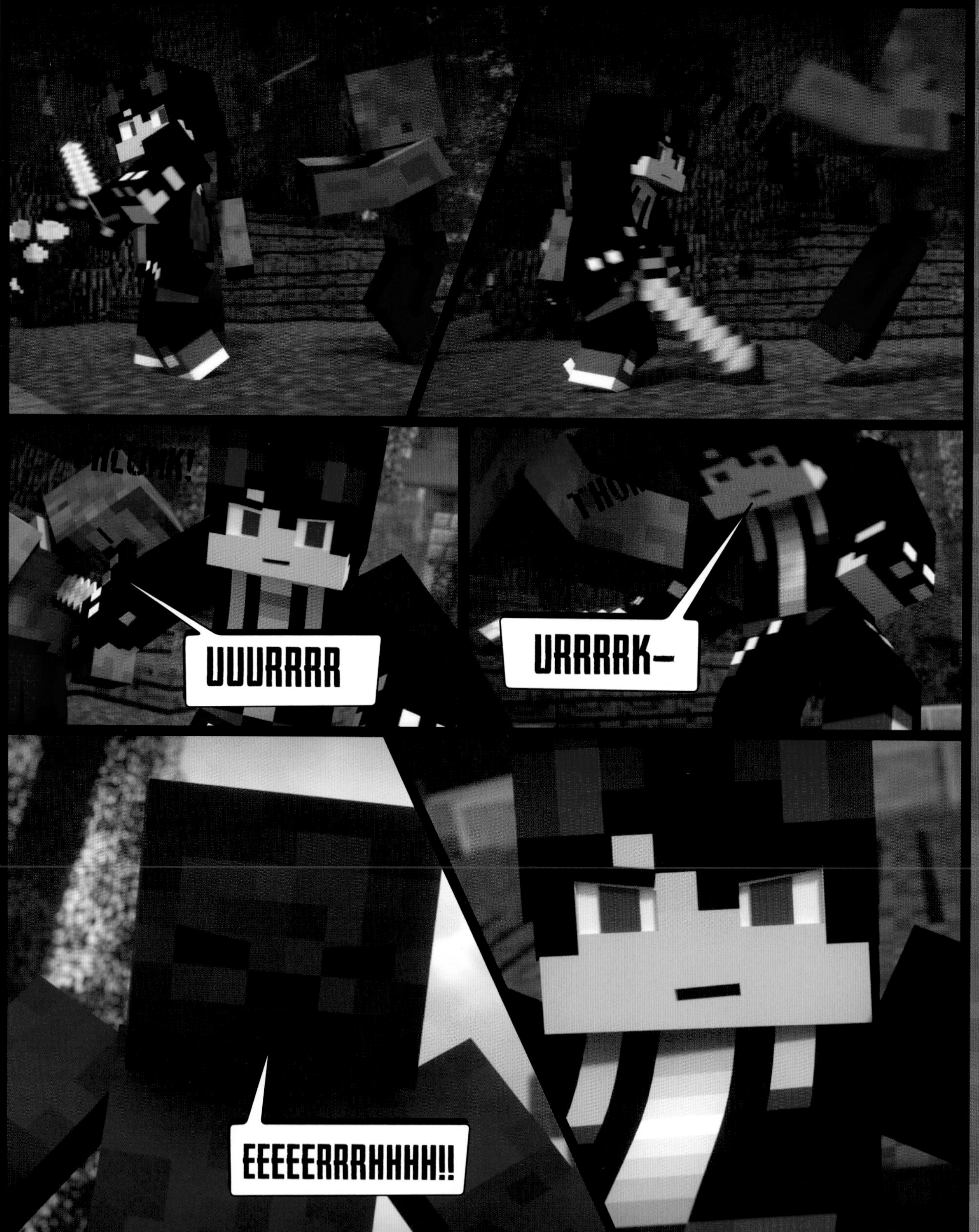
UUURRRR
URRRRK–
EEEEERRHHHH!!

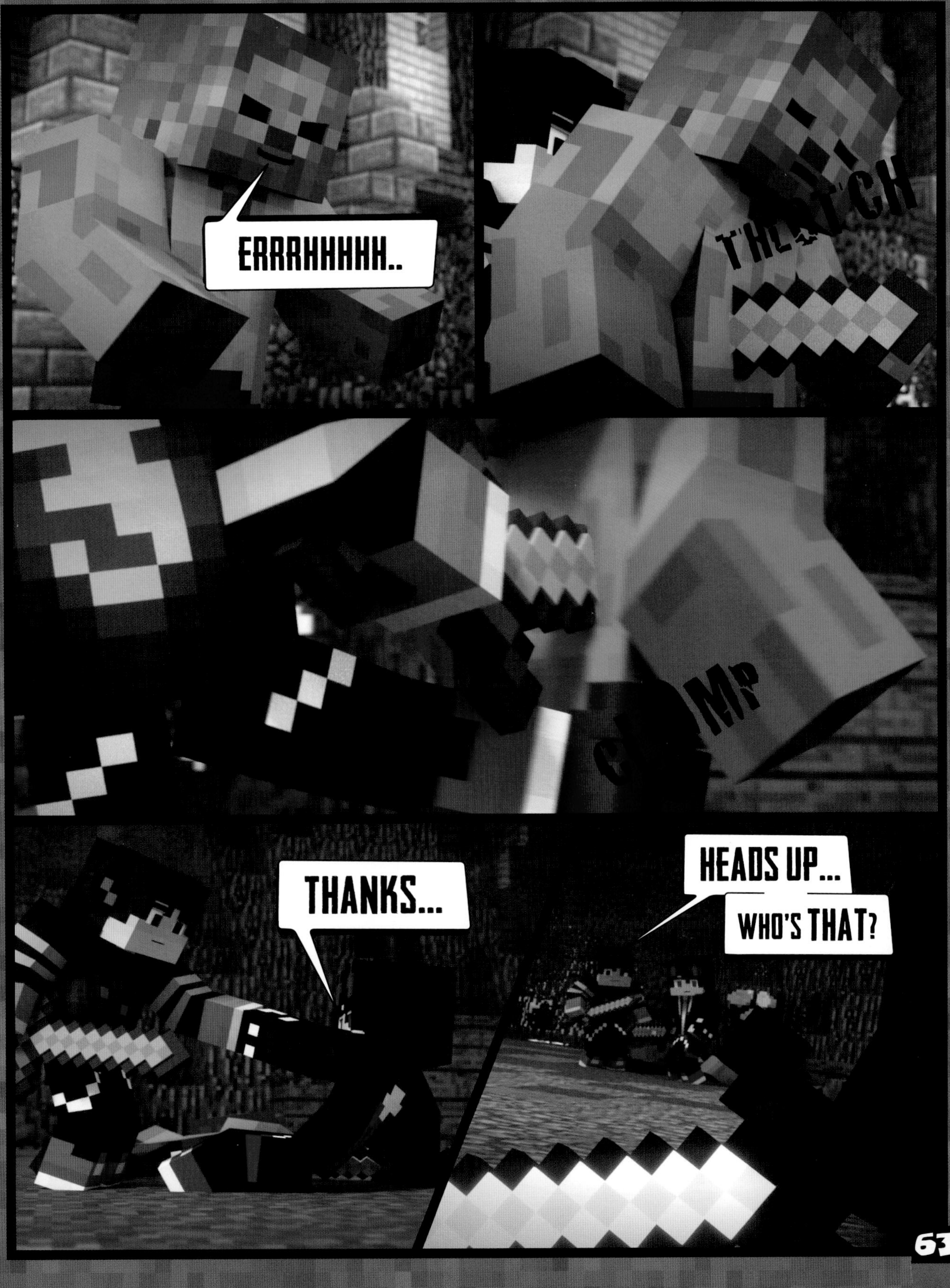
ERRRHHHHH..
THANKS...
HEADS UP...
WHO'S THAT?

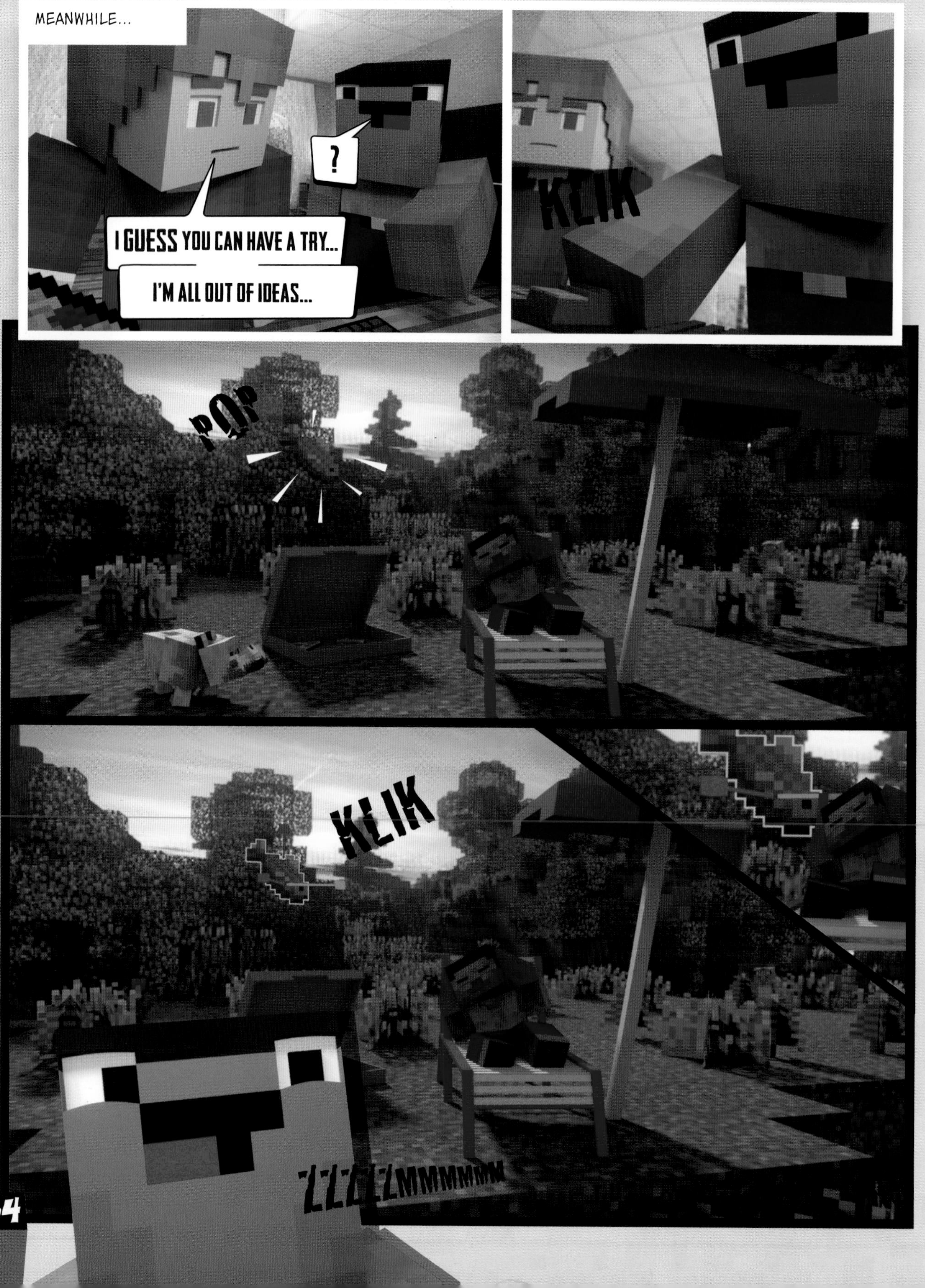
MEANWHILE...
?
I GUESS YOU CAN HAVE A TRY...
I'M ALL OUT OF IDEAS...
KLIK
POP
KLIK
ZZZZZMMMMMM

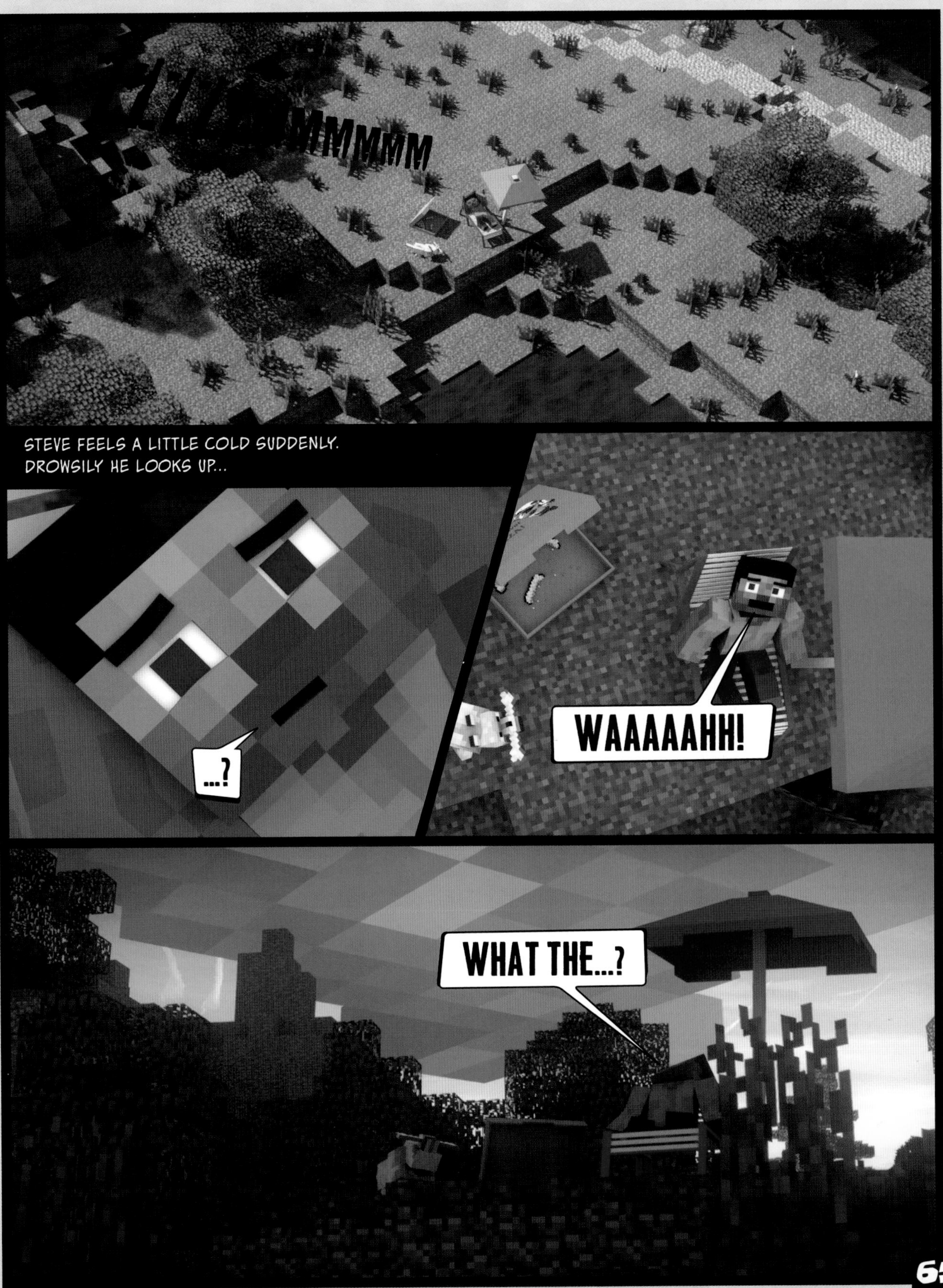
STEVE FEELS A LITTLE COLD SUDDENLY.
DROWSILY HE LOOKS UP...
...?
WAAAAAHH!
WHAT THE...?

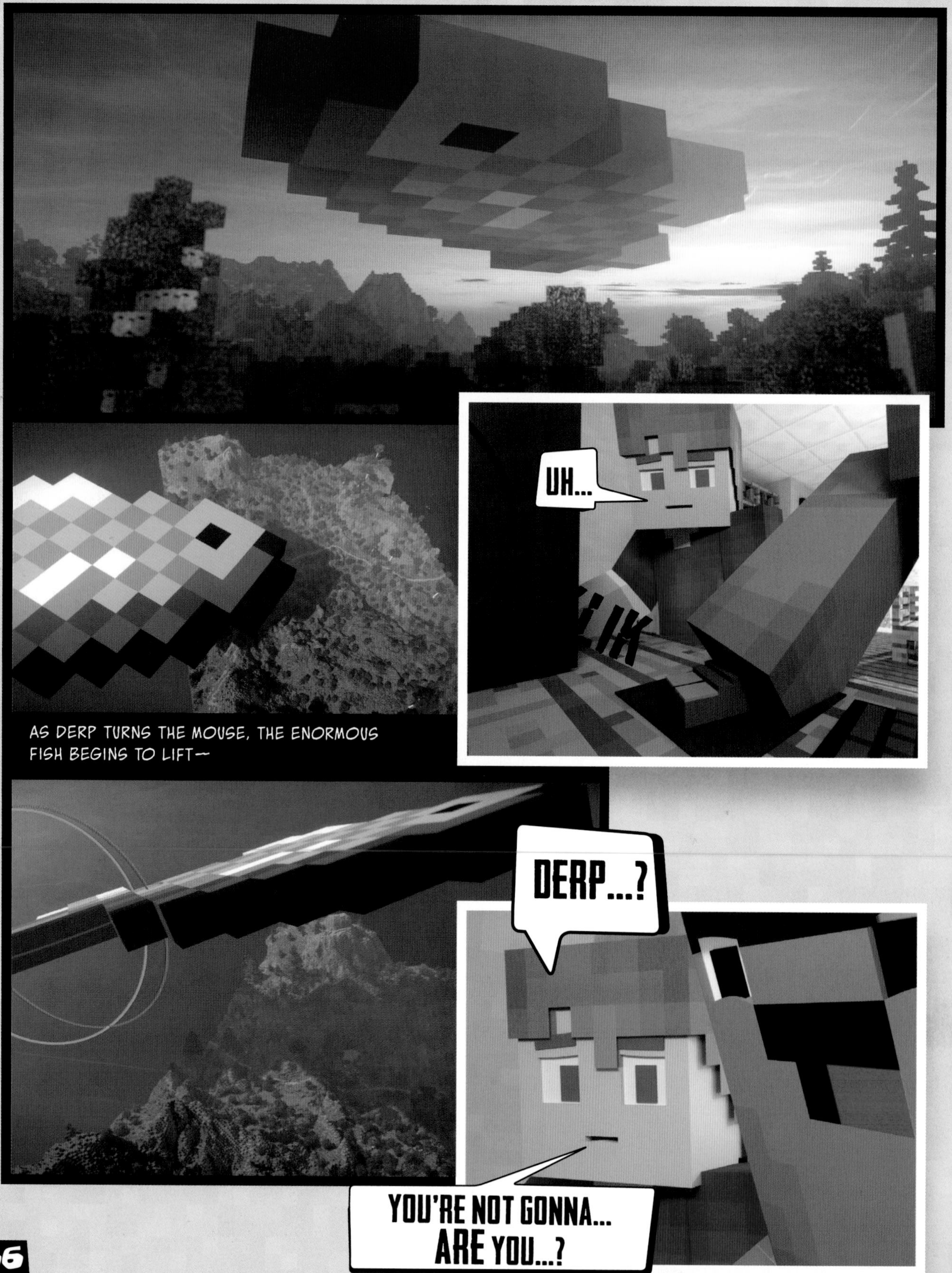
AS DERP TURNS THE MOUSE, THE ENORMOUS FISH BEGINS TO LIFT—
UH...
DERP...?
YOU'RE NOT GONNA... ARE YOU...?

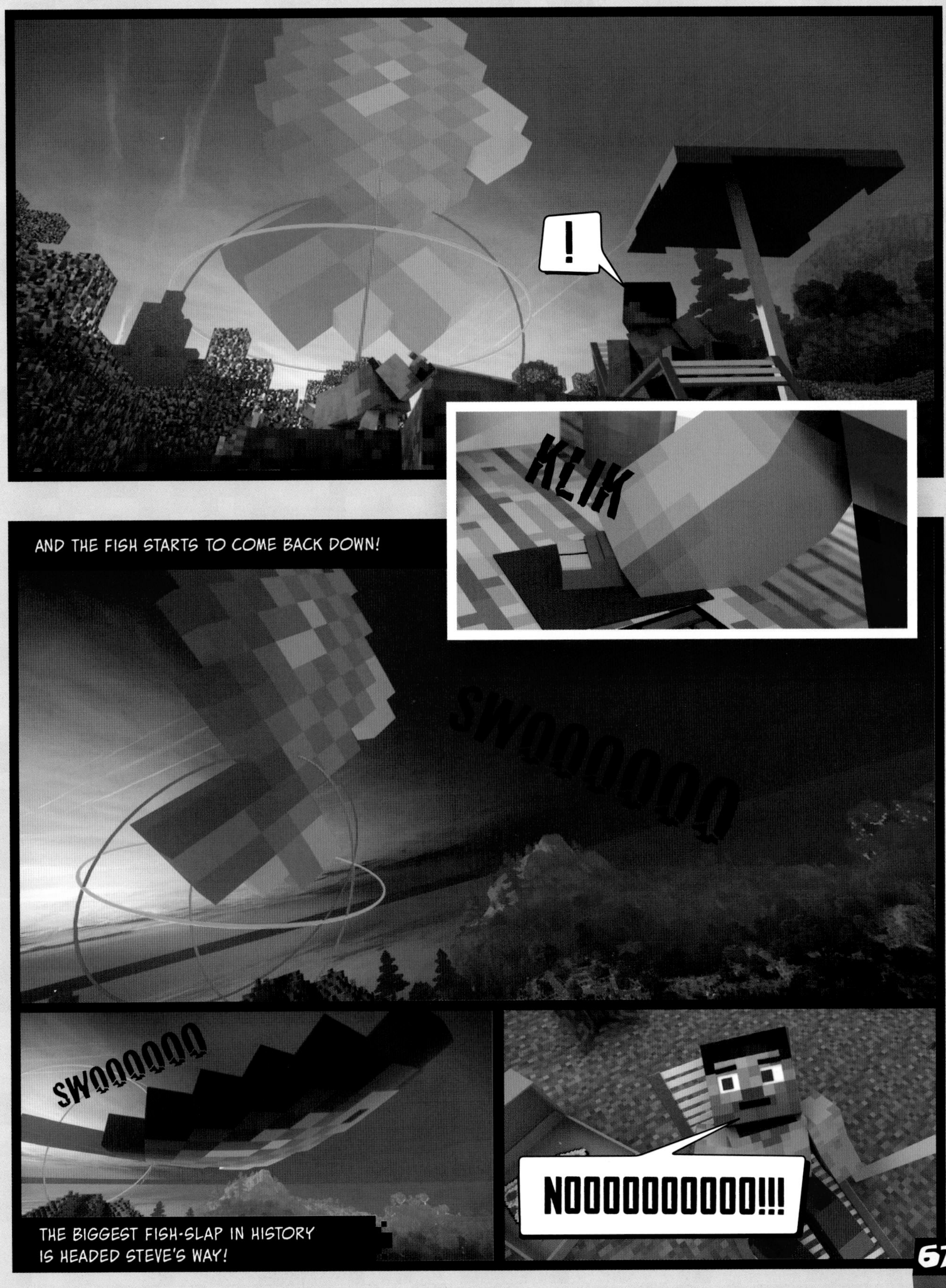
!
KLIK
AND THE FISH STARTS TO COME BACK DOWN!
SWOOOOOOO
SWOOOOOO
THE BIGGEST FISH-SLAP IN HISTORY IS HEADED STEVE'S WAY!
NOOOOOOOOOO!!!

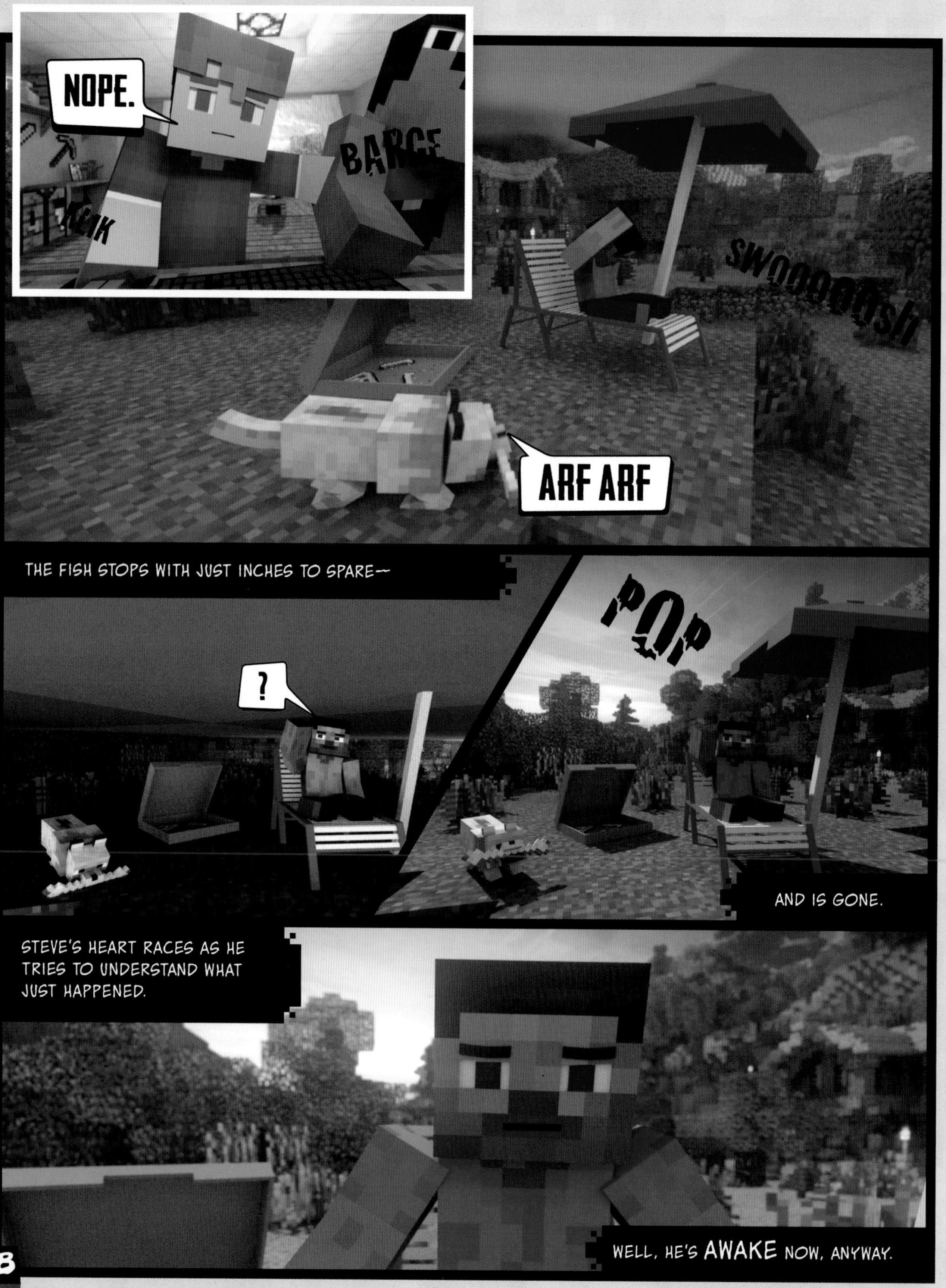
NOPE.
KLIK
BARGE
SWOOOOOSH
ARF ARF
THE FISH STOPS WITH JUST INCHES TO SPARE--
?
POP
AND IS GONE.
STEVE'S HEART RACES AS HE TRIES TO UNDERSTAND WHAT JUST HAPPENED.
WELL, HE'S AWAKE NOW, ANYWAY.

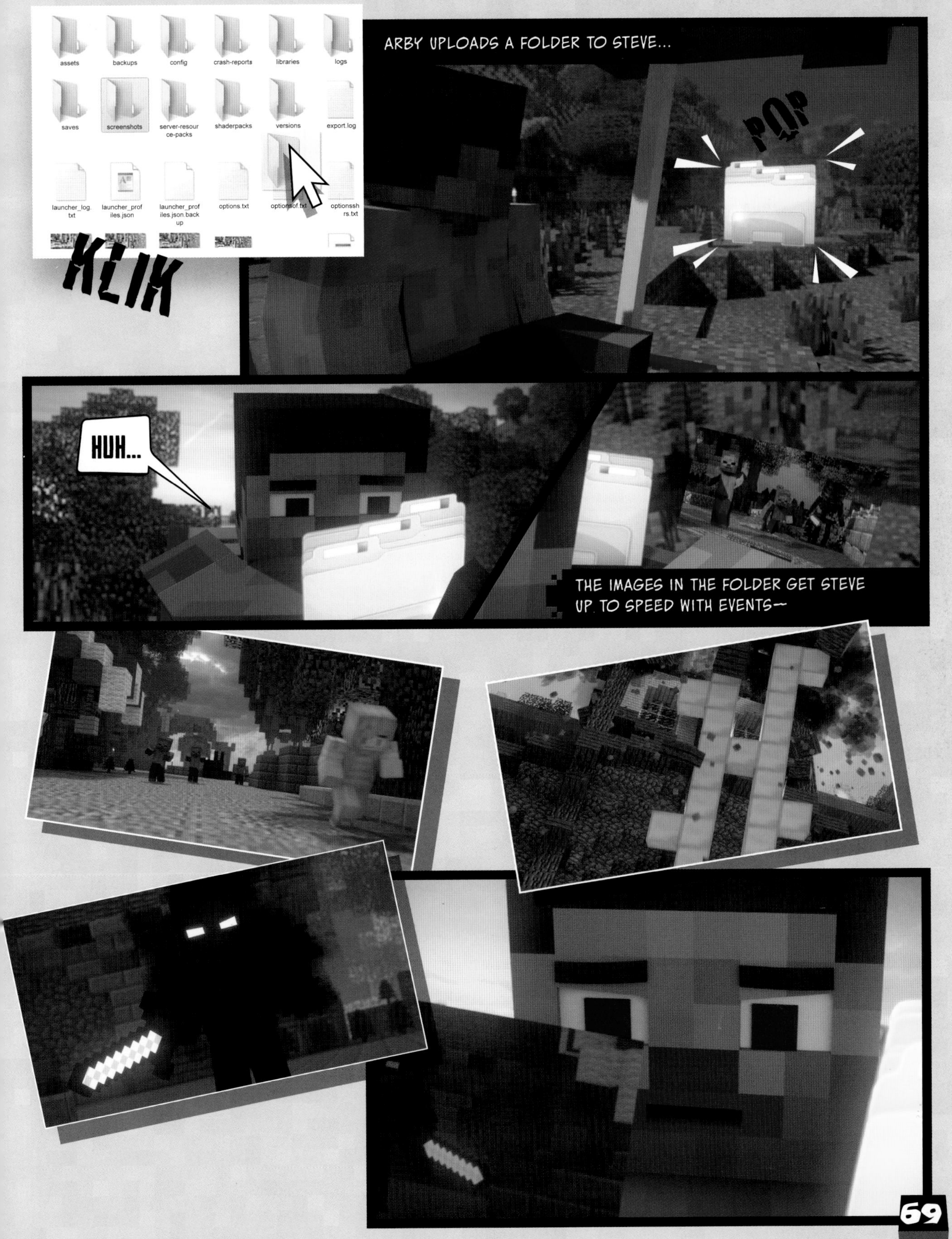
assets
backups
config
crash-reports
libraries
logs
saves
screenshots
server-resource-packs
shaderpacks
versions
export.log
launcher_log.txt
launcher_profiles.json
launcher_profiles.json.backup
options.txt
optionsof.txt
optionsshrs.txt
KLIK
ARBY UPLOADS A FOLDER TO STEVE...
POP
HUH...
THE IMAGES IN THE FOLDER GET STEVE UP TO SPEED WITH EVENTS—

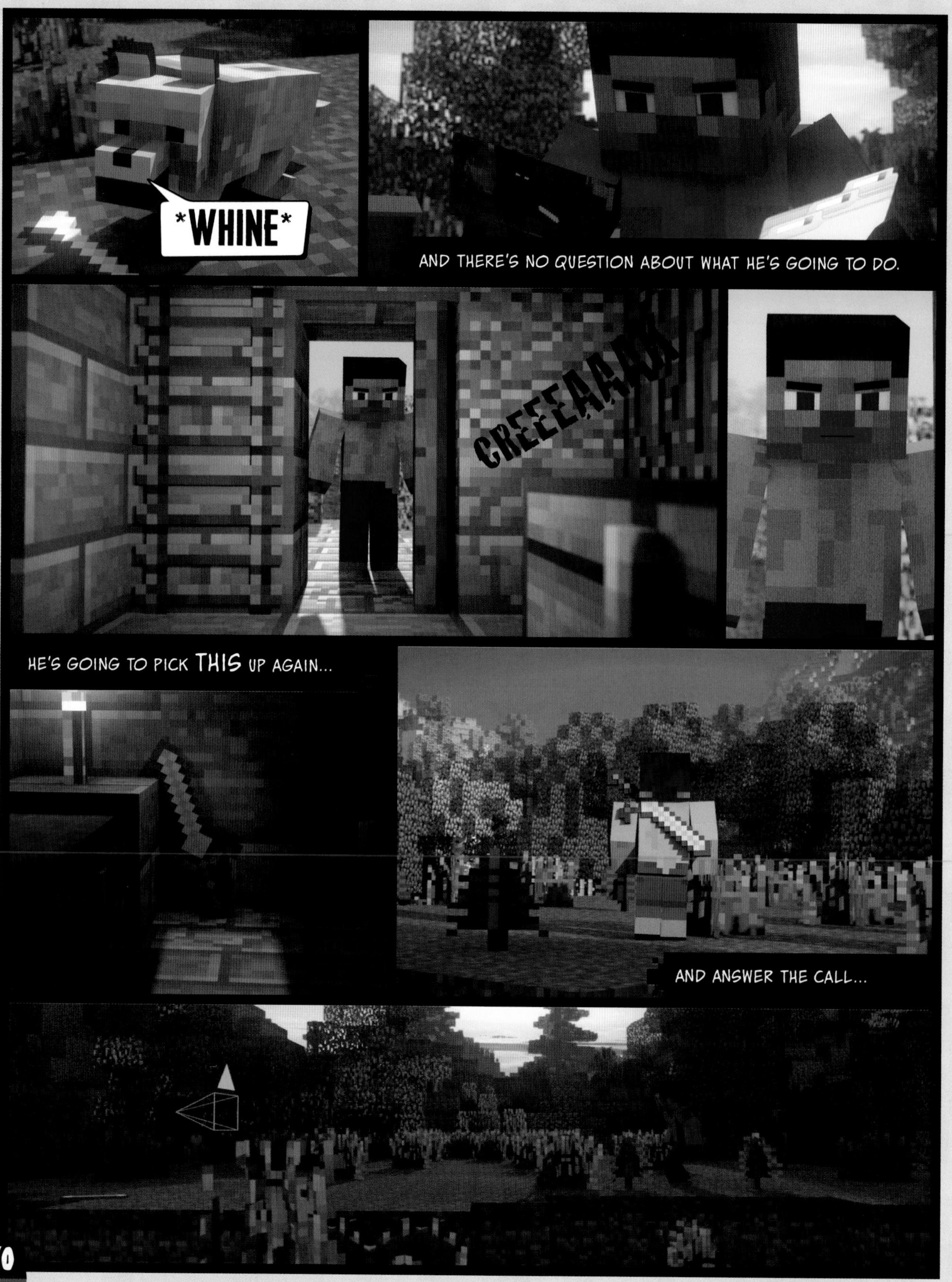
WHINE
AND THERE'S NO QUESTION ABOUT WHAT HE'S GOING TO DO.
CREEEAAR
HE'S GOING TO PICK THIS UP AGAIN...
AND ANSWER THE CALL...

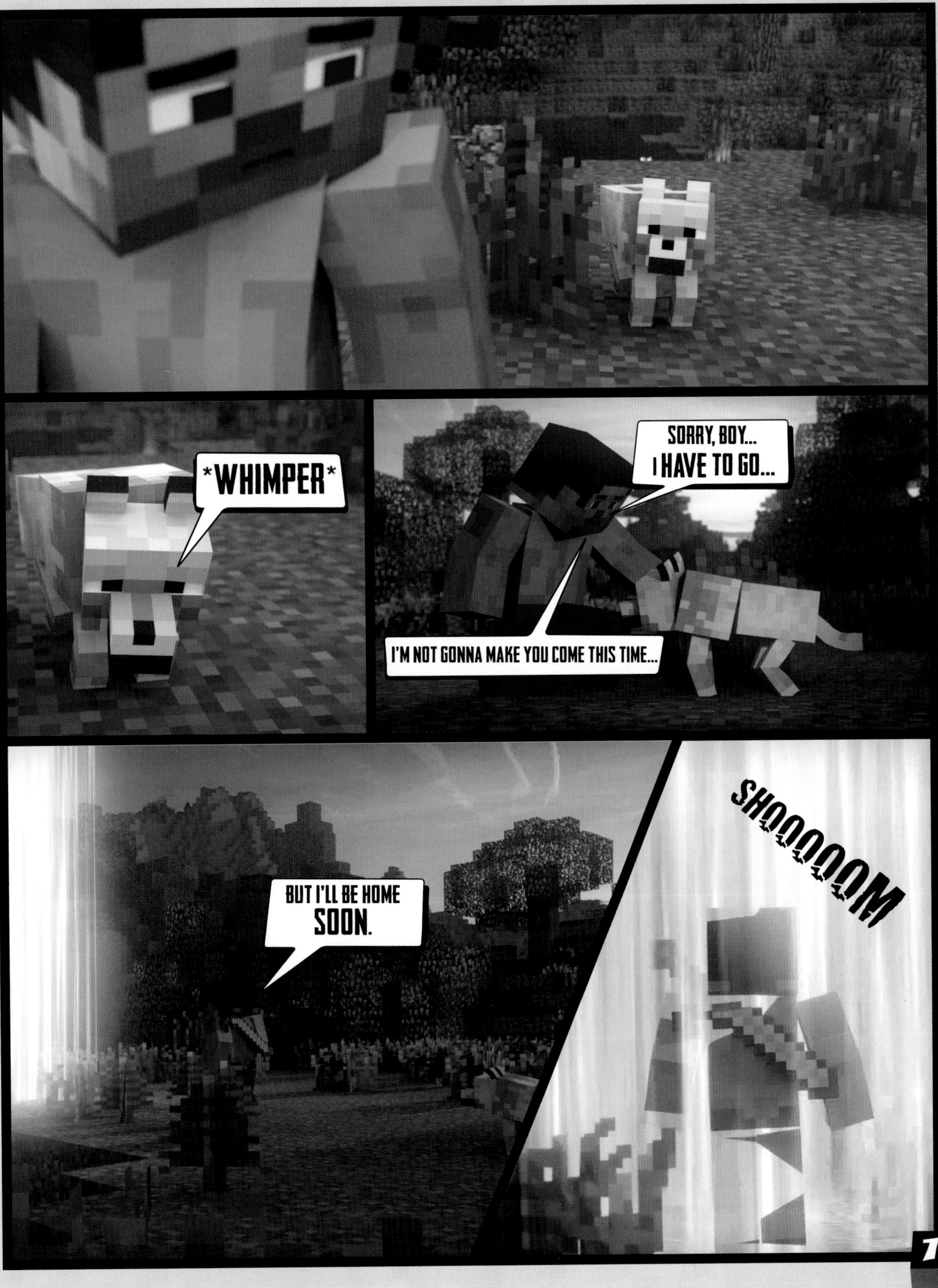
WHIMPER
SORRY, BOY...
I HAVE TO GO...
I'M NOT GONNA MAKE YOU COME THIS TIME...
BUT I'LL BE HOME
SOON.
SHOOOOOOM

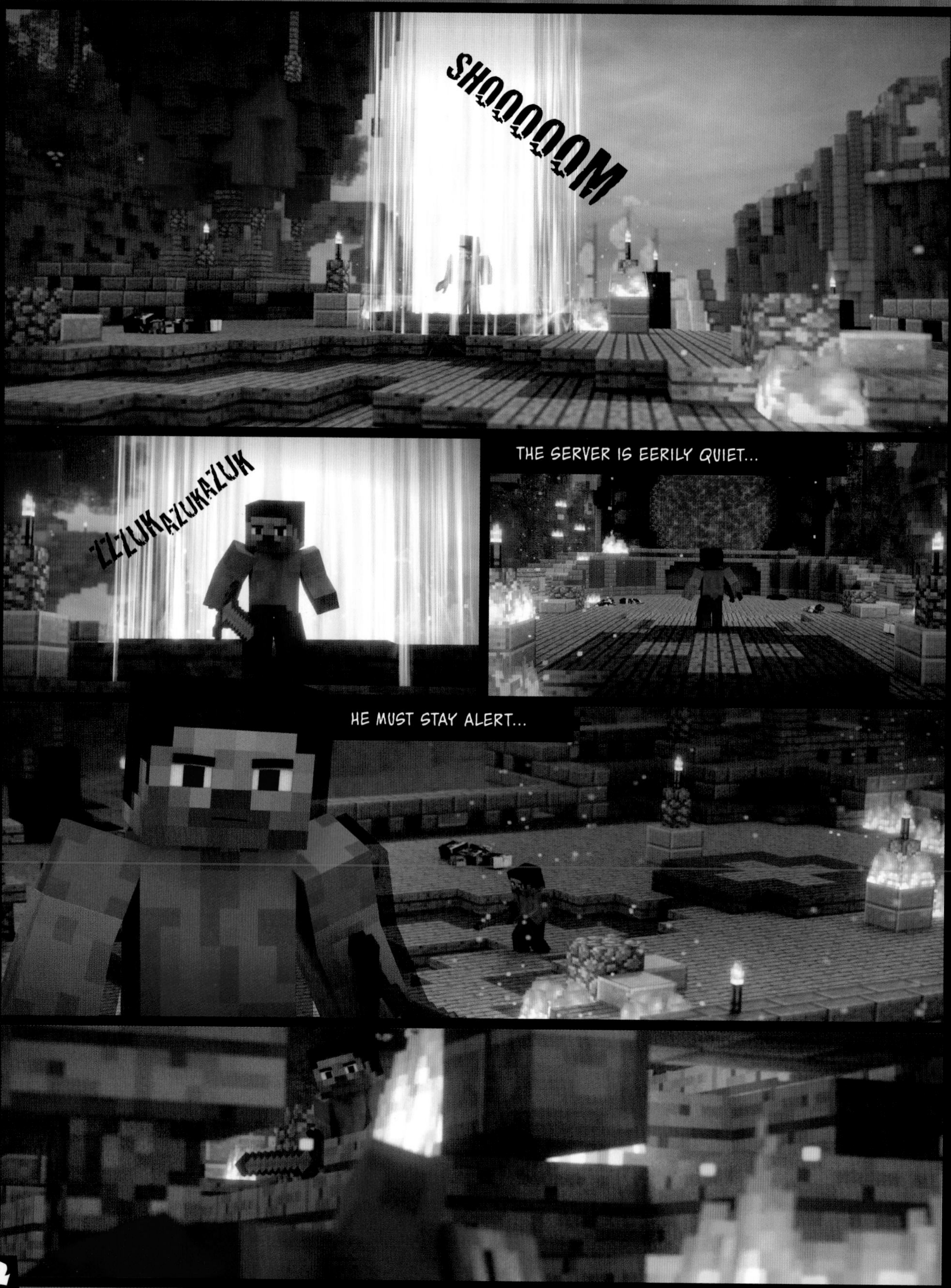
SHOOOOOOM
ZZZUKAZUKAZUK
THE SERVER IS EERILY QUIET...
HE MUST STAY ALERT...

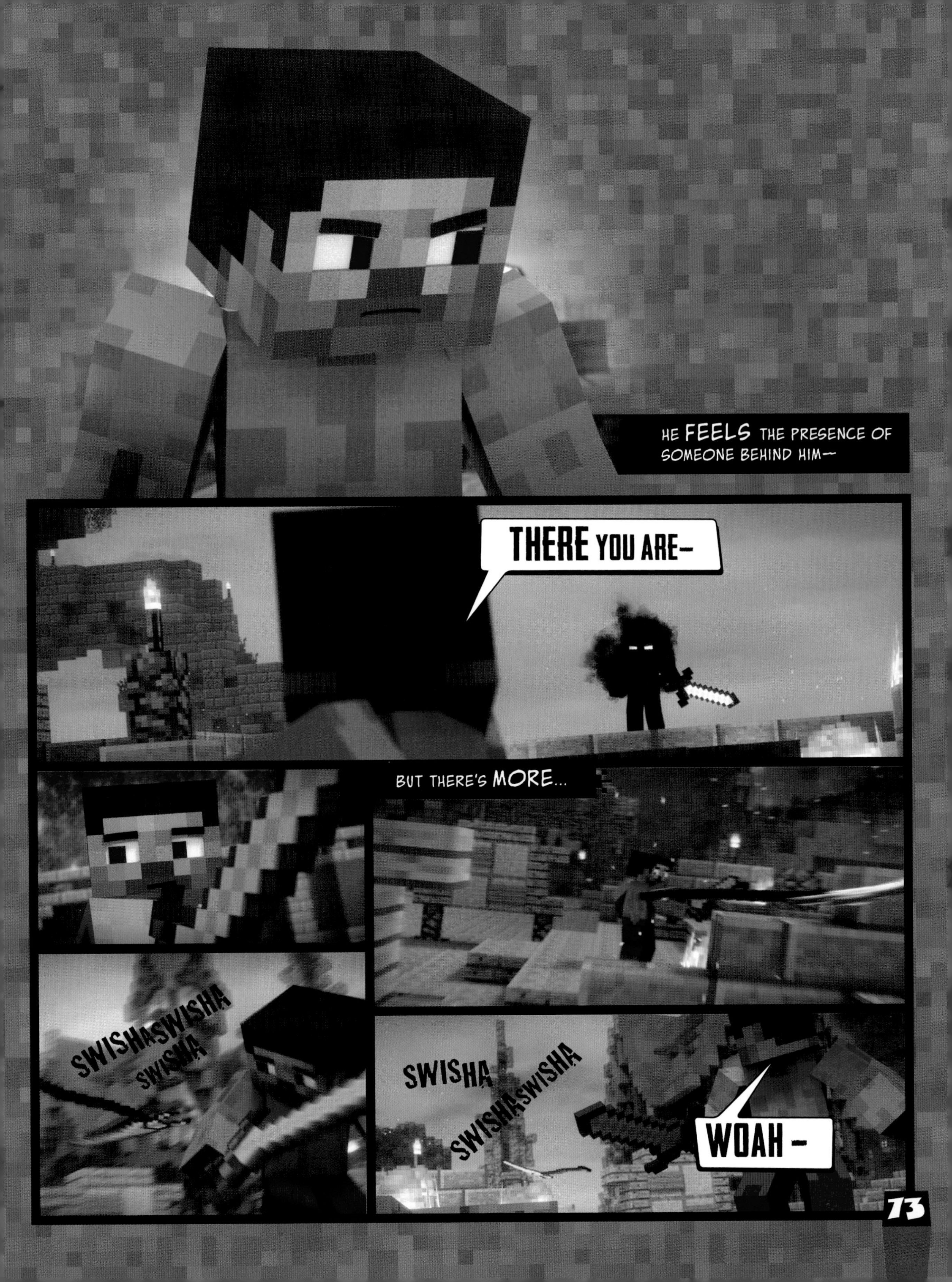
HE FEELS THE PRESENCE OF SOMEONE BEHIND HIM—
THERE YOU ARE-
BUT THERE'S MORE...
SWISHASWISHA
SWISHA
SWISHA
SWISHASWISHA
WOAH -

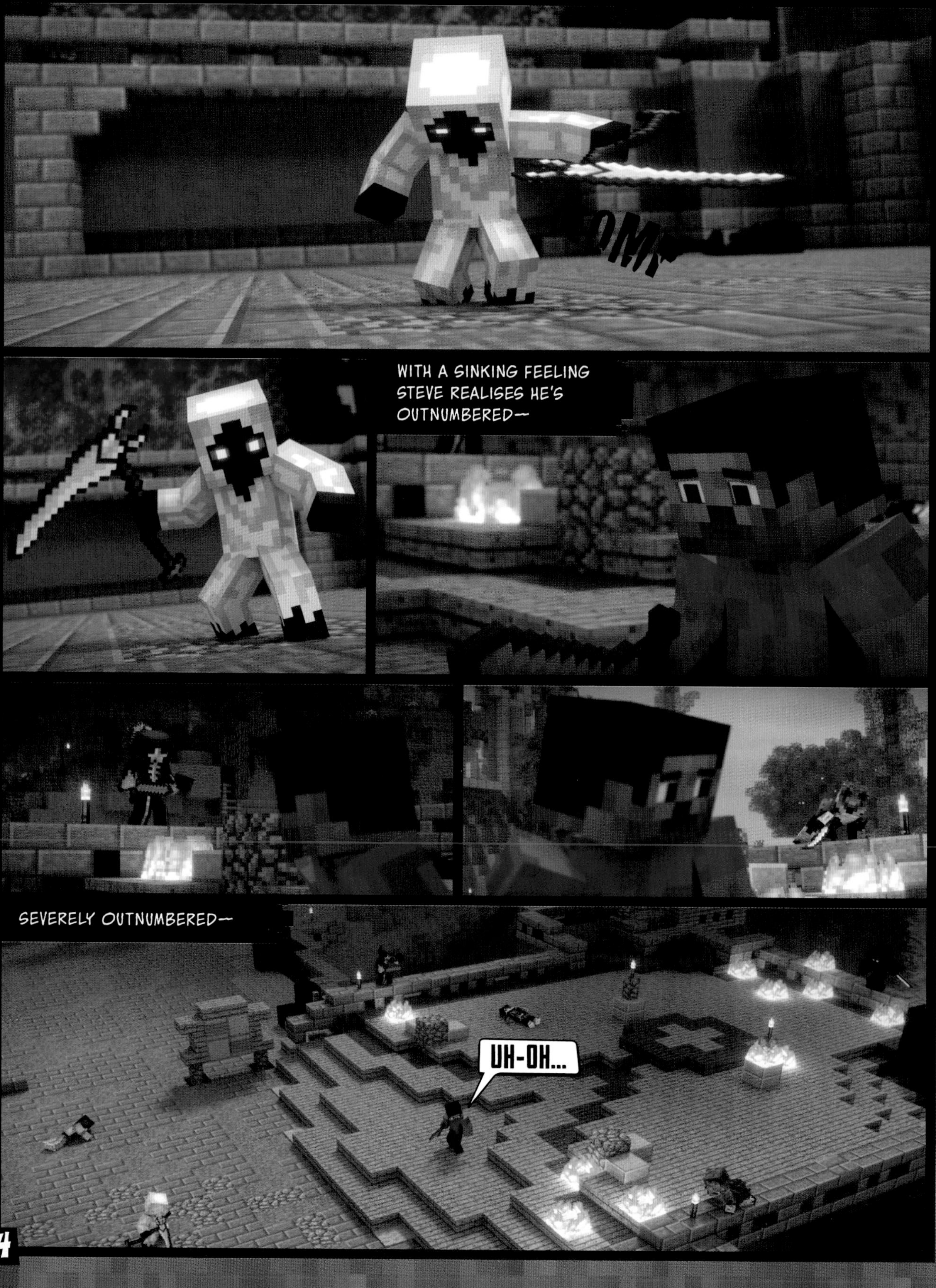
WITH A SINKING FEELING
STEVE REALISES HE'S
OUTNUMBERED—
SEVERELY OUTNUMBERED—
UH-OH...

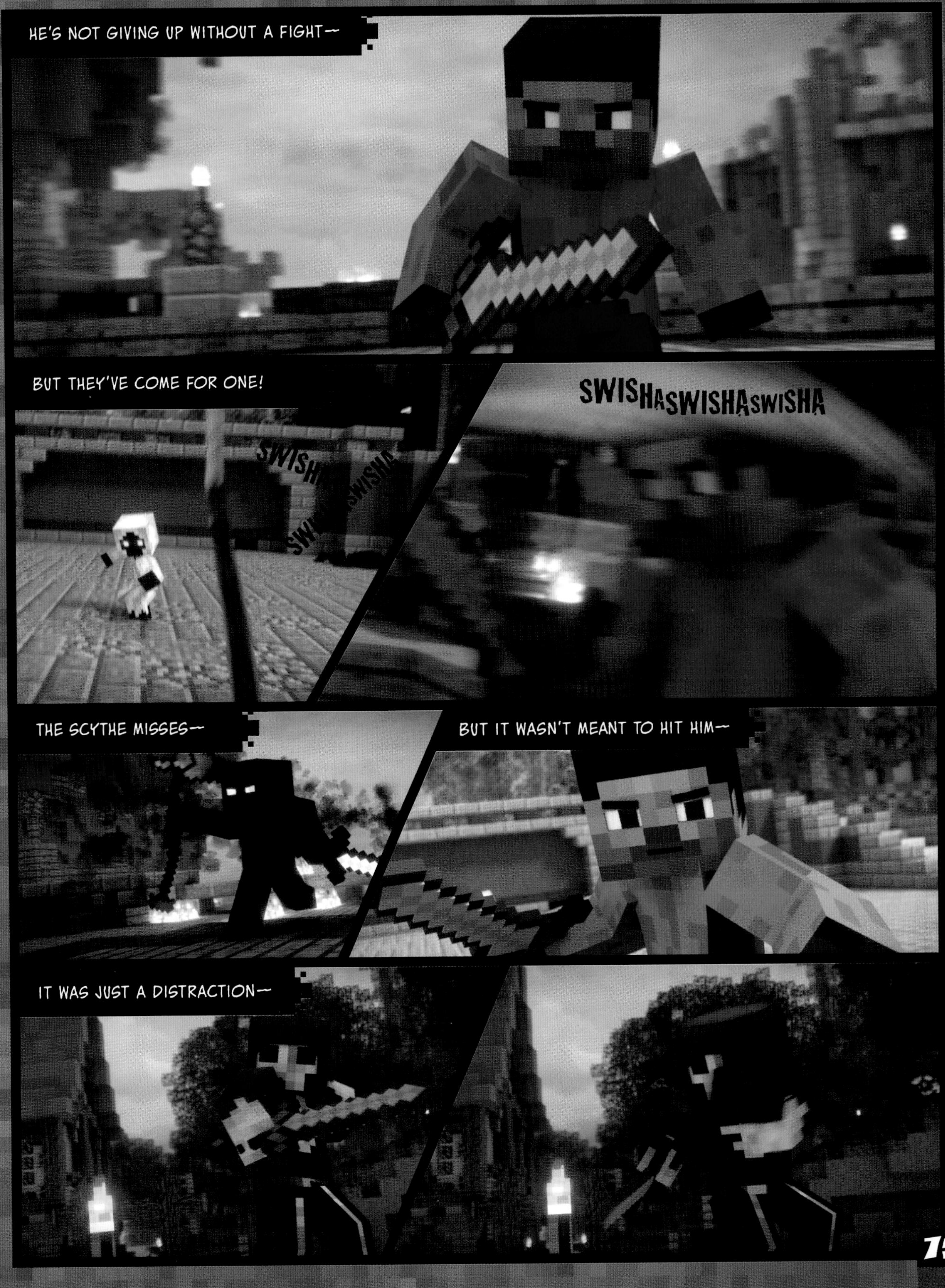
HE'S NOT GIVING UP WITHOUT A FIGHT—
BUT THEY'VE COME FOR ONE!
SWISHASWISHASWISHA
THE SCYTHE MISSES—
BUT IT WASN'T MEANT TO HIT HIM—
IT WAS JUST A DISTRACTION—

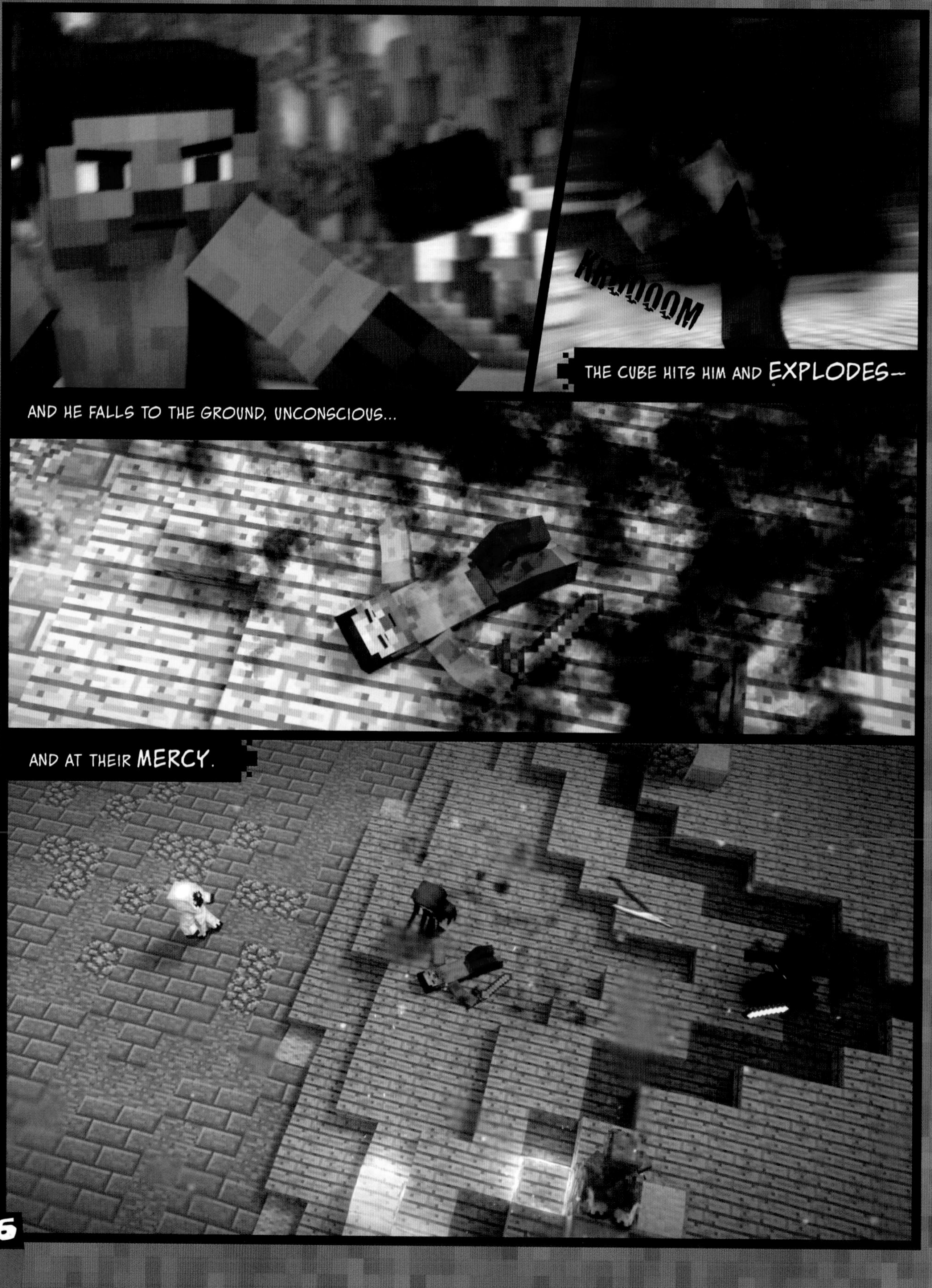
KRUOOOM
THE CUBE HITS HIM AND EXPLODES—
AND HE FALLS TO THE GROUND, UNCONSCIOUS...
AND AT THEIR MERCY.

CHAPTER 4

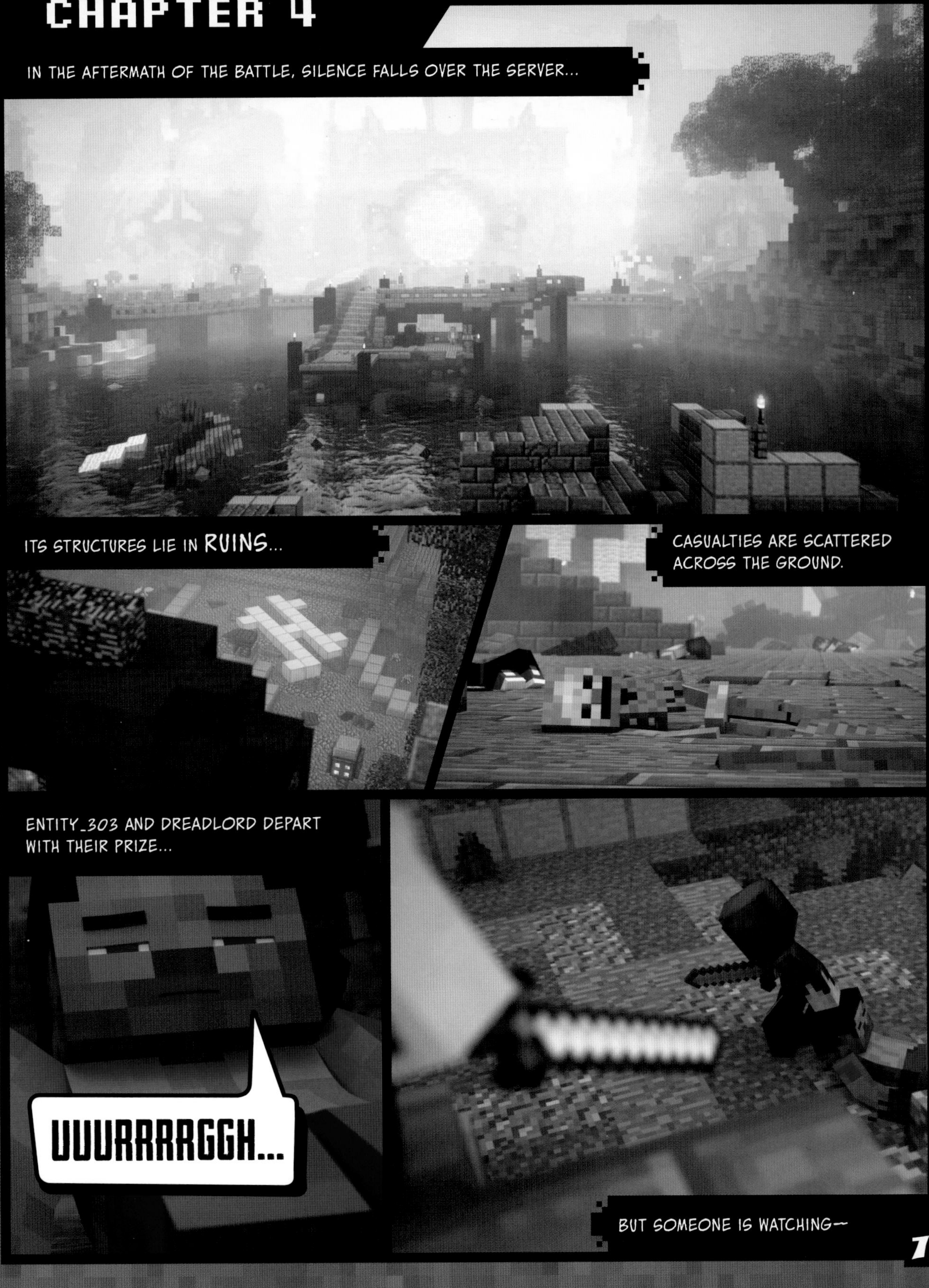

IN THE AFTERMATH OF THE BATTLE, SILENCE FALLS OVER THE SERVER...
ITS STRUCTURES LIE IN RUINS...
CASUALTIES ARE SCATTERED ACROSS THE GROUND.
ENTITY_303 AND DREADLORD DEPART WITH THEIR PRIZE...
UUURRRRGGH...
BUT SOMEONE IS WATCHING—

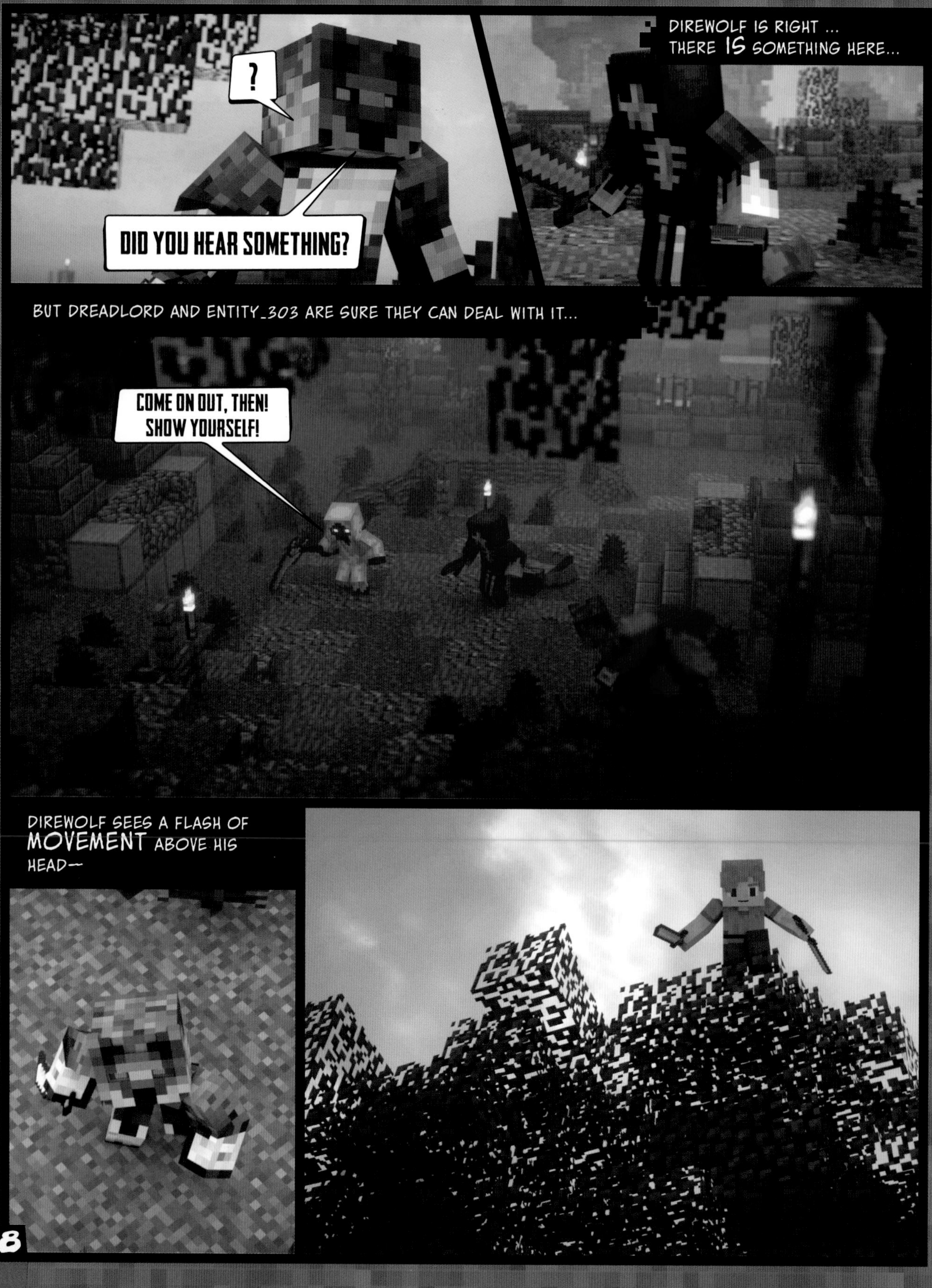
?
DID YOU HEAR SOMETHING?
DIREWOLF IS RIGHT ... THERE IS SOMETHING HERE...
BUT DREADLORD AND ENTITY_303 ARE SURE THEY CAN DEAL WITH IT...
COME ON OUT, THEN! SHOW YOURSELF!
DIREWOLF SEES A FLASH OF MOVEMENT ABOVE HIS HEAD—

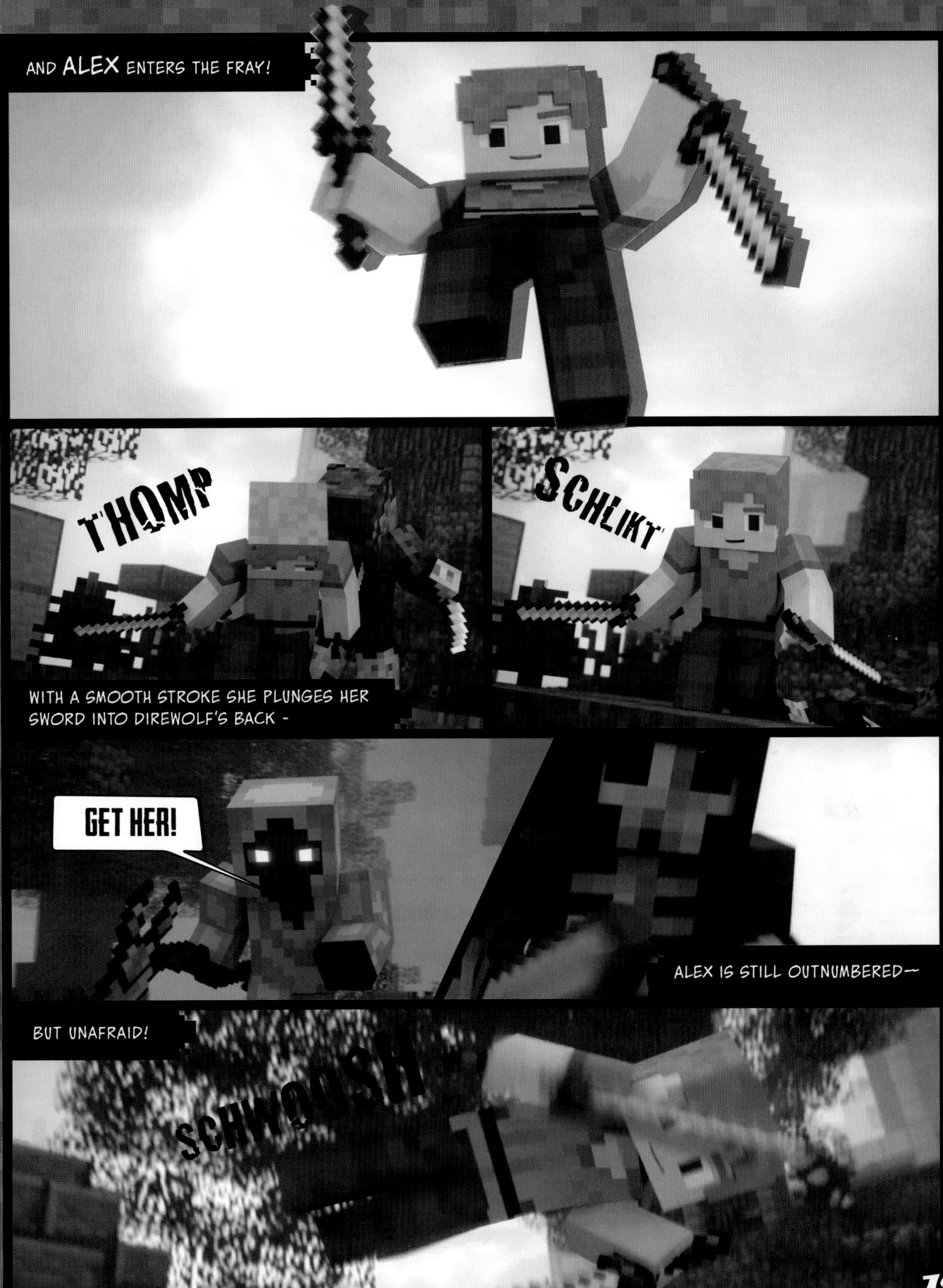

AND ALEX ENTERS THE FRAY!
THOMP
SCHLIKT
WITH A SMOOTH STROKE SHE PLUNGES HER SWORD INTO DIREWOLF'S BACK -
GET HER!
ALEX IS STILL OUTNUMBERED—
BUT UNAFRAID!
SCHWOOSH

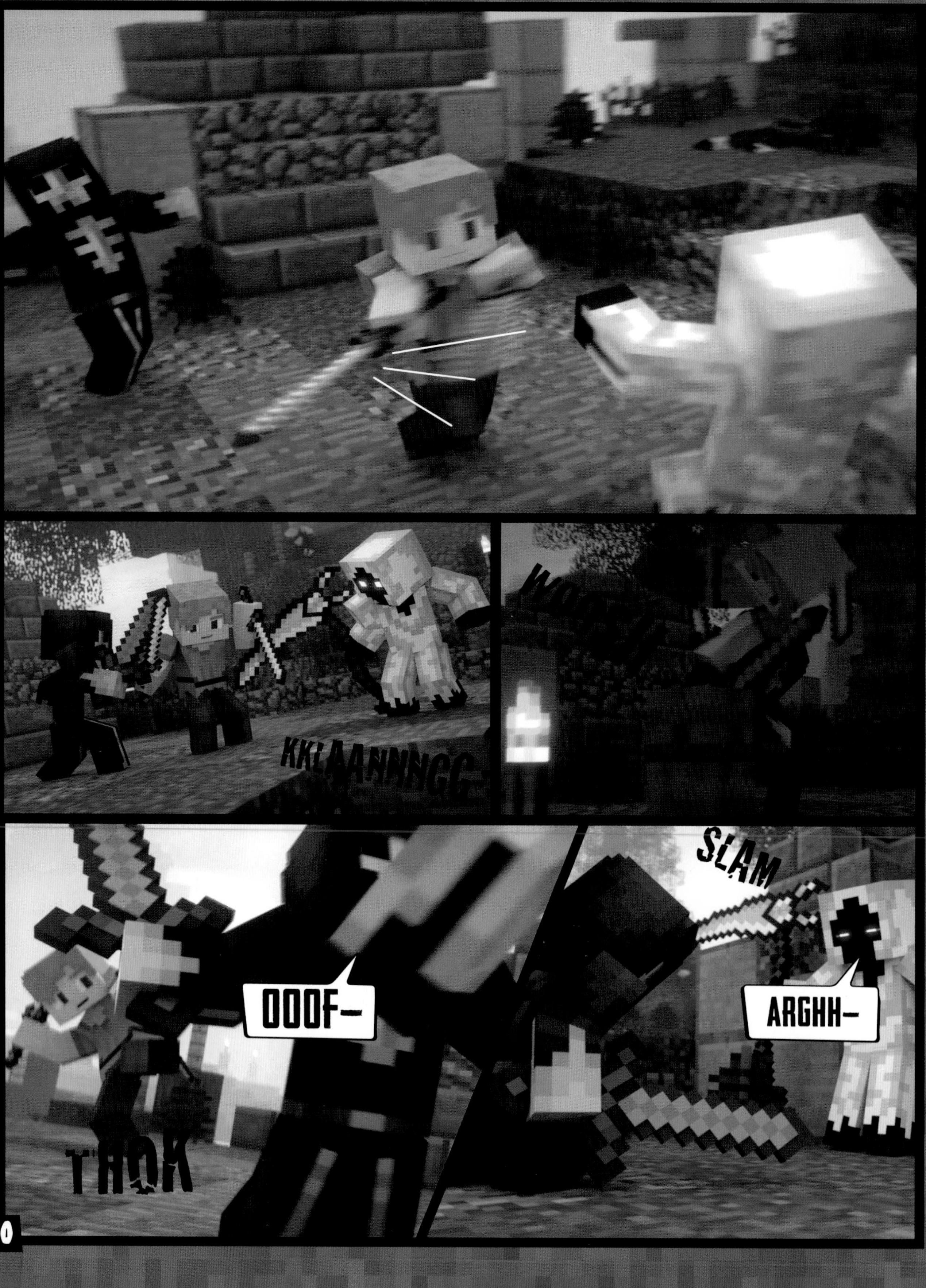
KKLAANNNGG
OOOF–
THOK
SLAM
ARGHH–

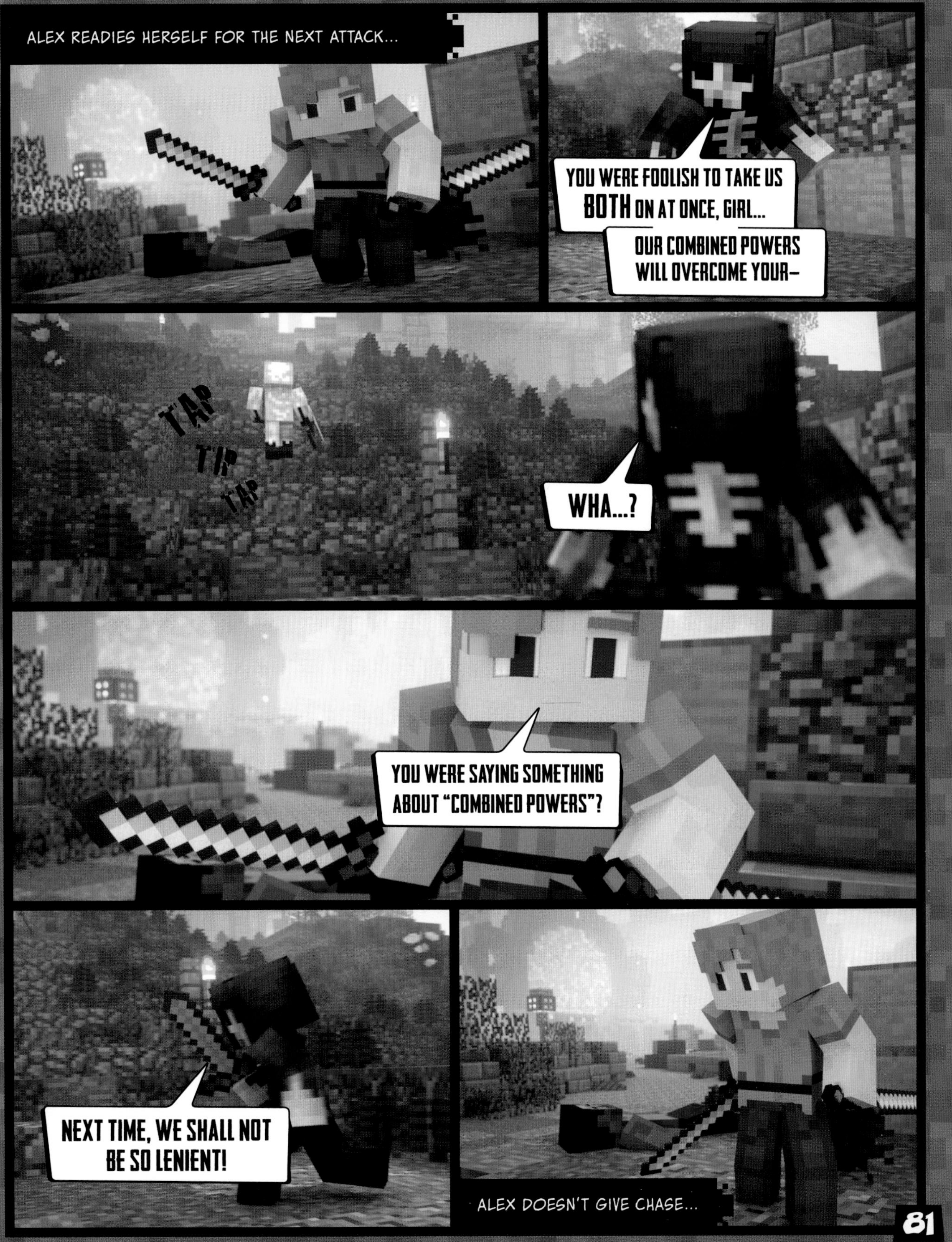
ALEX READIES HERSELF FOR THE NEXT ATTACK...
YOU WERE FOOLISH TO TAKE US BOTH ON AT ONCE, GIRL...
OUR COMBINED POWERS WILL OVERCOME YOUR–
TAP TAP TAP
WHA...?
YOU WERE SAYING SOMETHING ABOUT "COMBINED POWERS"?
NEXT TIME, WE SHALL NOT BE SO LENIENT!
ALEX DOESN'T GIVE CHASE...

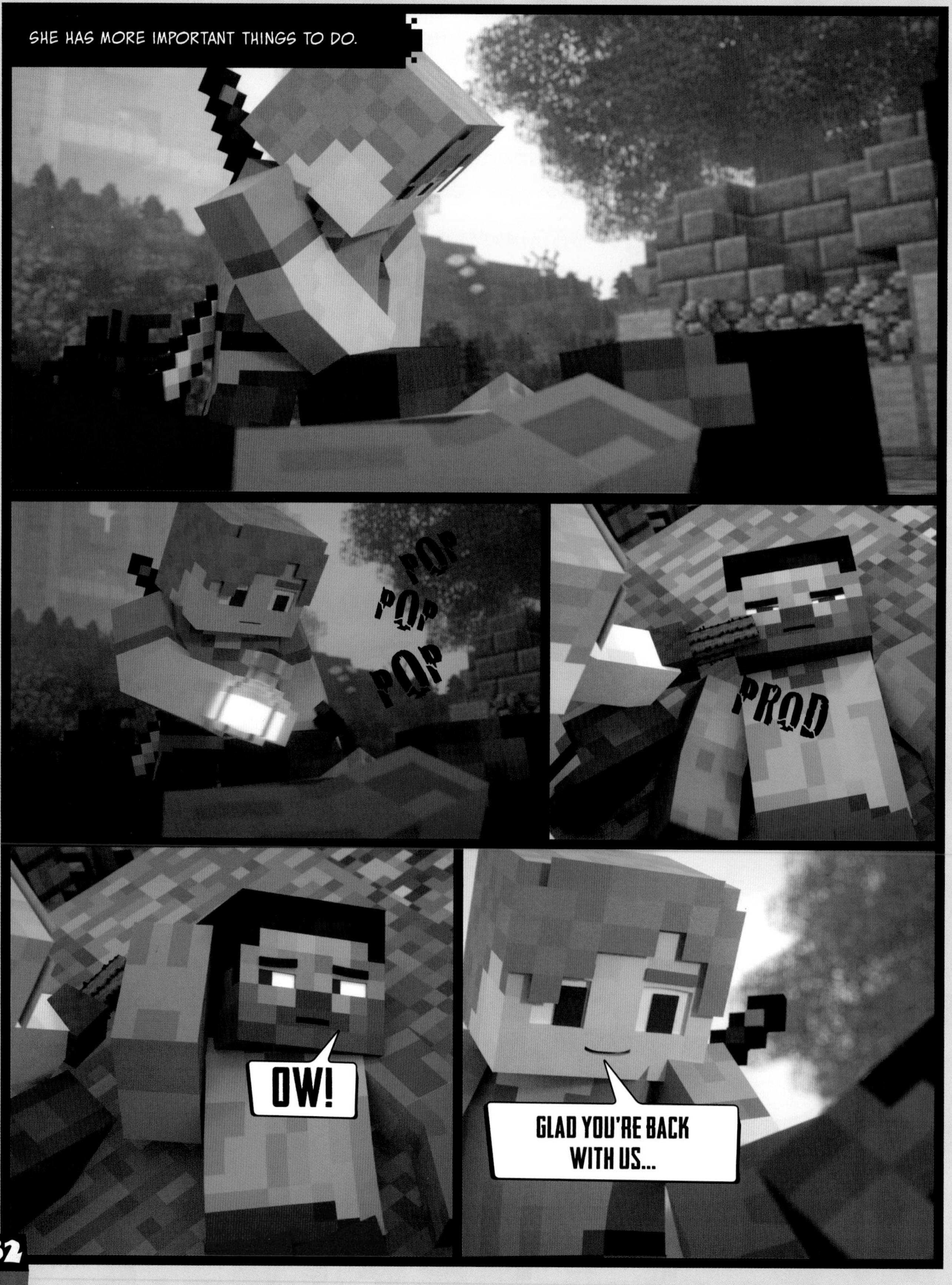
SHE HAS MORE IMPORTANT THINGS TO DO.
POP
POP
POP
PROD
OW!
GLAD YOU'RE BACK WITH US...

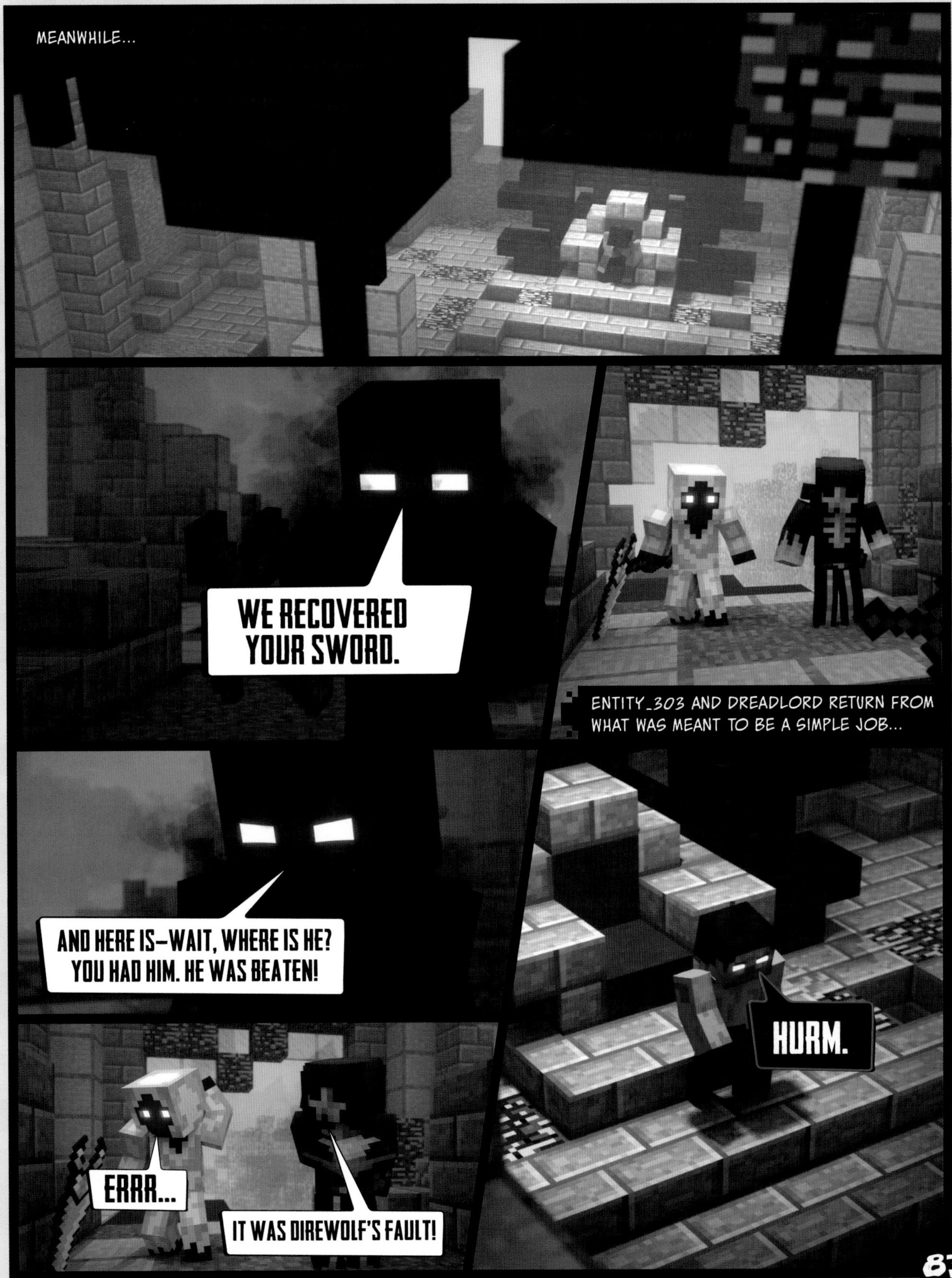
MEANWHILE...
WE RECOVERED YOUR SWORD.
ENTITY_303 AND DREADLORD RETURN FROM WHAT WAS MEANT TO BE A SIMPLE JOB...
AND HERE IS—WAIT, WHERE IS HE? YOU HAD HIM. HE WAS BEATEN!
HURM.
ERRR...
IT WAS DIREWOLF'S FAULT!

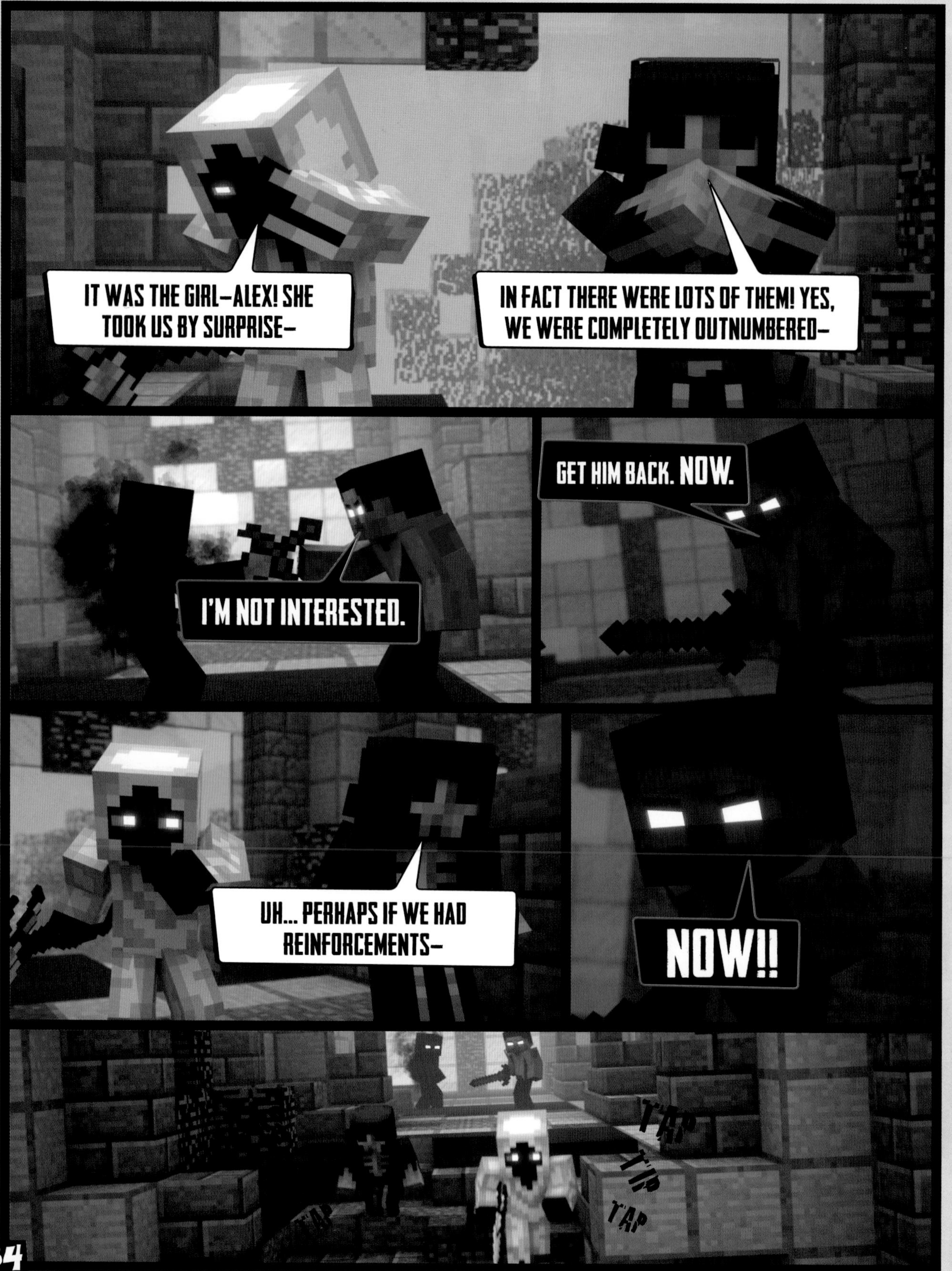
IT WAS THE GIRL—ALEX! SHE TOOK US BY SURPRISE—
IN FACT THERE WERE LOTS OF THEM! YES, WE WERE COMPLETELY OUTNUMBERED—
I'M NOT INTERESTED.
GET HIM BACK. NOW.
UH... PERHAPS IF WE HAD REINFORCEMENTS—
NOW!!
TAP
TAP
TAP
TAP

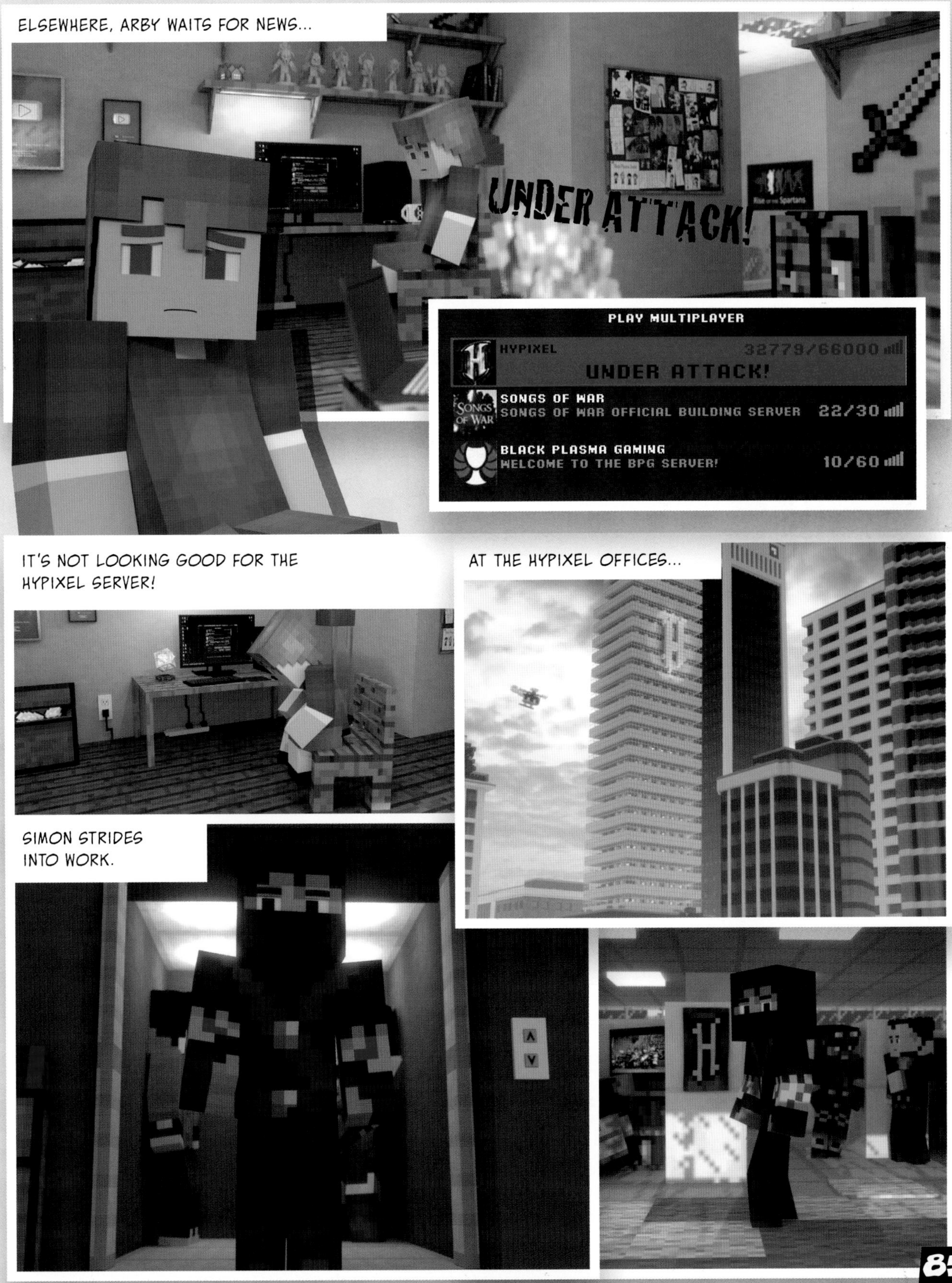
ELSEWHERE, ARBY WAITS FOR NEWS...
UNDER ATTACK!
PLAY MULTIPLAYER
HYPIXEL 32779/66000
UNDER ATTACK!
SONGS OF WAR
SONGS OF WAR OFFICIAL BUILDING SERVER 22/30
BLACK PLASMA GAMING
WELCOME TO THE BPG SERVER! 10/60
IT'S NOT LOOKING GOOD FOR THE HYPIXEL SERVER!
AT THE HYPIXEL OFFICES...
SIMON STRIDES INTO WORK.

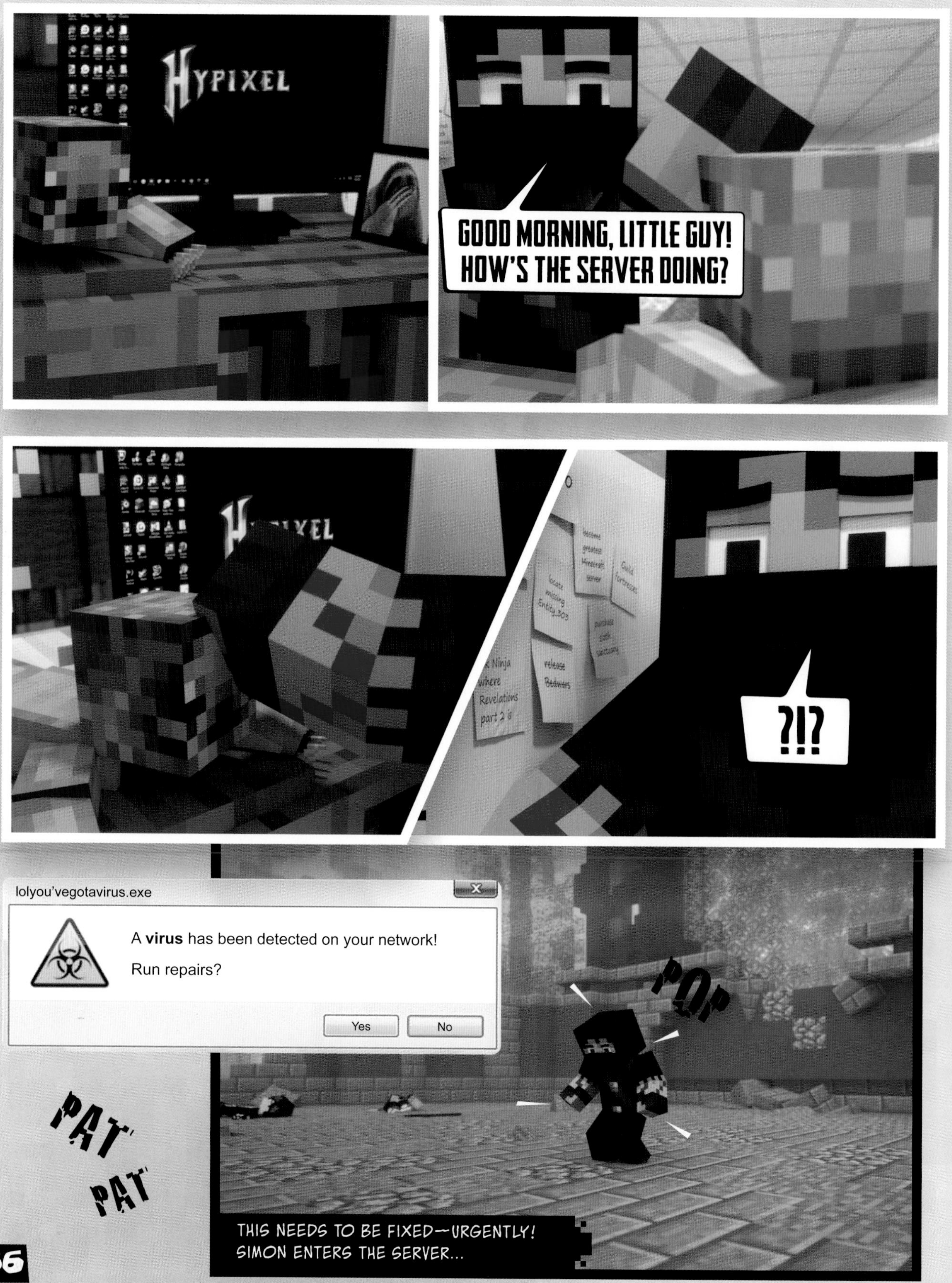
HYPIXEL
GOOD MORNING, LITTLE GUY! HOW'S THE SERVER DOING?
HYPIXEL
become greatest Minecraft server
Guild fortresses
locate missing Entity_303
purchase sloth sanctuary
release Bedwars
Ninja where Revelations part 2 is
?!?
lolyou'vegotavirus.exe
A **virus** has been detected on your network!
Run repairs?
Yes
No
POP
PAT
PAT
THIS NEEDS TO BE FIXED—URGENTLY! SIMON ENTERS THE SERVER...

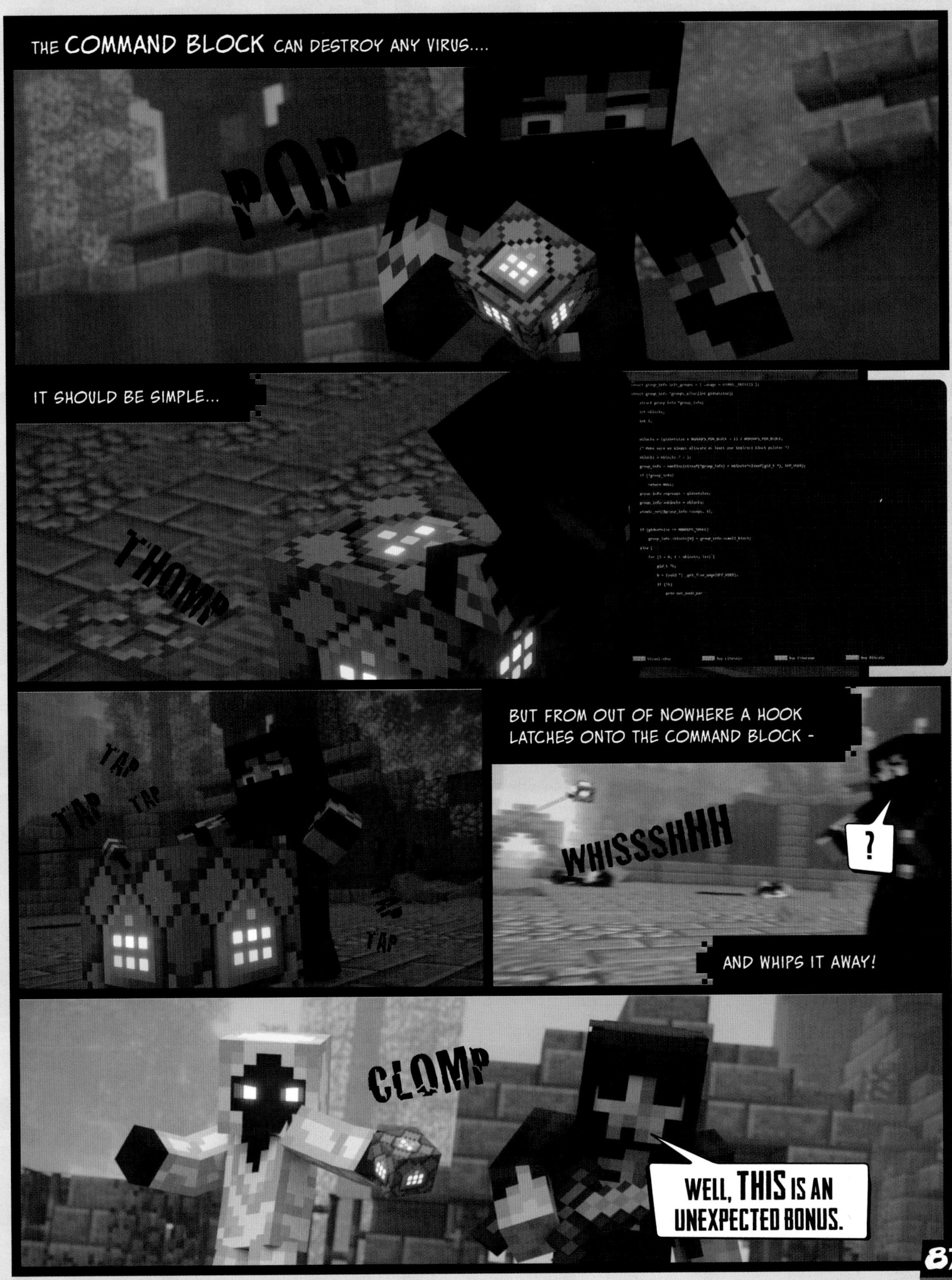
THE COMMAND BLOCK CAN DESTROY ANY VIRUS....
POP
IT SHOULD BE SIMPLE...
THOMP
TAP
TAP
TAP
TAP
BUT FROM OUT OF NOWHERE A HOOK LATCHES ONTO THE COMMAND BLOCK -
WHISSSHHH
?
AND WHIPS IT AWAY!
CLOMP
WELL, THIS IS AN UNEXPECTED BONUS.

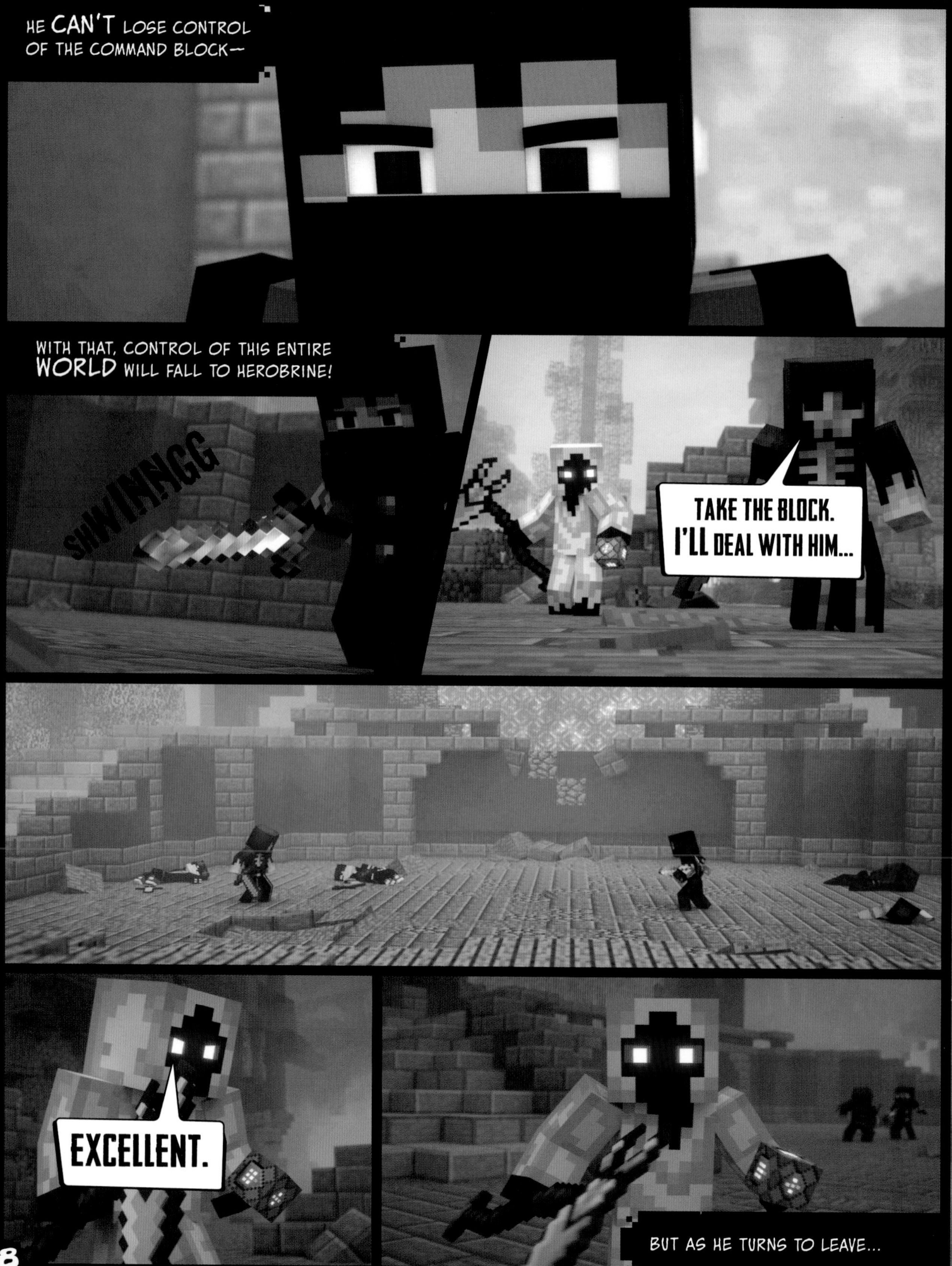
HE CAN'T LOSE CONTROL OF THE COMMAND BLOCK—
WITH THAT, CONTROL OF THIS ENTIRE WORLD WILL FALL TO HEROBRINE!
SHWINNGG
TAKE THE BLOCK. I'LL DEAL WITH HIM...
EXCELLENT.
BUT AS HE TURNS TO LEAVE...

HE ONCE MORE COMES FACE TO FACE WITH ALEX AND STEVE~

IS THAT A **COMMAND BLOCK**...?

IT'S **MINE**~

TAP
TIP
TAP

NO!!

ENTITY_303 THROWS HIS SCYTHE FORWARDS~

SWISHASWISHASWI

ITS FLIGHT CURVES **AROUND**~

AND COMES UP BEHIND THE CHASING STEVE
AND ALEX!

T'HODD

STEVE DROPS TO THE FLOOR JUST IN TIME~

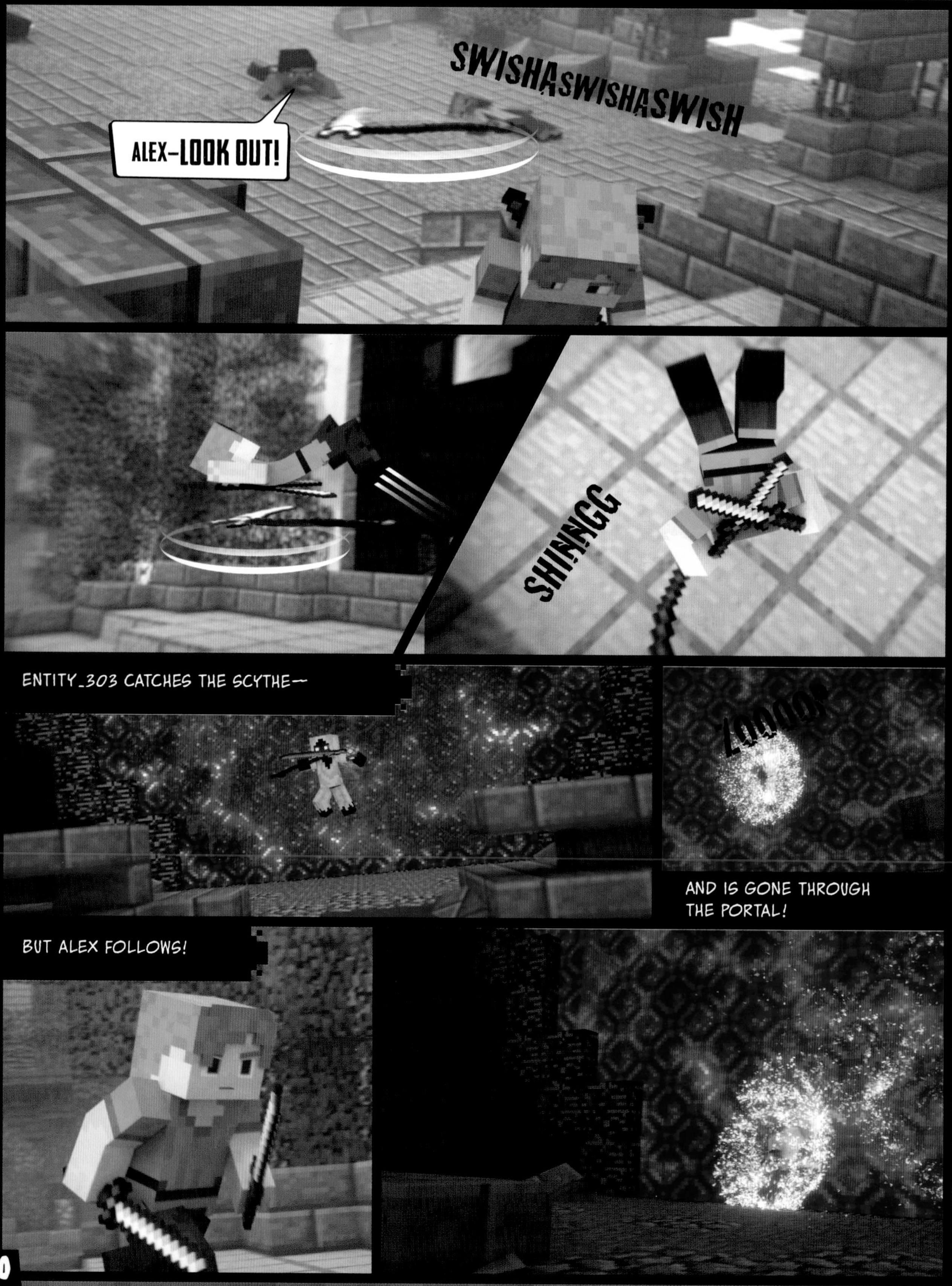
SWISHASWISHASWISH
ALEX—LOOK OUT!
SHINNGG
ENTITY_303 CATCHES THE SCYTHE—
ZOOOP
AND IS GONE THROUGH THE PORTAL!
BUT ALEX FOLLOWS!

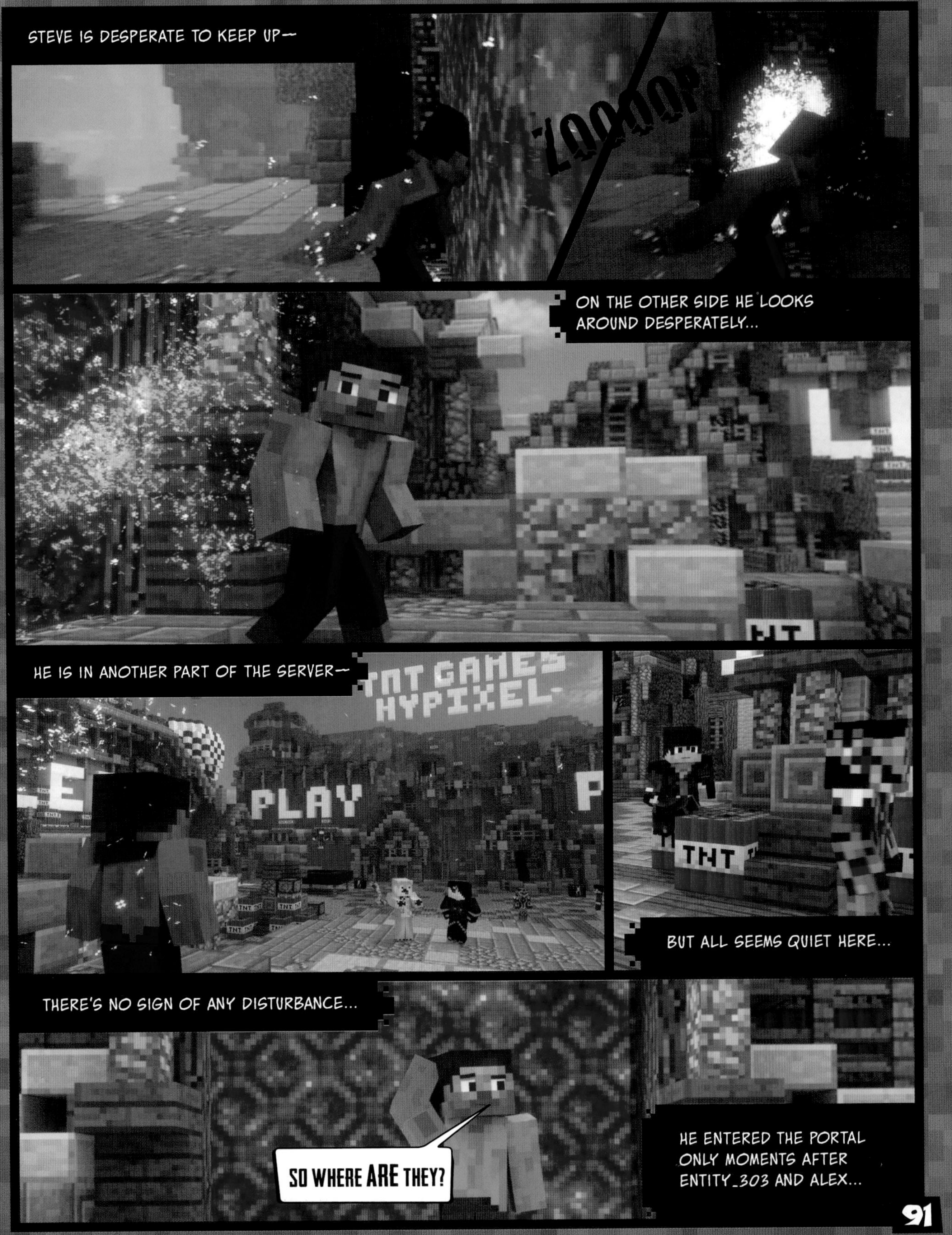

STEVE IS DESPERATE TO KEEP UP—
ZOOOOP
ON THE OTHER SIDE HE LOOKS AROUND DESPERATELY...
HE IS IN ANOTHER PART OF THE SERVER—
TNT GAMES
HYPIXEL
PLAY
BUT ALL SEEMS QUIET HERE...
THERE'S NO SIGN OF ANY DISTURBANCE...
SO WHERE ARE THEY?
HE ENTERED THE PORTAL ONLY MOMENTS AFTER ENTITY_303 AND ALEX...

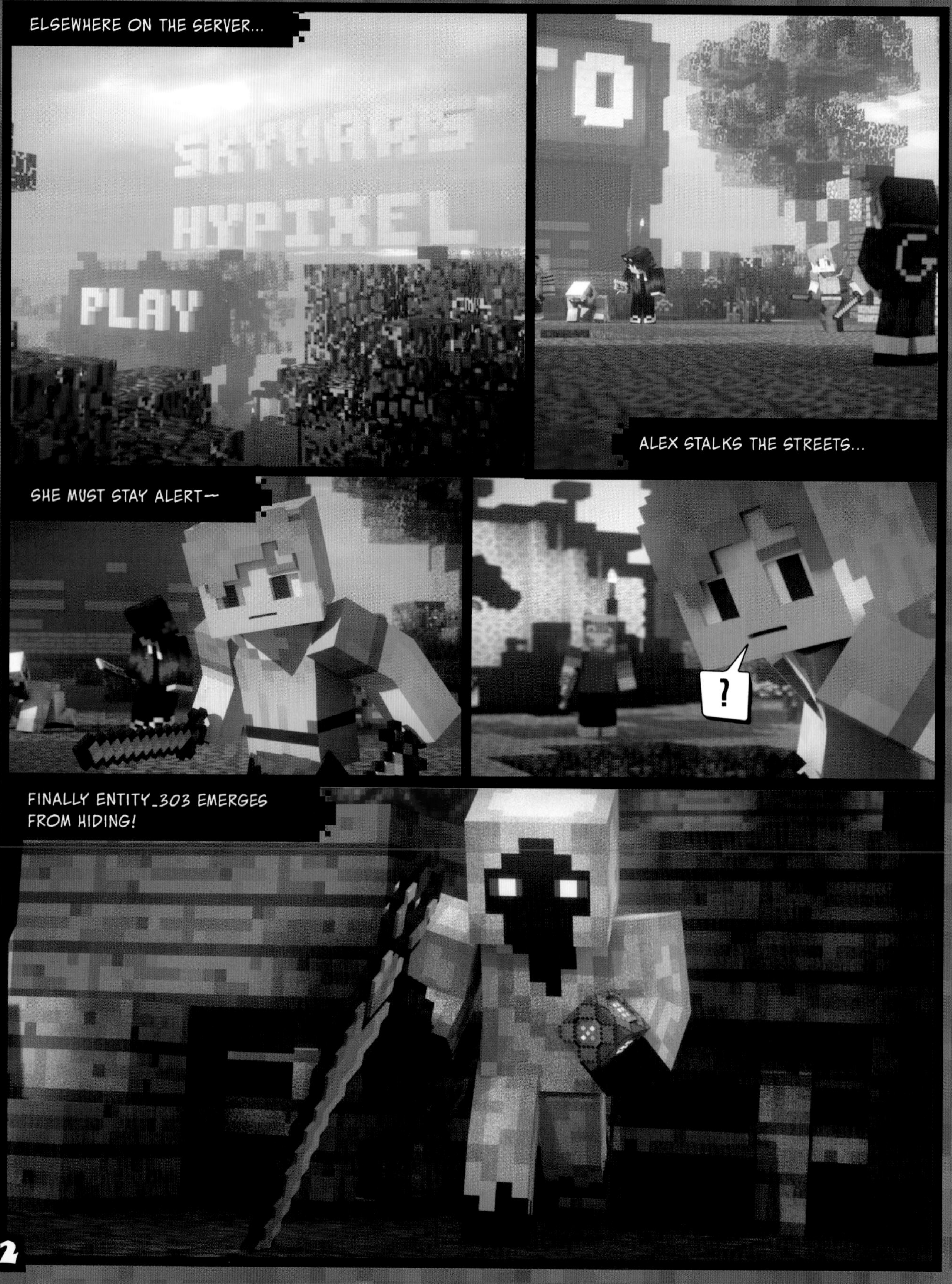
ELSEWHERE ON THE SERVER...
SKYWARS
HYPIXEL
PLAY
ALEX STALKS THE STREETS...
SHE MUST STAY ALERT—
?
FINALLY ENTITY_303 EMERGES
FROM HIDING!

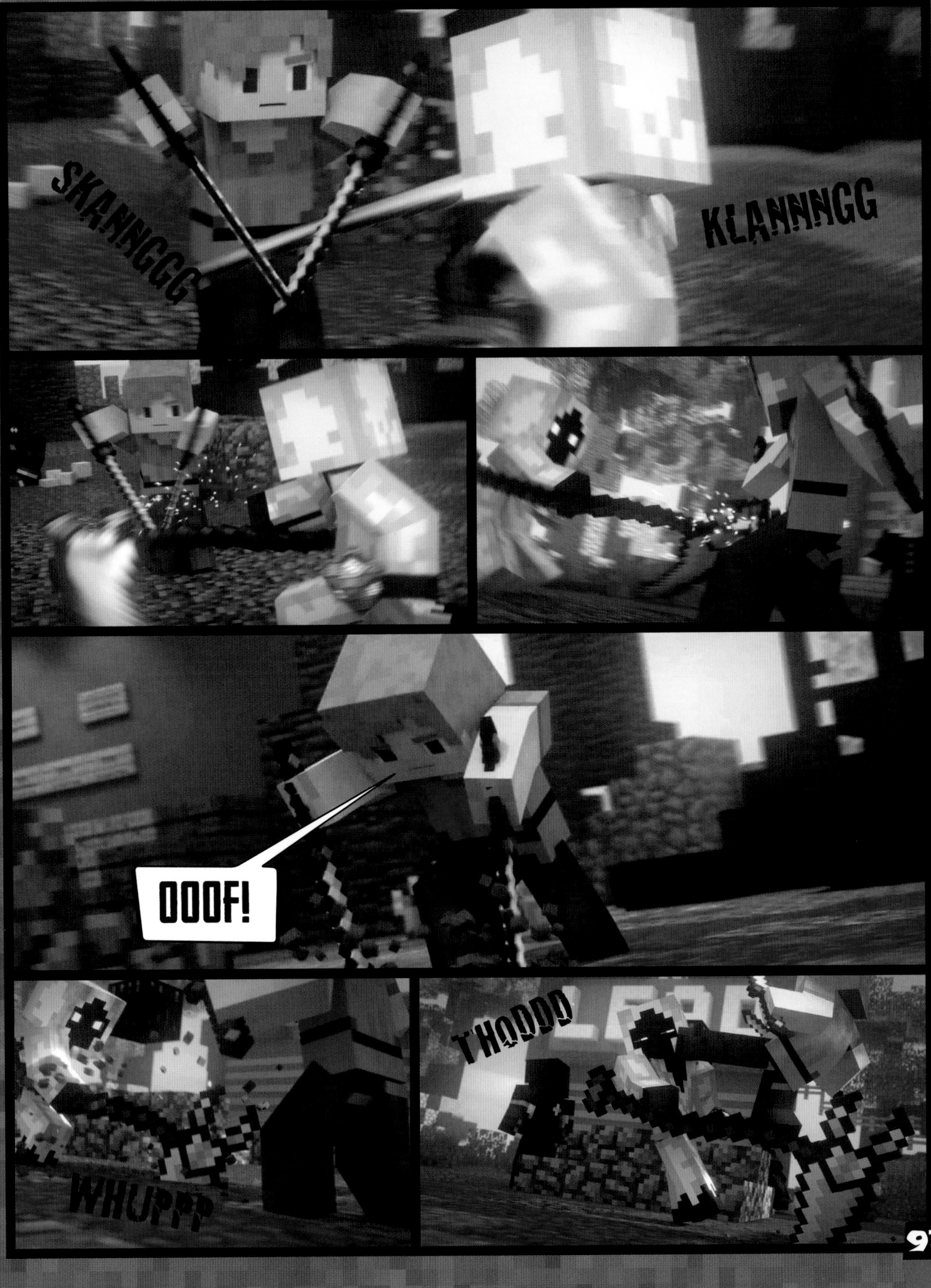
SKANNGGG
KLANNNGG
OOOF!
WHUPPP
THODDD

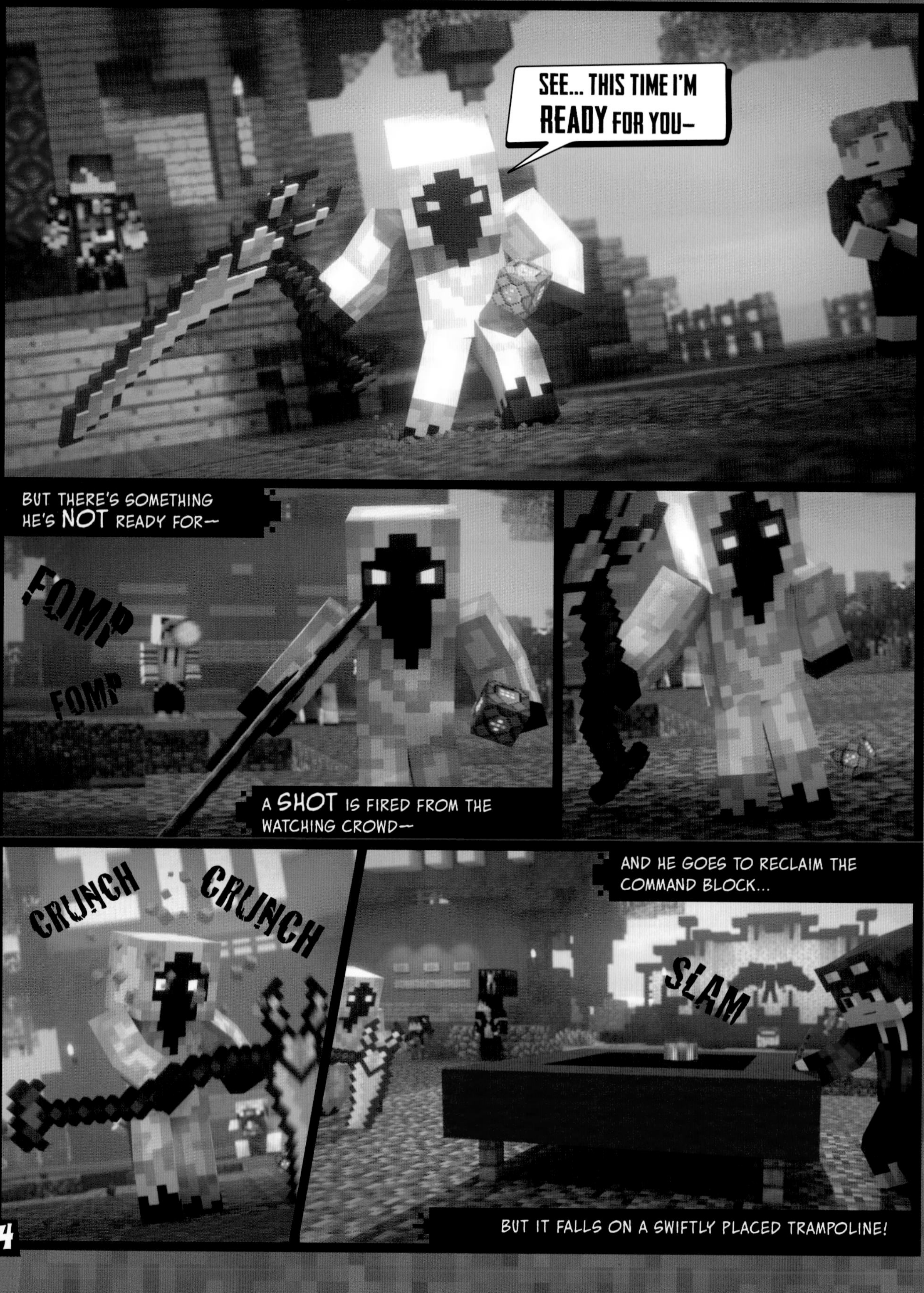

SEE... THIS TIME I'M READY FOR YOU—
BUT THERE'S SOMETHING HE'S NOT READY FOR—
FOMP
FOMP
A SHOT IS FIRED FROM THE WATCHING CROWD—
CRUNCH
CRUNCH
AND HE GOES TO RECLAIM THE COMMAND BLOCK...
SLAM
BUT IT FALLS ON A SWIFTLY PLACED TRAMPOLINE!

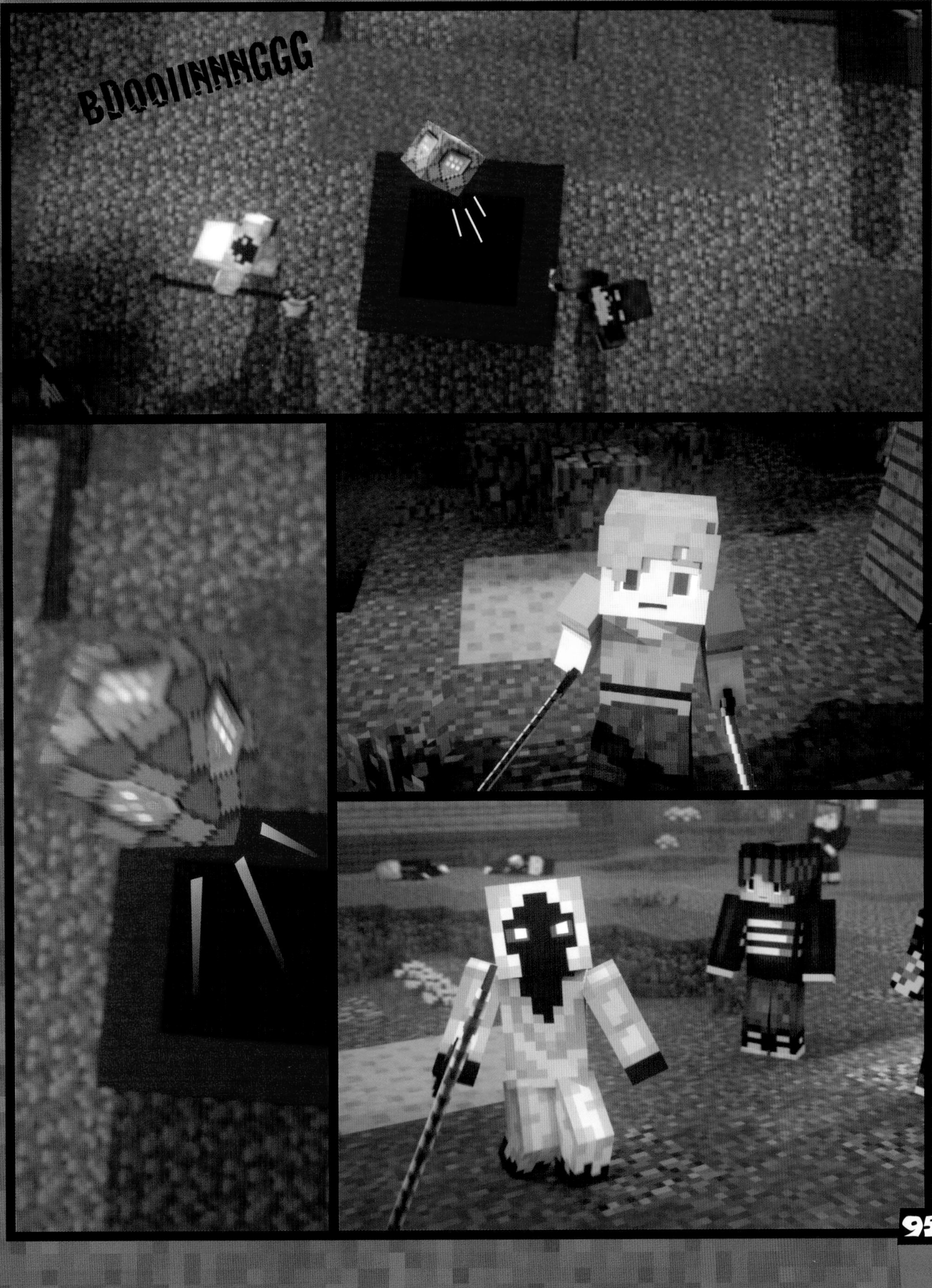
BDOOIINNNGGG

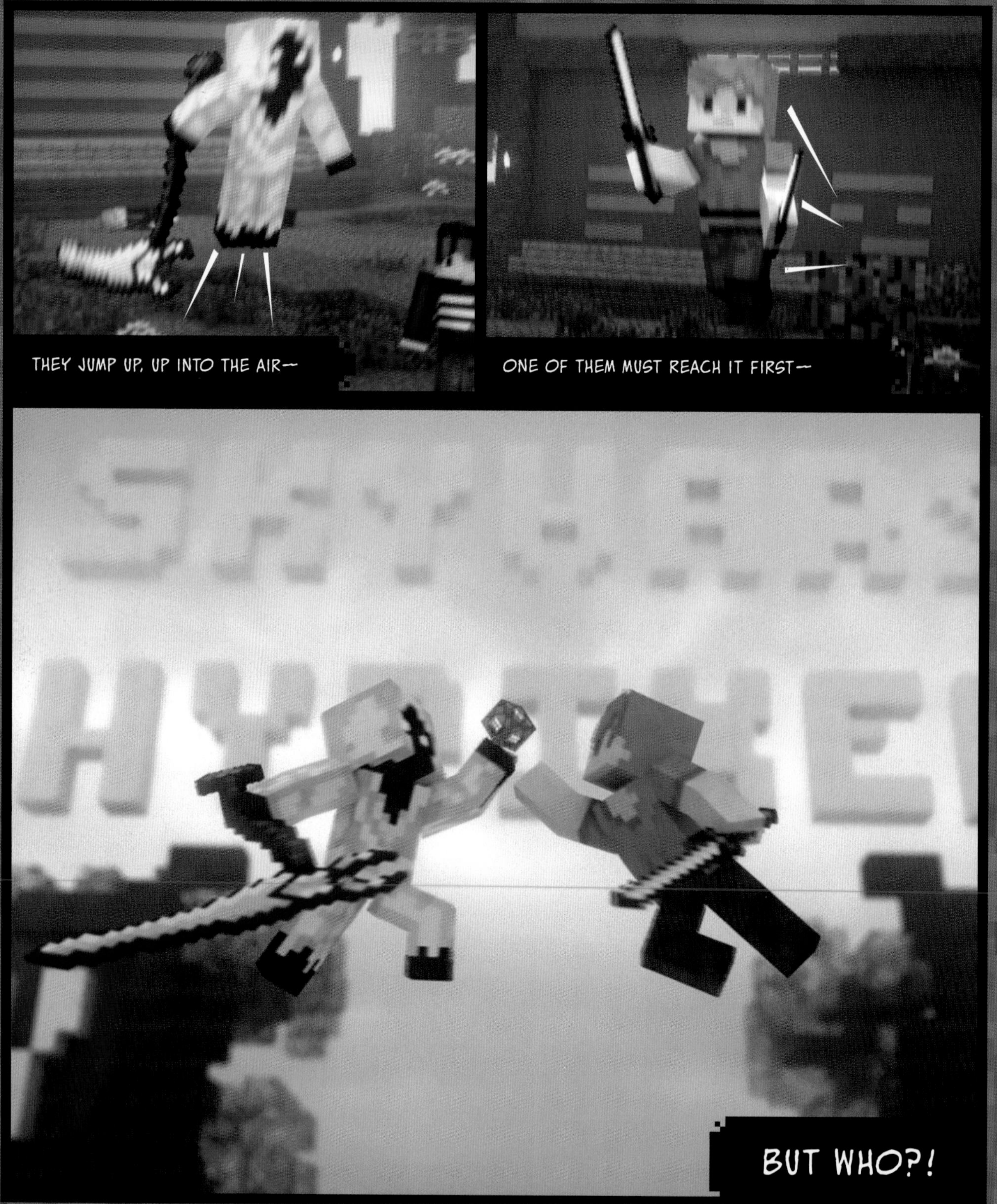
THEY JUMP UP, UP INTO THE AIR—
ONE OF THEM MUST REACH IT FIRST—
BUT WHO?!

PART II

THE MINDBENDING MINECRAFT GRAPHIC NOVEL ADVENTURE!

GOING VIRAL

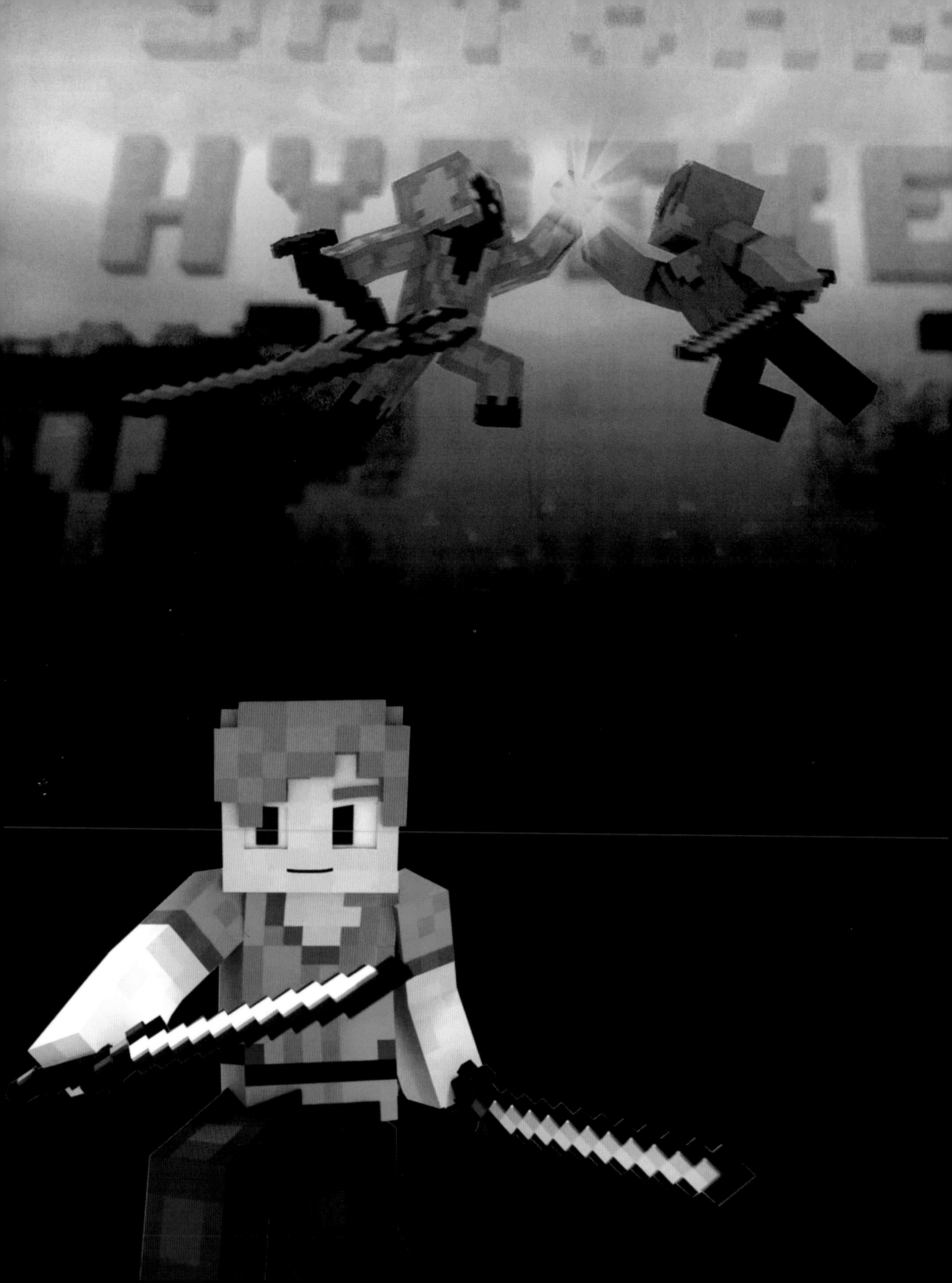

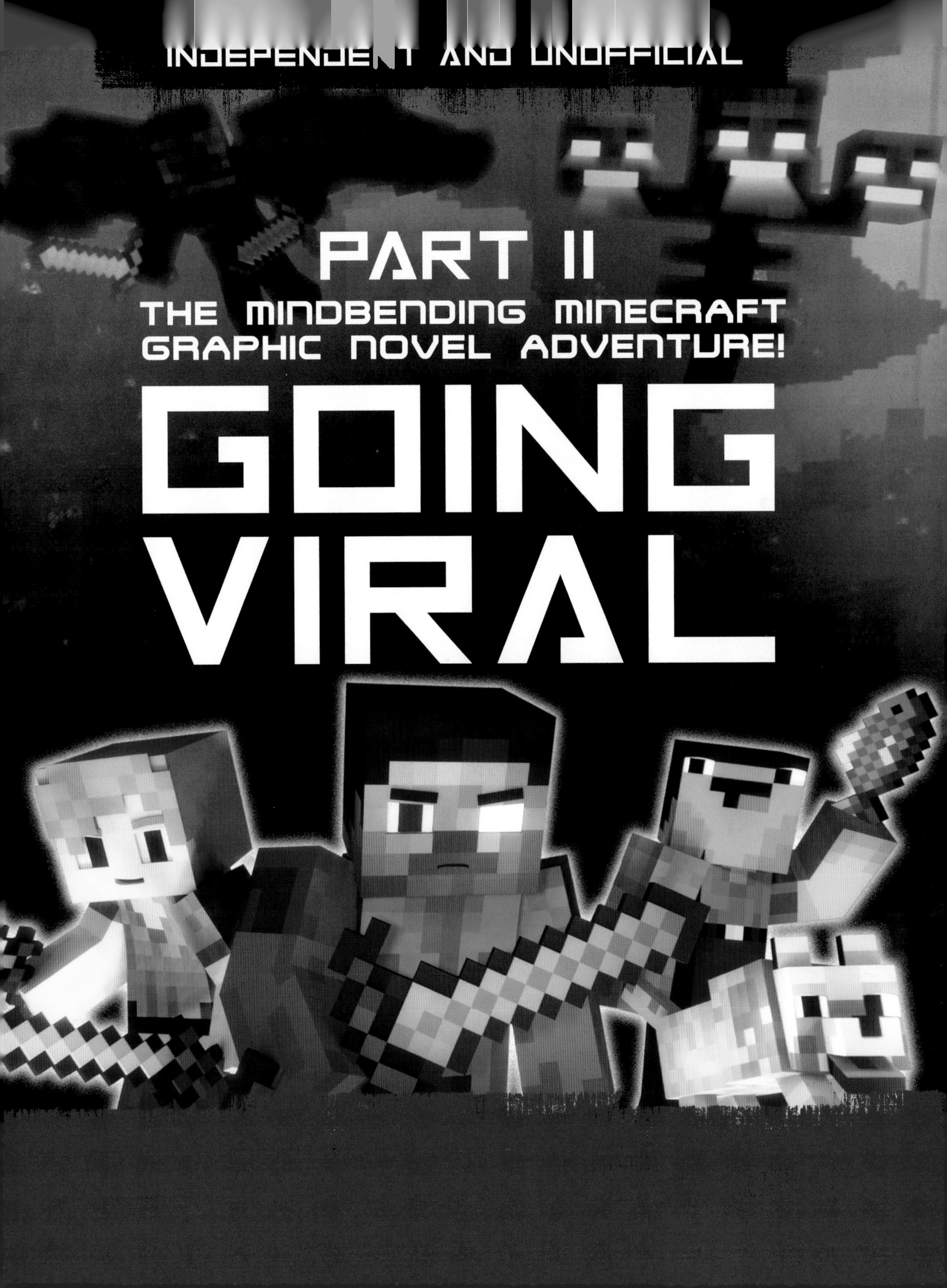
INDEPENDENT AND UNOFFICIAL
PART II
THE MINDBENDING MINECRAFT GRAPHIC NOVEL ADVENTURE!
GOING VIRAL

THE STORY SO FAR...

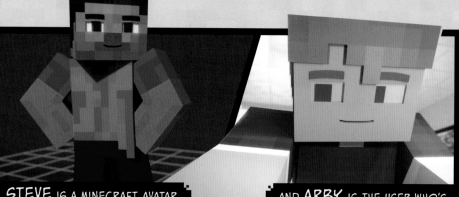

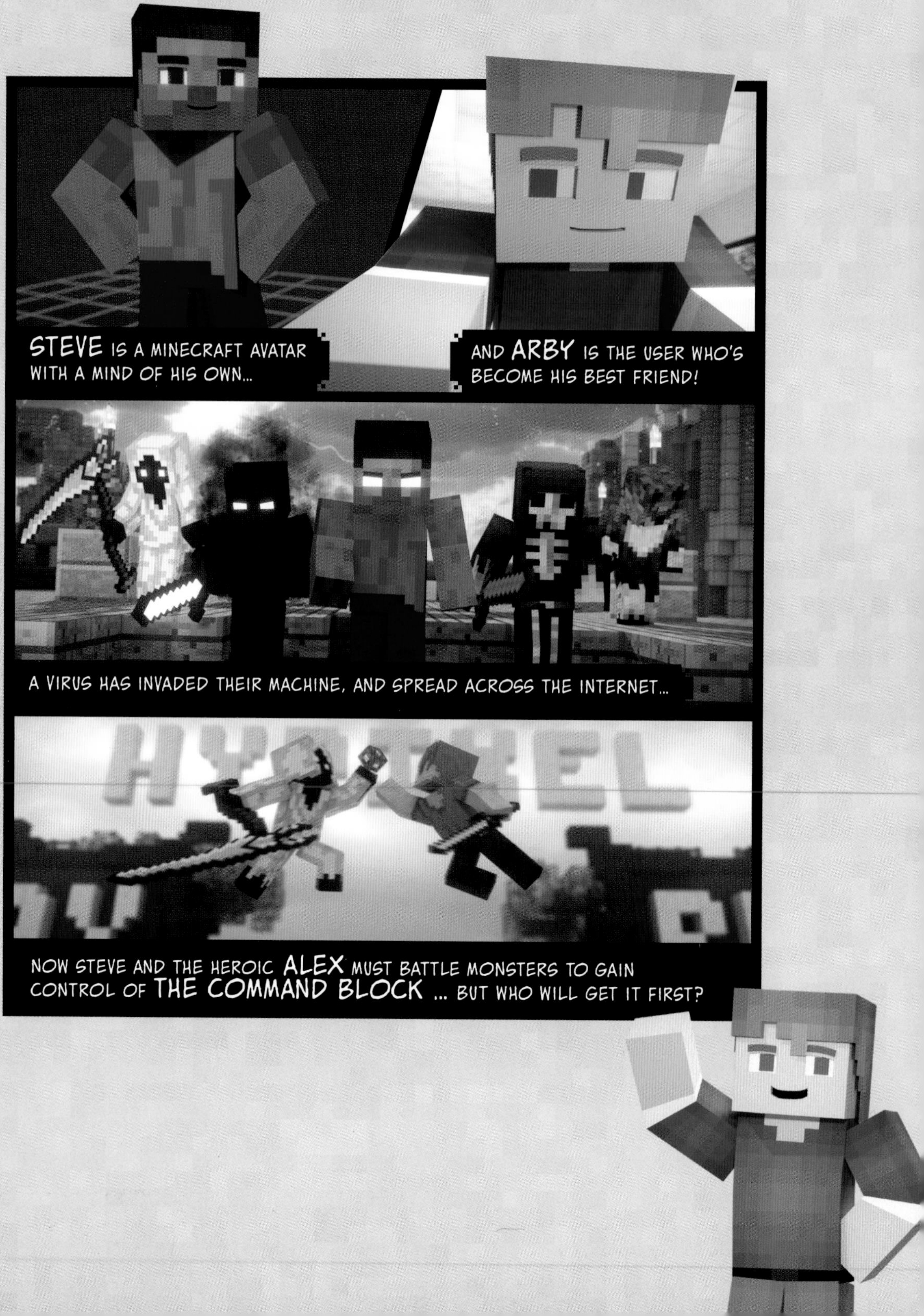

STEVE IS A MINECRAFT AVATAR WITH A MIND OF HIS OWN...

AND ARBY IS THE USER WHO'S BECOME HIS BEST FRIEND!

A VIRUS HAS INVADED THEIR MACHINE, AND SPREAD ACROSS THE INTERNET...

NOW STEVE AND THE HEROIC ALEX MUST BATTLE MONSTERS TO GAIN CONTROL OF THE COMMAND BLOCK ... BUT WHO WILL GET IT FIRST?

CHAPTER 5

AAAAAHH–
THOOOOOM
AS ALEX AND ENTITY_303 TOUCH THE COMMAND BLOCK—THEY COLLIDE AND FLY BACKWARDS—
OOF–
URRGGGHHH...
DOINK
NO!!

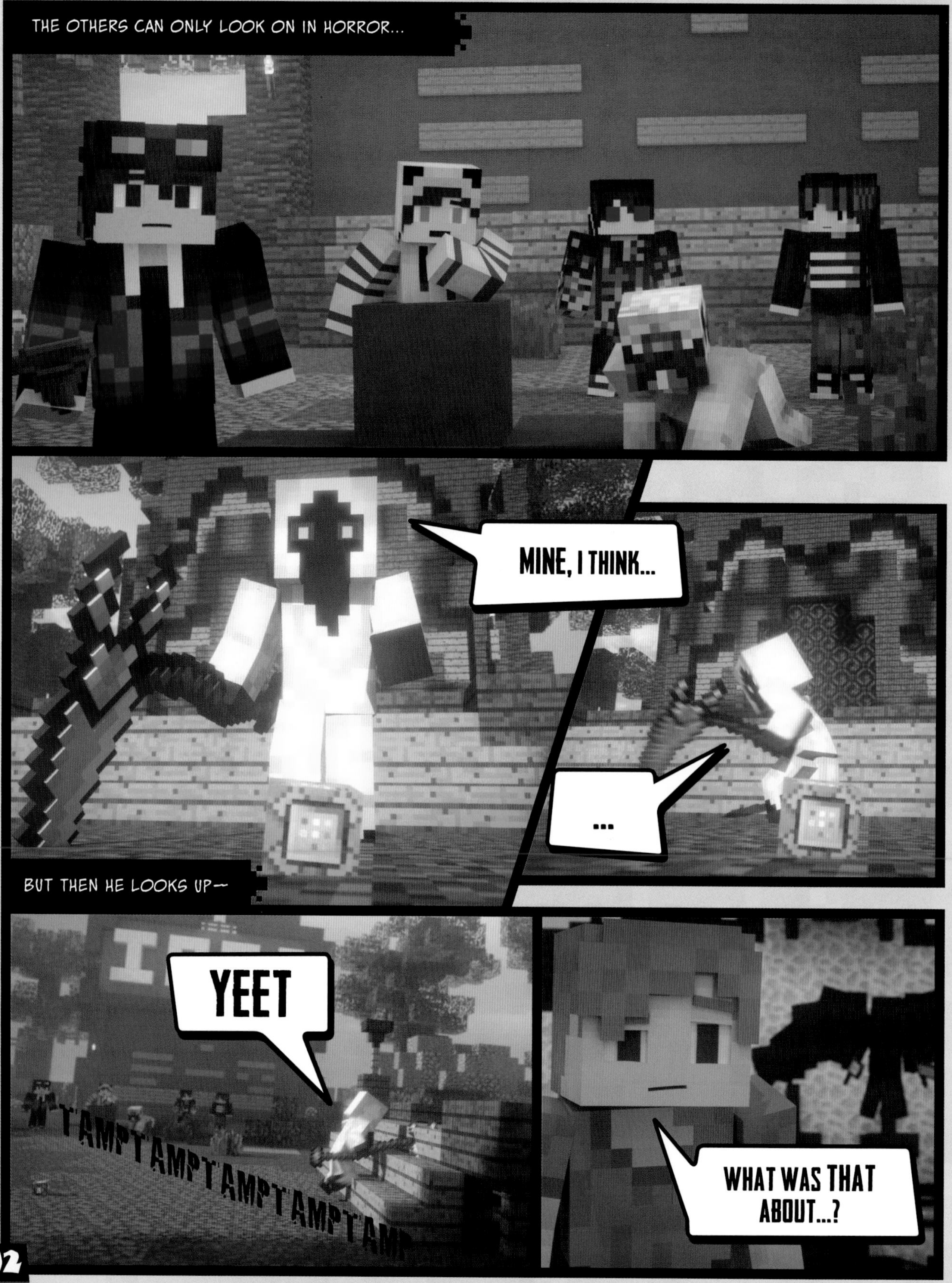

THE OTHERS CAN ONLY LOOK ON IN HORROR...
MINE, I THINK...
...
BUT THEN HE LOOKS UP—
YEET
TAMPTAMPTAMPTAMPTAMPTAMP
WHAT WAS THAT ABOUT...?

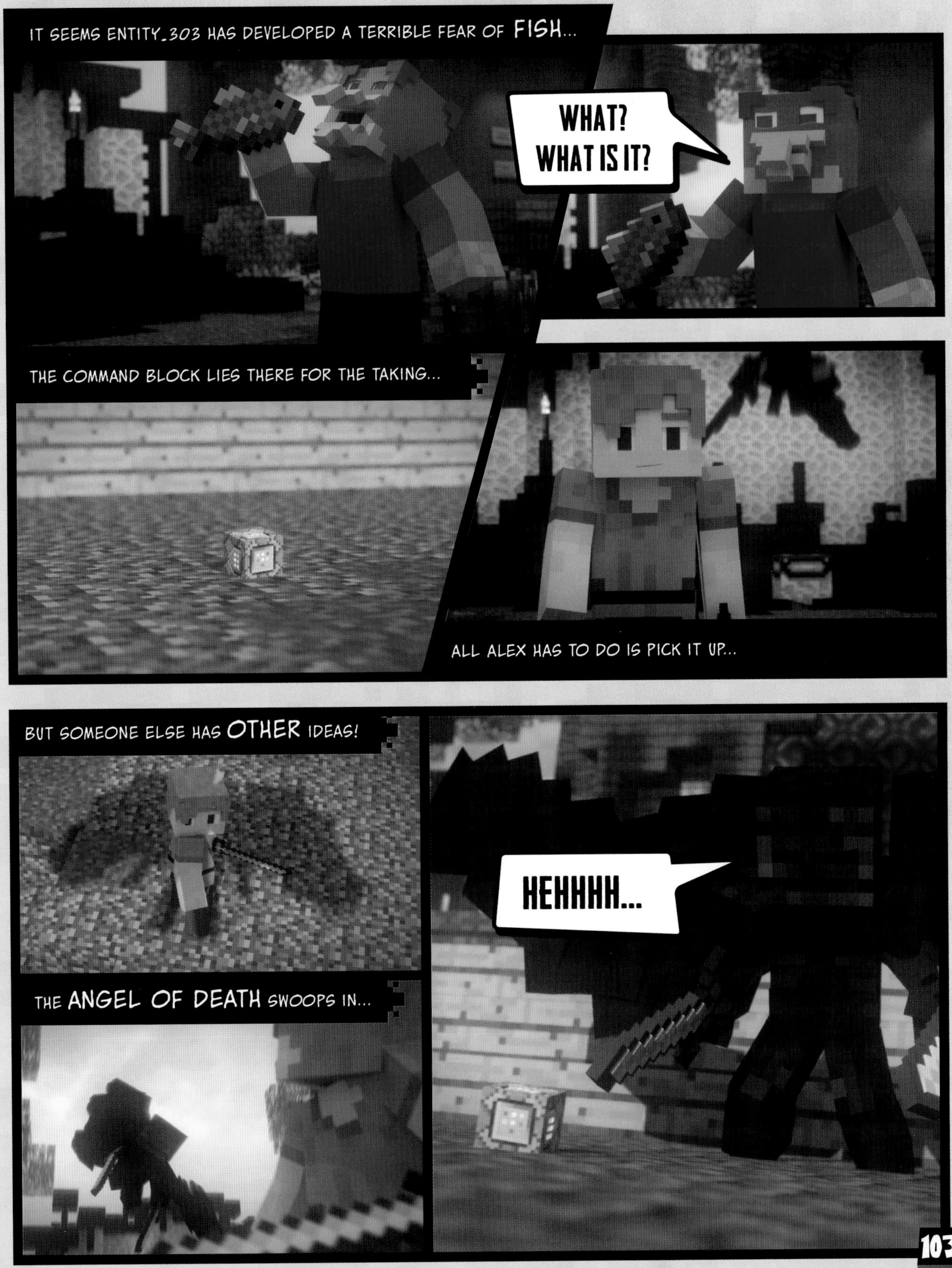
IT SEEMS ENTITY_303 HAS DEVELOPED A TERRIBLE FEAR OF FISH...
WHAT? WHAT IS IT?
THE COMMAND BLOCK LIES THERE FOR THE TAKING...
ALL ALEX HAS TO DO IS PICK IT UP...
BUT SOMEONE ELSE HAS OTHER IDEAS!
THE ANGEL OF DEATH SWOOPS IN...
HEHHHH...

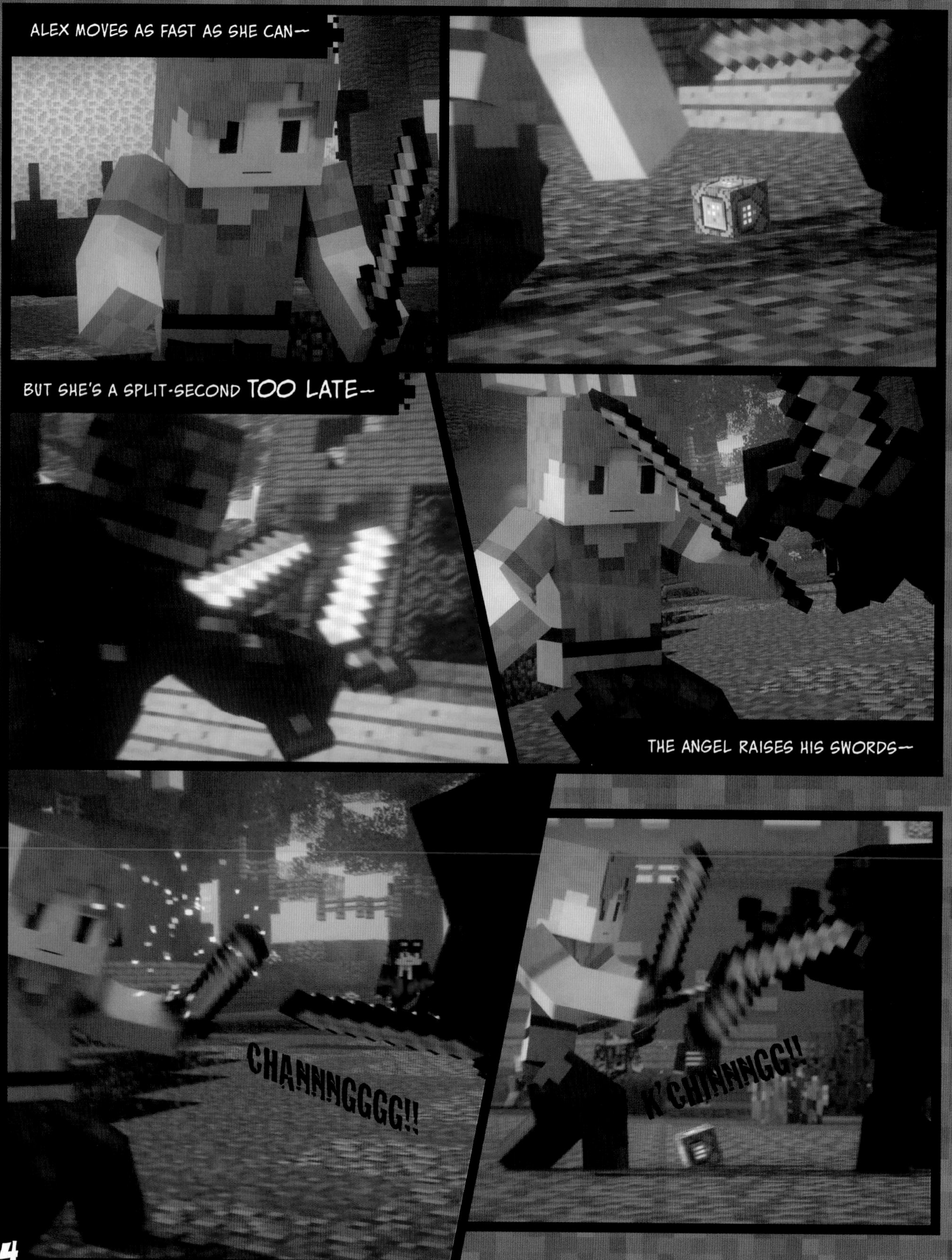
ALEX MOVES AS FAST AS SHE CAN—
BUT SHE'S A SPLIT-SECOND TOO LATE—
THE ANGEL RAISES HIS SWORDS—
CHANNNGGGGG!!
K'CHINNNGG!!

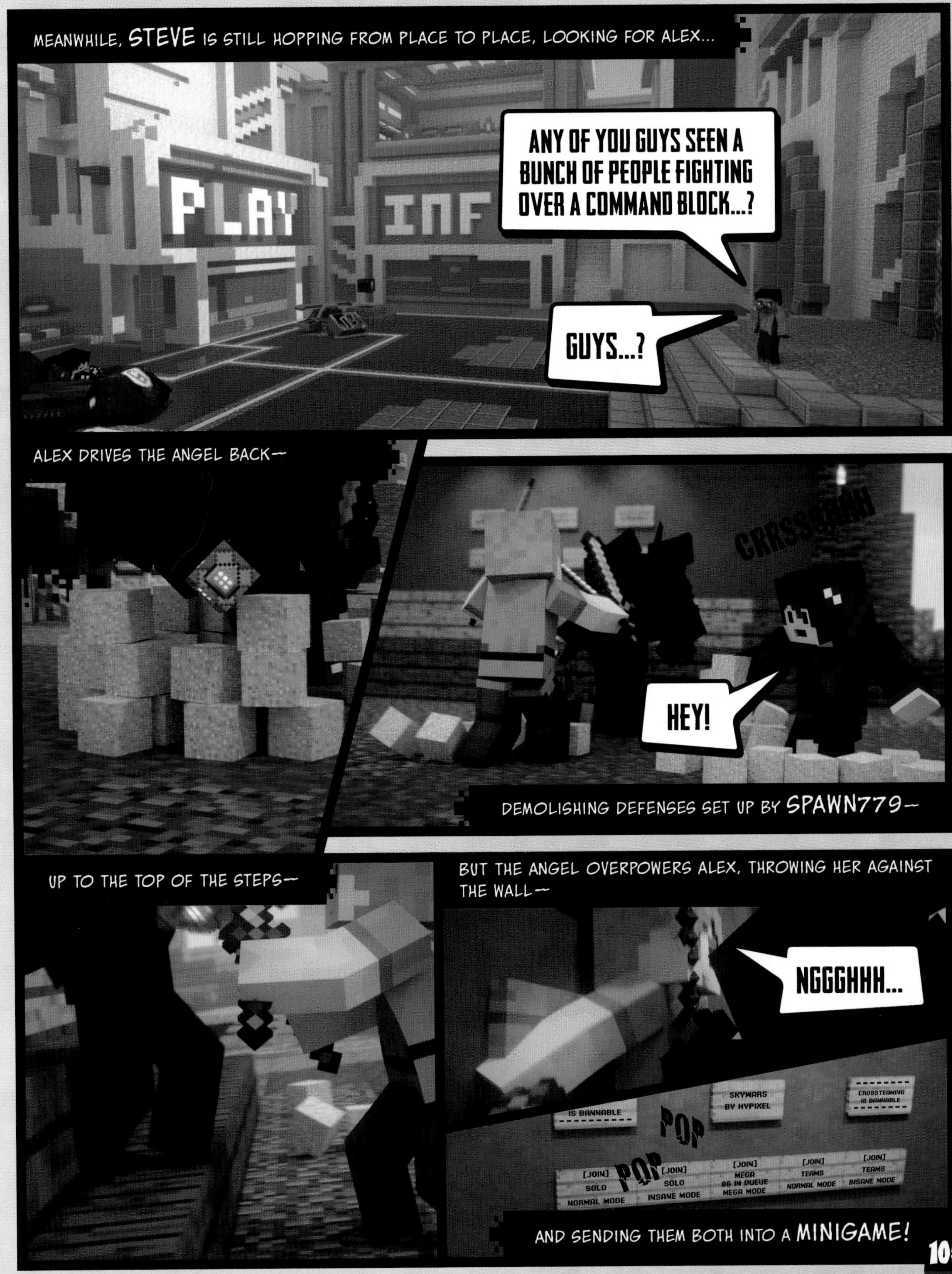
MEANWHILE, STEVE IS STILL HOPPING FROM PLACE TO PLACE, LOOKING FOR ALEX...
PLAY
INF
ANY OF YOU GUYS SEEN A BUNCH OF PEOPLE FIGHTING OVER A COMMAND BLOCK...?
GUYS...?
ALEX DRIVES THE ANGEL BACK—
CRRSSHHH
HEY!
DEMOLISHING DEFENSES SET UP BY SPAWN779—
UP TO THE TOP OF THE STEPS—
BUT THE ANGEL OVERPOWERS ALEX, THROWING HER AGAINST THE WALL—
NGGGHHH...
IS BANNABLE
SKYWARS BY HYPIXEL
CROSSTEAMING IS BANNABLE
POP
POP
[JOIN] SOLO NORMAL MODE
[JOIN] SOLO INSANE MODE
[JOIN] MEGA 86 IN QUEUE MEGA MODE
[JOIN] TEAMS NORMAL MODE
[JOIN] TEAMS INSANE MODE
AND SENDING THEM BOTH INTO A MINIGAME!

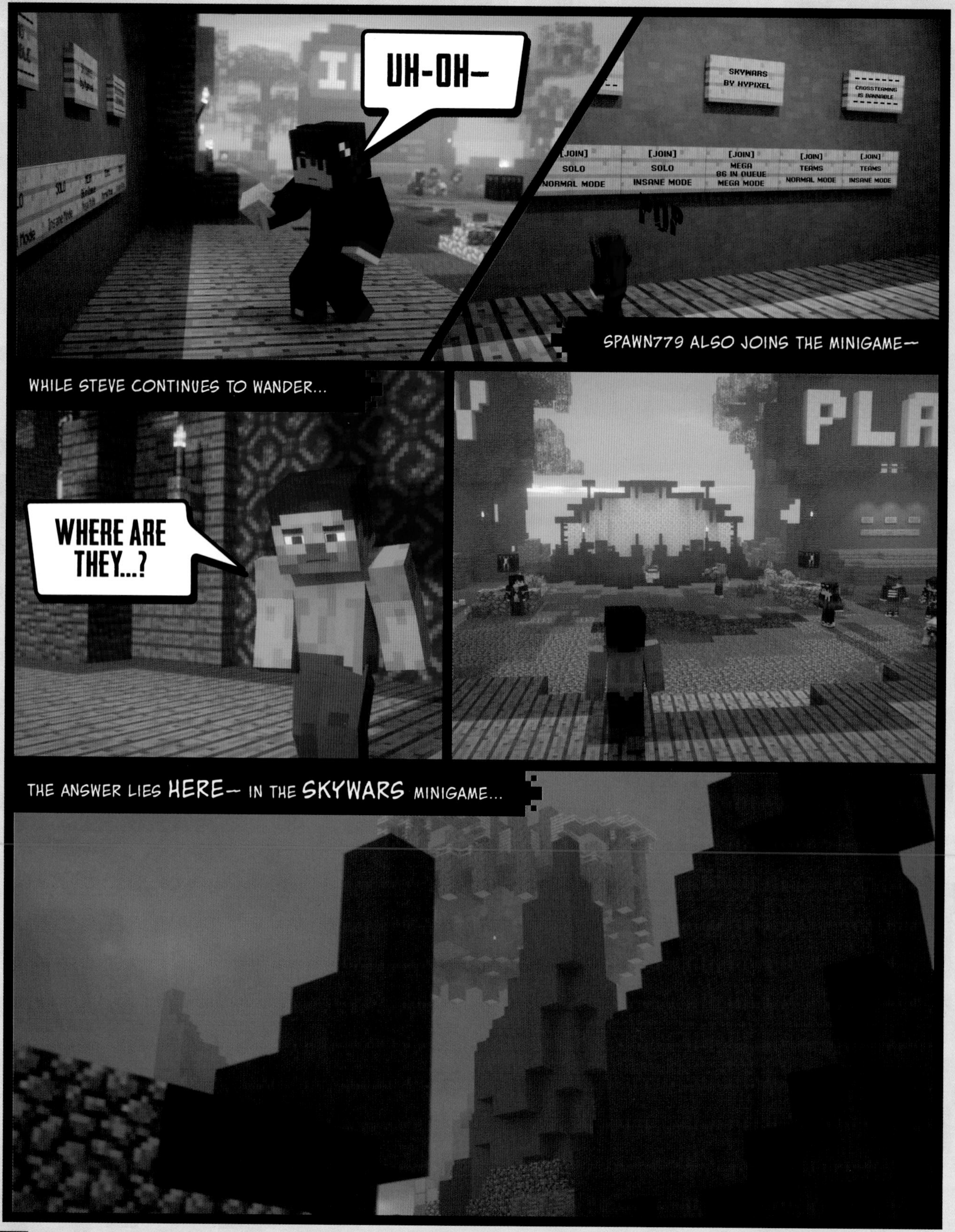
UH-OH—
SKYWARS BY HYPIXEL
CROSSTEAMING IS BANNABLE
[JOIN] SOLO NORMAL MODE
[JOIN] SOLO INSANE MODE
[JOIN] MEGA 86 IN QUEUE MEGA MODE
[JOIN] TEAMS NORMAL MODE
[JOIN] TEAMS INSANE MODE
POP
SPAWN779 ALSO JOINS THE MINIGAME—
WHILE STEVE CONTINUES TO WANDER...
WHERE ARE THEY...?
PLA
THE ANSWER LIES HERE— IN THE SKYWARS MINIGAME...

FROM OUT OF NOWHERE, ALEX AND THE ANGEL CRASH INTO THE MINIGAME—
AND THEIR FIGHT CONTINUES WITHOUT A PAUSE—
BUT THE ANGEL HAS THE UPPER HAND—
OOF!
SLAM!
THE COMMAND BLOCK IS THERE FOR THE TAKING...
POP

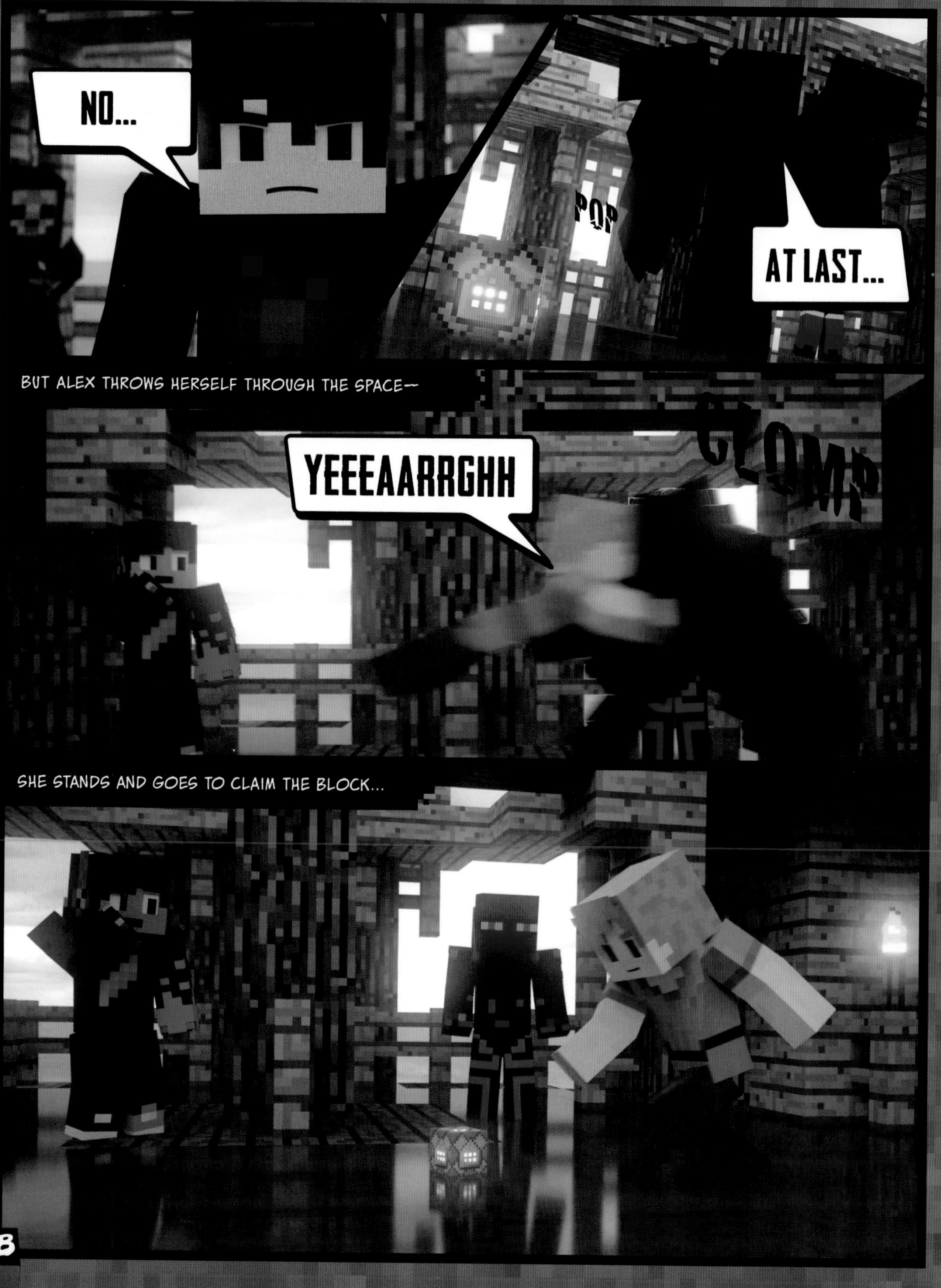
NO...
POP
AT LAST...
BUT ALEX THROWS HERSELF THROUGH THE SPACE—
YEEEAARRGHH
CLOMP
SHE STANDS AND GOES TO CLAIM THE BLOCK...

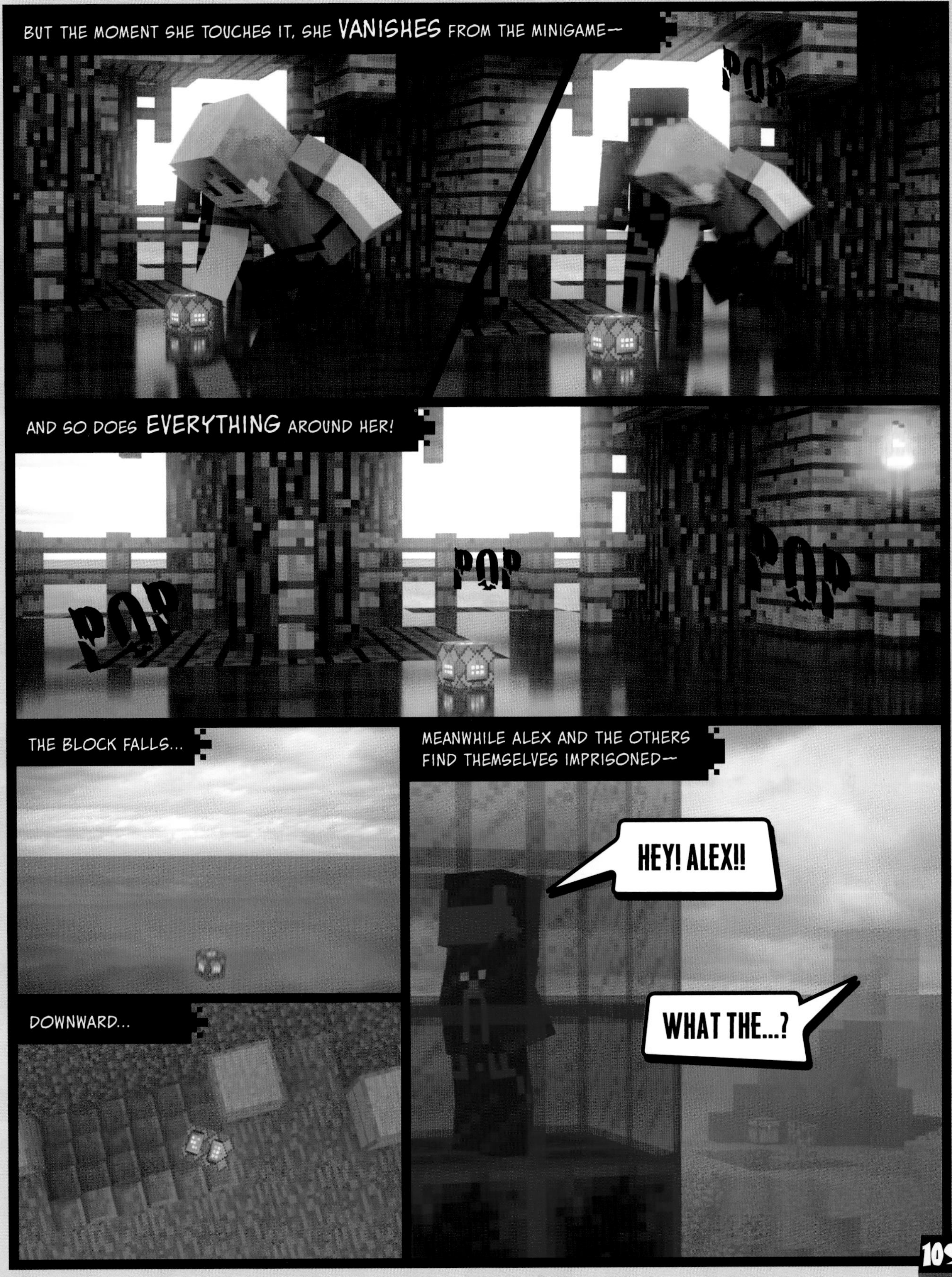

BUT THE MOMENT SHE TOUCHES IT, SHE VANISHES FROM THE MINIGAME—
POP
AND SO DOES EVERYTHING AROUND HER!
POP
POP
POP
THE BLOCK FALLS...
DOWNWARD...
MEANWHILE ALEX AND THE OTHERS FIND THEMSELVES IMPRISONED—
HEY! ALEX!!
WHAT THE...?

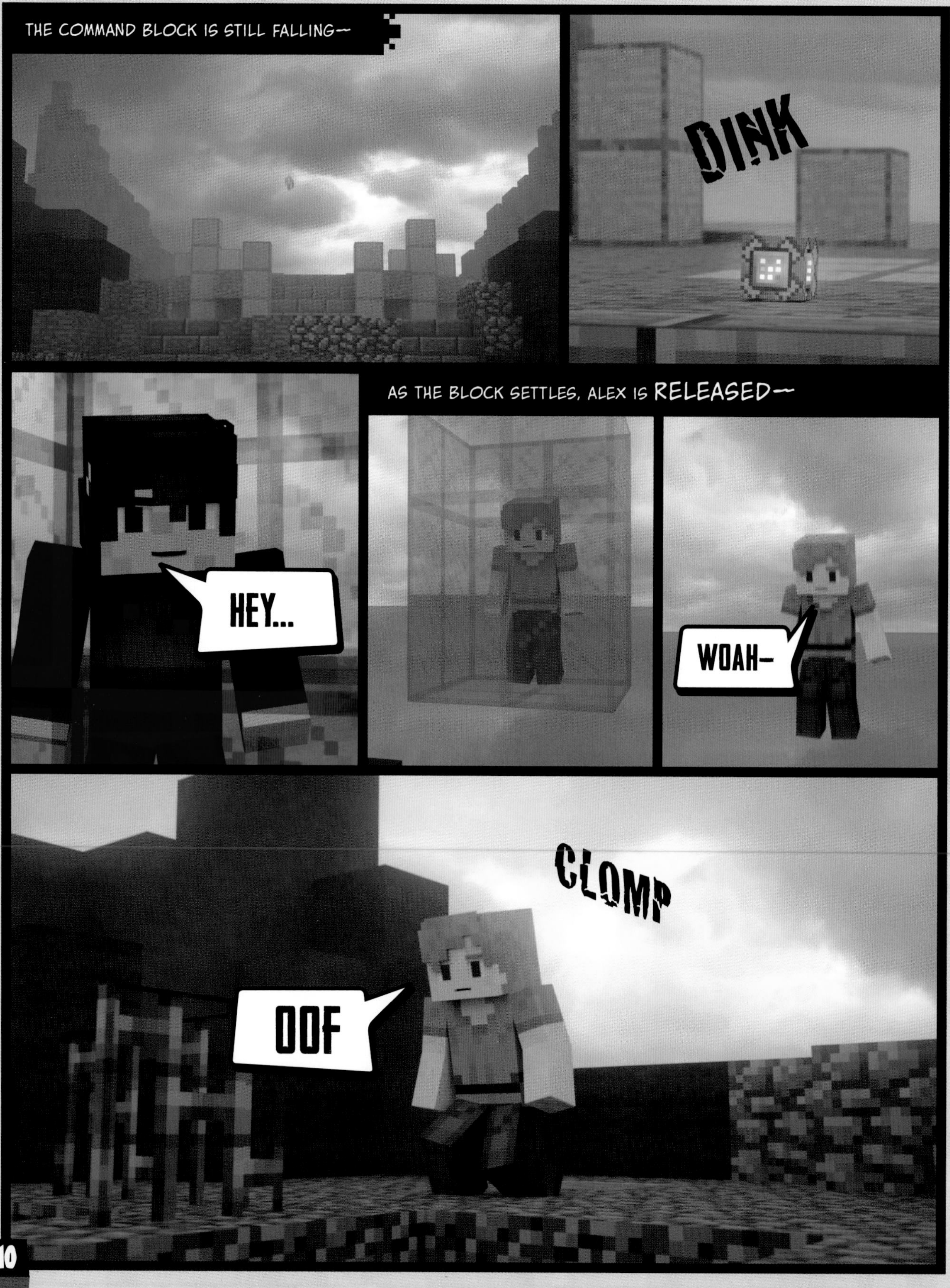
THE COMMAND BLOCK IS STILL FALLING—
DINK
AS THE BLOCK SETTLES, ALEX IS RELEASED—
HEY...
WOAH-
CLOMP
OOF

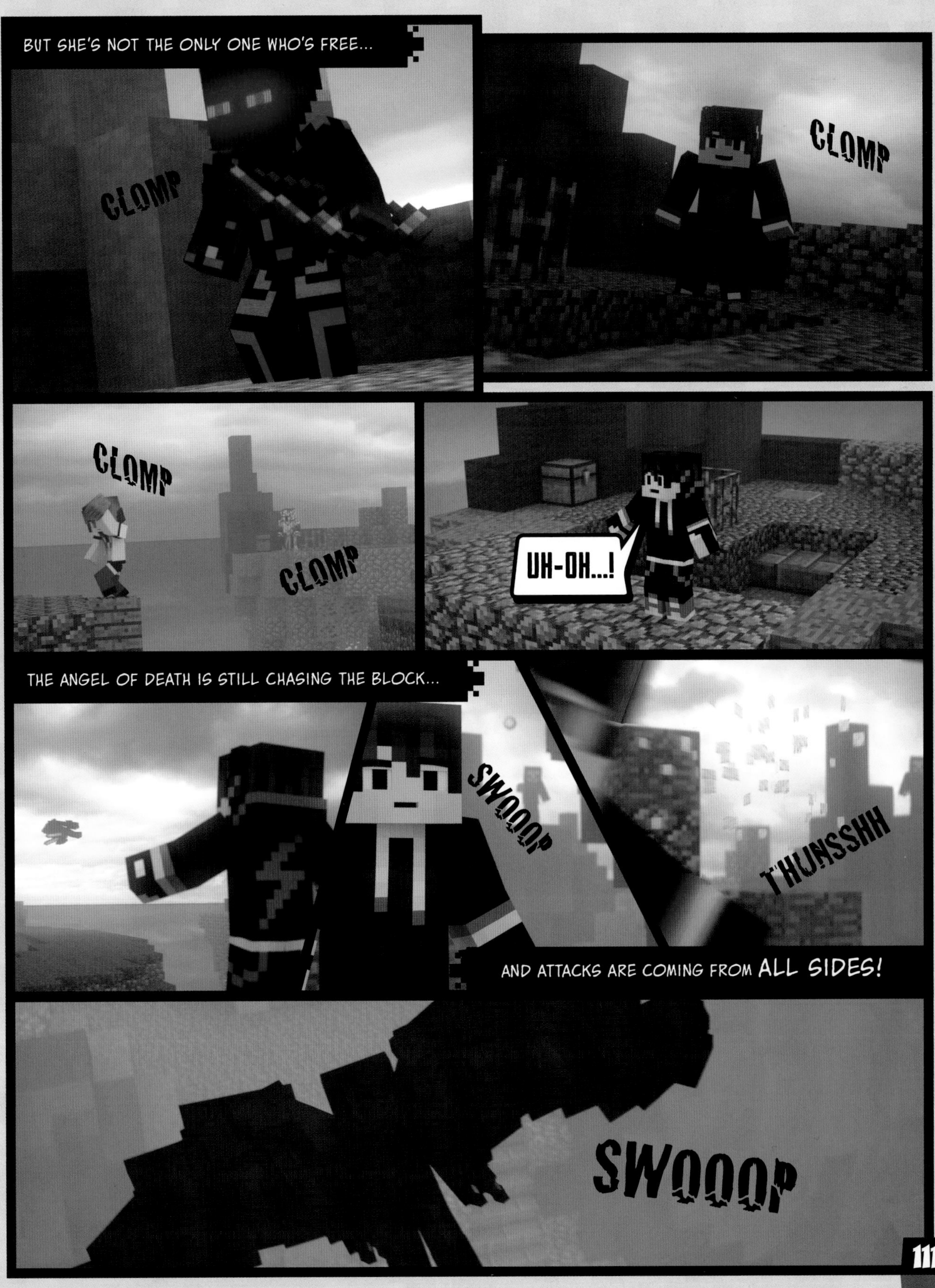
BUT SHE'S NOT THE ONLY ONE WHO'S FREE...
CLOMP
CLOMP
CLOMP
CLOMP
UH-OH...!
THE ANGEL OF DEATH IS STILL CHASING THE BLOCK...
SWOOOP
THUNSSHH
AND ATTACKS ARE COMING FROM ALL SIDES!
SWOOOP

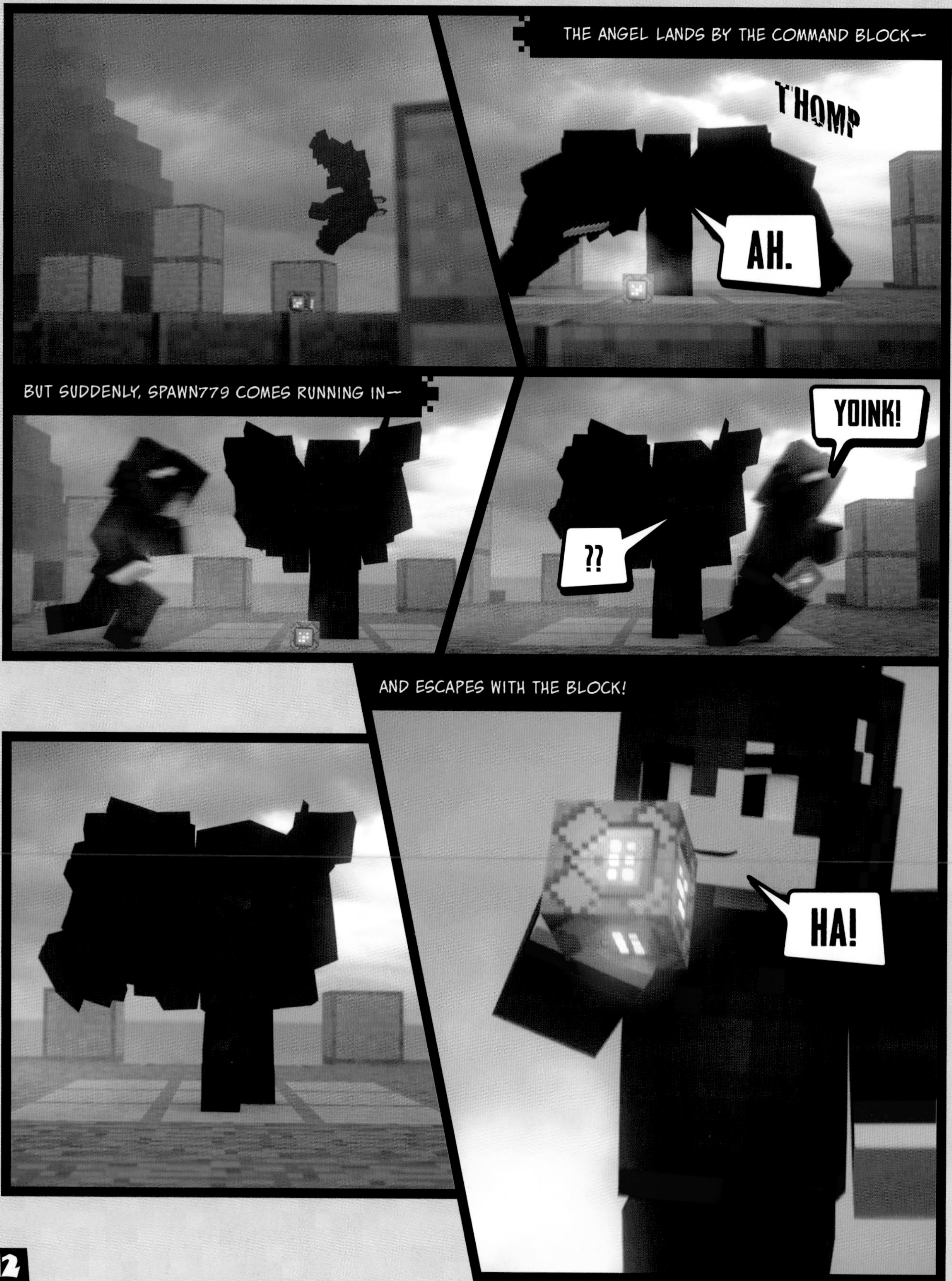
THE ANGEL LANDS BY THE COMMAND BLOCK—
THOMP
AH.
BUT SUDDENLY, SPAWN779 COMES RUNNING IN—
YOINK!
??
AND ESCAPES WITH THE BLOCK!
HA!

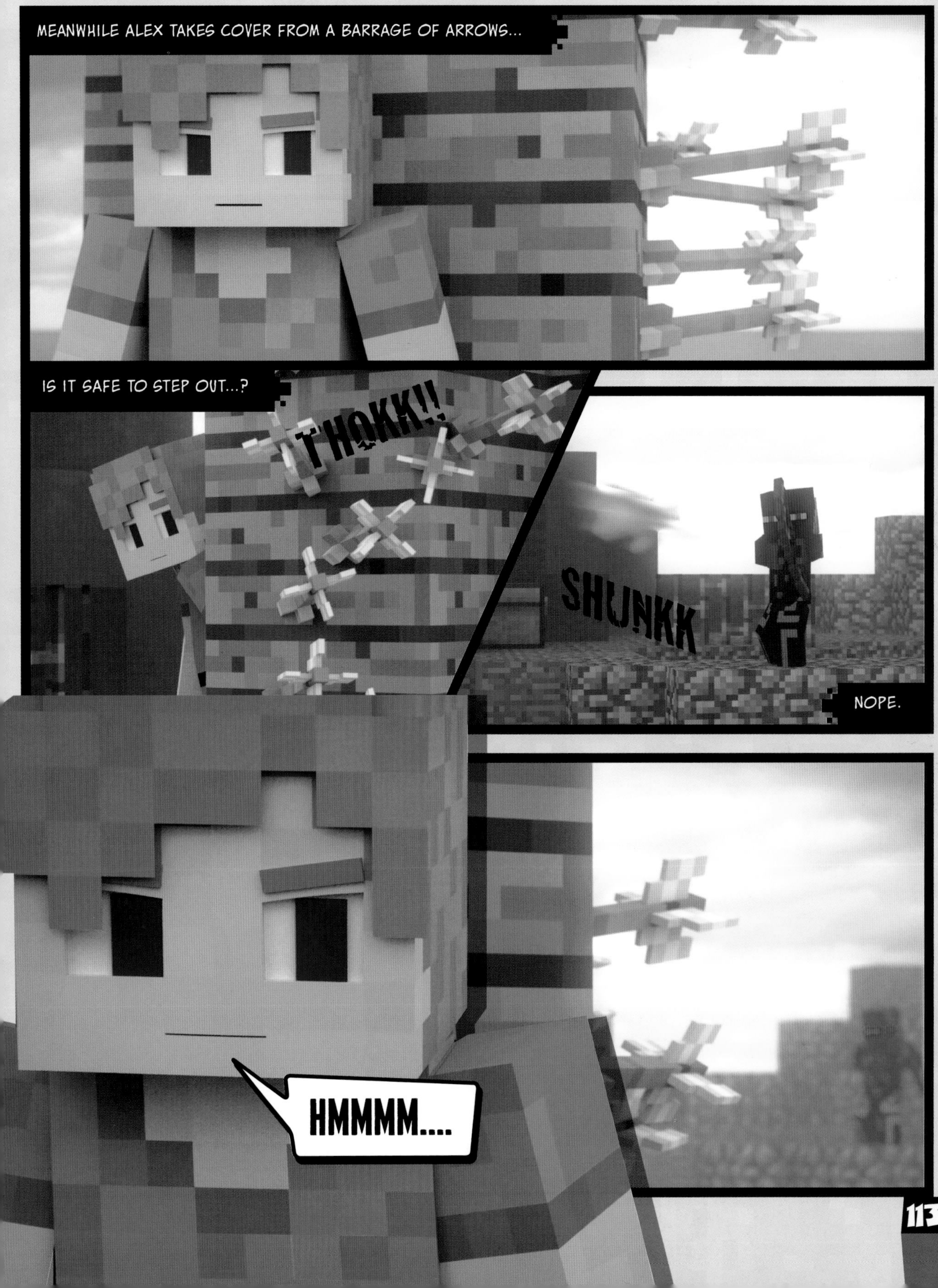

MEANWHILE ALEX TAKES COVER FROM A BARRAGE OF ARROWS...
IS IT SAFE TO STEP OUT...?
THOKK!!
SHUNKK
NOPE.
HMMMM....

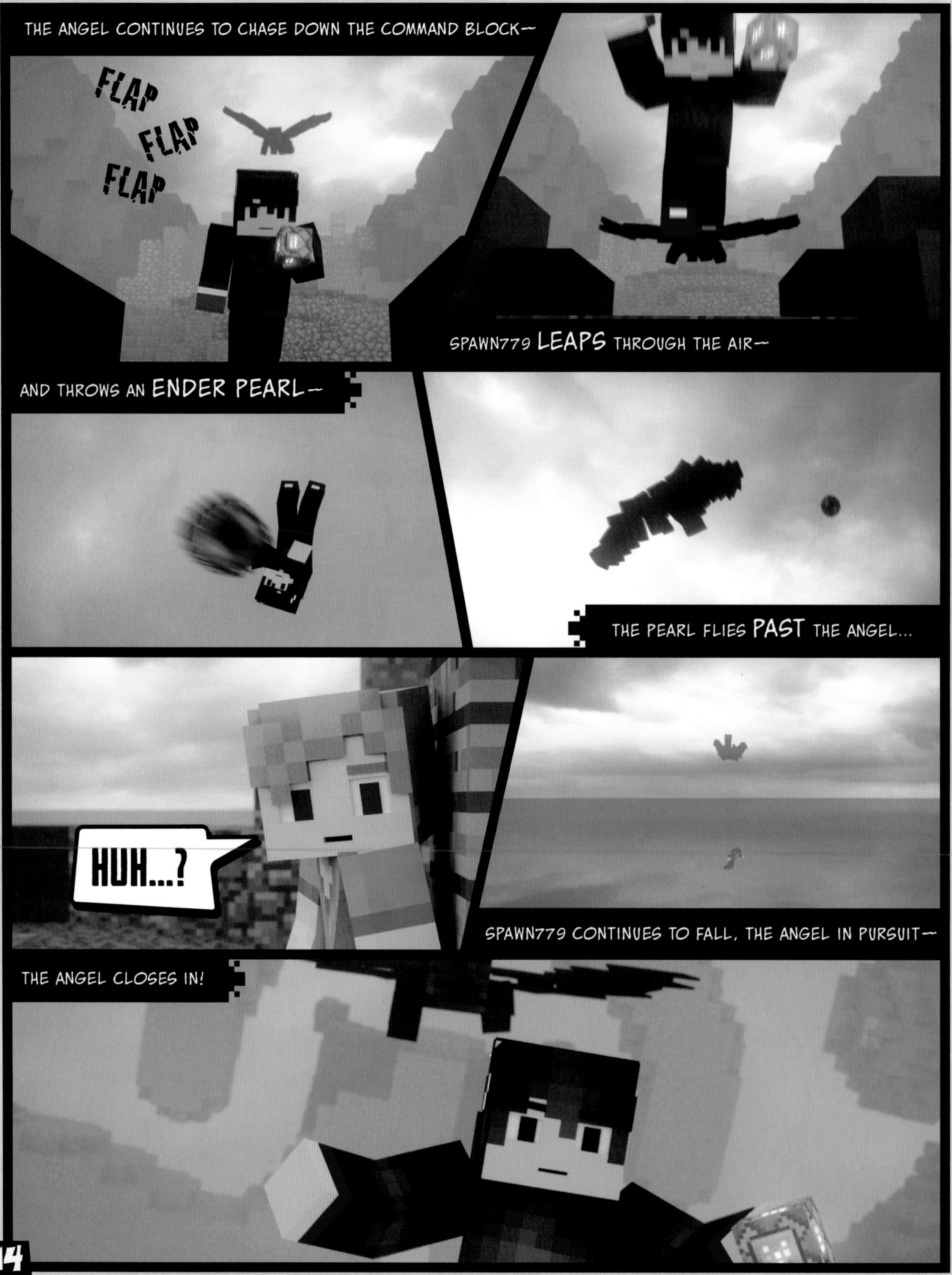
THE ANGEL CONTINUES TO CHASE DOWN THE COMMAND BLOCK—
FLAP
FLAP
FLAP
SPAWN779 LEAPS THROUGH THE AIR—
AND THROWS AN ENDER PEARL—
THE PEARL FLIES PAST THE ANGEL...
HUH...?
SPAWN779 CONTINUES TO FALL, THE ANGEL IN PURSUIT—
THE ANGEL CLOSES IN!

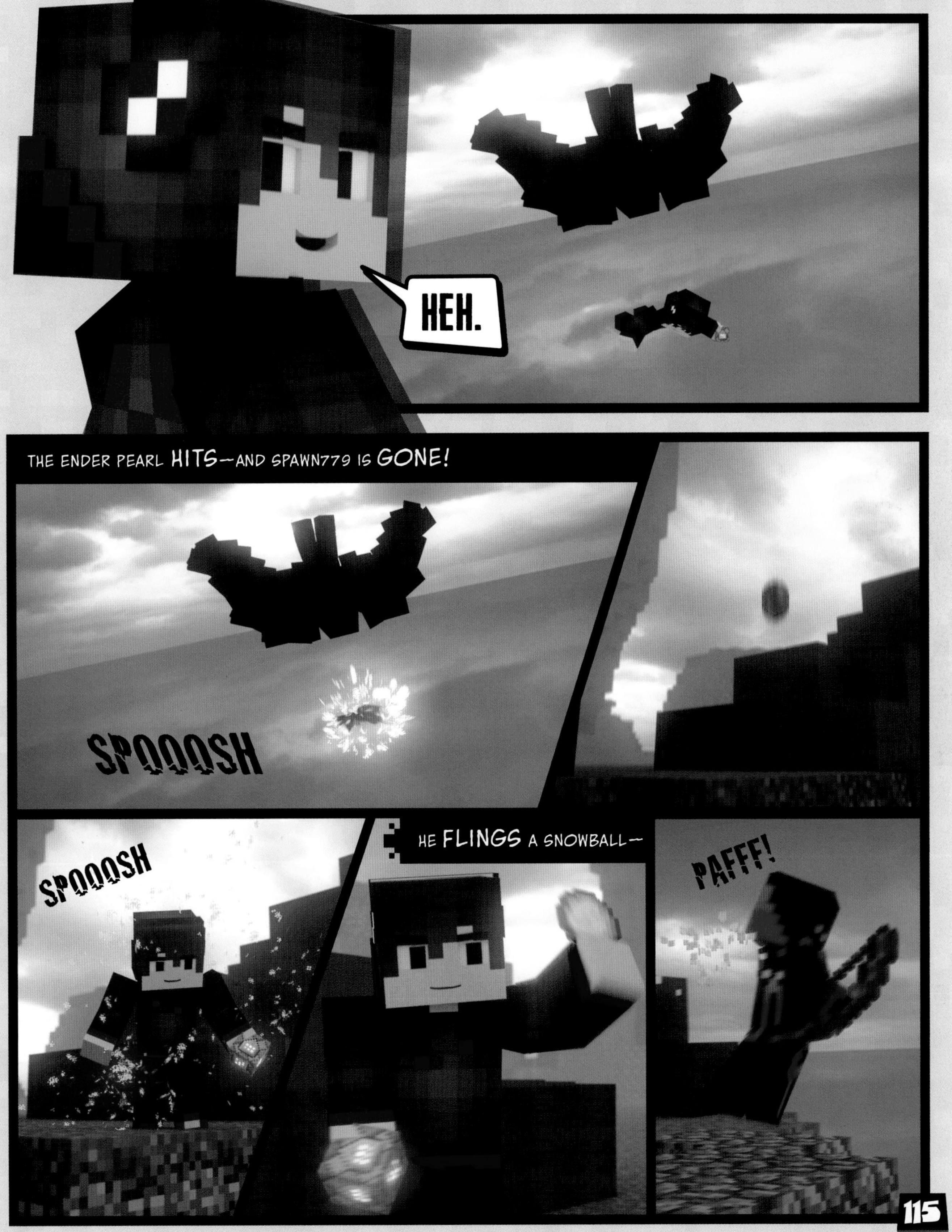

HEH.
THE ENDER PEARL HITS—AND SPAWN779 IS GONE!
SPOOOSH
SPOOOSH
HE FLINGS A SNOWBALL—
PAFFF!

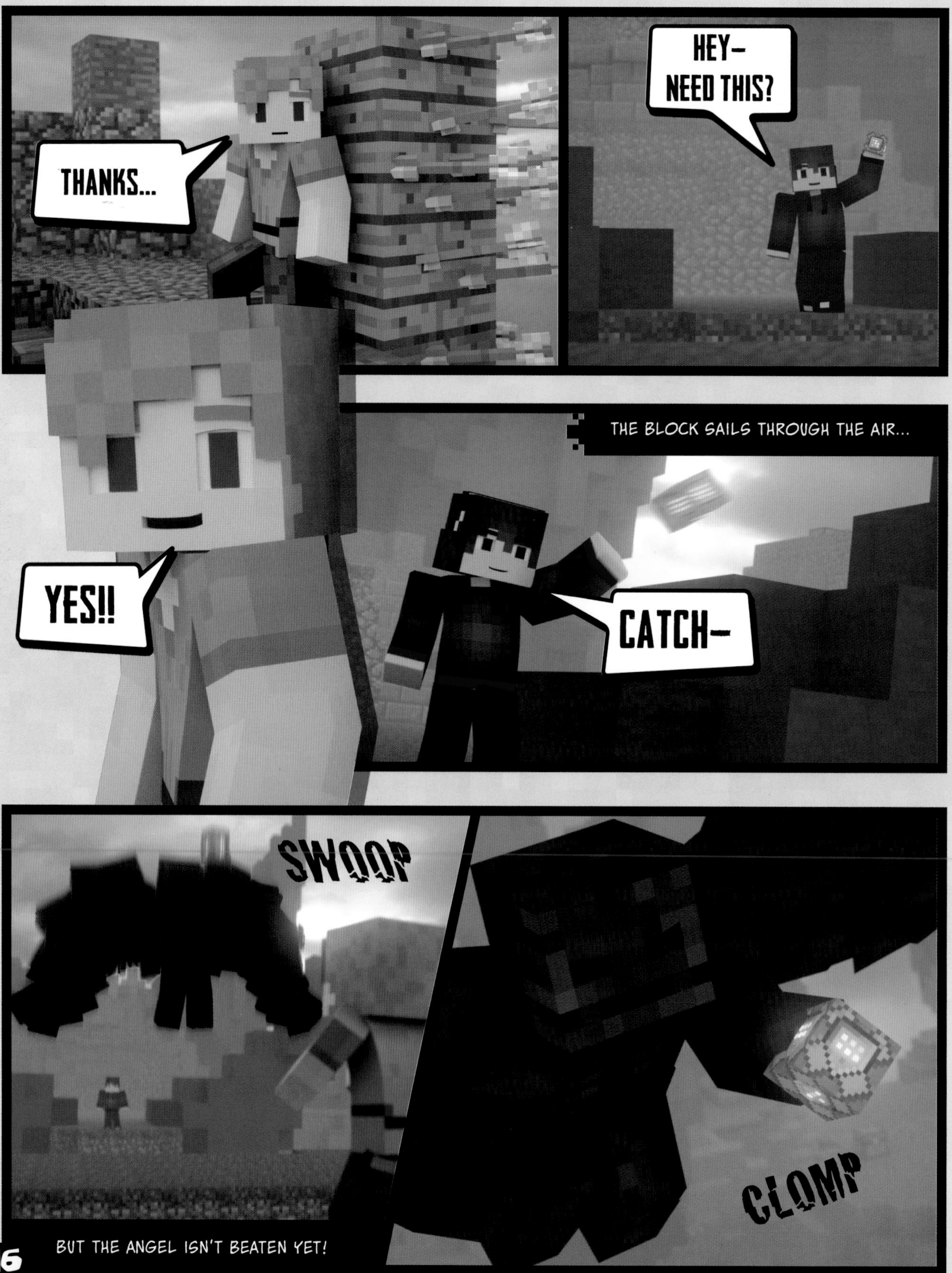
THANKS...
HEY-
NEED THIS?
YES!!
THE BLOCK SAILS THROUGH THE AIR...
CATCH-
SWOOP
CLOMP
BUT THE ANGEL ISN'T BEATEN YET!

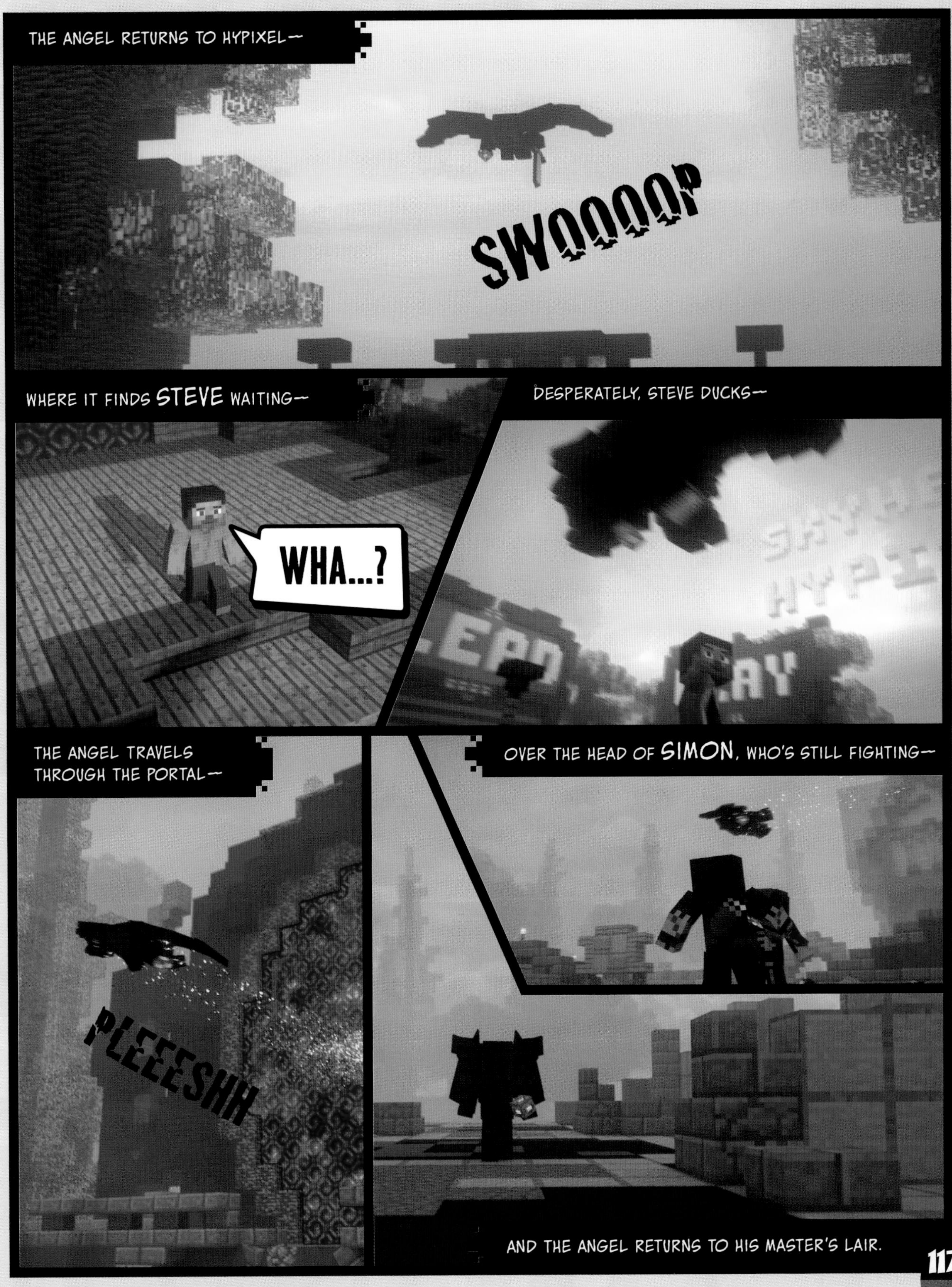

THE ANGEL RETURNS TO HYPIXEL—
SWOOOOP
WHERE IT FINDS STEVE WAITING—
WHA...?
DESPERATELY, STEVE DUCKS—
THE ANGEL TRAVELS THROUGH THE PORTAL—
PLEEESHH
OVER THE HEAD OF SIMON, WHO'S STILL FIGHTING—
AND THE ANGEL RETURNS TO HIS MASTER'S LAIR.

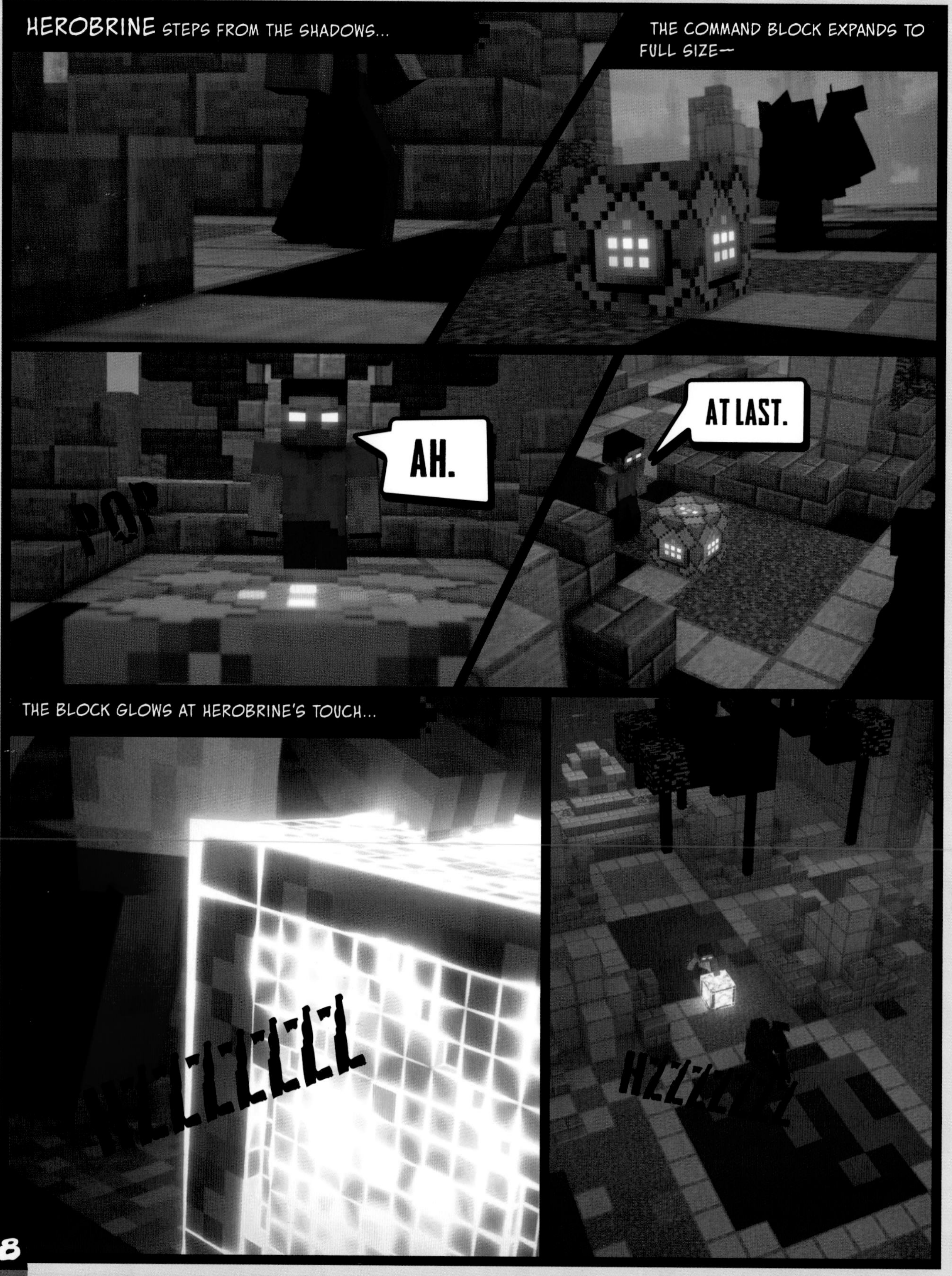
HEROBRINE STEPS FROM THE SHADOWS...
THE COMMAND BLOCK EXPANDS TO FULL SIZE—
POP
AH.
AT LAST.
THE BLOCK GLOWS AT HEROBRINE'S TOUCH...

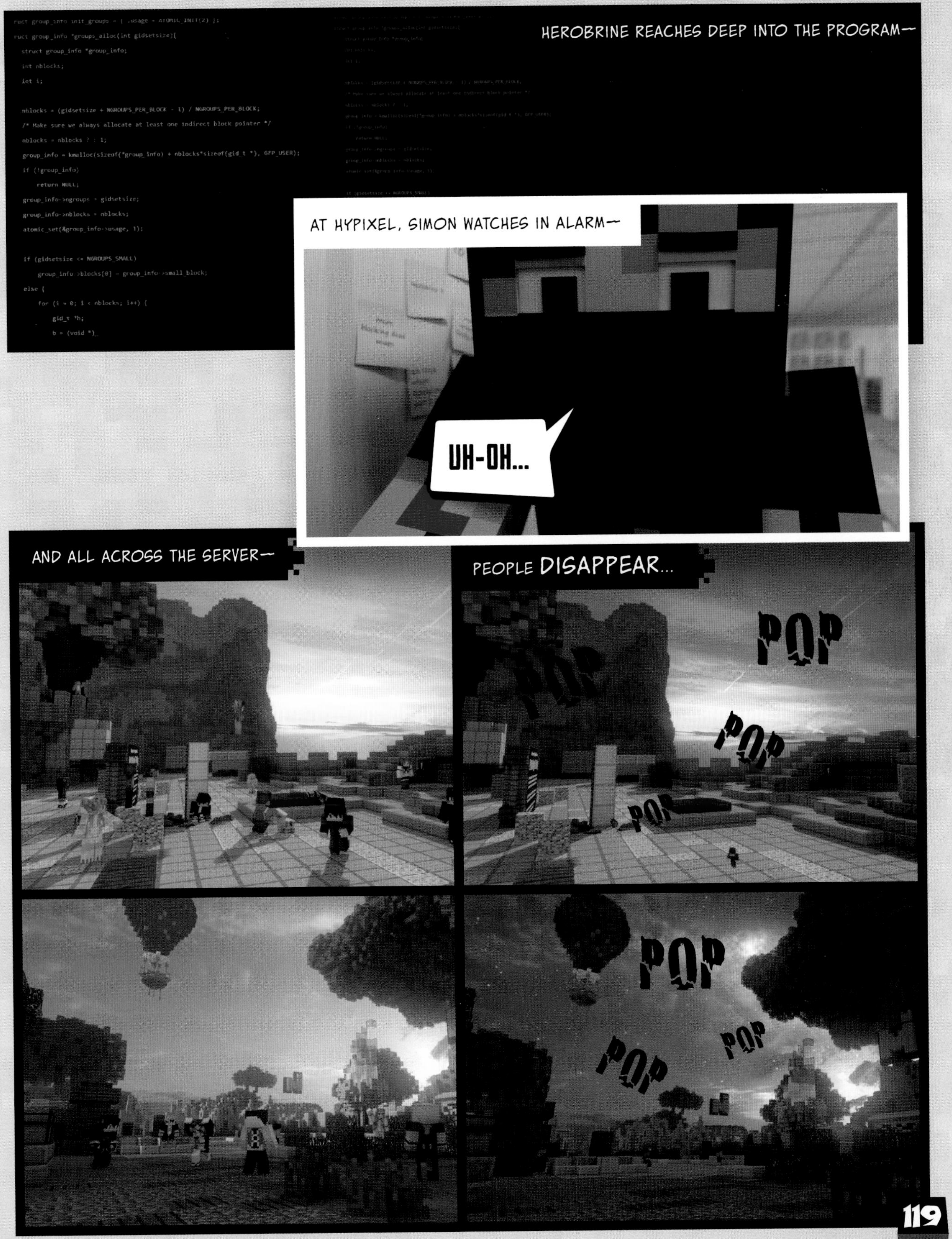
HEROBRINE REACHES DEEP INTO THE PROGRAM—
AT HYPIXEL, SIMON WATCHES IN ALARM—
UH-OH...
AND ALL ACROSS THE SERVER—
PEOPLE DISAPPEAR...
POP
POP
POP
POP
POP
POP
POP
POP

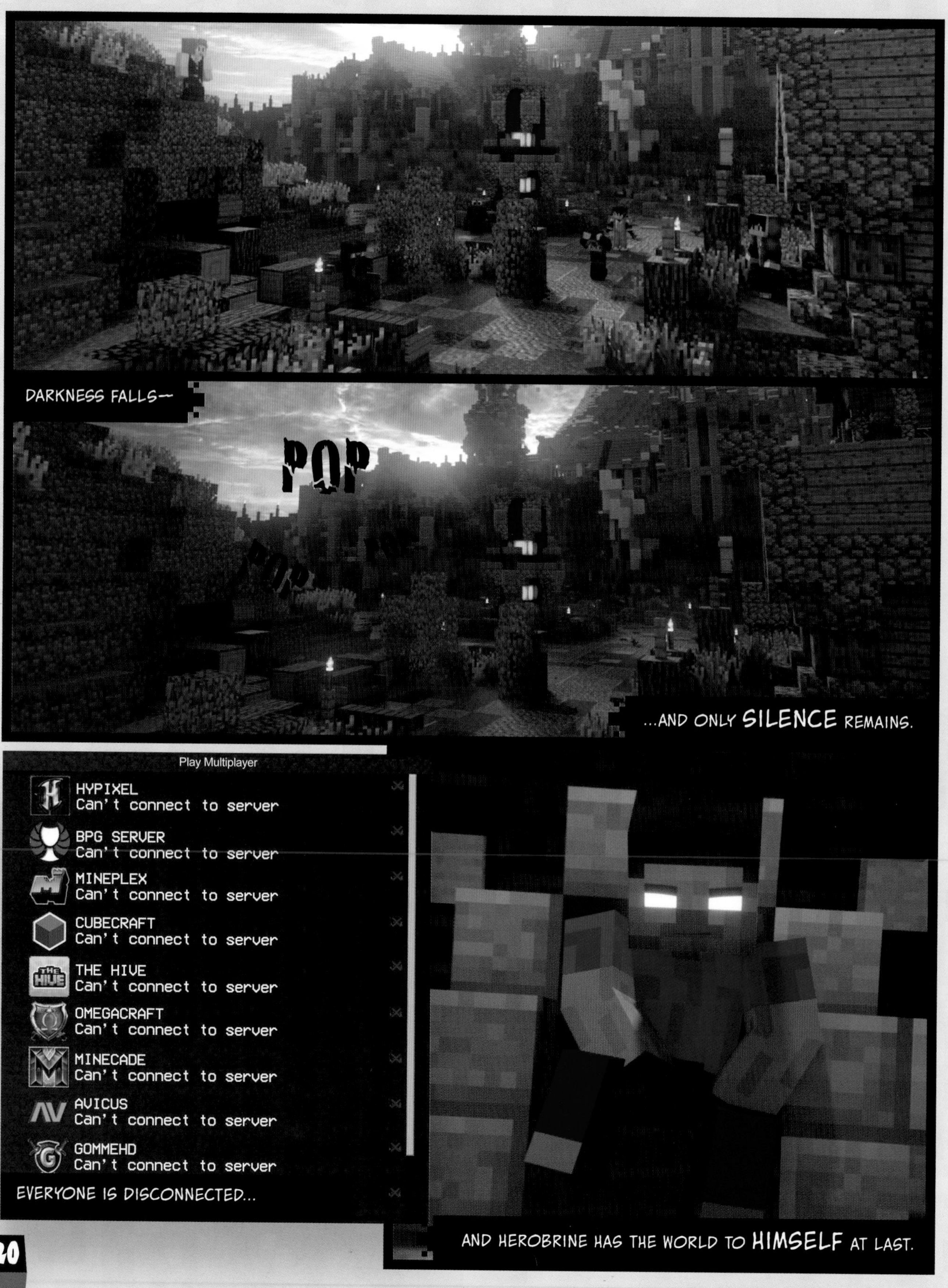
DARKNESS FALLS—
POP
POP
...AND ONLY SILENCE REMAINS.
Play Multiplayer
HYPIXEL
Can't connect to server
BPG SERVER
Can't connect to server
MINEPLEX
Can't connect to server
CUBECRAFT
Can't connect to server
THE HIVE
Can't connect to server
OMEGACRAFT
Can't connect to server
MINECADE
Can't connect to server
AVICUS
Can't connect to server
GOMMEHD
Can't connect to server
EVERYONE IS DISCONNECTED...
AND HEROBRINE HAS THE WORLD TO HIMSELF AT LAST.

CHAPTER 6

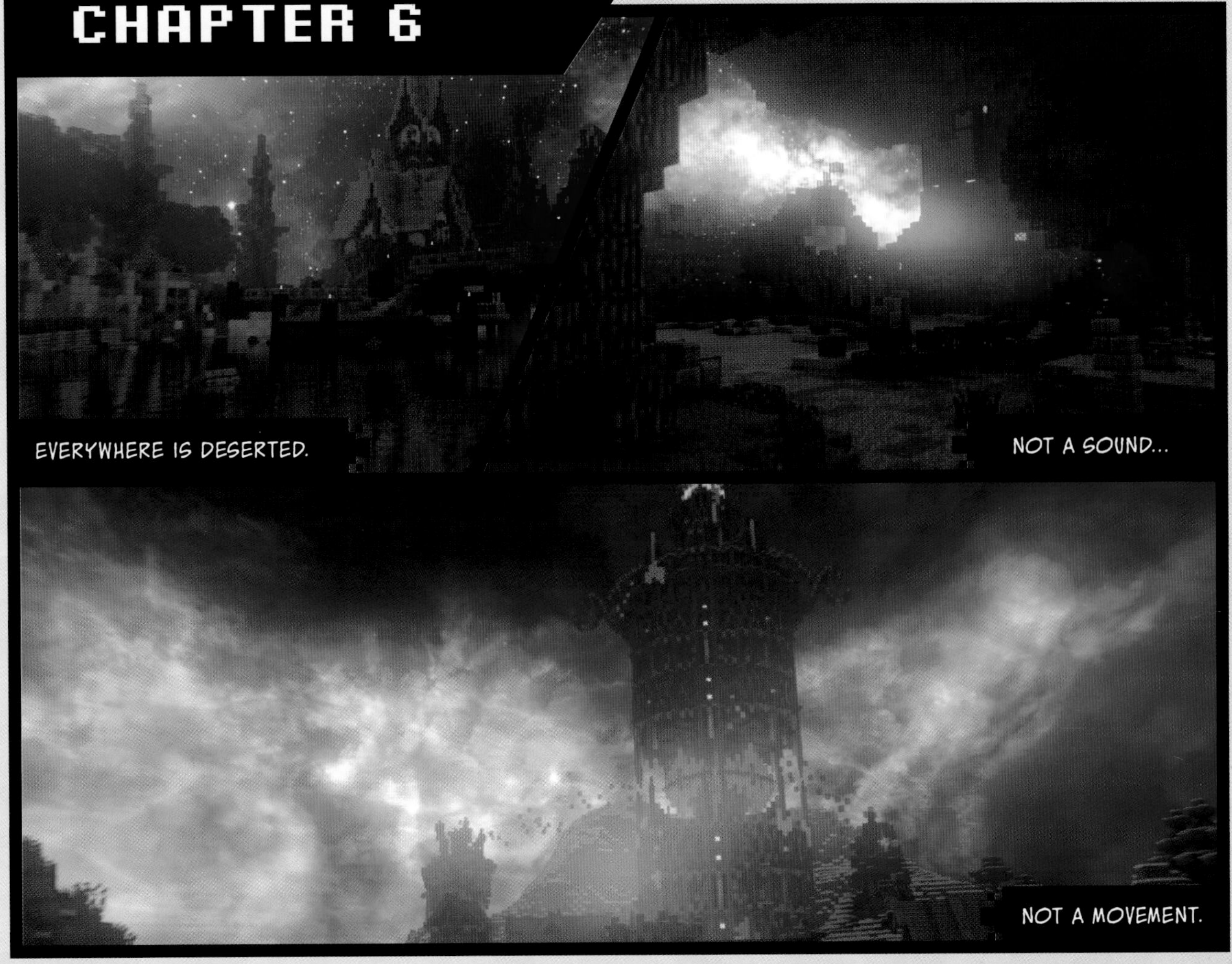
EVERYWHERE IS DESERTED.
NOT A SOUND...
NOT A MOVEMENT.

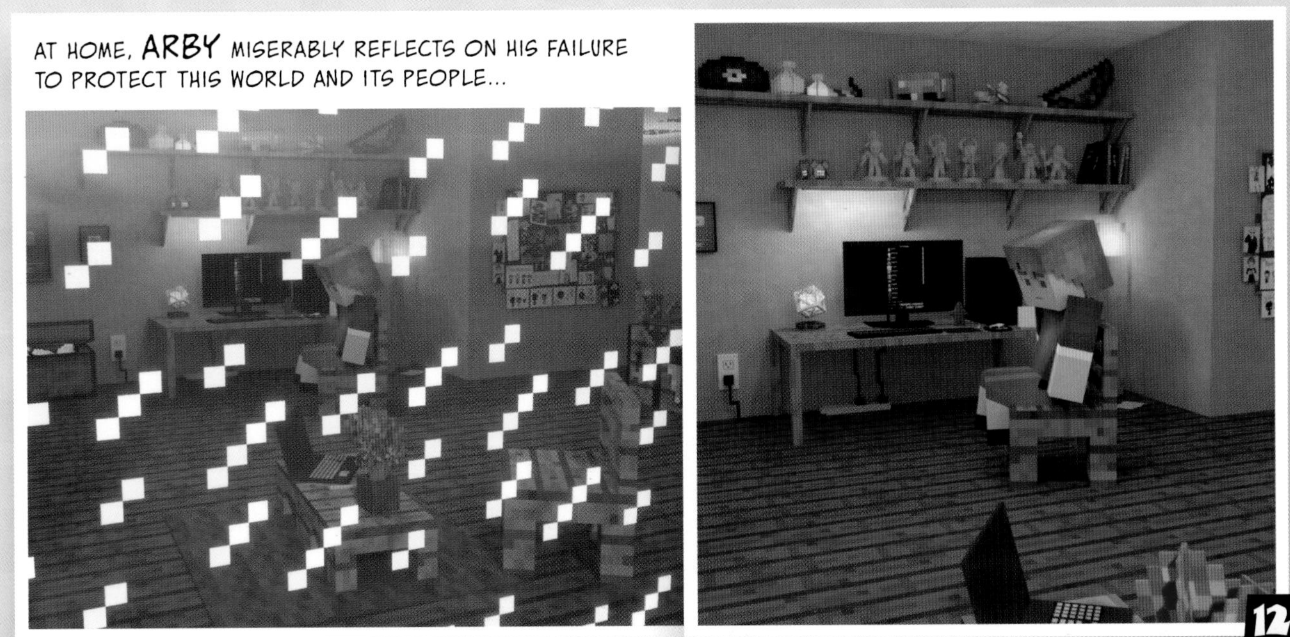
AT HOME, ARBY MISERABLY REFLECTS ON HIS FAILURE TO PROTECT THIS WORLD AND ITS PEOPLE...

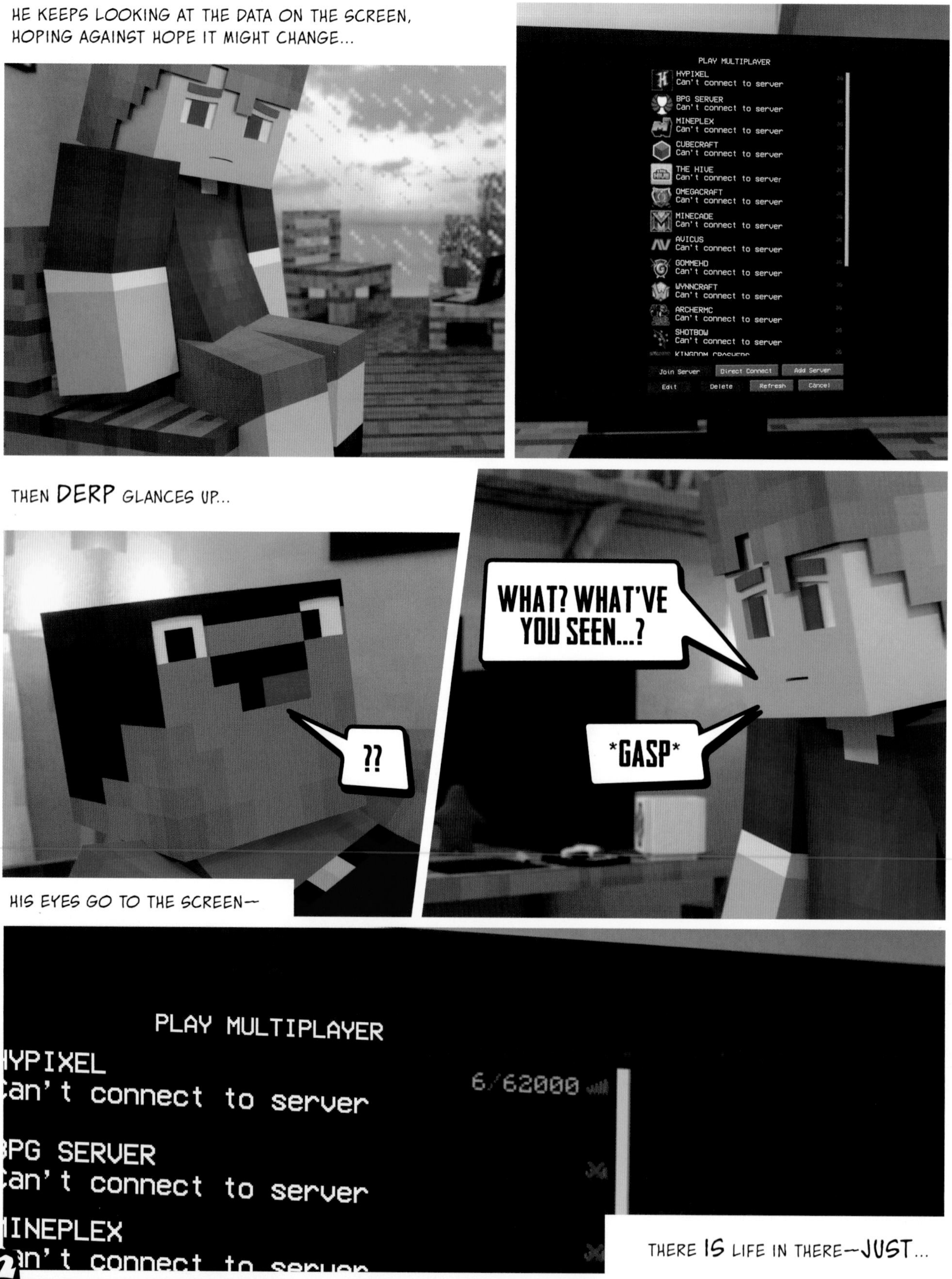
HE KEEPS LOOKING AT THE DATA ON THE SCREEN, HOPING AGAINST HOPE IT MIGHT CHANGE...
PLAY MULTIPLAYER
HYPIXEL
Can't connect to server
BPG SERVER
Can't connect to server
MINEPLEX
Can't connect to server
CUBECRAFT
Can't connect to server
THE HIVE
Can't connect to server
OMEGACRAFT
Can't connect to server
MINECADE
Can't connect to server
AVICUS
Can't connect to server
GOMMEHD
Can't connect to server
WYNNCRAFT
Can't connect to server
ARCHERMC
Can't connect to server
SHOTBOW
Can't connect to server
Join Server
Direct Connect
Add Server
Edit
Delete
Refresh
Cancel
THEN DERP GLANCES UP...
??
WHAT? WHAT'VE YOU SEEN...?
GASP
HIS EYES GO TO THE SCREEN—
PLAY MULTIPLAYER
HYPIXEL
Can't connect to server
6/62000
BPG SERVER
Can't connect to server
MINEPLEX
THERE IS LIFE IN THERE—JUST...

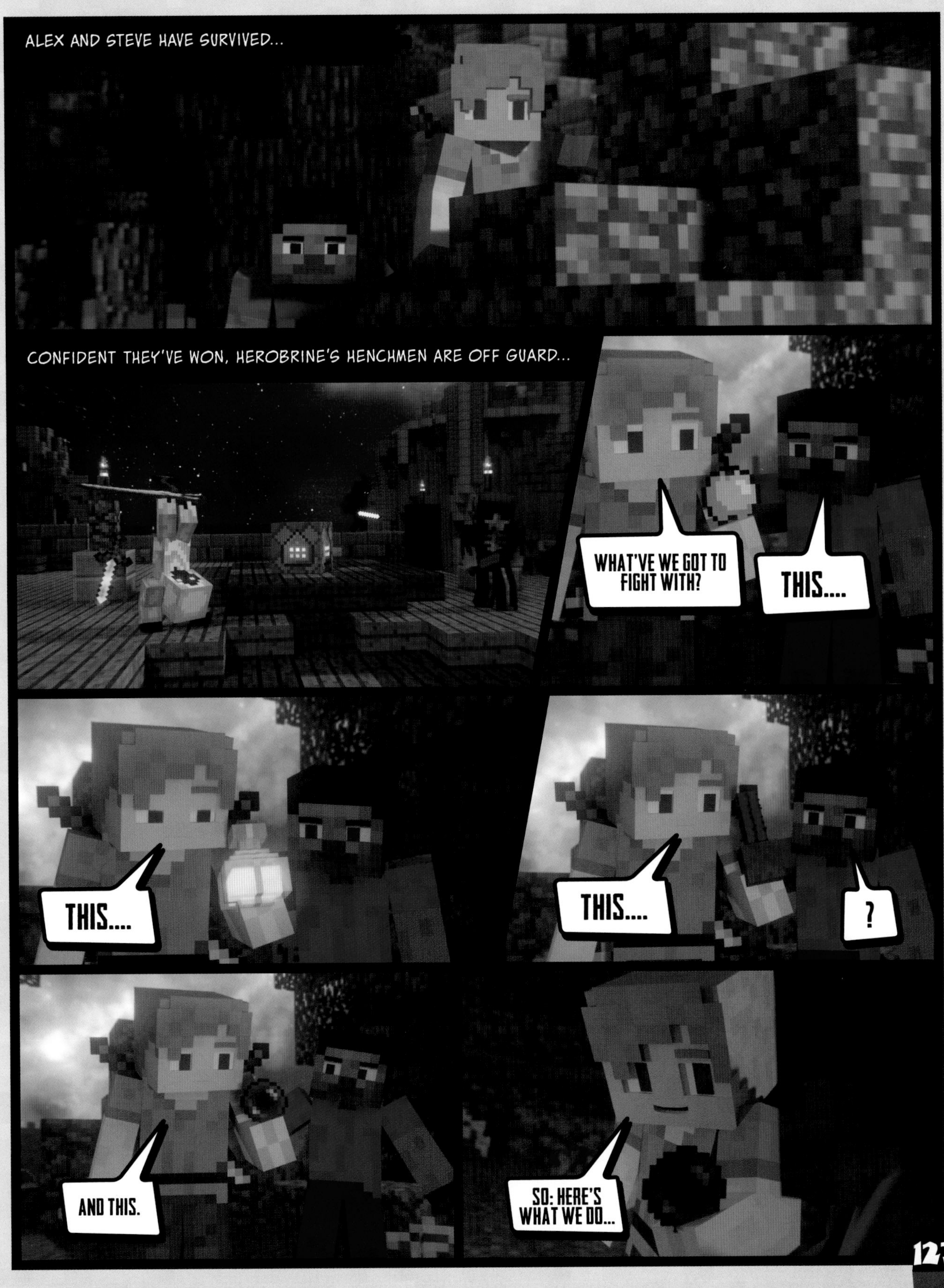
ALEX AND STEVE HAVE SURVIVED...
CONFIDENT THEY'VE WON, HEROBRINE'S HENCHMEN ARE OFF GUARD...
WHAT'VE WE GOT TO FIGHT WITH?
THIS....
THIS....
THIS....
?
AND THIS.
SO: HERE'S WHAT WE DO...

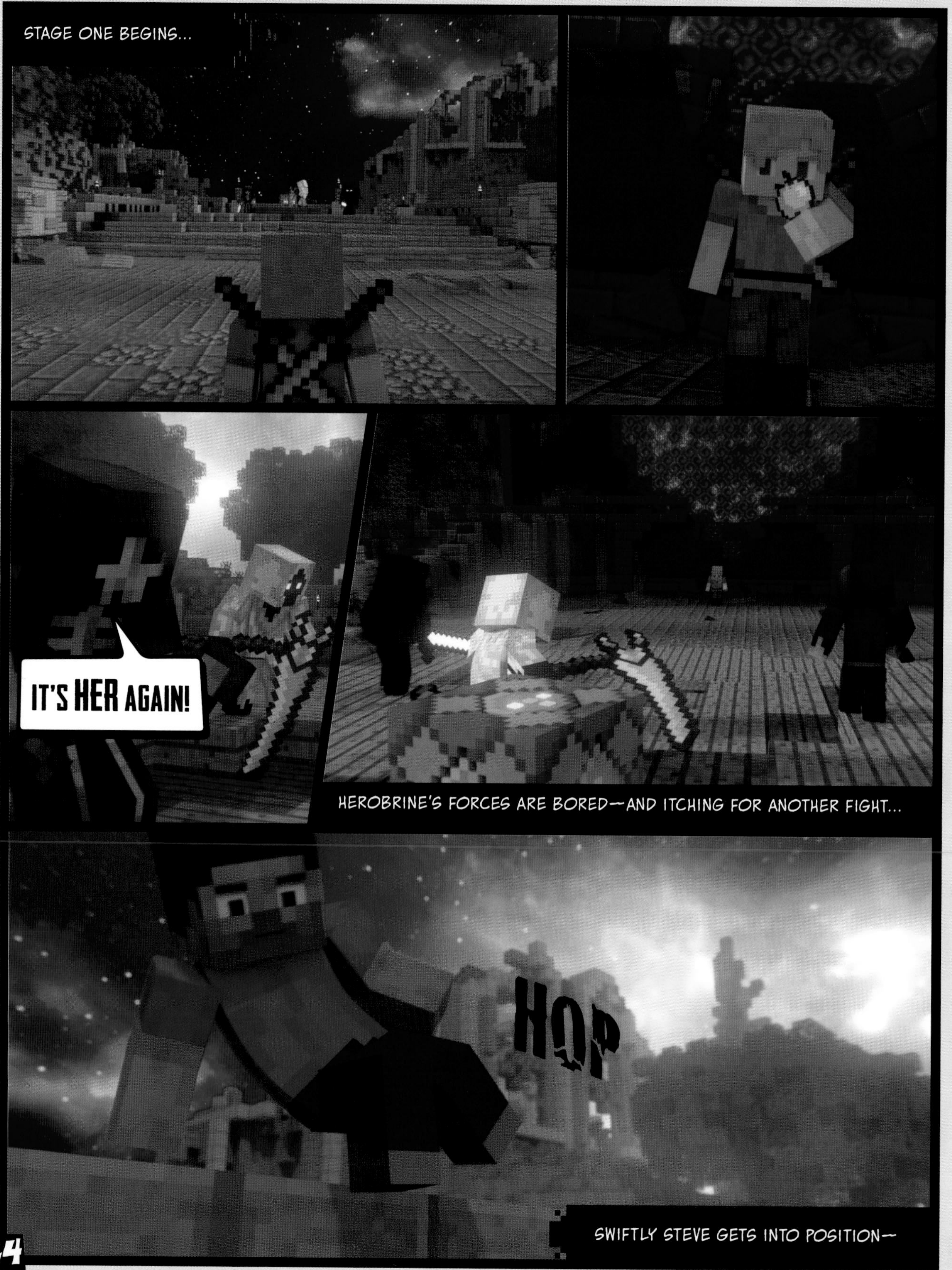
STAGE ONE BEGINS...
IT'S HER AGAIN!
HEROBRINE'S FORCES ARE BORED—AND ITCHING FOR ANOTHER FIGHT...
HOP
SWIFTLY STEVE GETS INTO POSITION—

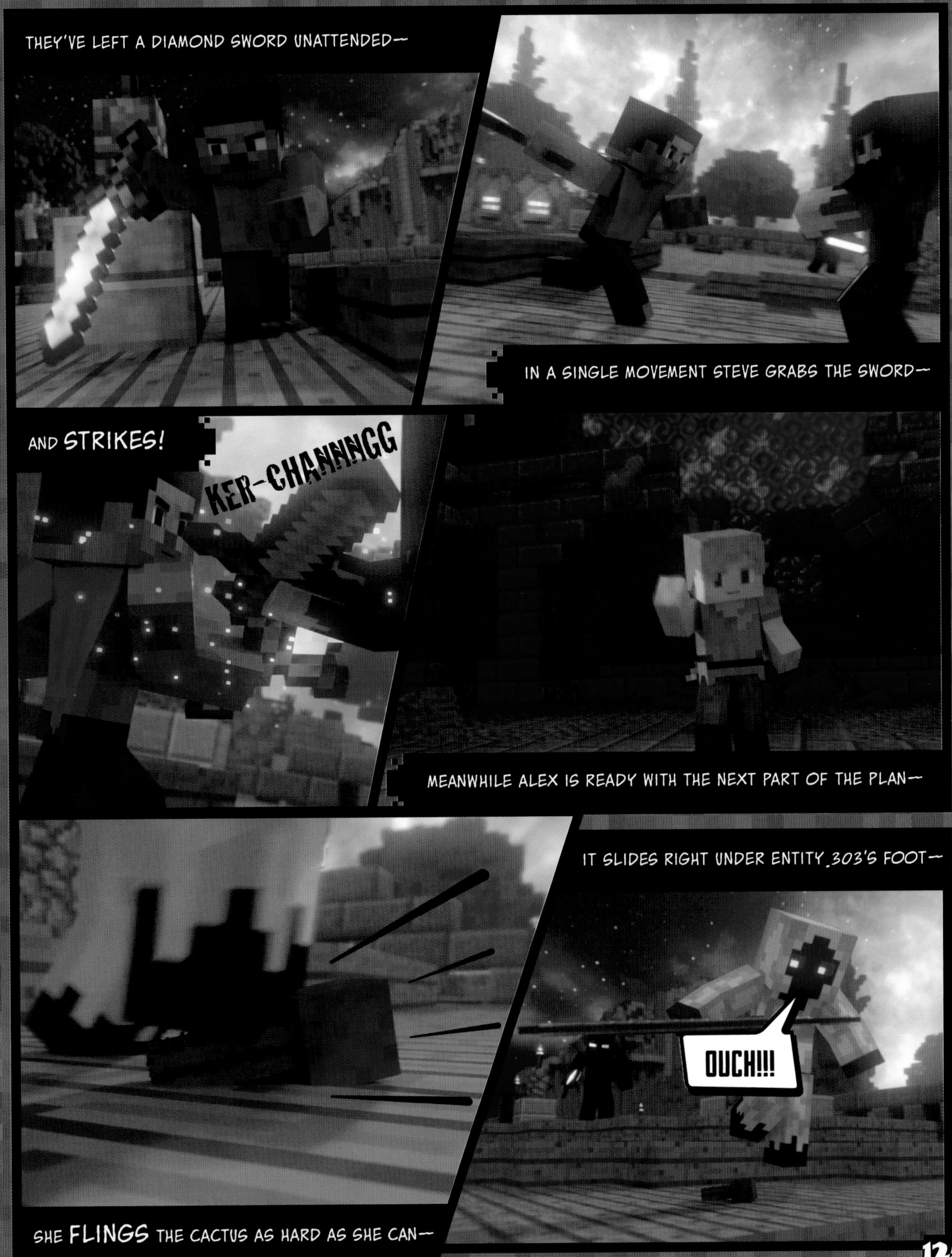

THEY'VE LEFT A DIAMOND SWORD UNATTENDED—
IN A SINGLE MOVEMENT STEVE GRABS THE SWORD—
AND STRIKES!
KER-CHANNNGG
MEANWHILE ALEX IS READY WITH THE NEXT PART OF THE PLAN—
SHE FLINGS THE CACTUS AS HARD AS SHE CAN—
IT SLIDES RIGHT UNDER ENTITY_303'S FOOT—
OUCH!!!

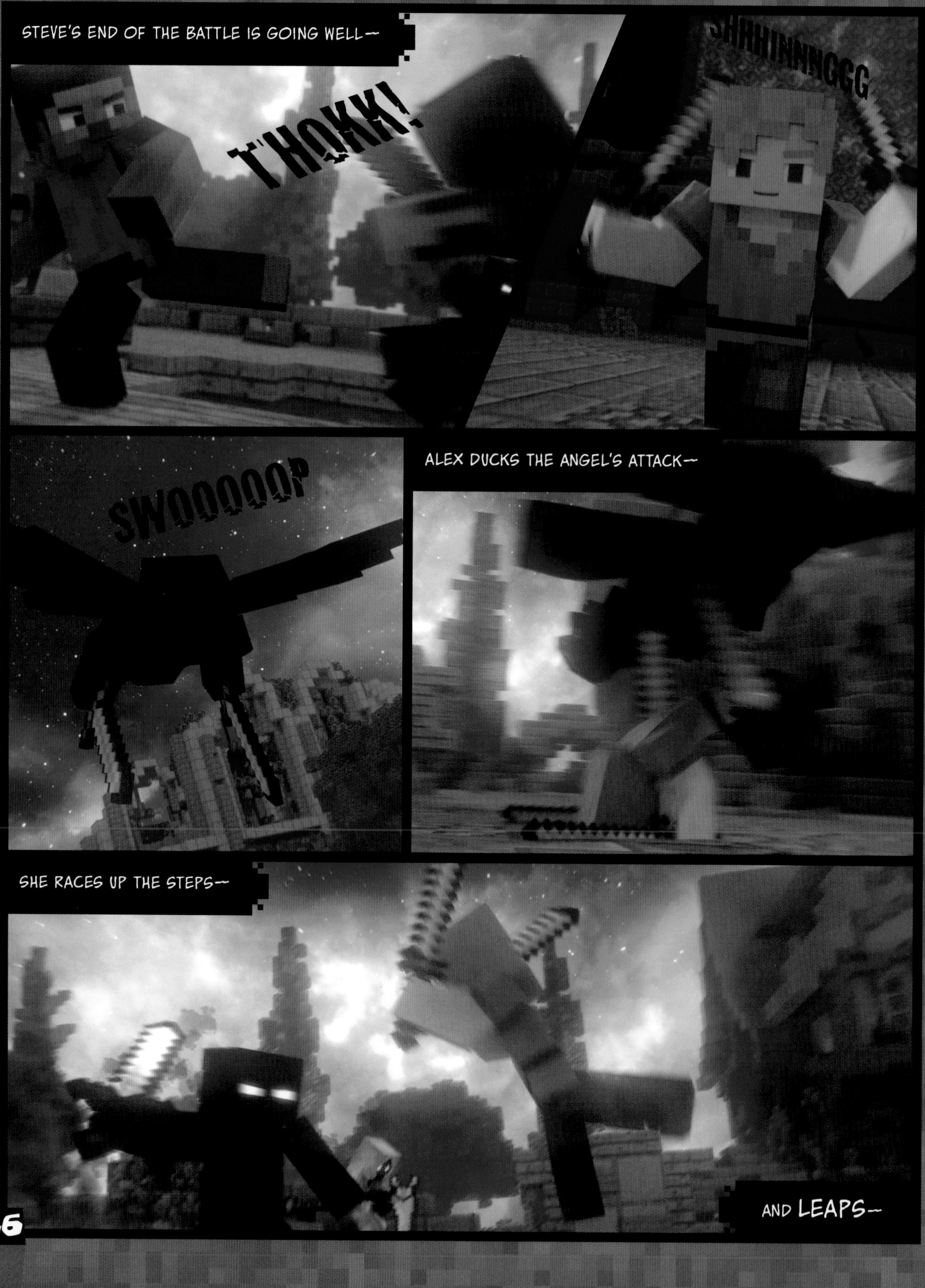
STEVE'S END OF THE BATTLE IS GOING WELL—
T'HOKK!
SHHHINNNNGGG
SWOOOOOP
ALEX DUCKS THE ANGEL'S ATTACK—
SHE RACES UP THE STEPS—
AND LEAPS—

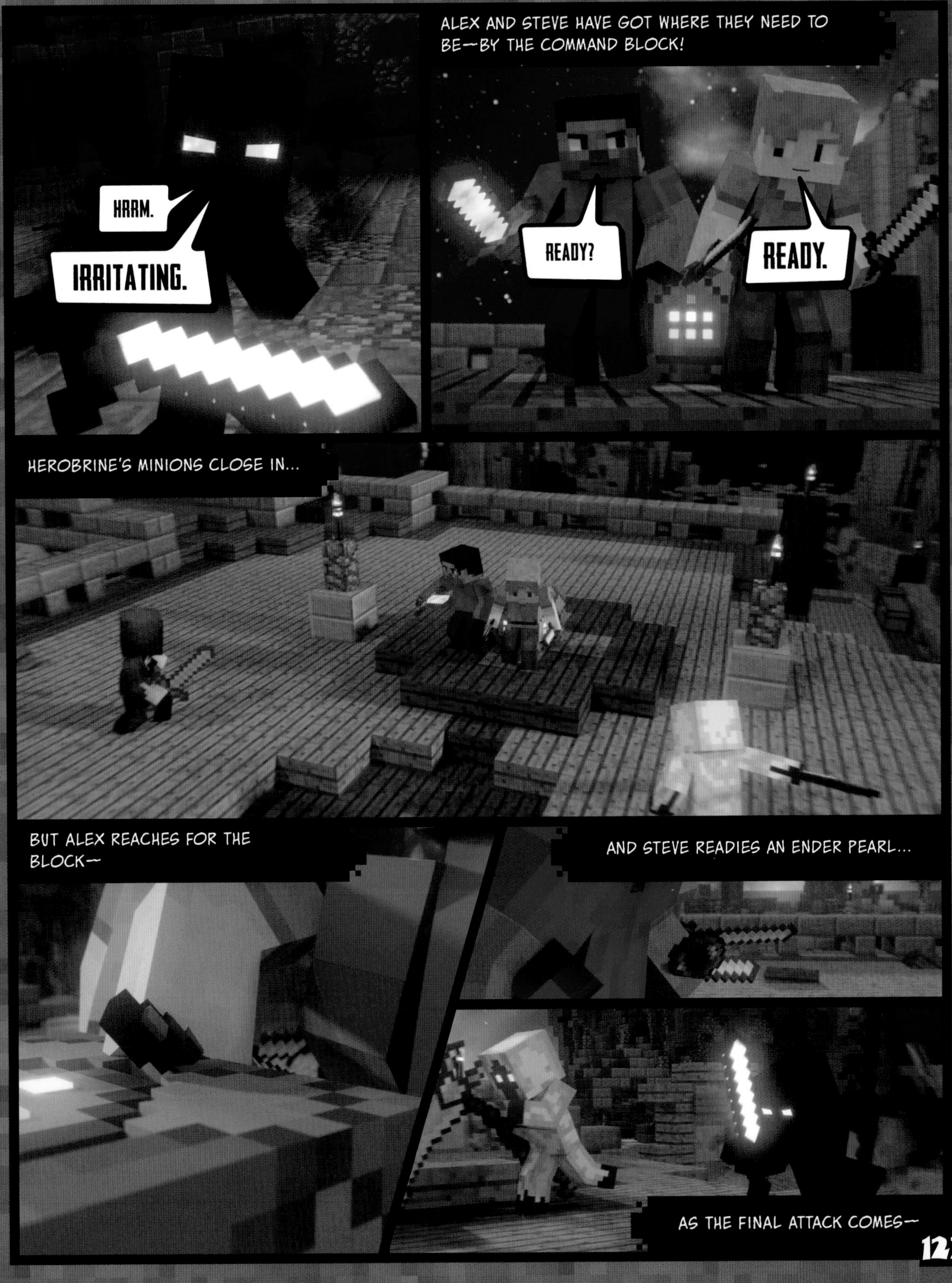
HRRM.
IRRITATING.
ALEX AND STEVE HAVE GOT WHERE THEY NEED TO BE—BY THE COMMAND BLOCK!
READY?
READY.
HEROBRINE'S MINIONS CLOSE IN...
BUT ALEX REACHES FOR THE BLOCK—
AND STEVE READIES AN ENDER PEARL...
AS THE FINAL ATTACK COMES—

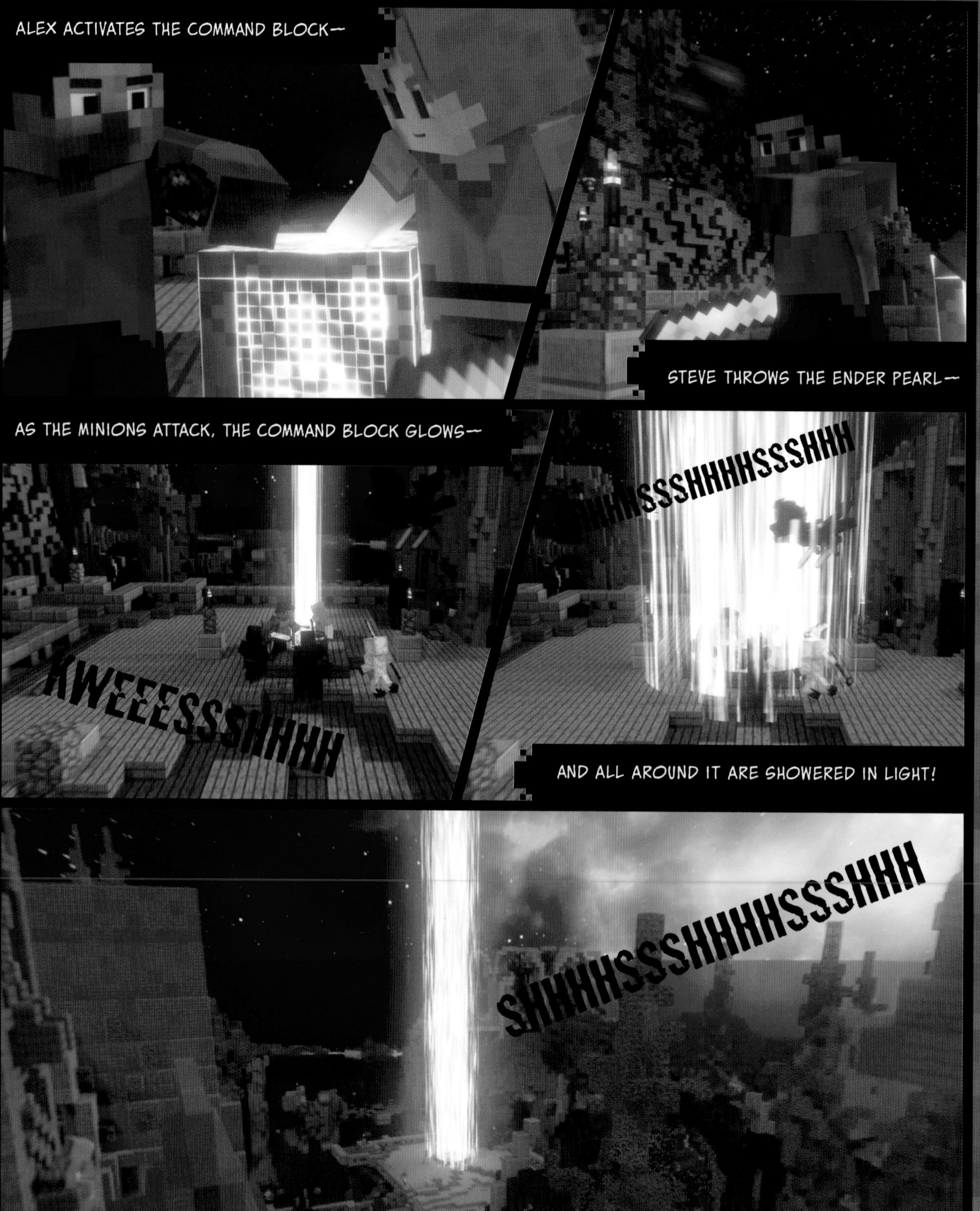
ALEX ACTIVATES THE COMMAND BLOCK—
STEVE THROWS THE ENDER PEARL—
AS THE MINIONS ATTACK, THE COMMAND BLOCK GLOWS—
KWEEESSSHHHH
HHHSSSHHHHHSSSHHH
AND ALL AROUND IT ARE SHOWERED IN LIGHT!
SHHHHSSSHHHHHSSSHHH

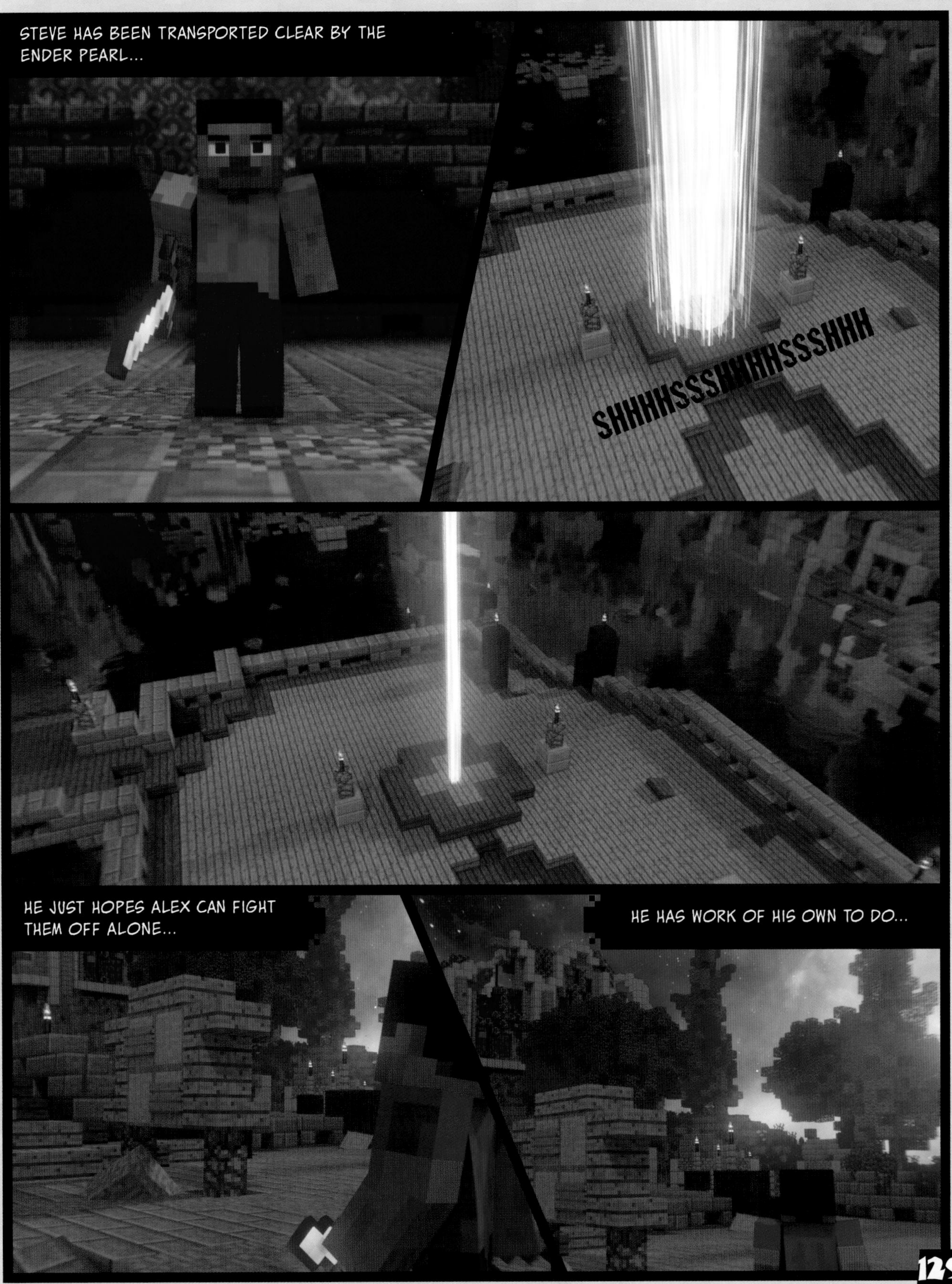
STEVE HAS BEEN TRANSPORTED CLEAR BY THE ENDER PEARL...
SHHHHSSSHHHHHSSSHHH
HE JUST HOPES ALEX CAN FIGHT THEM OFF ALONE...
HE HAS WORK OF HIS OWN TO DO...

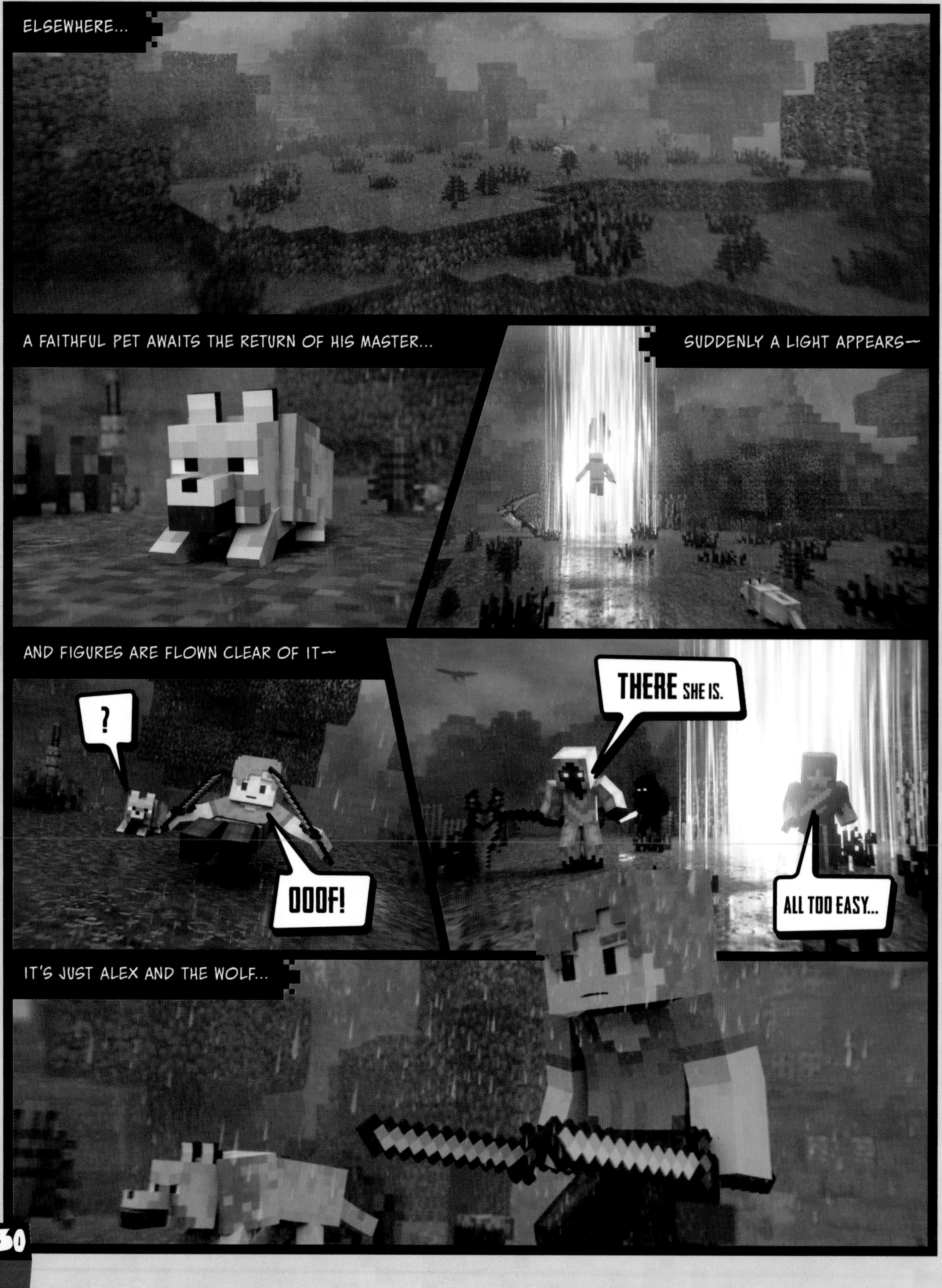
ELSEWHERE...
A FAITHFUL PET AWAITS THE RETURN OF HIS MASTER...
SUDDENLY A LIGHT APPEARS—
AND FIGURES ARE FLOWN CLEAR OF IT—
?
OOOF!
THERE SHE IS.
ALL TOO EASY...
IT'S JUST ALEX AND THE WOLF...

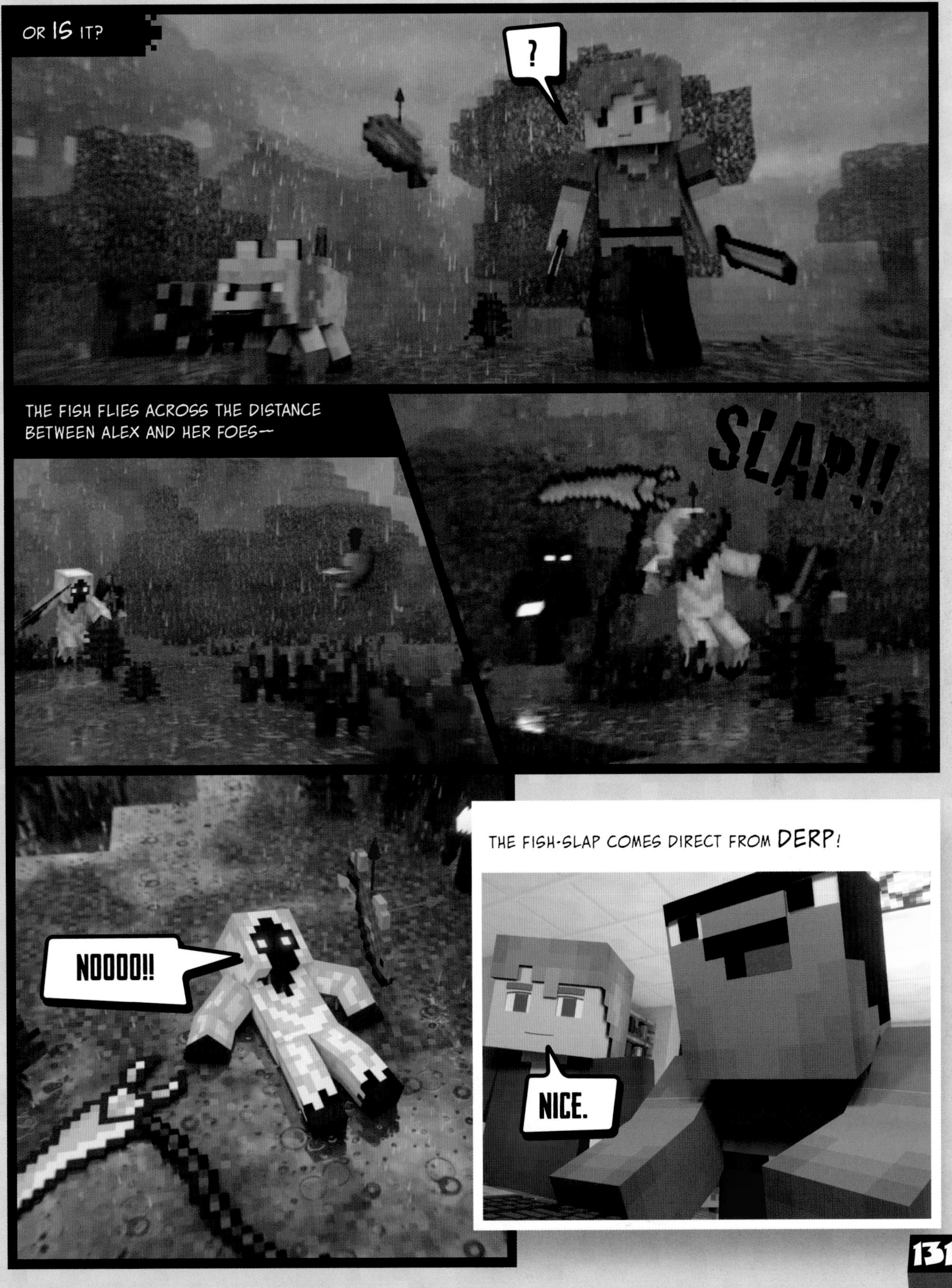
OR IS IT?
?
THE FISH FLIES ACROSS THE DISTANCE BETWEEN ALEX AND HER FOES—
SLAP!!
NOOOO!!
THE FISH-SLAP COMES DIRECT FROM DERP!
NICE.

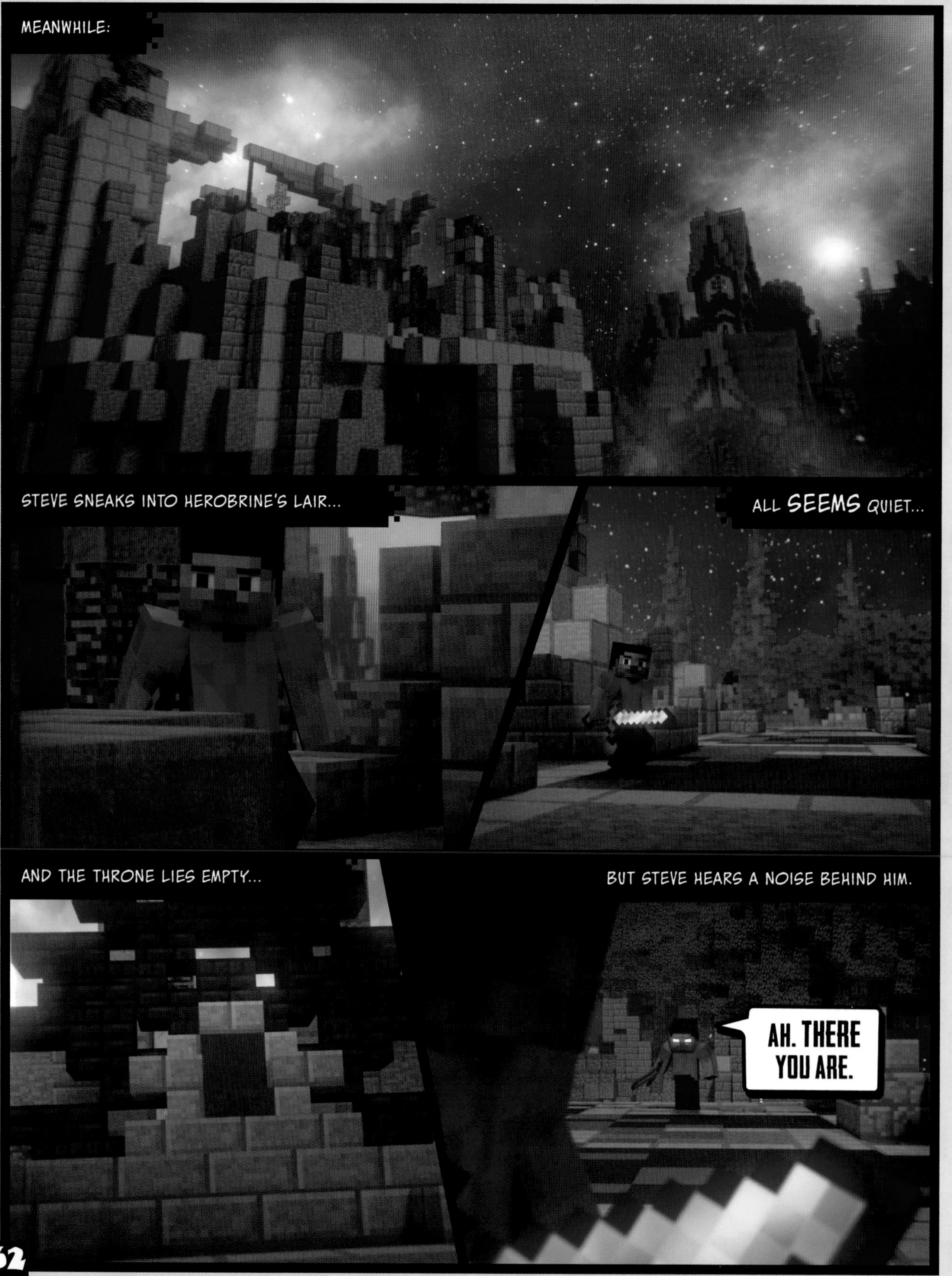
MEANWHILE:
STEVE SNEAKS INTO HEROBRINE'S LAIR...
ALL SEEMS QUIET...
AND THE THRONE LIES EMPTY...
BUT STEVE HEARS A NOISE BEHIND HIM.
AH. THERE YOU ARE.

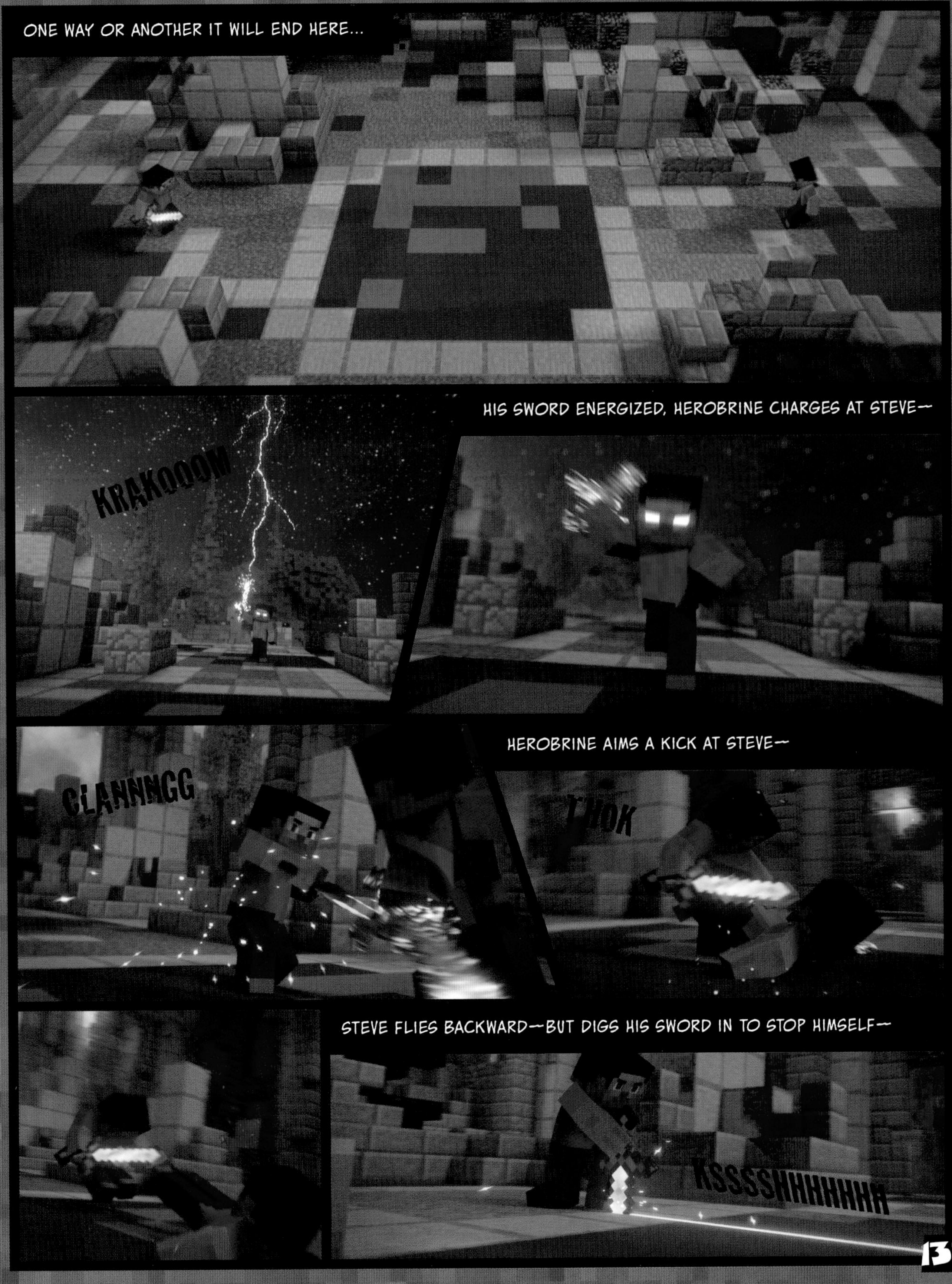
ONE WAY OR ANOTHER IT WILL END HERE...
KRAKOOOM
HIS SWORD ENERGIZED, HEROBRINE CHARGES AT STEVE—
CLANNNGG
HEROBRINE AIMS A KICK AT STEVE—
THOK
STEVE FLIES BACKWARD—BUT DIGS HIS SWORD IN TO STOP HIMSELF—
KSSSSHHHHHHH

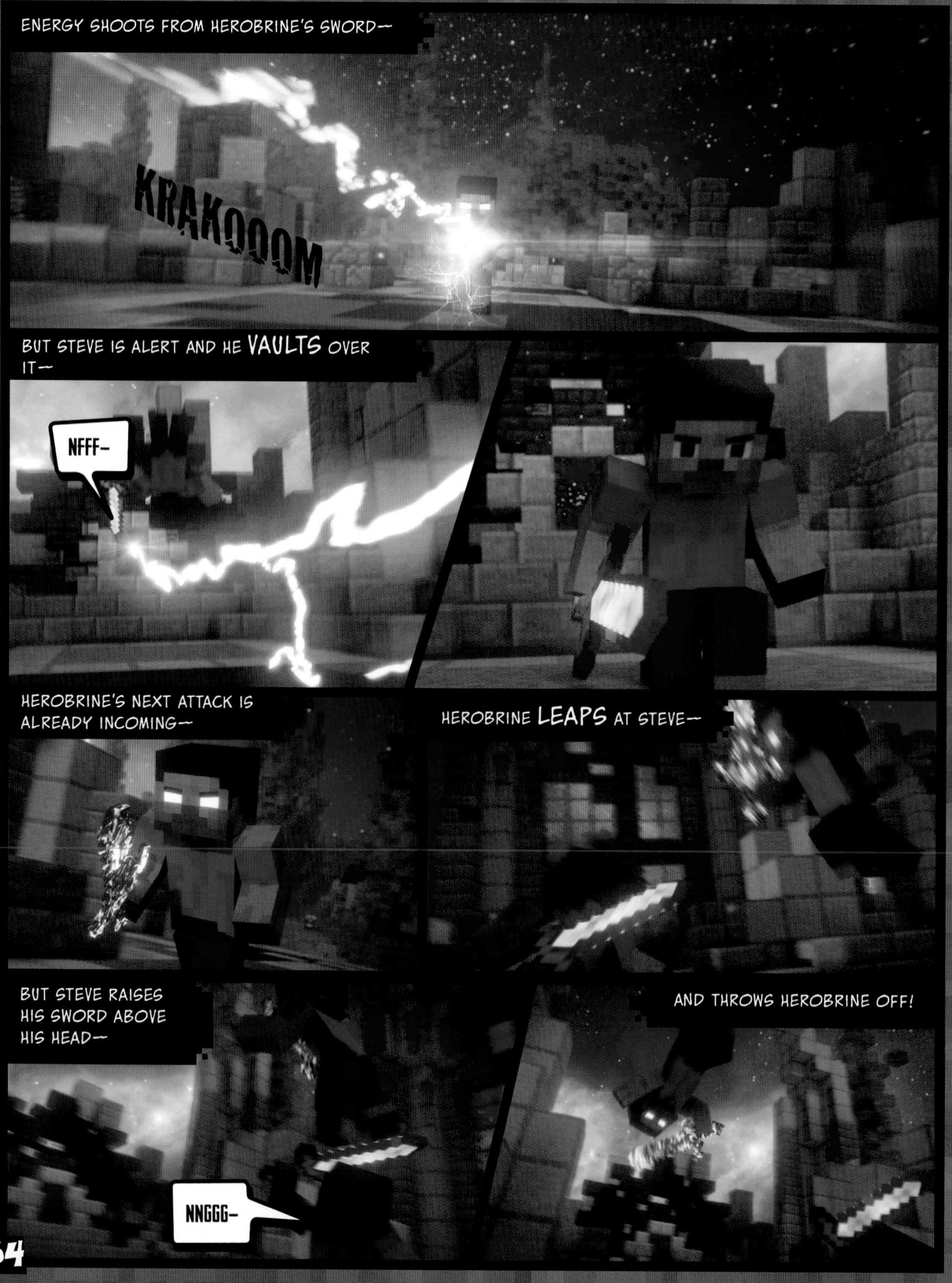

ENERGY SHOOTS FROM HEROBRINE'S SWORD—
KRAKOOOM
BUT STEVE IS ALERT AND HE VAULTS OVER IT—
NFFF-
HEROBRINE'S NEXT ATTACK IS ALREADY INCOMING—
HEROBRINE LEAPS AT STEVE—
BUT STEVE RAISES HIS SWORD ABOVE HIS HEAD—
NNGGG-
AND THROWS HEROBRINE OFF!

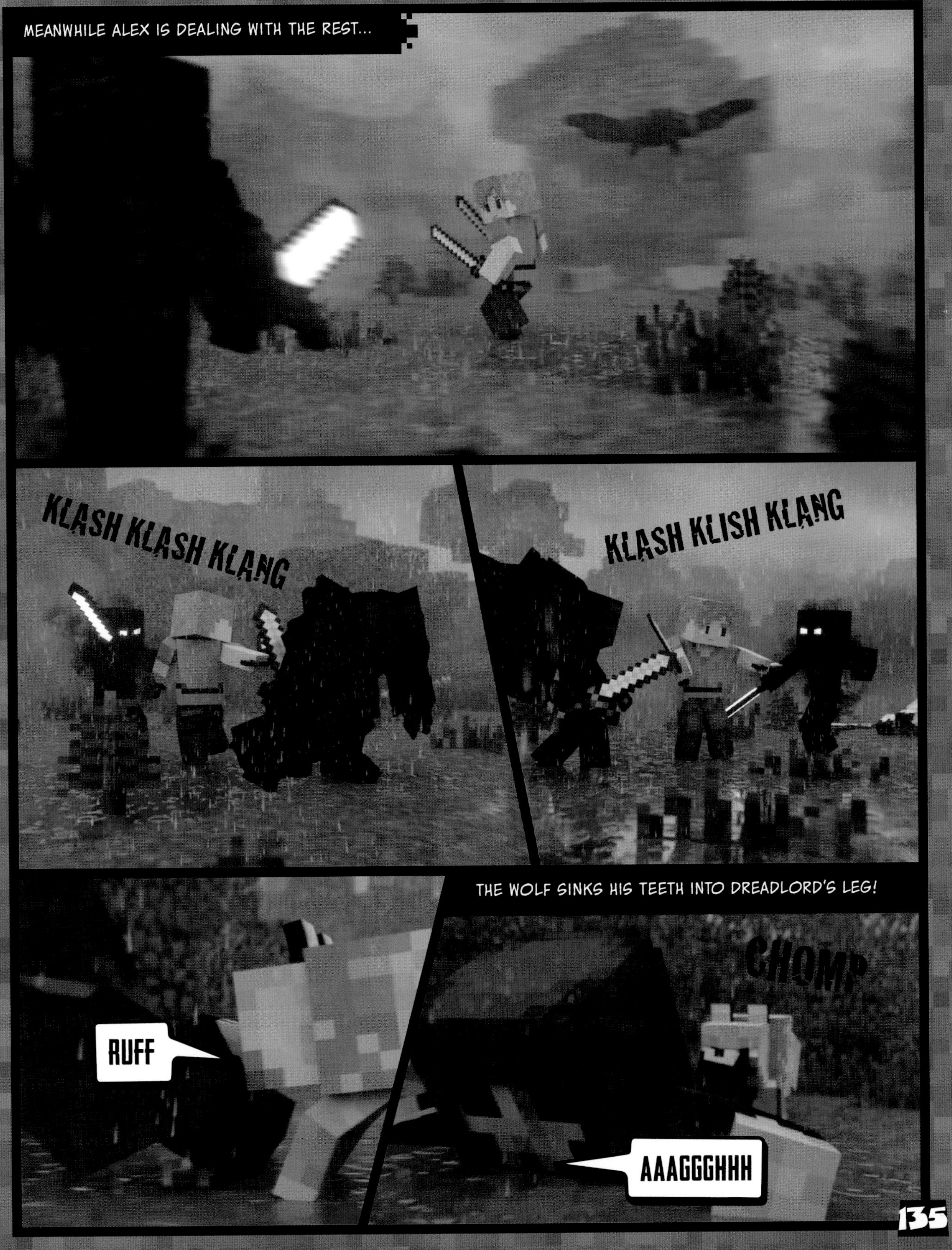
MEANWHILE ALEX IS DEALING WITH THE REST...
KLASH KLASH KLANG
KLASH KLISH KLANG
RUFF
THE WOLF SINKS HIS TEETH INTO DREADLORD'S LEG!
CHOMP
AAAGGGHHH

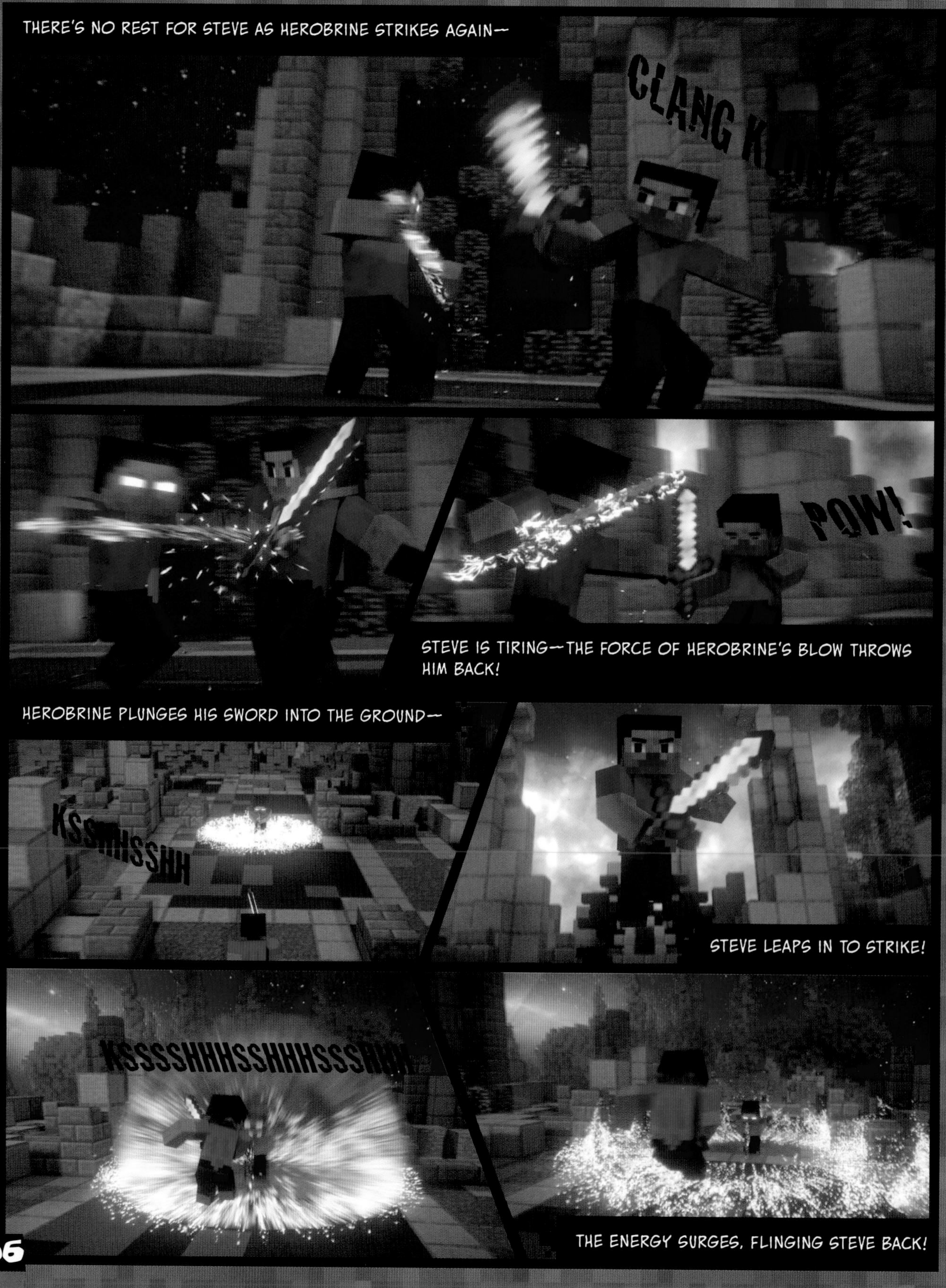
THERE'S NO REST FOR STEVE AS HEROBRINE STRIKES AGAIN—
CLANG
POW!
STEVE IS TIRING—THE FORCE OF HEROBRINE'S BLOW THROWS HIM BACK!
HEROBRINE PLUNGES HIS SWORD INTO THE GROUND—
KSSHHSSHH
STEVE LEAPS IN TO STRIKE!
KSSSSHHHSSHHHSSSSHHH
THE ENERGY SURGES, FLINGING STEVE BACK!

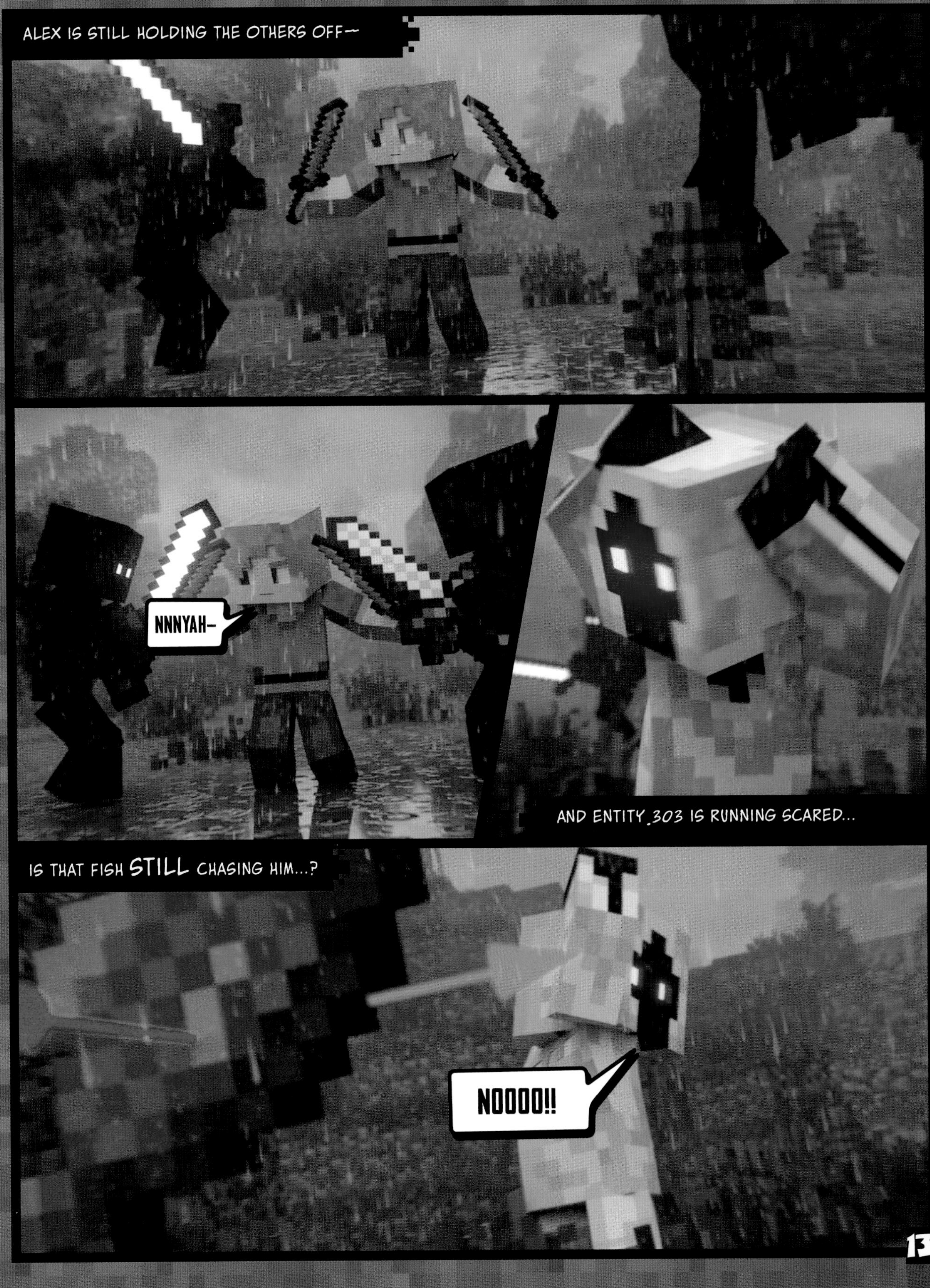
ALEX IS STILL HOLDING THE OTHERS OFF—
NNNYAH-
AND ENTITY_303 IS RUNNING SCARED...
IS THAT FISH STILL CHASING HIM...?
NOOOO!!

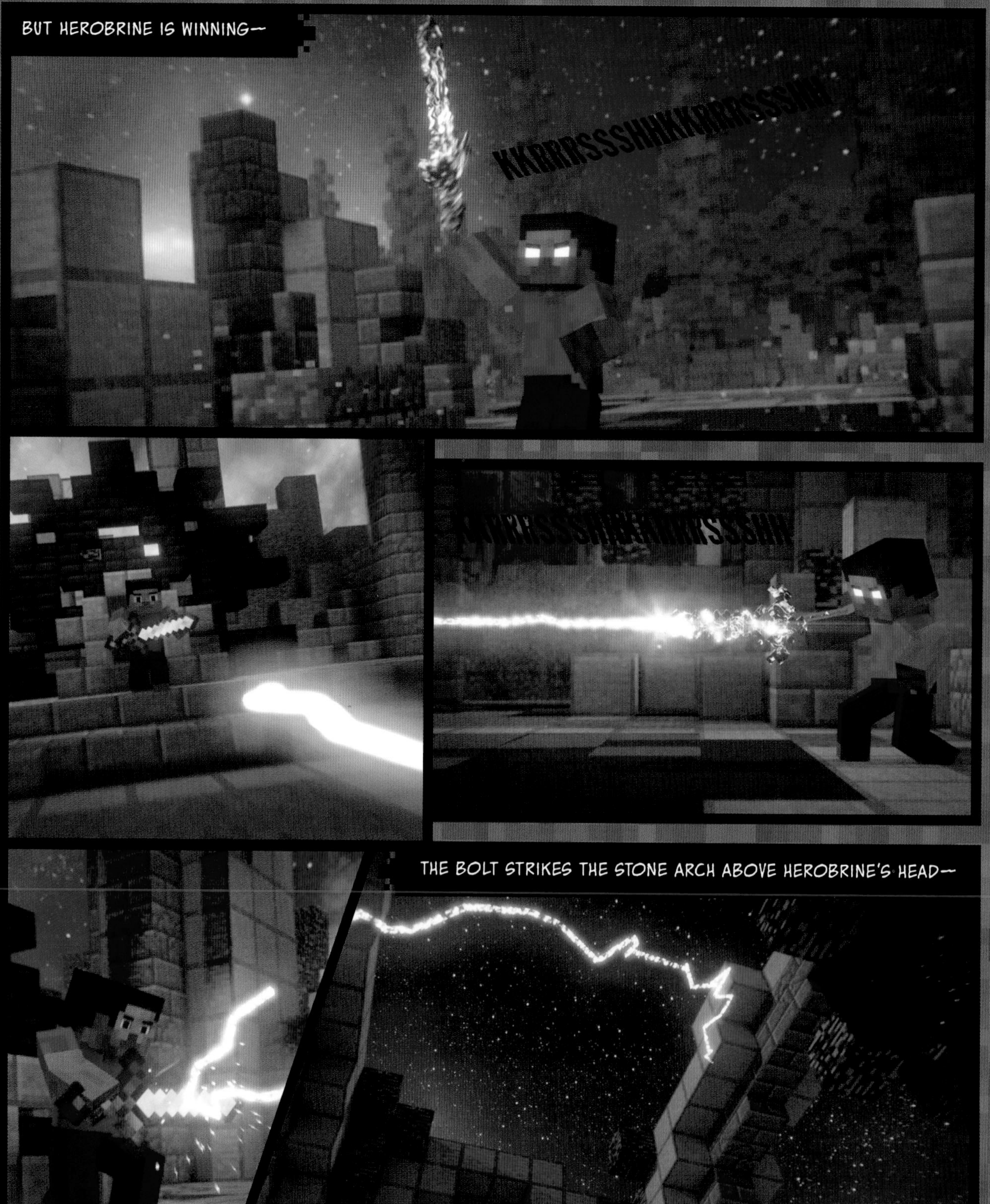

BUT HEROBRINE IS WINNING—
KKRRRSSSHHKKRRRSSSHH
THE BOLT STRIKES THE STONE ARCH ABOVE HEROBRINE'S HEAD—

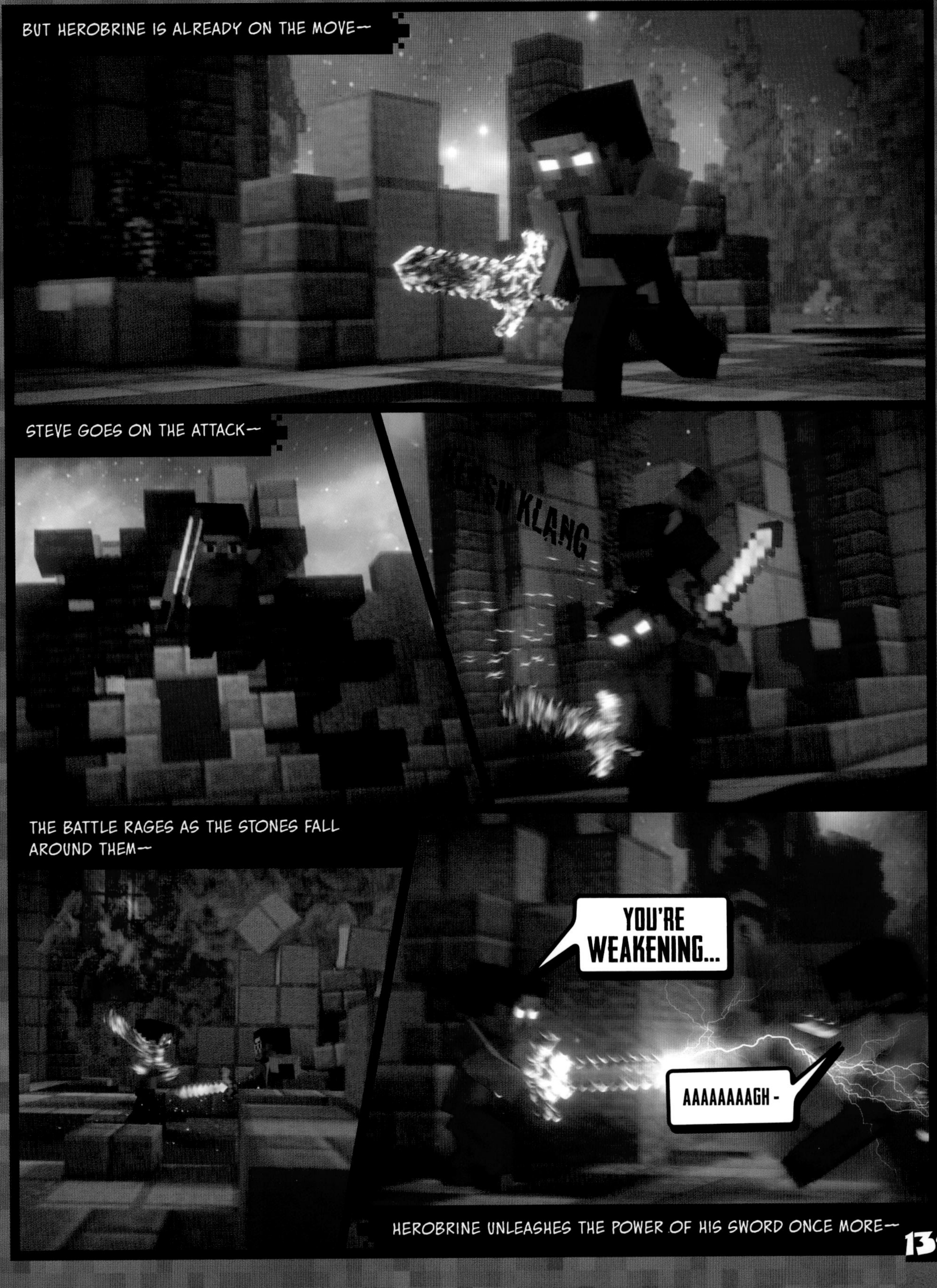
BUT HEROBRINE IS ALREADY ON THE MOVE—
STEVE GOES ON THE ATTACK—
KLANG
THE BATTLE RAGES AS THE STONES FALL AROUND THEM—
YOU'RE WEAKENING...
AAAAAAAAGH -
HEROBRINE UNLEASHES THE POWER OF HIS SWORD ONCE MORE—

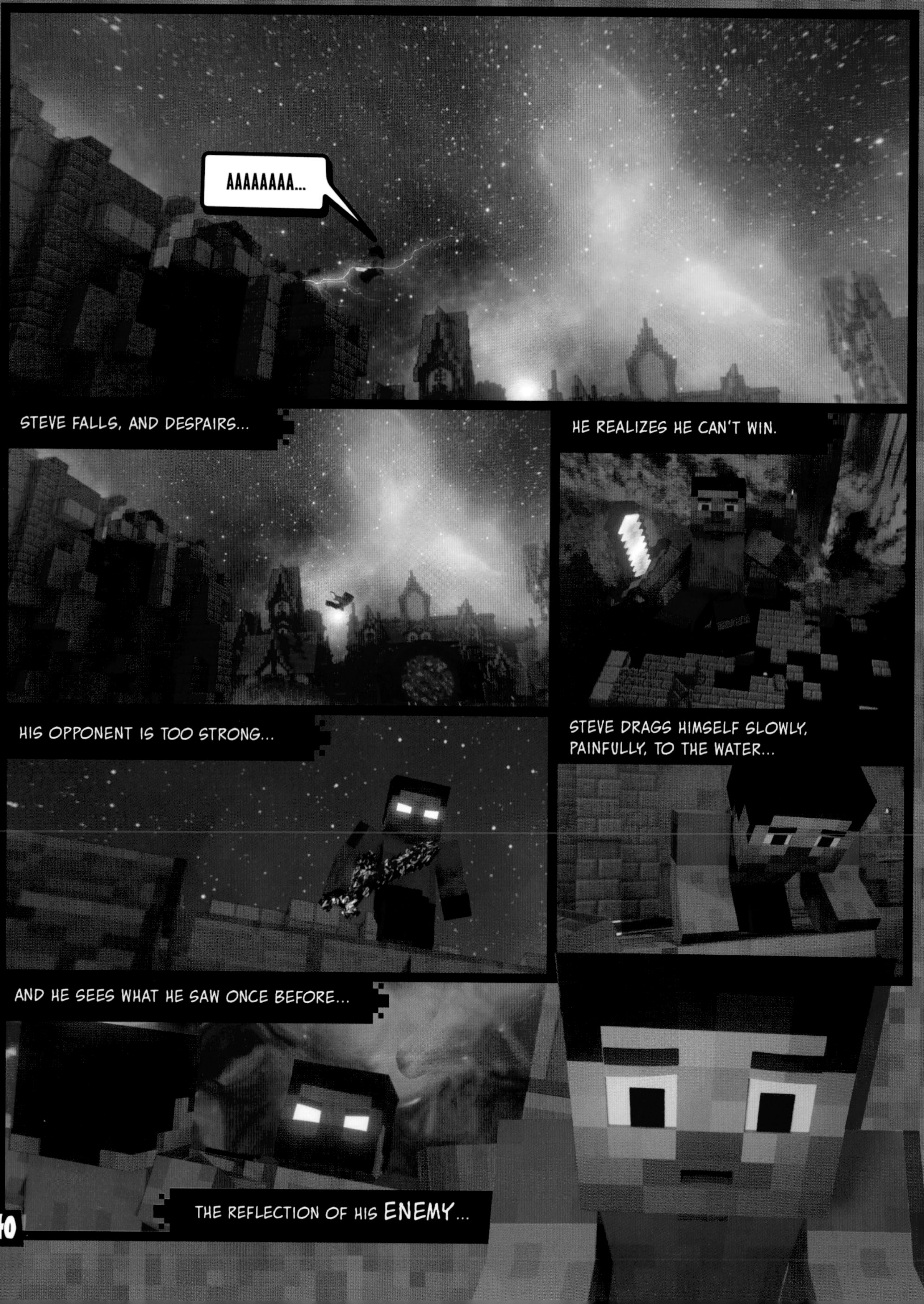
AAAAAAAA...
STEVE FALLS, AND DESPAIRS...
HE REALIZES HE CAN'T WIN.
HIS OPPONENT IS TOO STRONG...
STEVE DRAGS HIMSELF SLOWLY, PAINFULLY, TO THE WATER...
AND HE SEES WHAT HE SAW ONCE BEFORE...
THE REFLECTION OF HIS ENEMY...

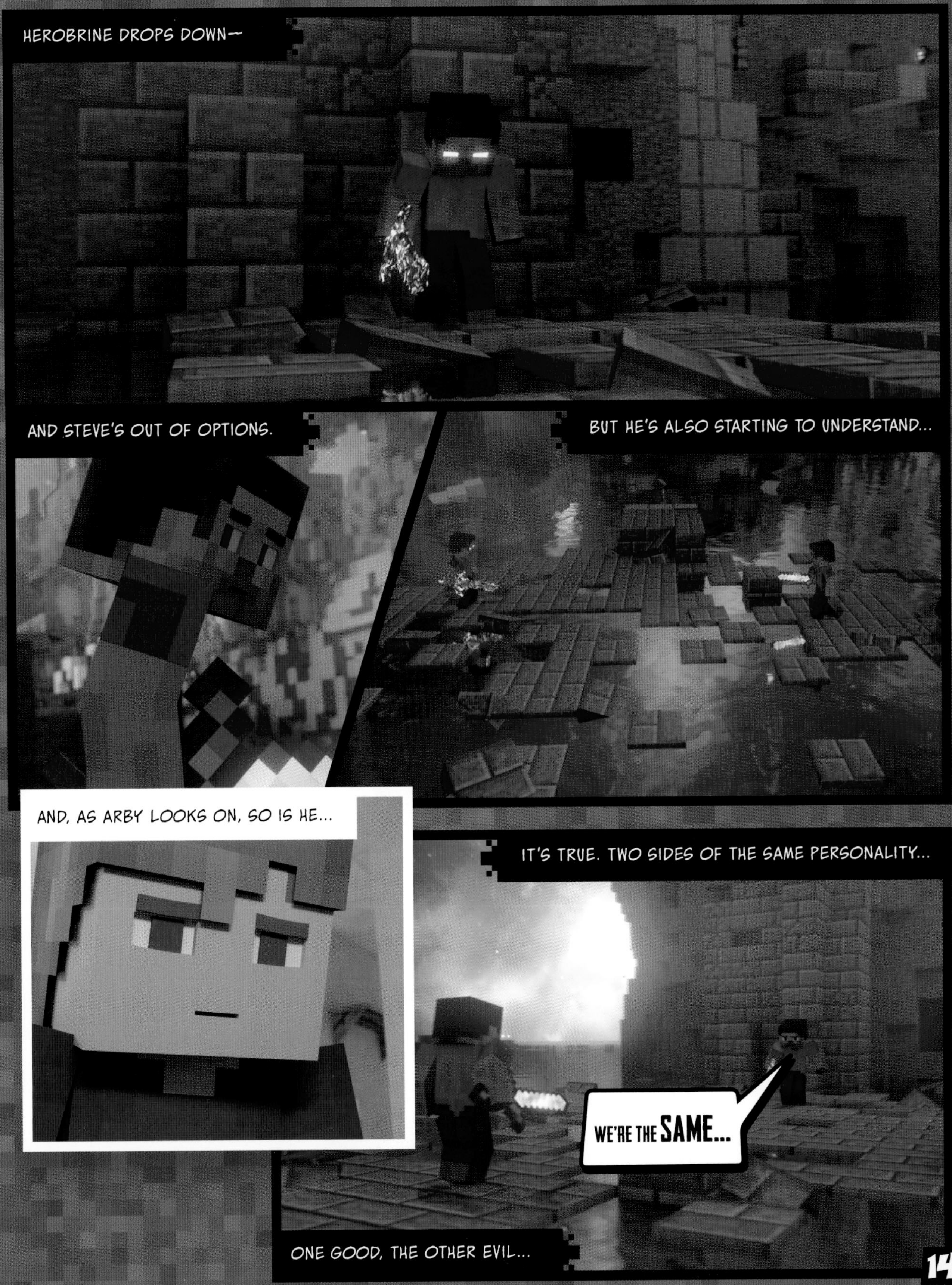
HEROBRINE DROPS DOWN—
AND STEVE'S OUT OF OPTIONS.
BUT HE'S ALSO STARTING TO UNDERSTAND...
AND, AS ARBY LOOKS ON, SO IS HE...
IT'S TRUE. TWO SIDES OF THE SAME PERSONALITY...
WE'RE THE SAME...
ONE GOOD, THE OTHER EVIL...

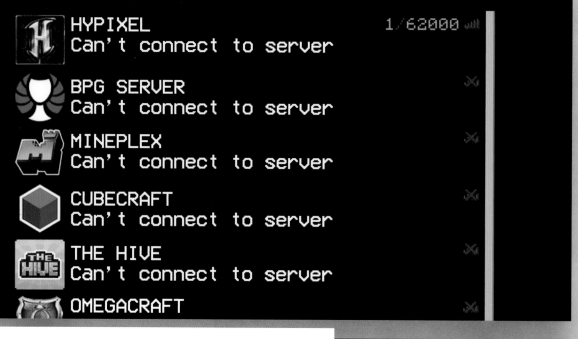

PLAY MULTIPLAYER

HYPIXEL
Can't connect to server

1/62000

BPG SERVER
Can't connect to server

MINEPLEX
Can't connect to server

CUBECRAFT
Can't connect to server

THE HIVE
Can't connect to server

OMEGACRAFT

THERE'S ONLY ONE PERSON IN HYPIXEL—BECAUSE STEVE AND HEROBRINE ARE THE **SAME PERSON!**

WOAH...

STEVE THINKS BACK THROUGH THE MOMENTS OF HIS LIFE SO FAR...

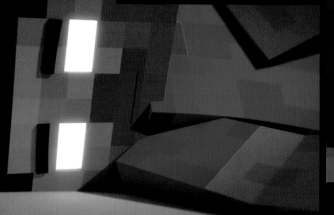

SOMETHING HE FELT THE MOMENT HE WOKE UP—

THOUGH IT ONLY LASTED A SECOND ...
THE REFLECTION HE SAW AT THE LAKE—

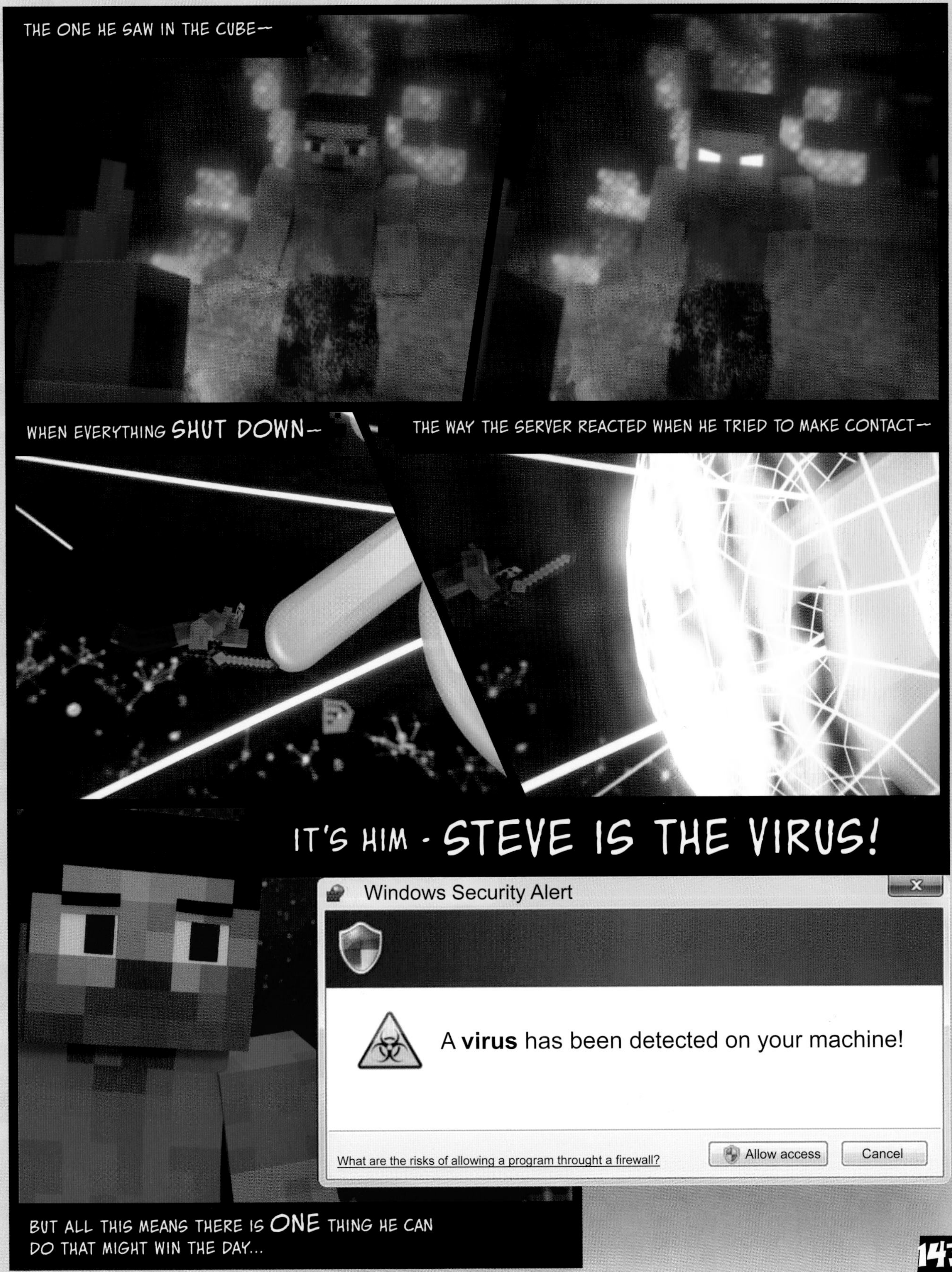

THE ONE HE SAW IN THE CUBE—
WHEN EVERYTHING SHUT DOWN—
THE WAY THE SERVER REACTED WHEN HE TRIED TO MAKE CONTACT—
IT'S HIM - STEVE IS THE VIRUS!
Windows Security Alert
A virus has been detected on your machine!
What are the risks of allowing a program throught a firewall?
Allow access
Cancel
BUT ALL THIS MEANS THERE IS ONE THING HE CAN DO THAT MIGHT WIN THE DAY...

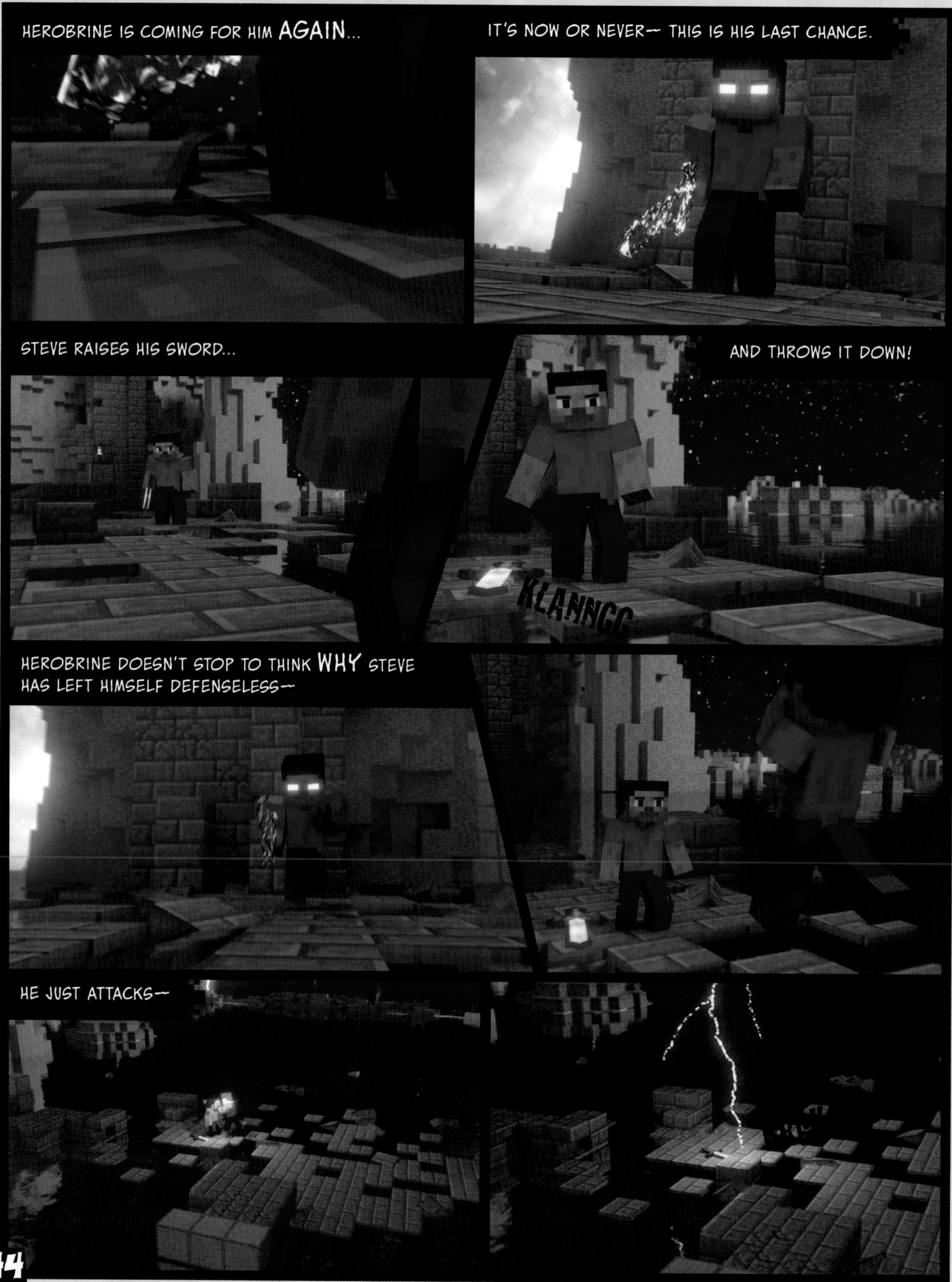
HEROBRINE IS COMING FOR HIM AGAIN...
IT'S NOW OR NEVER— THIS IS HIS LAST CHANCE.
STEVE RAISES HIS SWORD...
AND THROWS IT DOWN!
KLANNGG
HEROBRINE DOESN'T STOP TO THINK WHY STEVE HAS LEFT HIMSELF DEFENSELESS—
HE JUST ATTACKS—

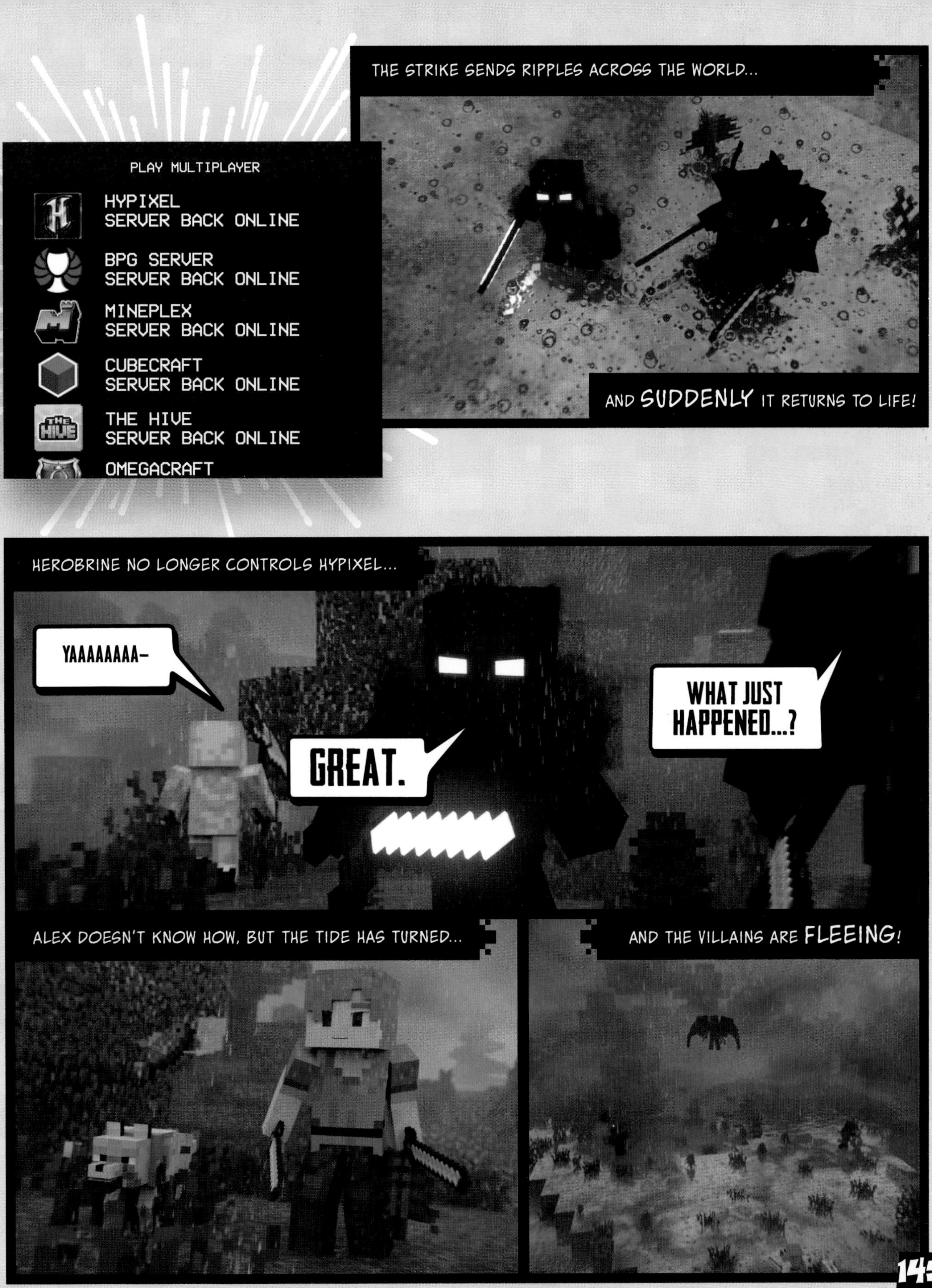
THE STRIKE SENDS RIPPLES ACROSS THE WORLD...
PLAY MULTIPLAYER
HYPIXEL
SERVER BACK ONLINE
BPG SERVER
SERVER BACK ONLINE
MINEPLEX
SERVER BACK ONLINE
CUBECRAFT
SERVER BACK ONLINE
THE HIVE
SERVER BACK ONLINE
OMEGACRAFT
AND SUDDENLY IT RETURNS TO LIFE!
HEROBRINE NO LONGER CONTROLS HYPIXEL...
YAAAAAAAA-
GREAT.
WHAT JUST HAPPENED...?
ALEX DOESN'T KNOW HOW, BUT THE TIDE HAS TURNED...
AND THE VILLAINS ARE FLEEING!

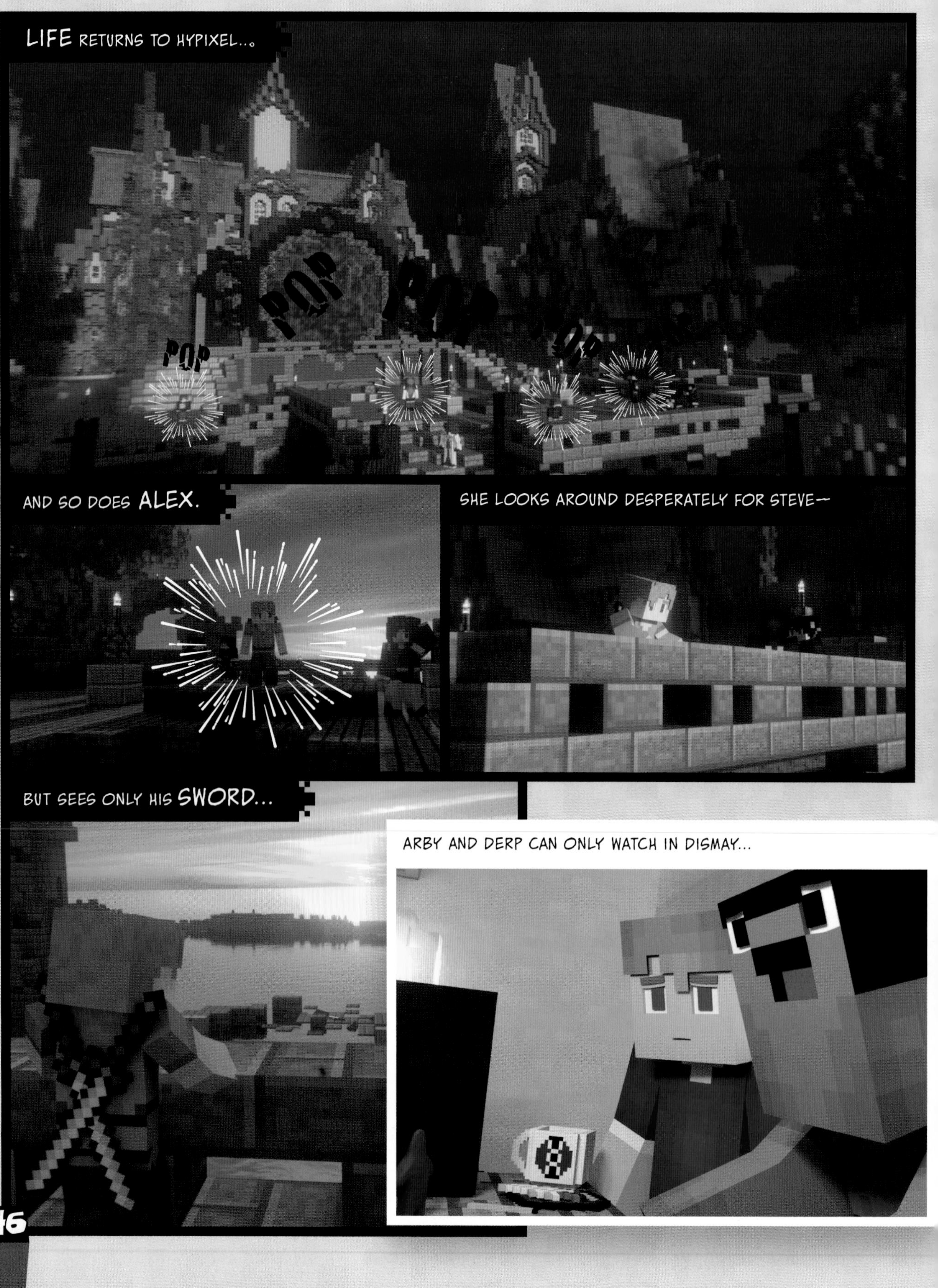
LIFE RETURNS TO HYPIXEL...
POP
POP
AND SO DOES ALEX.
SHE LOOKS AROUND DESPERATELY FOR STEVE—
BUT SEES ONLY HIS SWORD...
ARBY AND DERP CAN ONLY WATCH IN DISMAY...

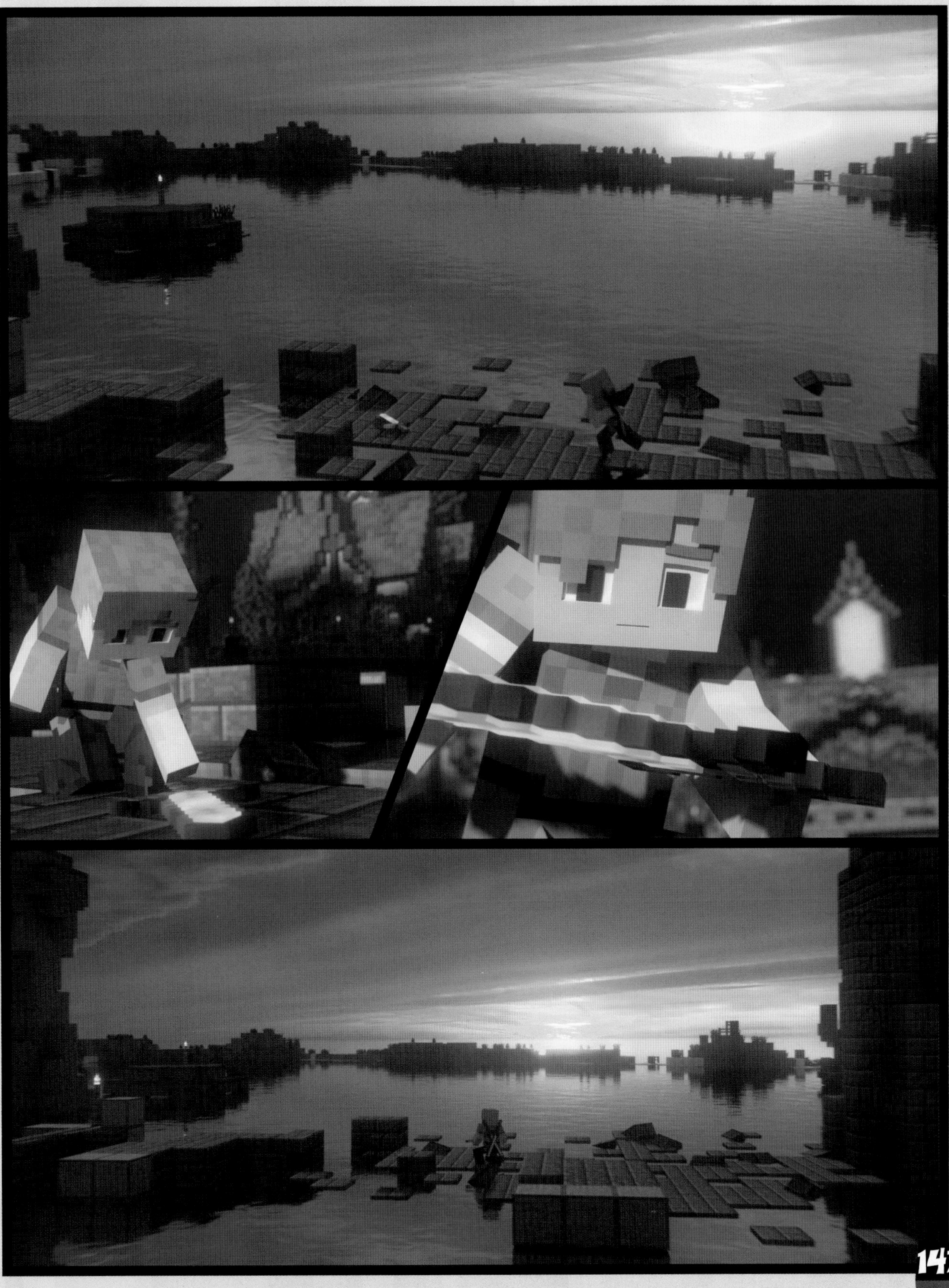

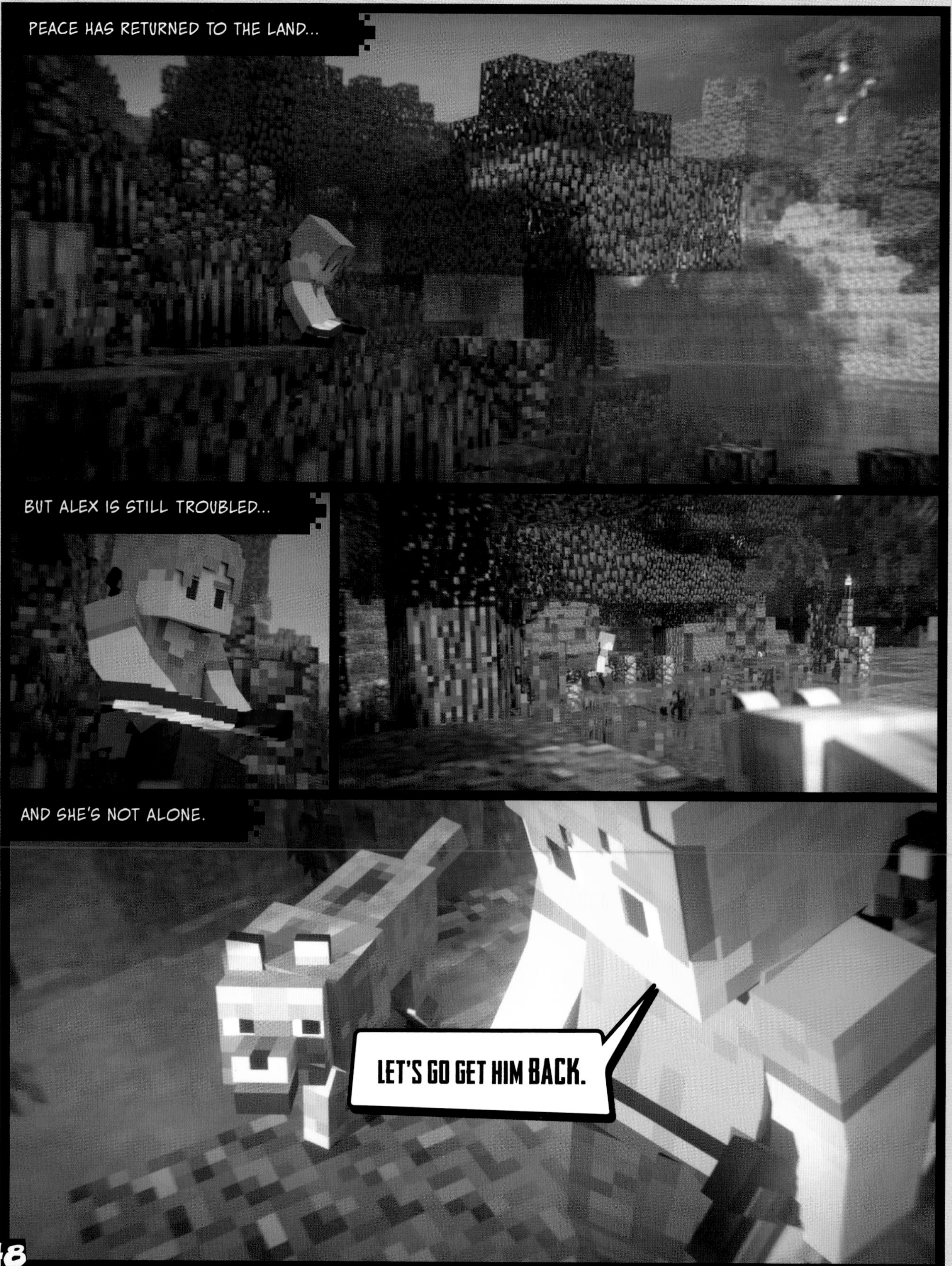

PEACE HAS RETURNED TO THE LAND...
BUT ALEX IS STILL TROUBLED...
AND SHE'S NOT ALONE.
LET'S GO GET HIM BACK.

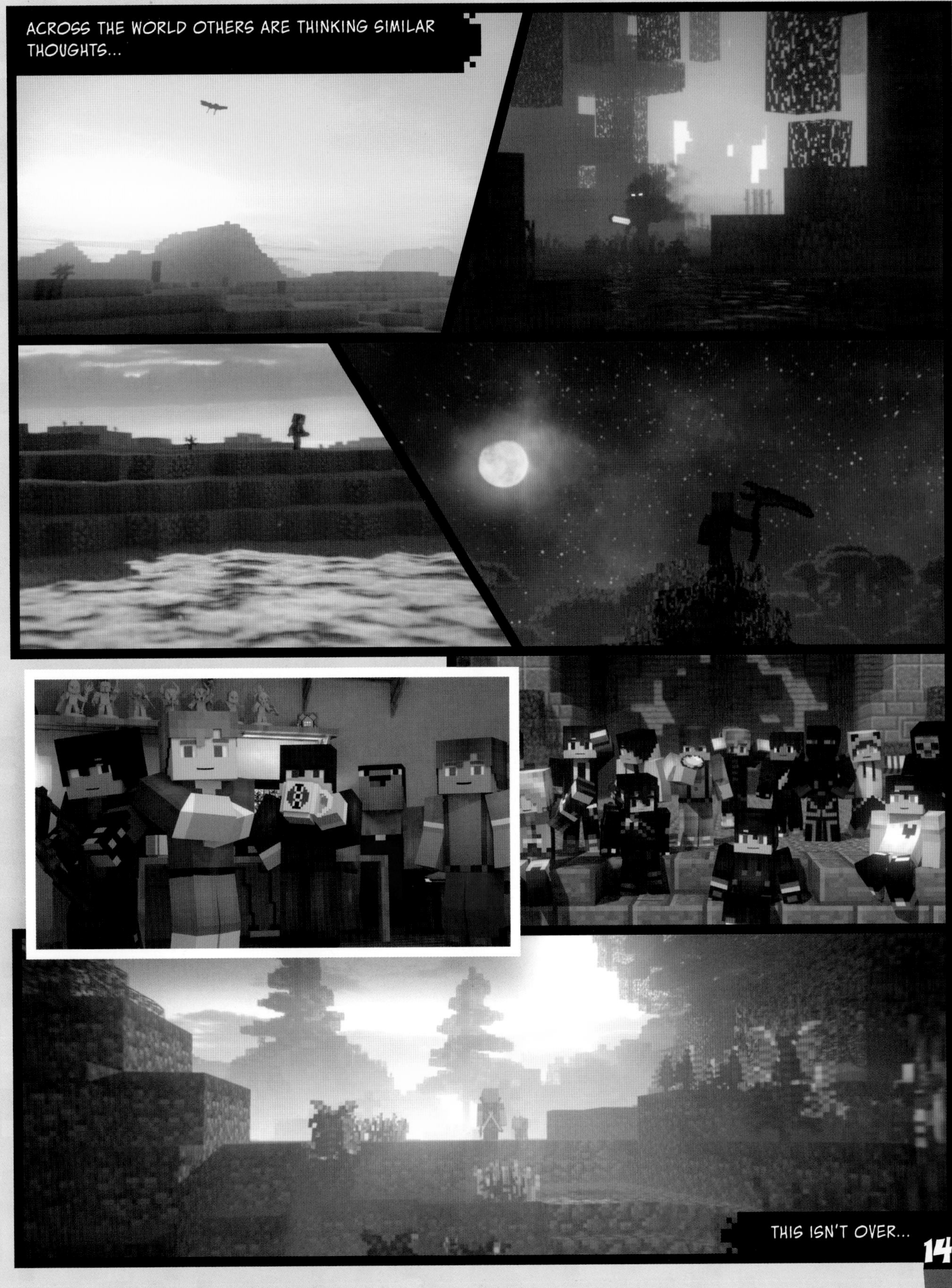
ACROSS THE WORLD OTHERS ARE THINKING SIMILAR THOUGHTS...
THIS ISN'T OVER...

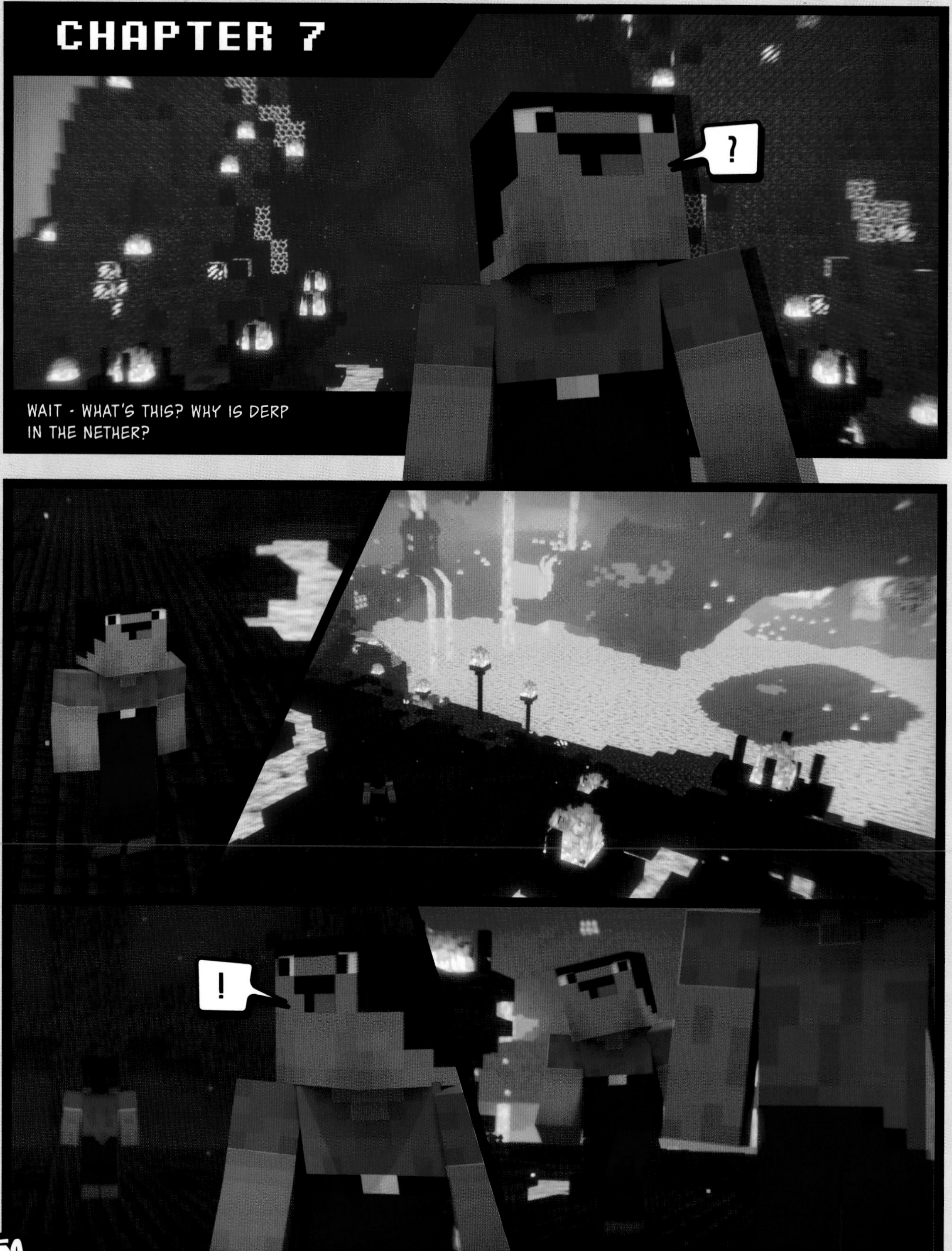
CHAPTER 7
?
WAIT - WHAT'S THIS? WHY IS DERP IN THE NETHER?
!

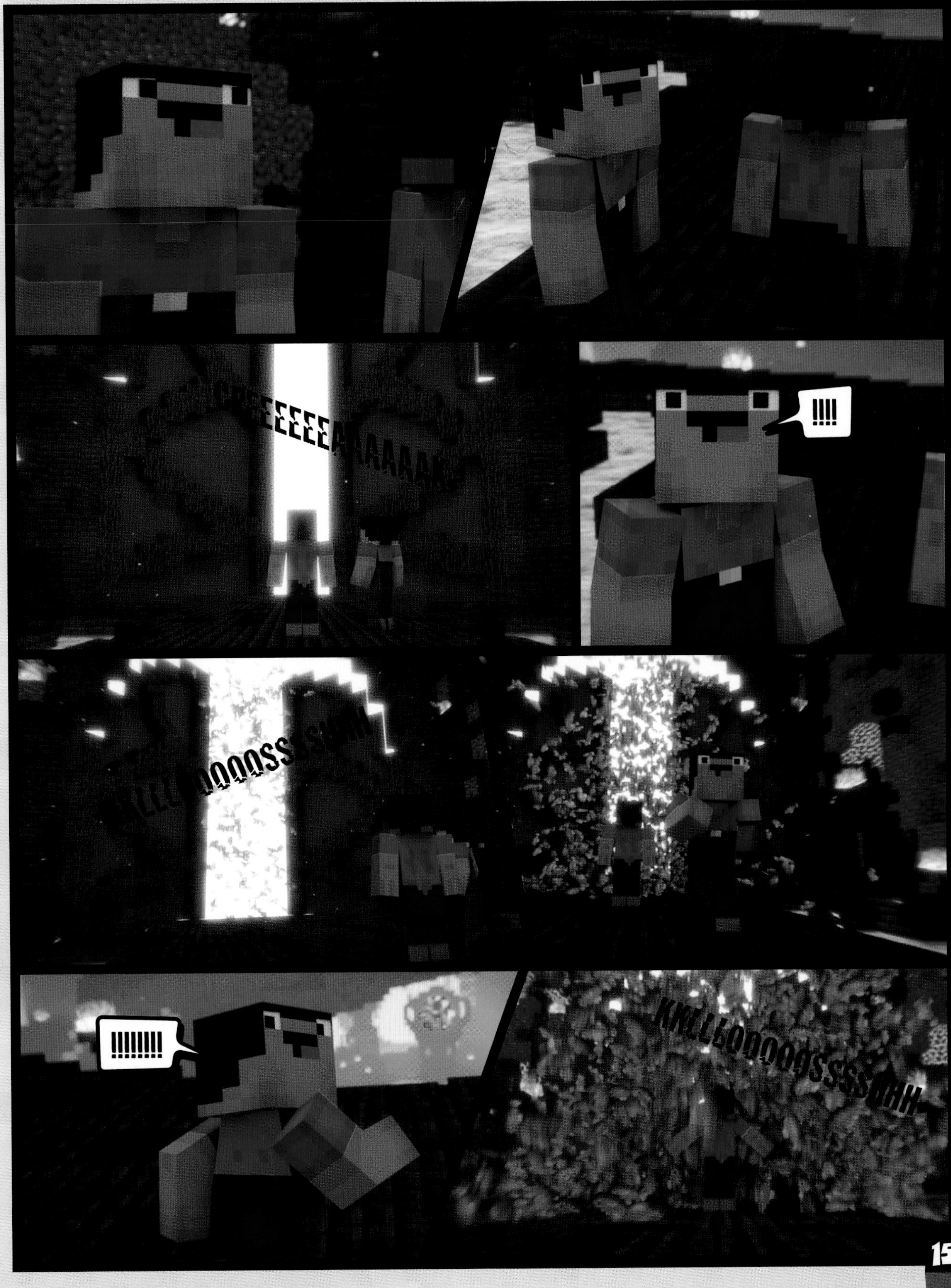
CREEEEEEAAAAAAK
!!!!
OOOOSSSSHHH
!!!!!!!!
KHLLLOOOOOSSSSSHHH

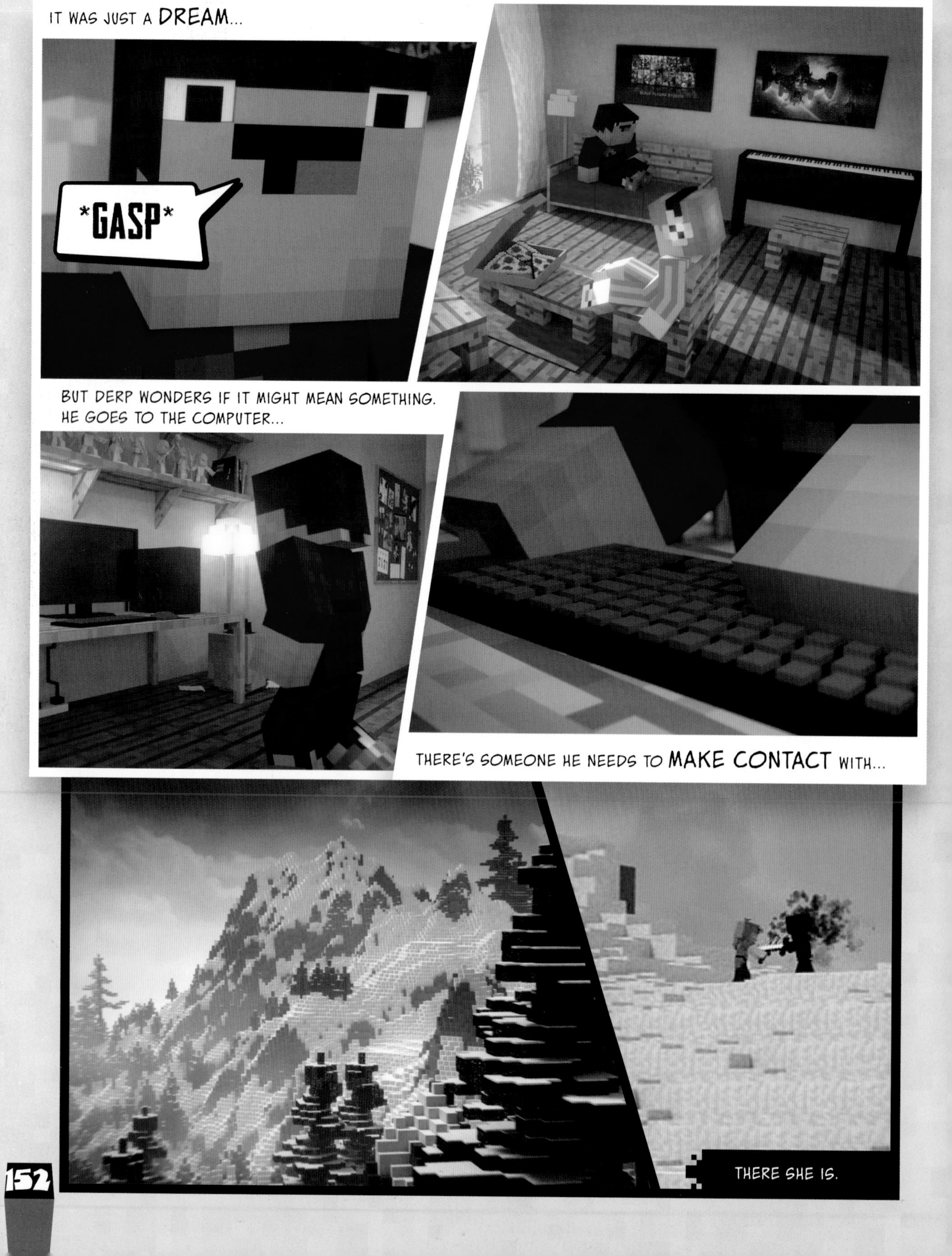
IT WAS JUST A DREAM...
GASP
BUT DERP WONDERS IF IT MIGHT MEAN SOMETHING. HE GOES TO THE COMPUTER...
THERE'S SOMEONE HE NEEDS TO MAKE CONTACT WITH...
THERE SHE IS.

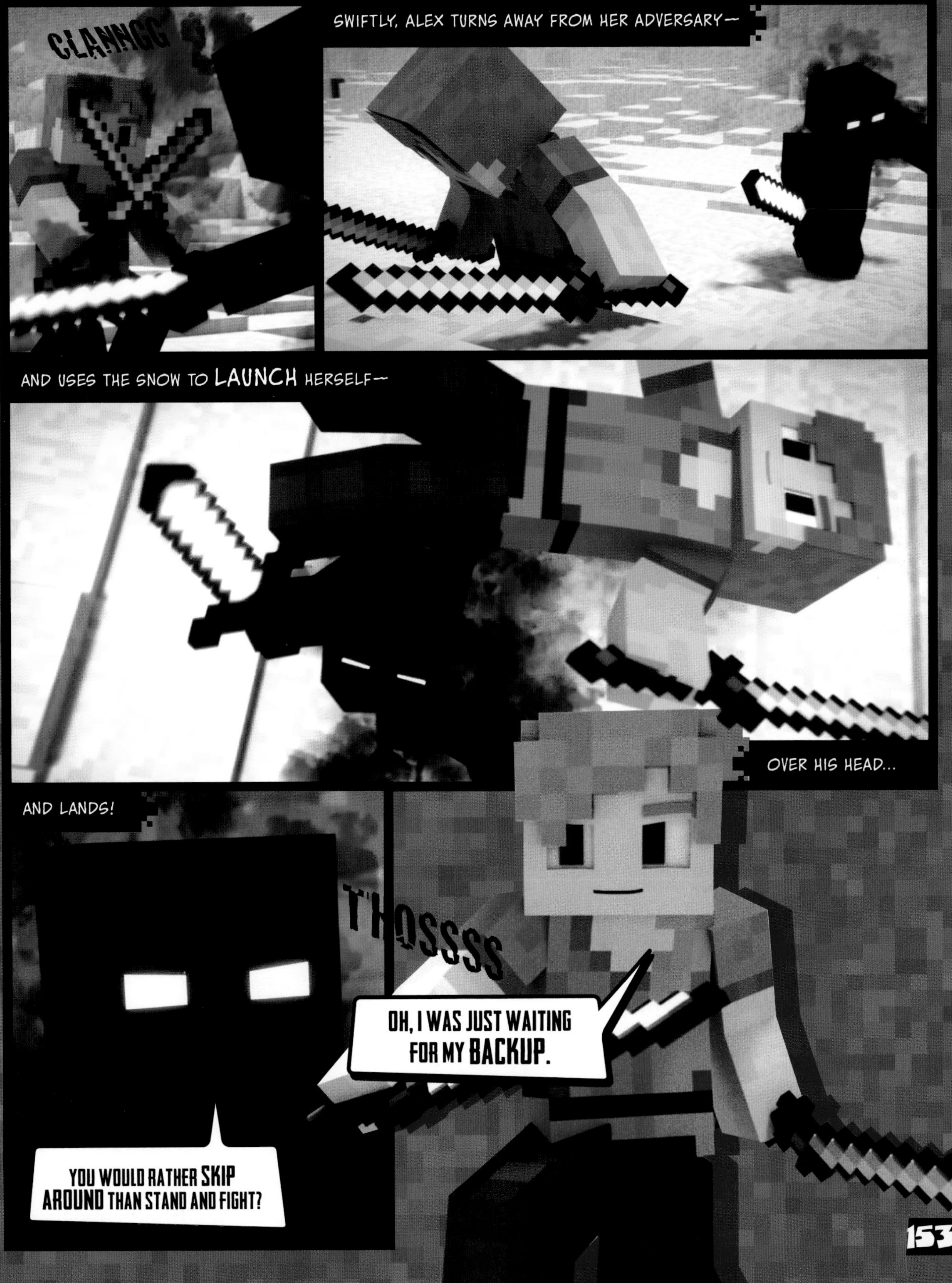
CLANNGG
SWIFTLY, ALEX TURNS AWAY FROM HER ADVERSARY—
AND USES THE SNOW TO LAUNCH HERSELF—
OVER HIS HEAD...
AND LANDS!
THOSSSS
OH, I WAS JUST WAITING FOR MY BACKUP.
YOU WOULD RATHER SKIP AROUND THAN STAND AND FIGHT?

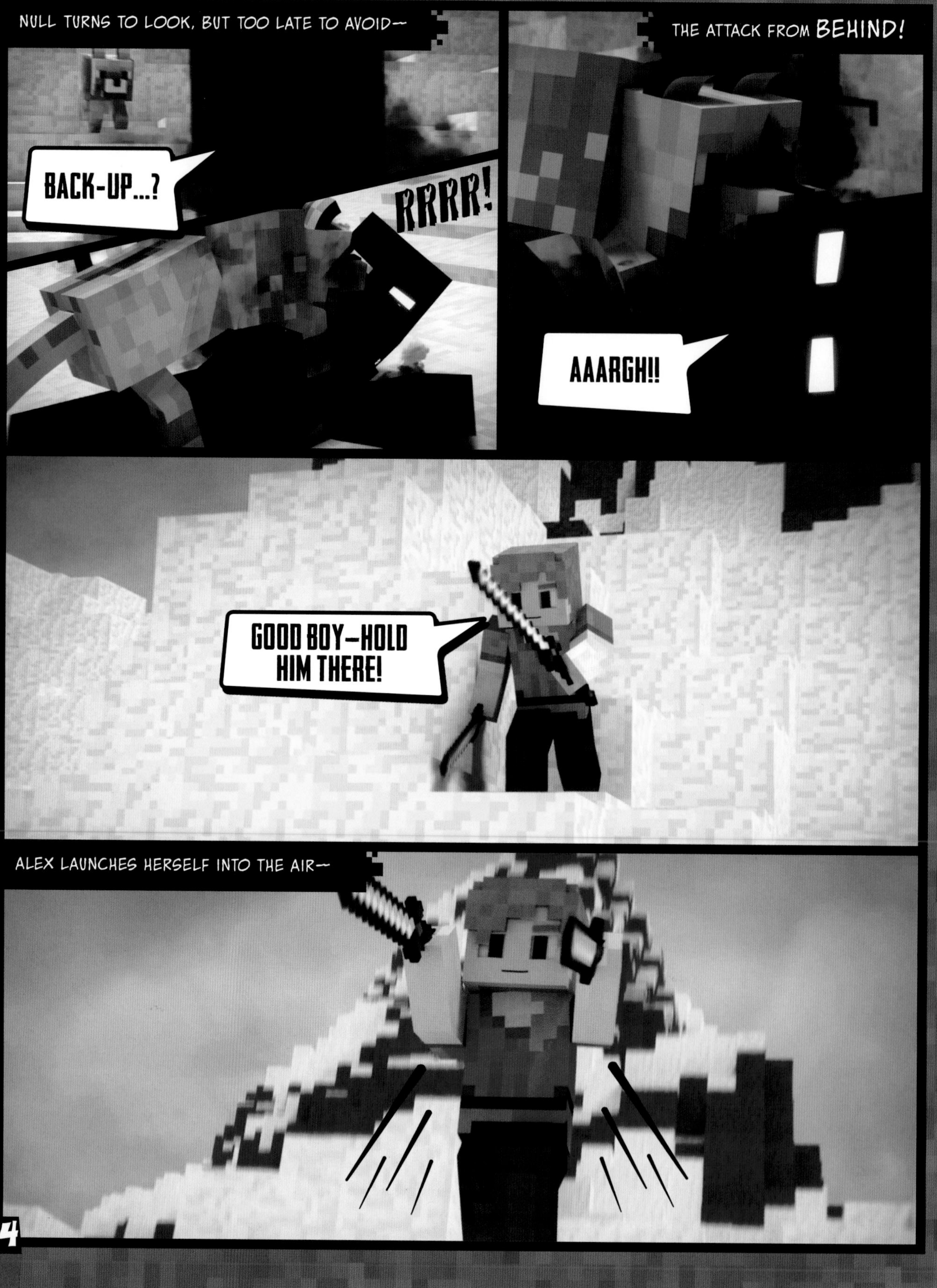
NULL TURNS TO LOOK, BUT TOO LATE TO AVOID—
BACK-UP...?
RRRR!
THE ATTACK FROM BEHIND!
AAARGH!!
GOOD BOY—HOLD HIM THERE!
ALEX LAUNCHES HERSELF INTO THE AIR—

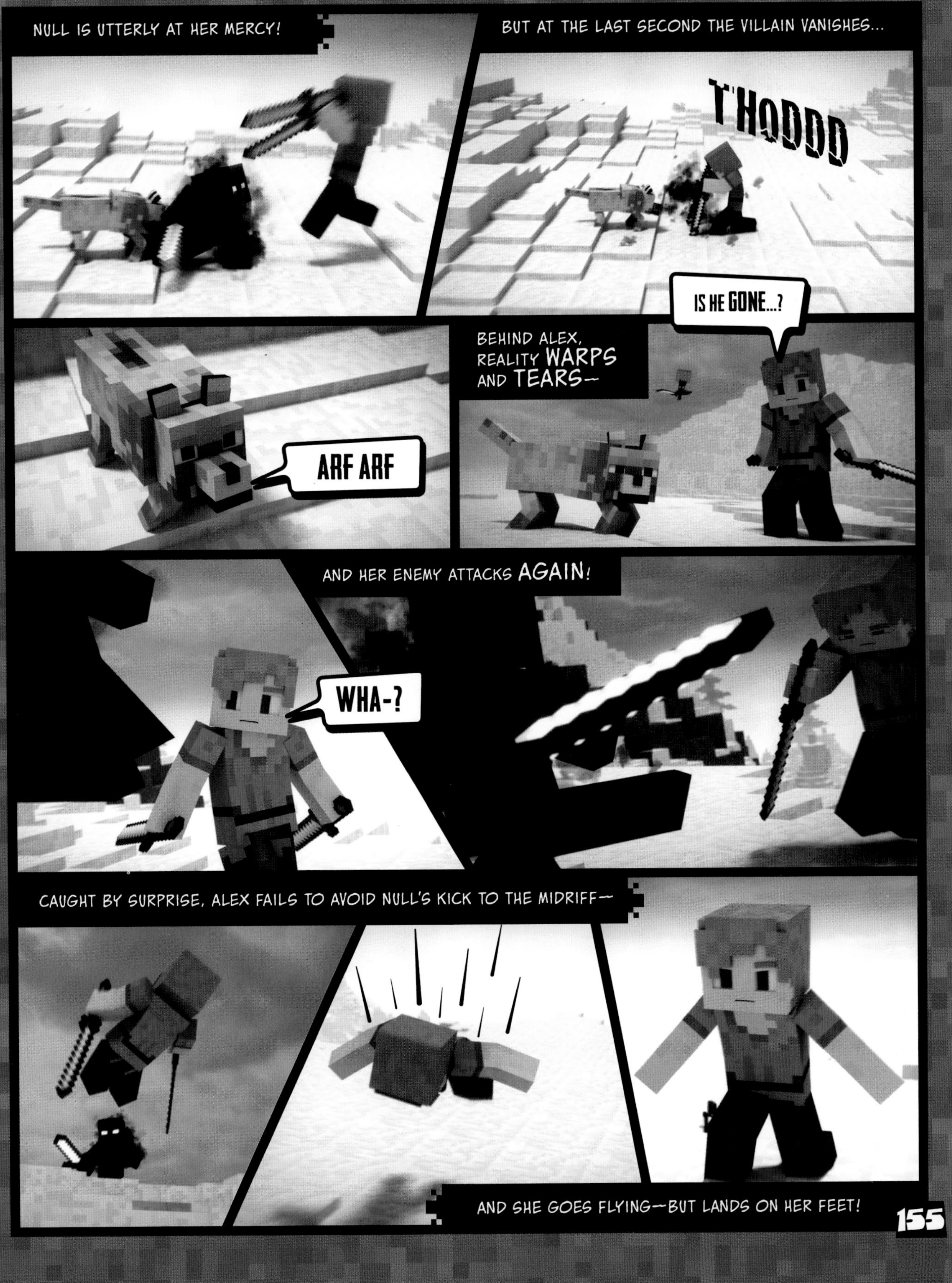
NULL IS UTTERLY AT HER MERCY!
BUT AT THE LAST SECOND THE VILLAIN VANISHES...
T'HODDD
IS HE GONE...?
ARF ARF
BEHIND ALEX, REALITY WARPS AND TEARS—
AND HER ENEMY ATTACKS AGAIN!
WHA-?
CAUGHT BY SURPRISE, ALEX FAILS TO AVOID NULL'S KICK TO THE MIDRIFF—
AND SHE GOES FLYING—BUT LANDS ON HER FEET!

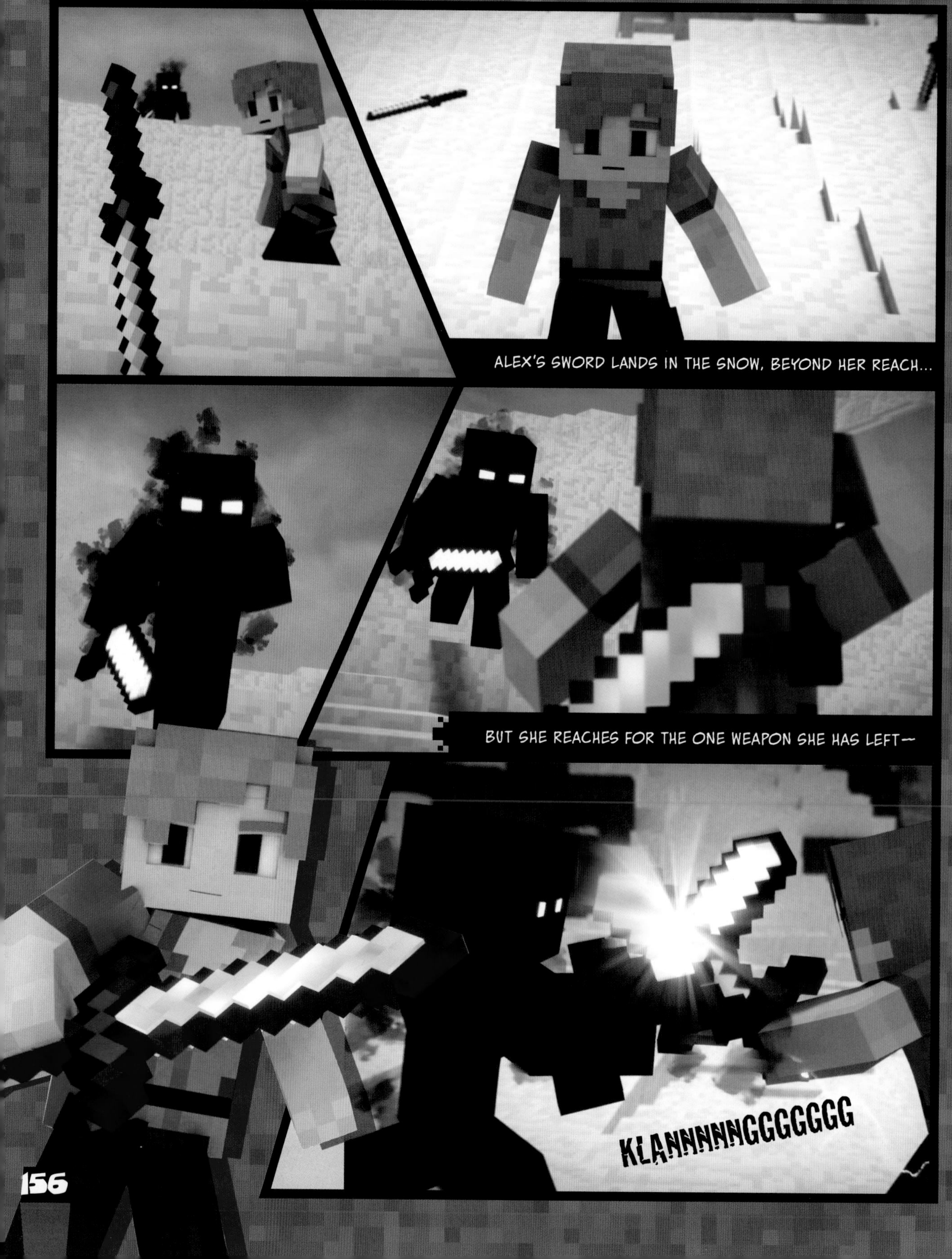

ALEX'S SWORD LANDS IN THE SNOW, BEYOND HER REACH...
BUT SHE REACHES FOR THE ONE WEAPON SHE HAS LEFT—
KLANNNNNGGGGGGG

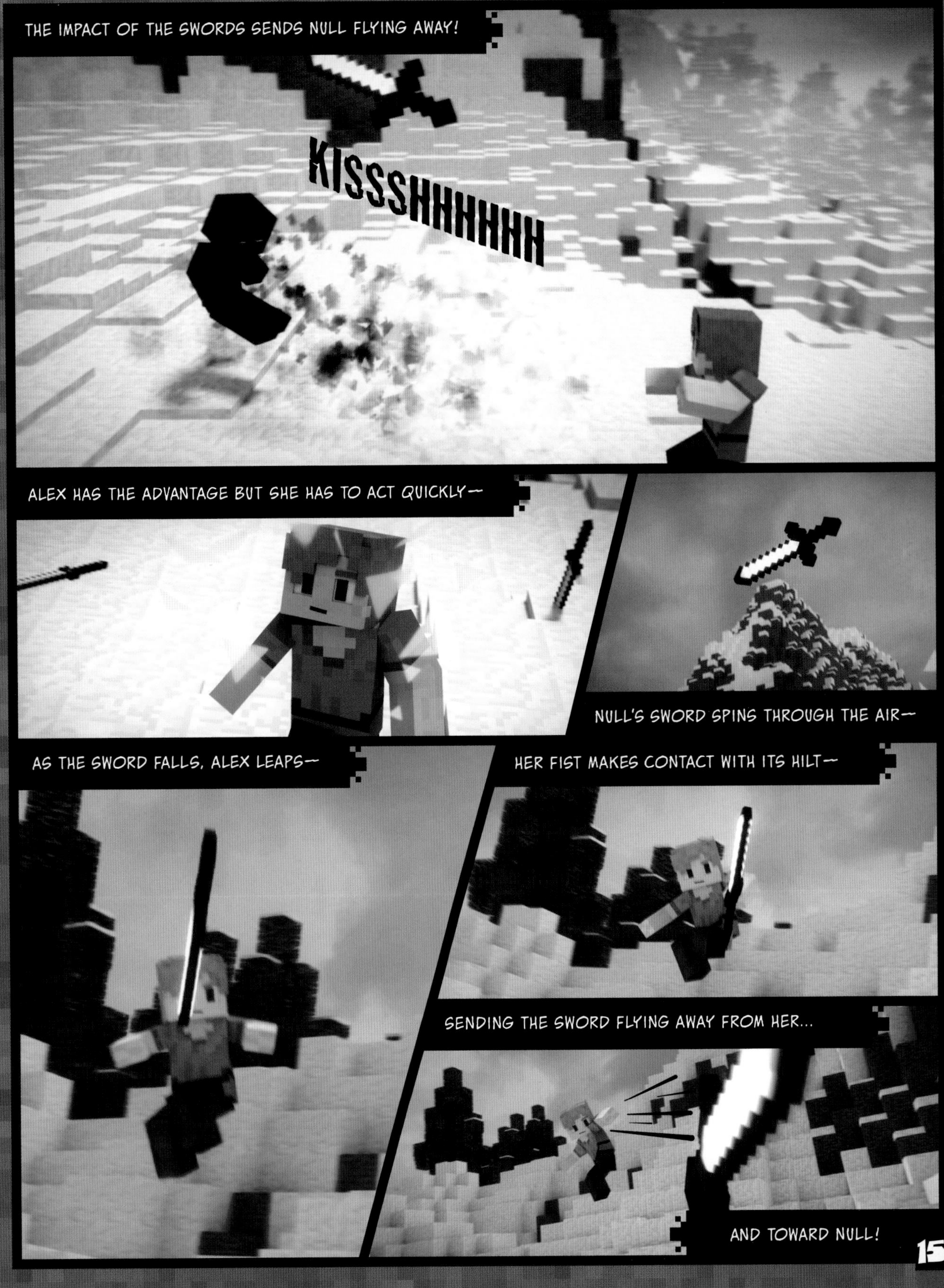

THE IMPACT OF THE SWORDS SENDS NULL FLYING AWAY!

KISSSHHHHHH

ALEX HAS THE ADVANTAGE BUT SHE HAS TO ACT QUICKLY~

NULL'S SWORD SPINS THROUGH THE AIR~

AS THE SWORD FALLS, ALEX LEAPS~

HER FIST MAKES CONTACT WITH ITS HILT~

SENDING THE SWORD FLYING AWAY FROM HER...

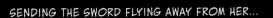

AND TOWARD NULL!

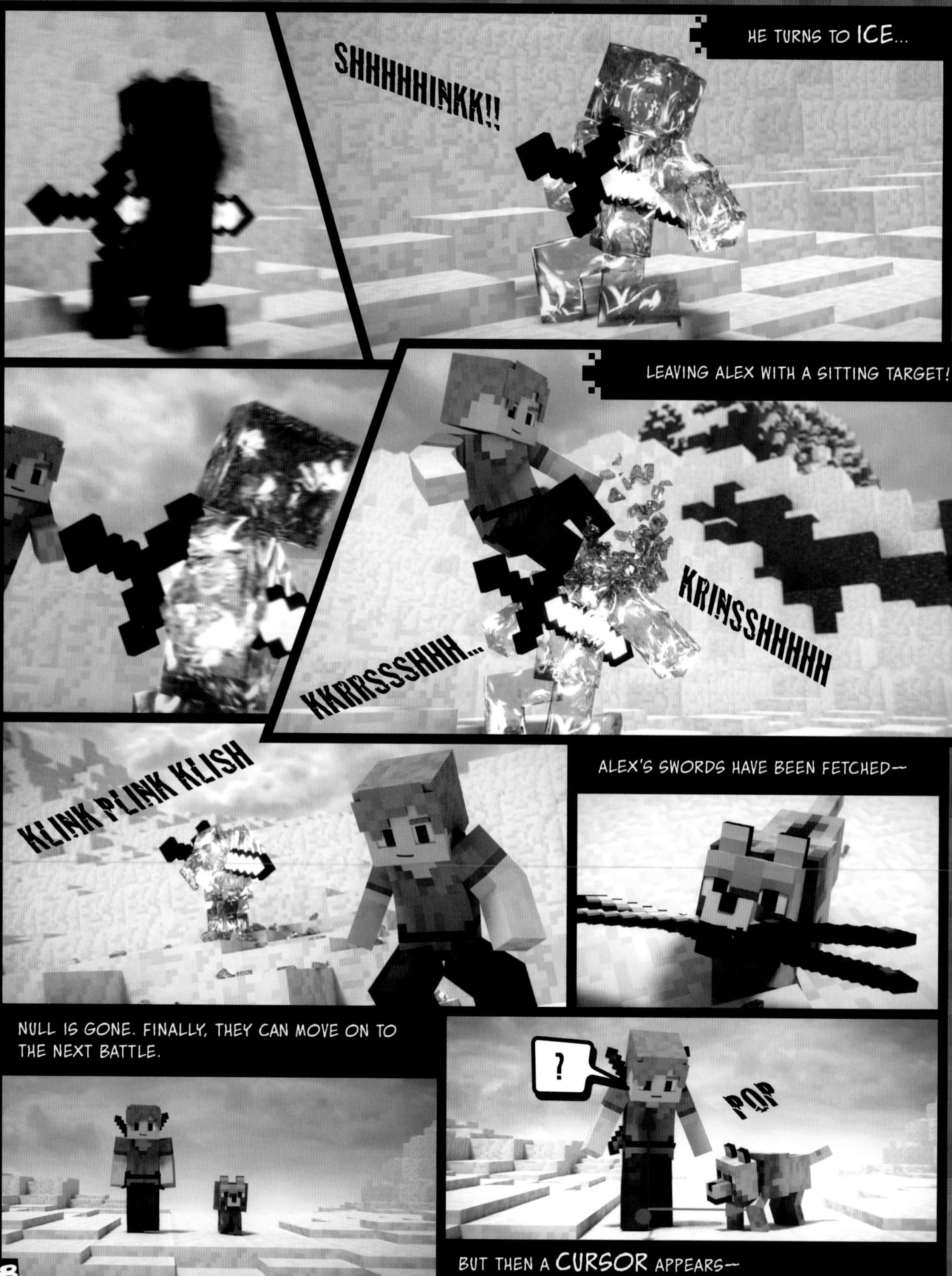

HE TURNS TO ICE...
SHHHHHINKK!!
LEAVING ALEX WITH A SITTING TARGET!
KRRSSSHHH...
KRINSSHHHHHH
KLINK PLINK KLISH
ALEX'S SWORDS HAVE BEEN FETCHED—
NULL IS GONE. FINALLY, THEY CAN MOVE ON TO THE NEXT BATTLE.
?
POP
BUT THEN A CURSOR APPEARS—

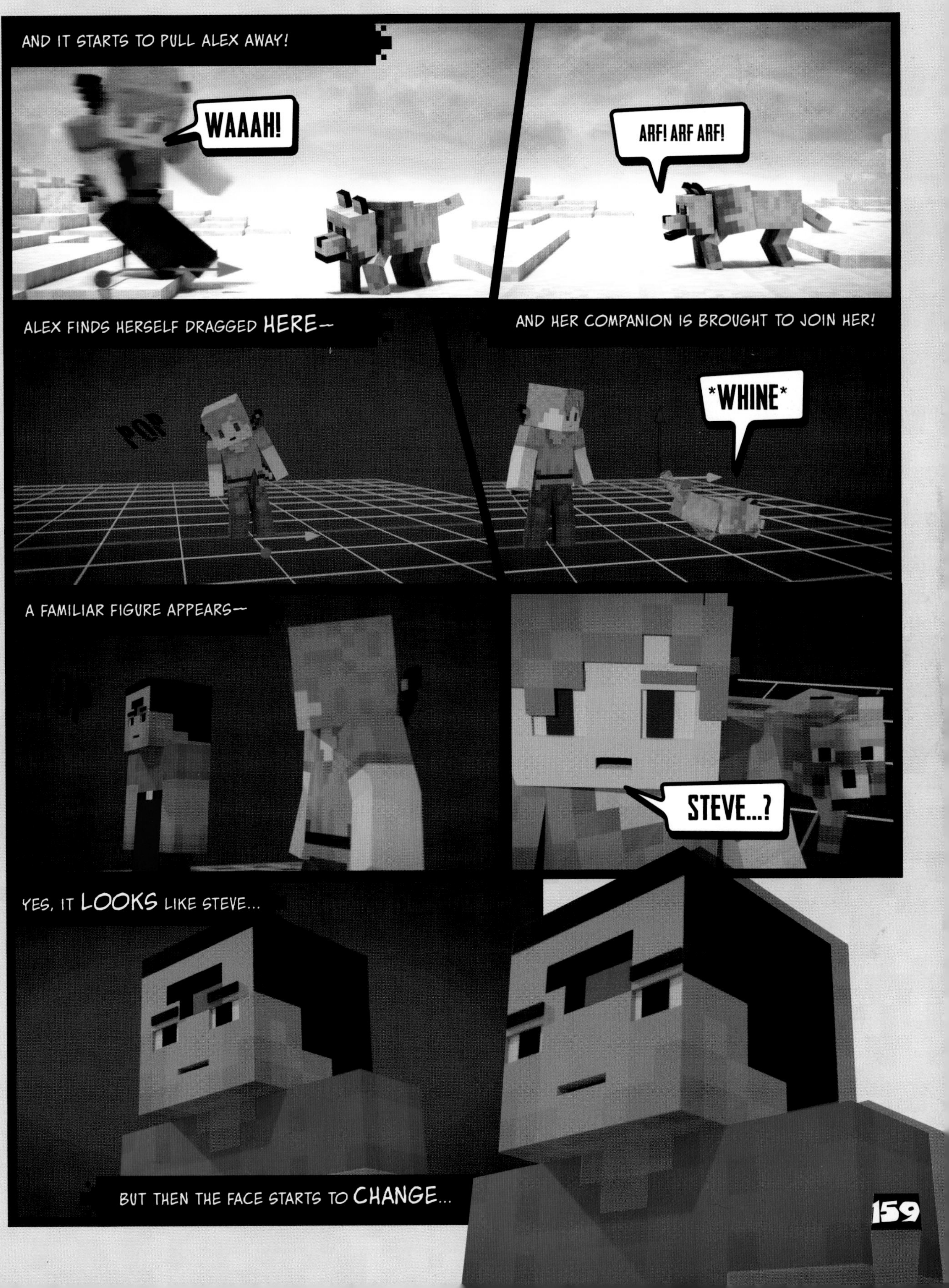
AND IT STARTS TO PULL ALEX AWAY!
WAAAH!
ARF! ARF ARF!
ALEX FINDS HERSELF DRAGGED HERE–
POP
AND HER COMPANION IS BROUGHT TO JOIN HER!
WHINE
A FAMILIAR FIGURE APPEARS–
STEVE...?
YES, IT LOOKS LIKE STEVE...
BUT THEN THE FACE STARTS TO CHANGE...

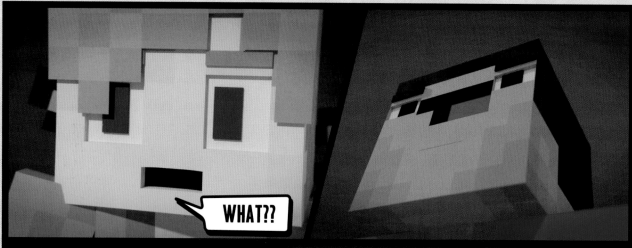

THE FACE IS DIFFERENT—BUT STILL FAMILIAR!

AND AT LEAST IT'S A FRIENDLY FACE...

UM ... WHAT'S UP, DERP?

HE HANDS A PICTURE TO ALEX...

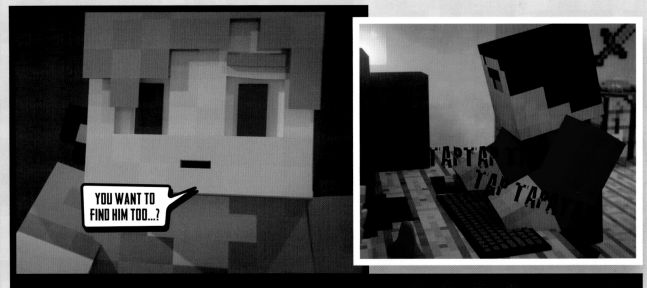

YOU WANT TO FIND HIM TOO...?

ALEX FEELS A SUDDEN MOVEMENT BEHIND HER~

SWOOOOSH

AND SHE TURNS TO SEE AN IMPRESSIVE **RIG**...

DERP SWIPES HIS HAND~

SWOOOOSH

AND THE RIG MOVES ON, TO BE REPLACED BY~

AN **INVENTORY**...

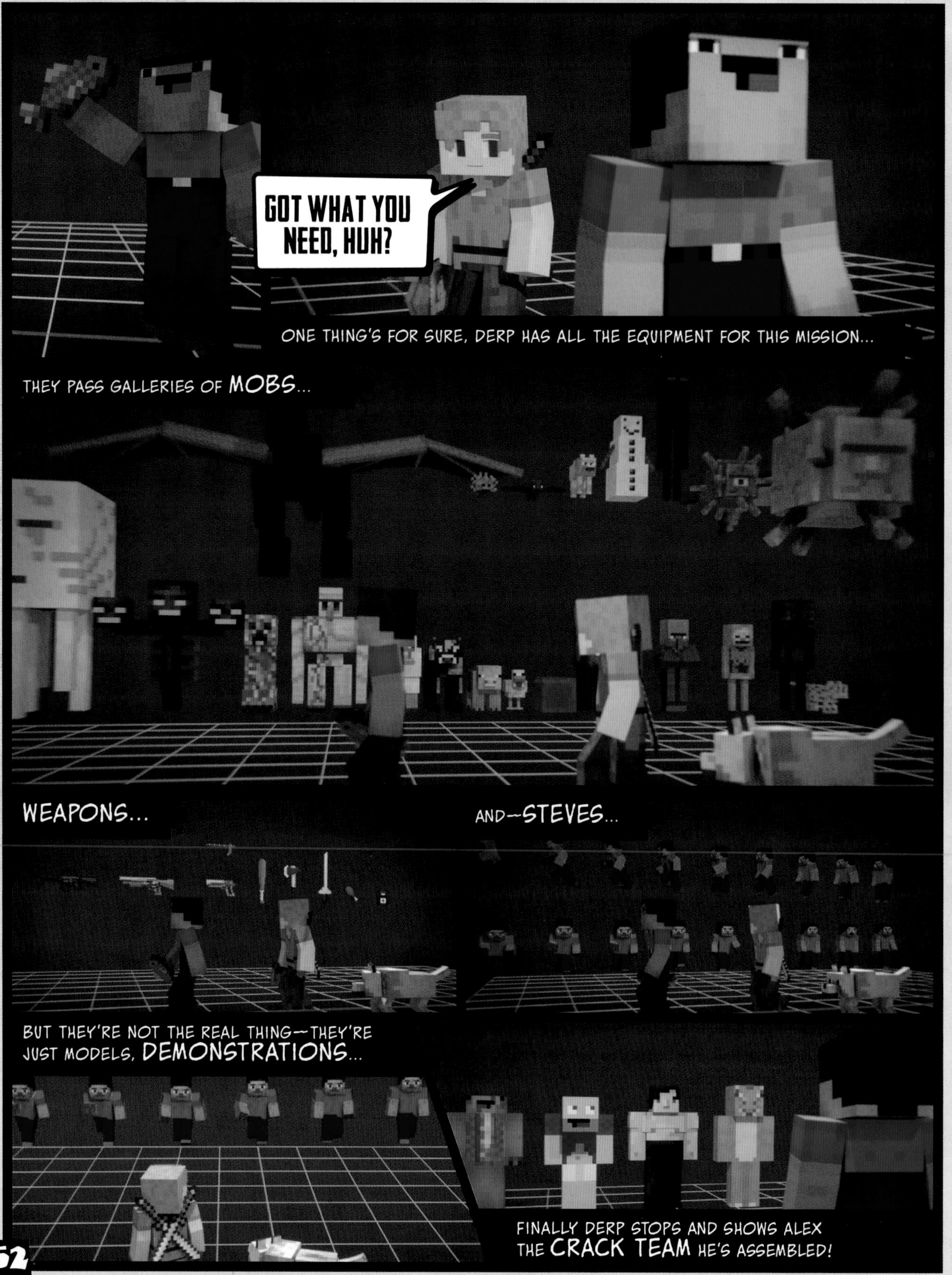
GOT WHAT YOU NEED, HUH?
ONE THING'S FOR SURE, DERP HAS ALL THE EQUIPMENT FOR THIS MISSION...
THEY PASS GALLERIES OF MOBS...
WEAPONS...
AND—STEVES...
BUT THEY'RE NOT THE REAL THING—THEY'RE JUST MODELS, DEMONSTRATIONS...
FINALLY DERP STOPS AND SHOWS ALEX THE CRACK TEAM HE'S ASSEMBLED!

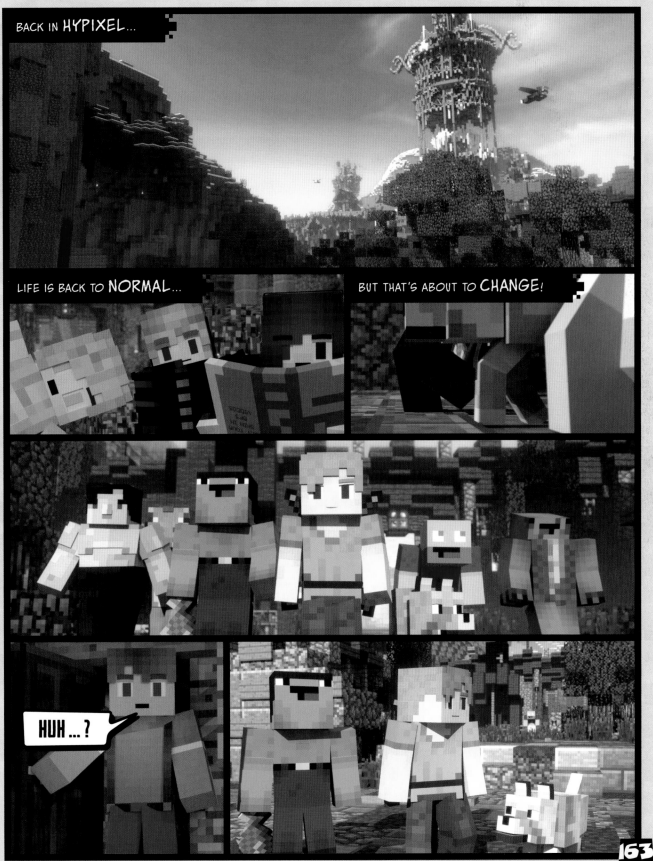

BACK IN **HYPIXEL**...

LIFE IS BACK TO **NORMAL**...

BUT THAT'S ABOUT TO **CHANGE!**

HUH ... ?

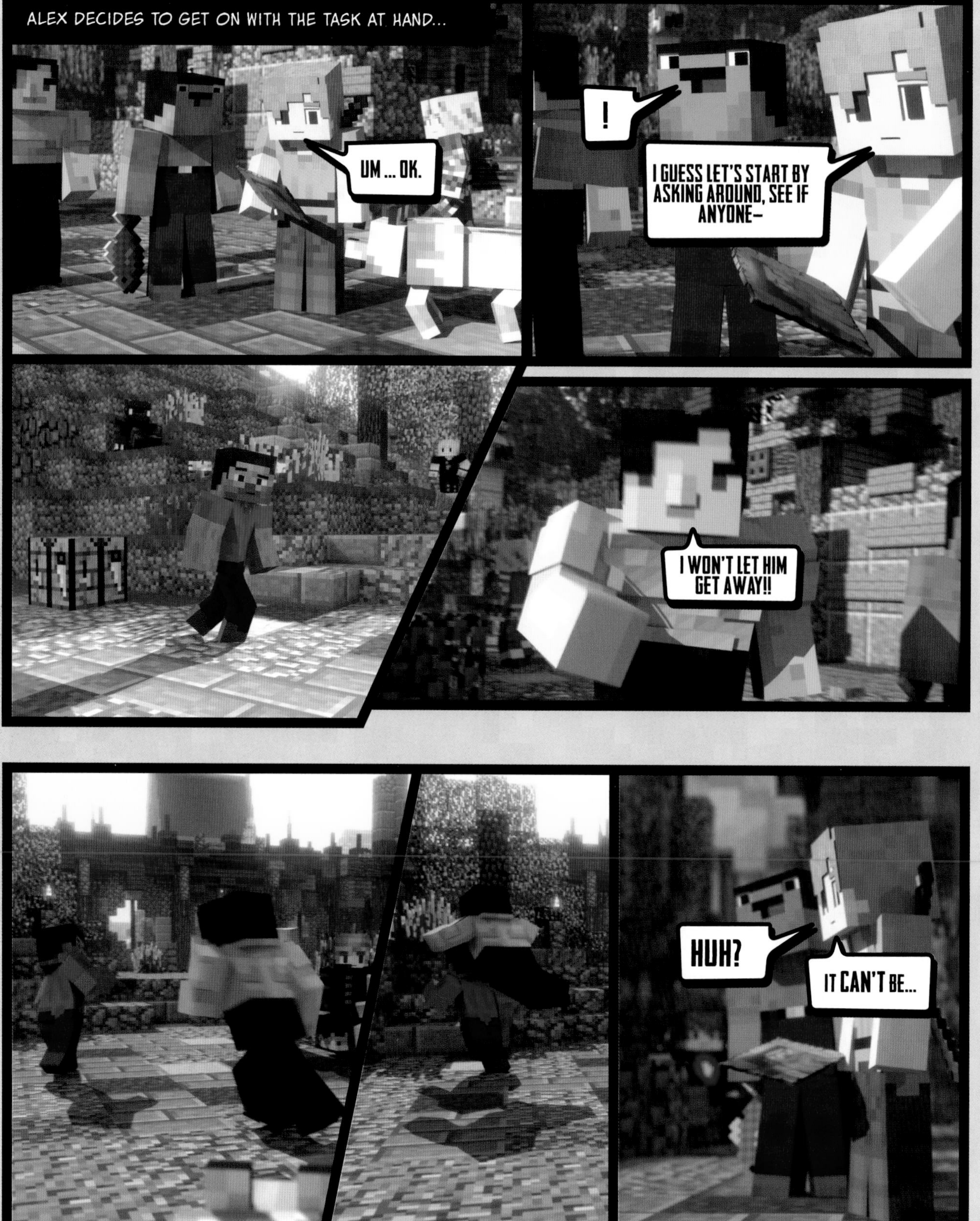
ALEX DECIDES TO GET ON WITH THE TASK AT HAND...
UM ... OK.
!
I GUESS LET'S START BY ASKING AROUND, SEE IF ANYONE–
I WON'T LET HIM GET AWAY!!
HUH?
IT CAN'T BE...

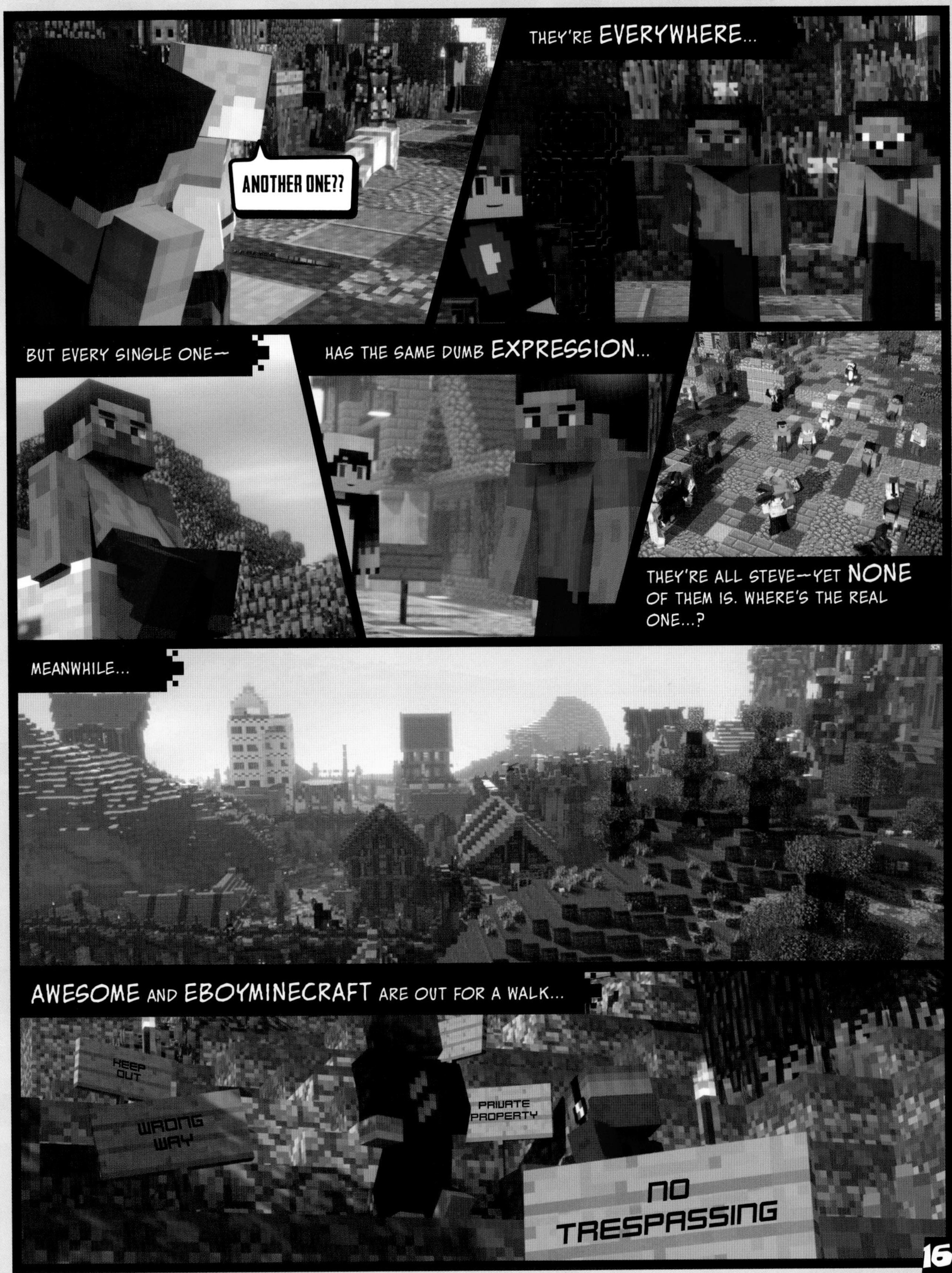
ANOTHER ONE??
THEY'RE EVERYWHERE...
BUT EVERY SINGLE ONE—
HAS THE SAME DUMB EXPRESSION...
THEY'RE ALL STEVE—YET NONE OF THEM IS. WHERE'S THE REAL ONE...?
MEANWHILE...
AWESOME AND EBOYMINECRAFT ARE OUT FOR A WALK...
KEEP OUT
WRONG WAY
PRIVATE PROPERTY
NO TRESPASSING

I WONDER WHY NO ONE COMES UP HERE...

THIS PLACE IS COOL...

WOAH—WAIT...

THE FIGURE TURNS TO FACE THEM~

AND THEY BOTH FLEE!

YAAAAAA

BUT IF THEY'D STUCK AROUND, THEY MIGHT HAVE NOTICED THE FIGURE'S **OTHER** EYE...

STEVE IS TORMENTED BY VISIONS OF HIS LIFE BEFORE~

A BATTLE IS GOING ON INSIDE HIM~

BECAUSE WHILE HE LIVES, SO DOES **HEROBRINE!**

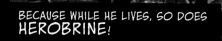

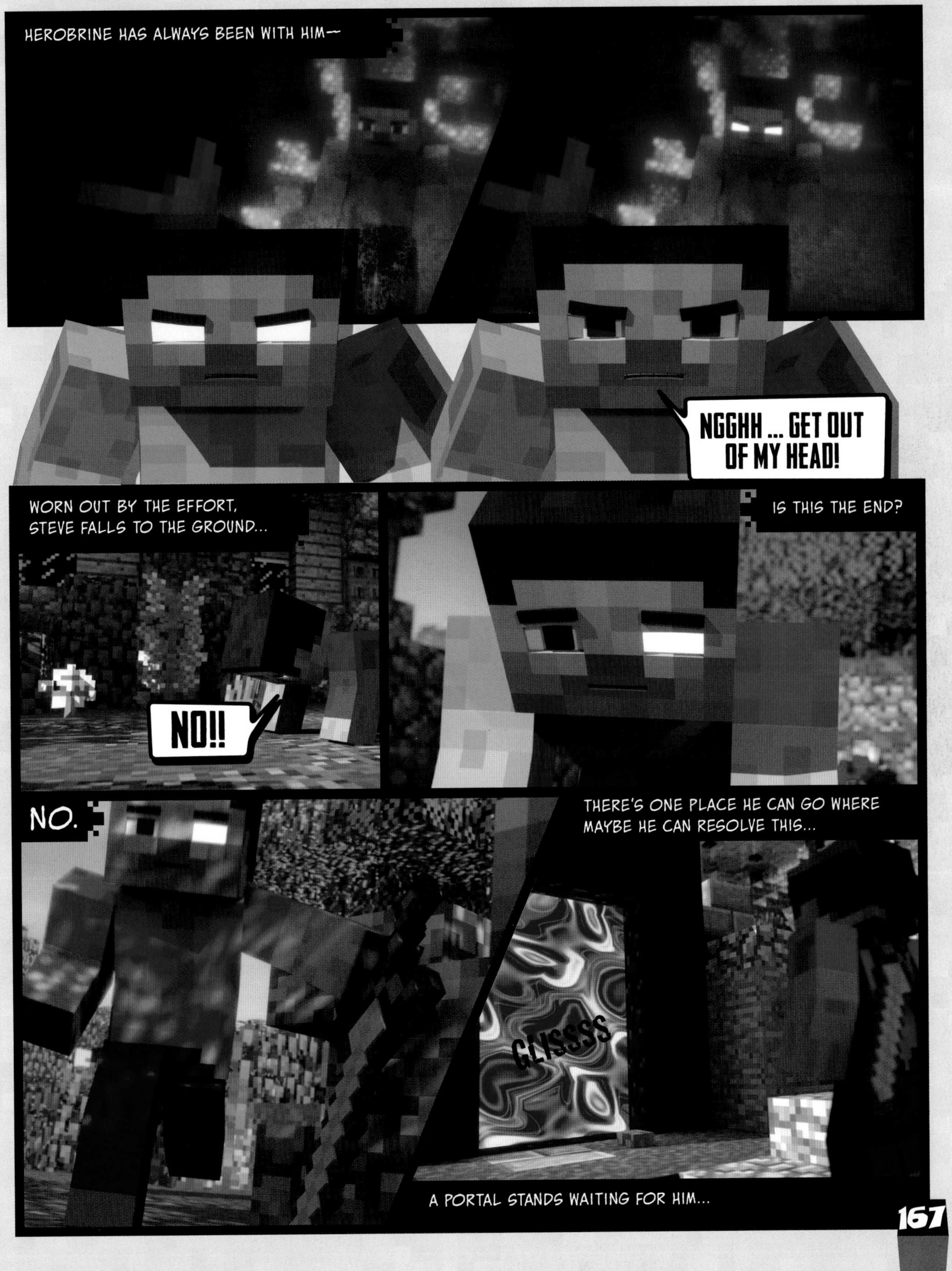

HEROBRINE HAS ALWAYS BEEN WITH HIM—
NGGHH ... GET OUT OF MY HEAD!
WORN OUT BY THE EFFORT, STEVE FALLS TO THE GROUND...
NO!!
IS THIS THE END?
NO.
THERE'S ONE PLACE HE CAN GO WHERE MAYBE HE CAN RESOLVE THIS...
GLISSSS
A PORTAL STANDS WAITING FOR HIM...

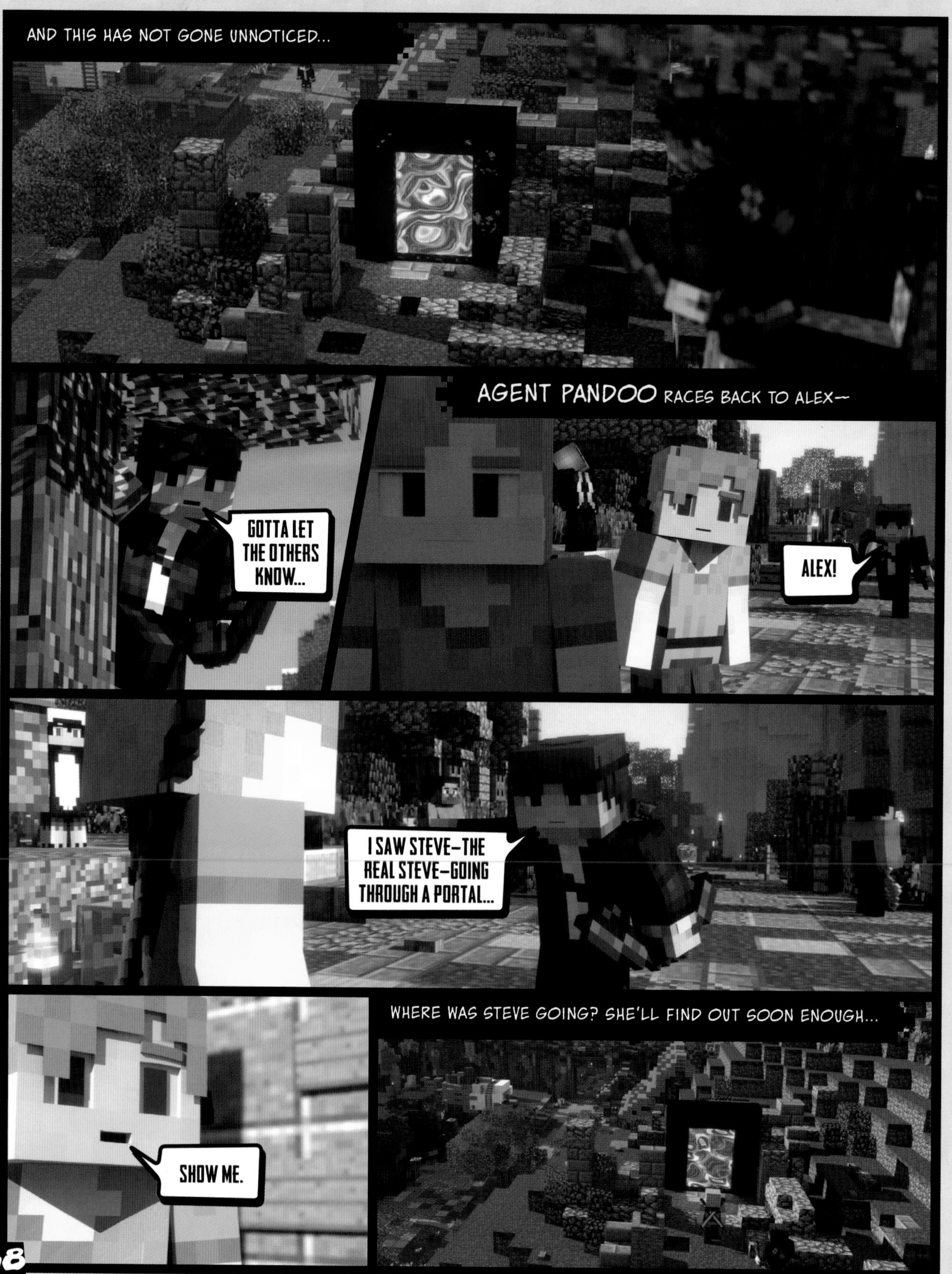
AND THIS HAS NOT GONE UNNOTICED...
GOTTA LET THE OTHERS KNOW...
AGENT PANDOO RACES BACK TO ALEX—
ALEX!
I SAW STEVE—THE REAL STEVE—GOING THROUGH A PORTAL...
SHOW ME.
WHERE WAS STEVE GOING? SHE'LL FIND OUT SOON ENOUGH...

CHAPTER 8

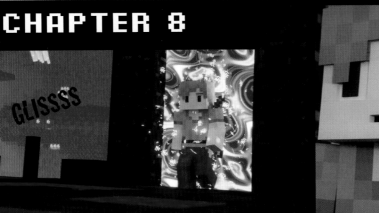

GLISSSS

HUH.

THE NETHER.

AND ALEX WON'T BE FACING IT ALONE~

TOGETHER THEY WALK THROUGH VALLEYS OF FIRE...

GLISSSS

BUT DERP SENSES ONE OF THEM SNEAKING UP ON HIM...

IGNORE THE ZOMBIE PIGMEN AND MAYBE THEY'LL IGNORE US...

AND HE PREPARES TO STRIKE FIRST!

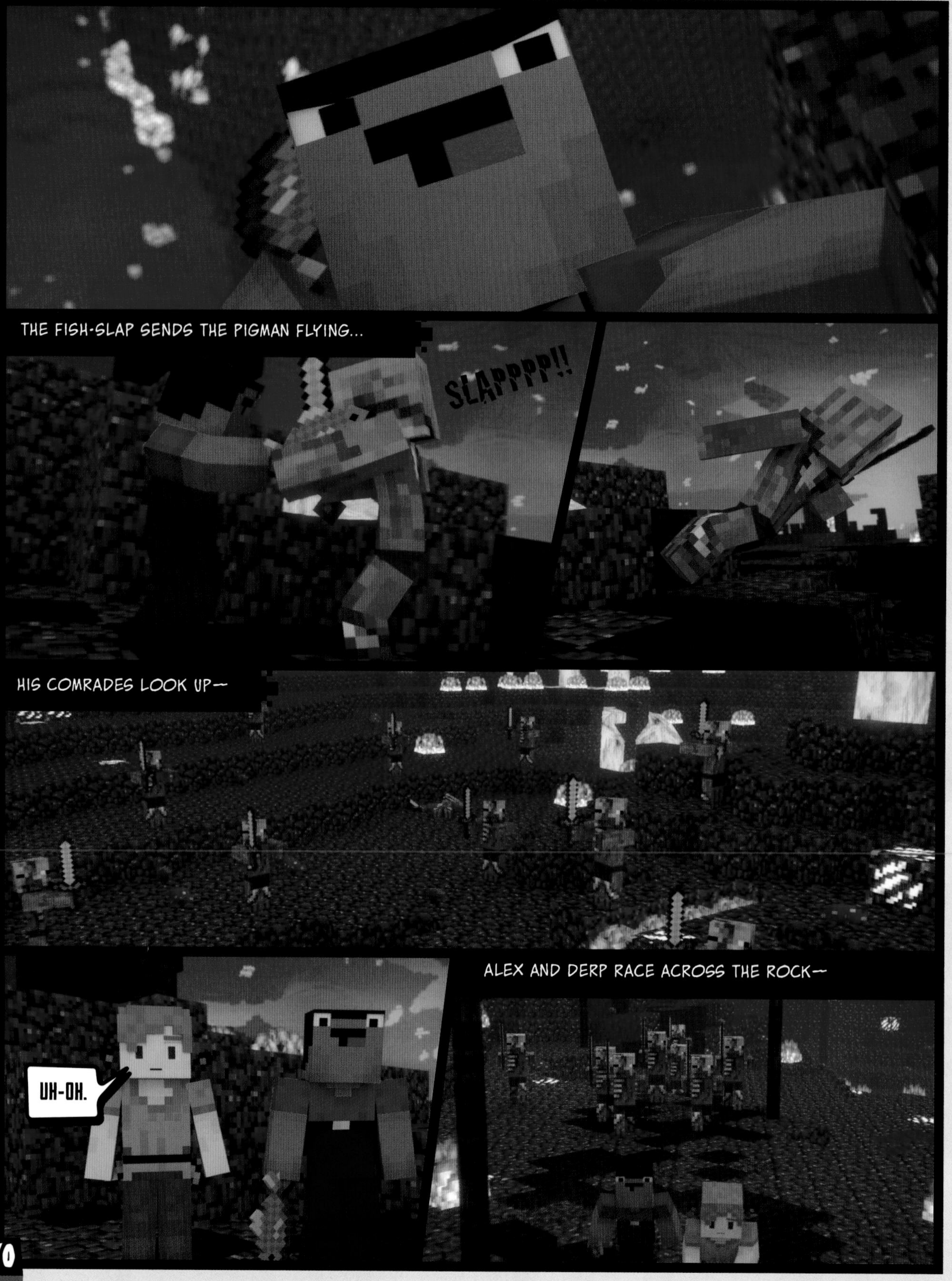
THE FISH-SLAP SENDS THE PIGMAN FLYING...
SLAPPPP!!
HIS COMRADES LOOK UP—
UH-OH.
ALEX AND DERP RACE ACROSS THE ROCK—

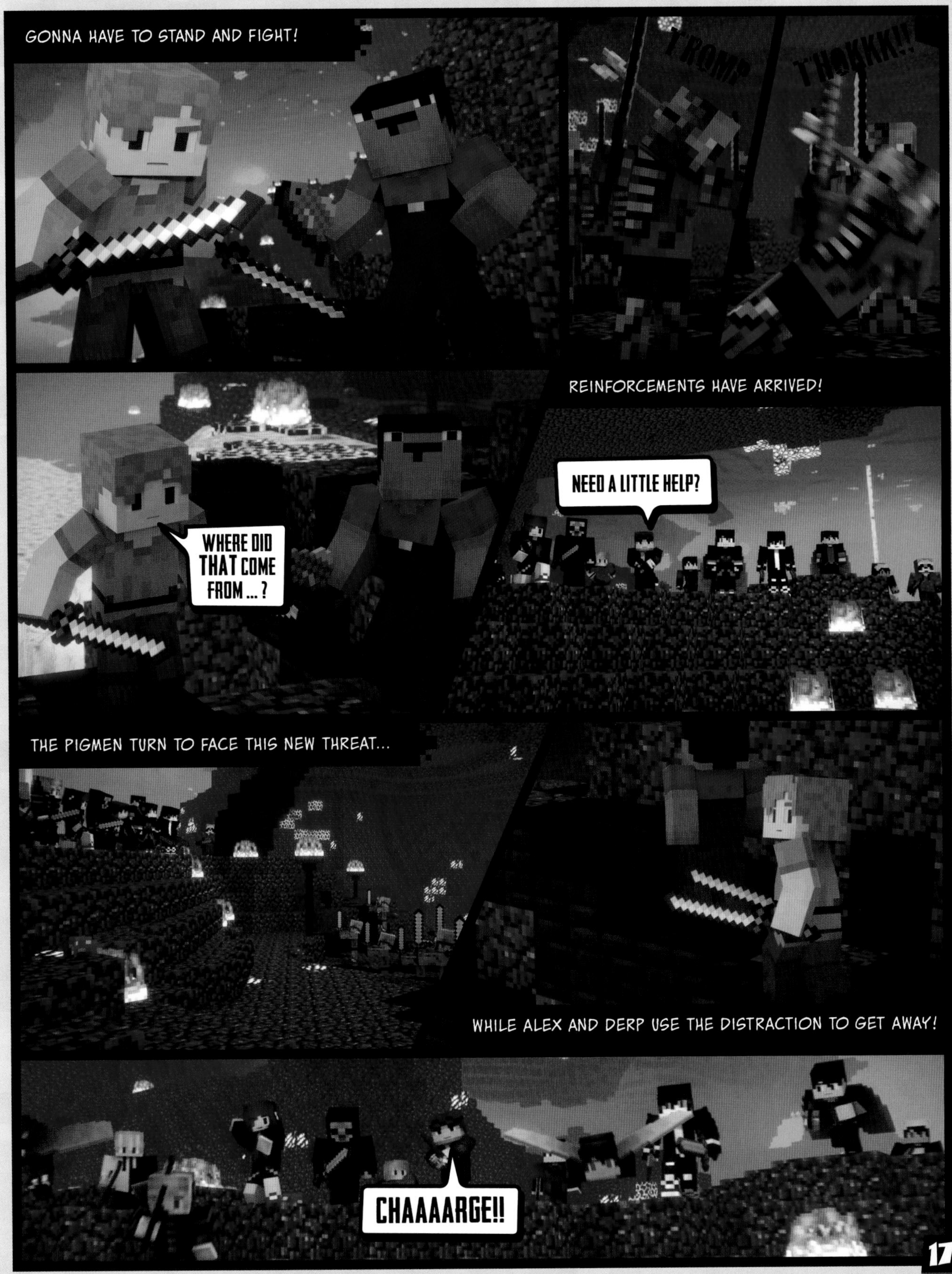
GONNA HAVE TO STAND AND FIGHT!
T'ROMP
T'HOKKK!!
REINFORCEMENTS HAVE ARRIVED!
WHERE DID THAT COME FROM ... ?
NEED A LITTLE HELP?
THE PIGMEN TURN TO FACE THIS NEW THREAT...
WHILE ALEX AND DERP USE THE DISTRACTION TO GET AWAY!
CHAAAARGE!!

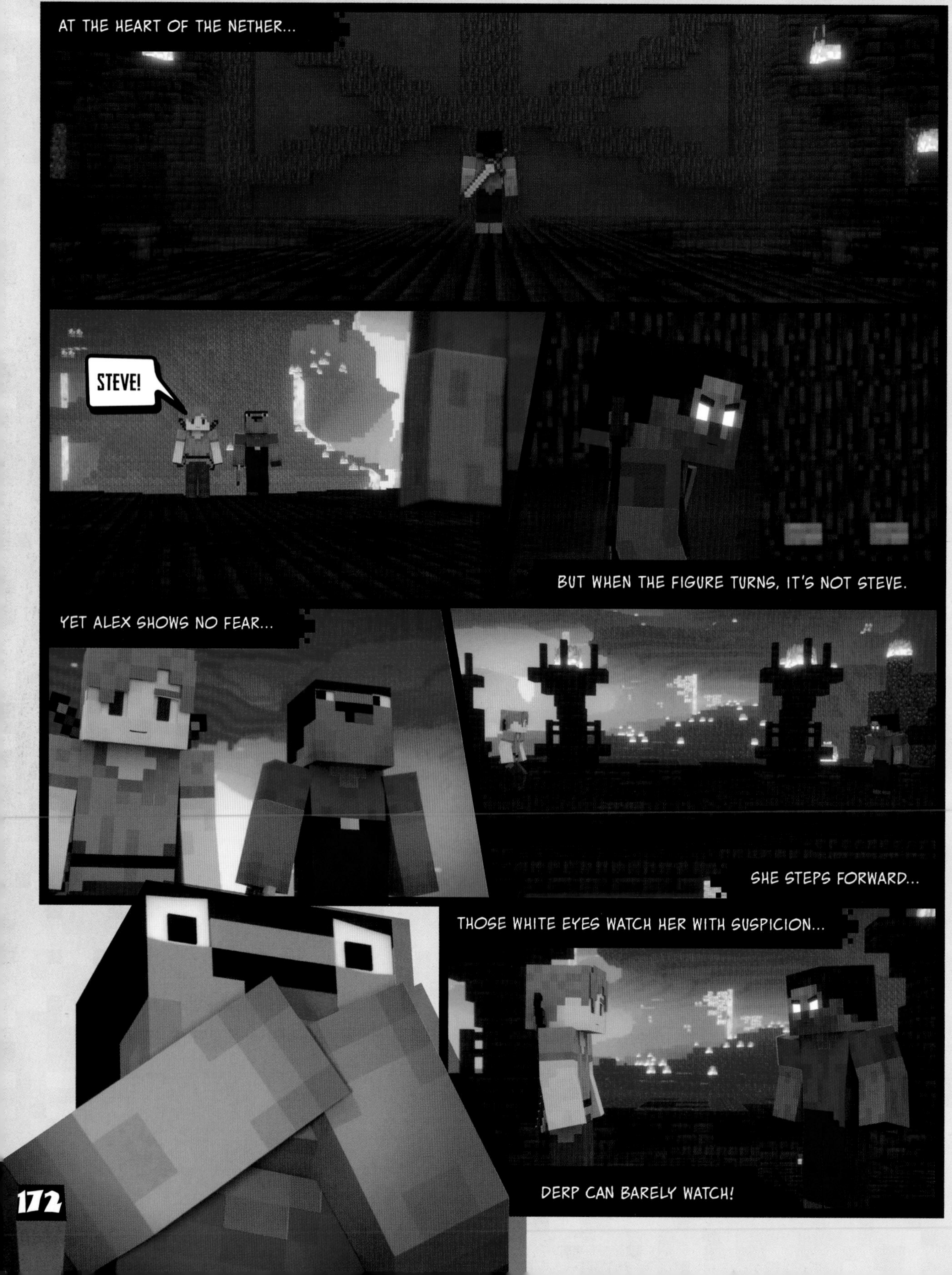
AT THE HEART OF THE NETHER...
STEVE!
BUT WHEN THE FIGURE TURNS, IT'S NOT STEVE.
YET ALEX SHOWS NO FEAR...
SHE STEPS FORWARD...
THOSE WHITE EYES WATCH HER WITH SUSPICION...
DERP CAN BARELY WATCH!

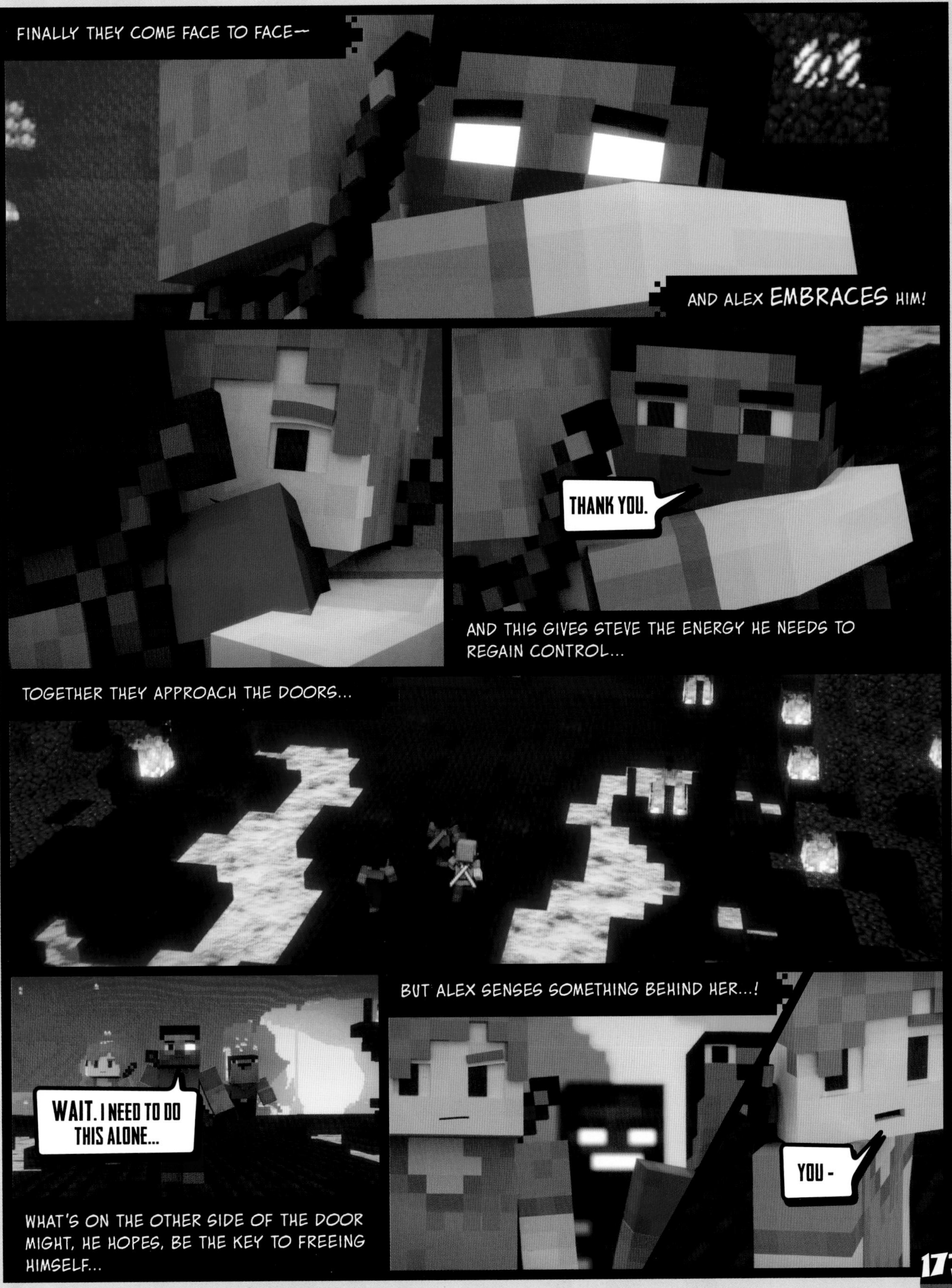
FINALLY THEY COME FACE TO FACE—
AND ALEX EMBRACES HIM!
THANK YOU.
AND THIS GIVES STEVE THE ENERGY HE NEEDS TO REGAIN CONTROL...
TOGETHER THEY APPROACH THE DOORS...
WAIT. I NEED TO DO THIS ALONE...
WHAT'S ON THE OTHER SIDE OF THE DOOR MIGHT, HE HOPES, BE THE KEY TO FREEING HIMSELF...
BUT ALEX SENSES SOMETHING BEHIND HER...!
YOU -

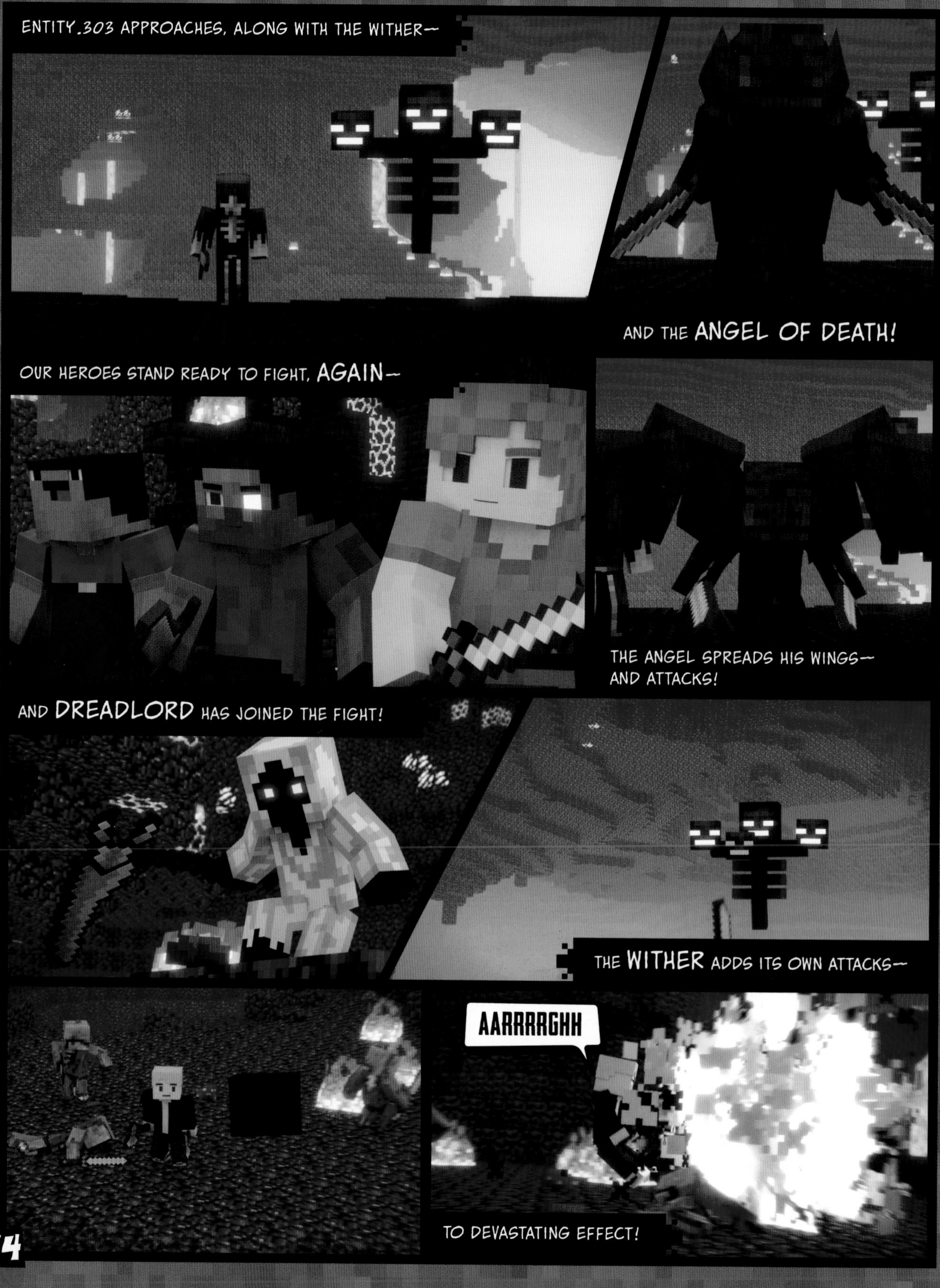
ENTITY_303 APPROACHES, ALONG WITH THE WITHER—
AND THE ANGEL OF DEATH!
OUR HEROES STAND READY TO FIGHT, AGAIN—
THE ANGEL SPREADS HIS WINGS—
AND ATTACKS!
AND DREADLORD HAS JOINED THE FIGHT!
THE WITHER ADDS ITS OWN ATTACKS—
AARRRRGHH
TO DEVASTATING EFFECT!

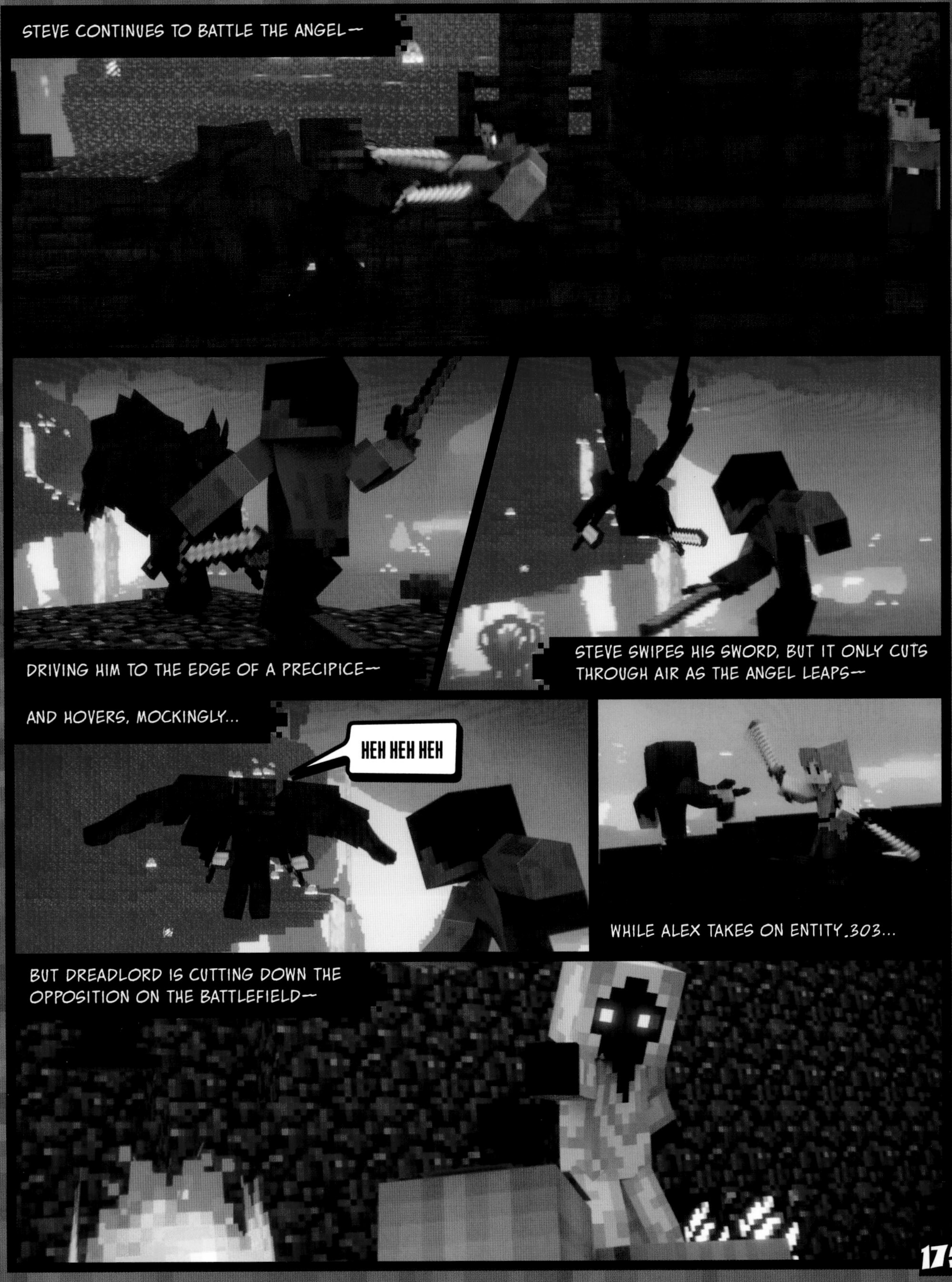
STEVE CONTINUES TO BATTLE THE ANGEL—
DRIVING HIM TO THE EDGE OF A PRECIPICE—
STEVE SWIPES HIS SWORD, BUT IT ONLY CUTS THROUGH AIR AS THE ANGEL LEAPS—
AND HOVERS, MOCKINGLY...
HEH HEH HEH
WHILE ALEX TAKES ON ENTITY_303...
BUT DREADLORD IS CUTTING DOWN THE OPPOSITION ON THE BATTLEFIELD—

THE SCYTHE FLIES BACK THROUGH THE AIR TOWARD DREADLORD...

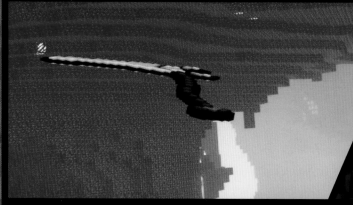

BUT THEN IT'S CAUGHT BY ANOTHER HAND~

AS ARBY'S FRIEND **SPINTOWN** TAUNTS HIM~

I'VE GOT YOUR TOY.

DREADLORD CAN ONLY LOOK ON IN AMAZEMENT~

DREADLORD LOOKS AROUND, AND COMES TO A QUICK DECISION~

I SURRENDER!

STEVE IS RUSHING TO HIS FRIEND'S AID~

ALEX! I'M COMING!

BUT BEHIND HIM, THE WITHER IS RETURNING~

176

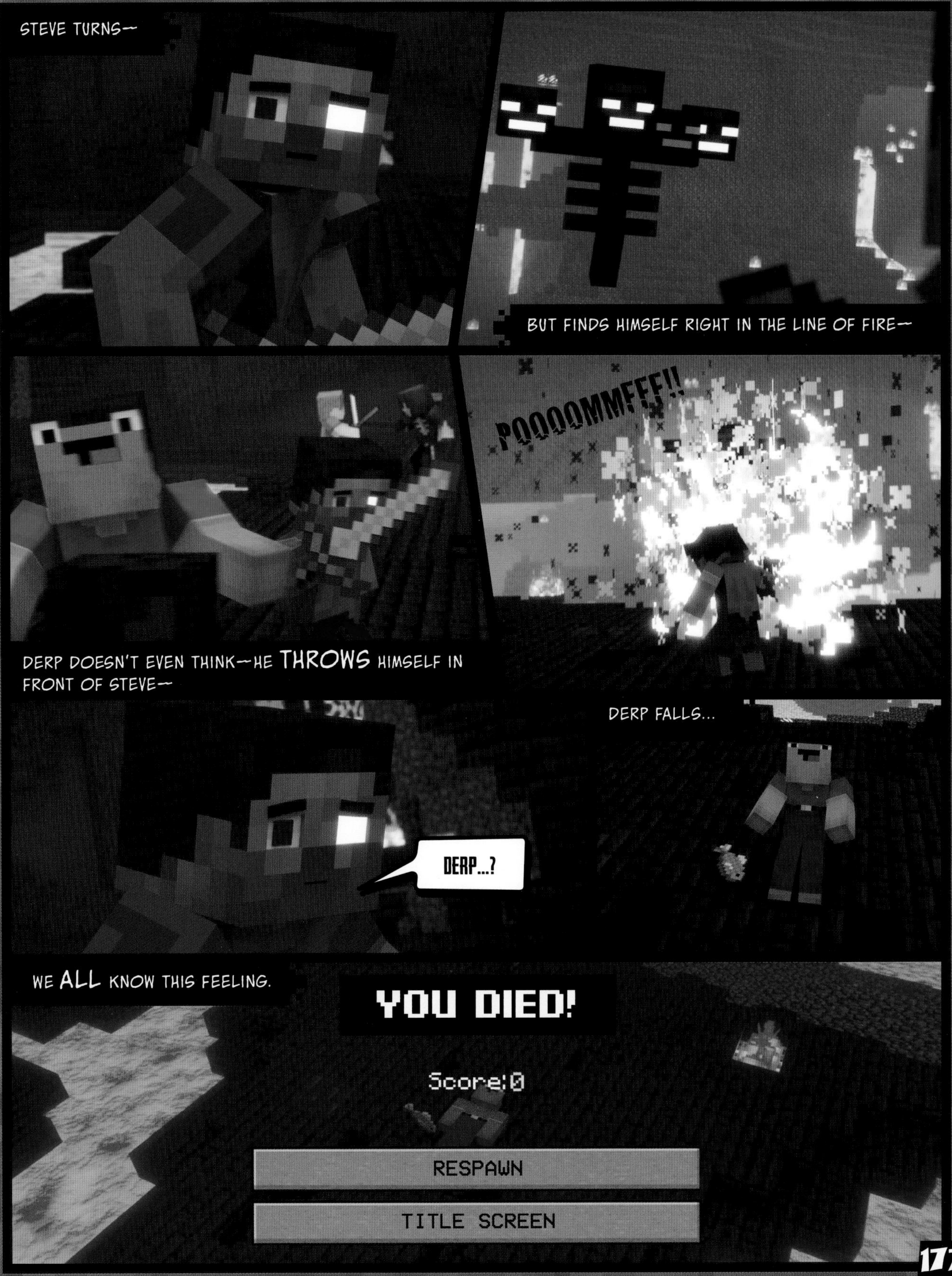
STEVE TURNS—
BUT FINDS HIMSELF RIGHT IN THE LINE OF FIRE—
DERP DOESN'T EVEN THINK—HE THROWS HIMSELF IN FRONT OF STEVE—
POOOOMMFFF!!
DERP FALLS...
DERP...?
WE ALL KNOW THIS FEELING.
YOU DIED!
Score: 0
RESPAWN
TITLE SCREEN

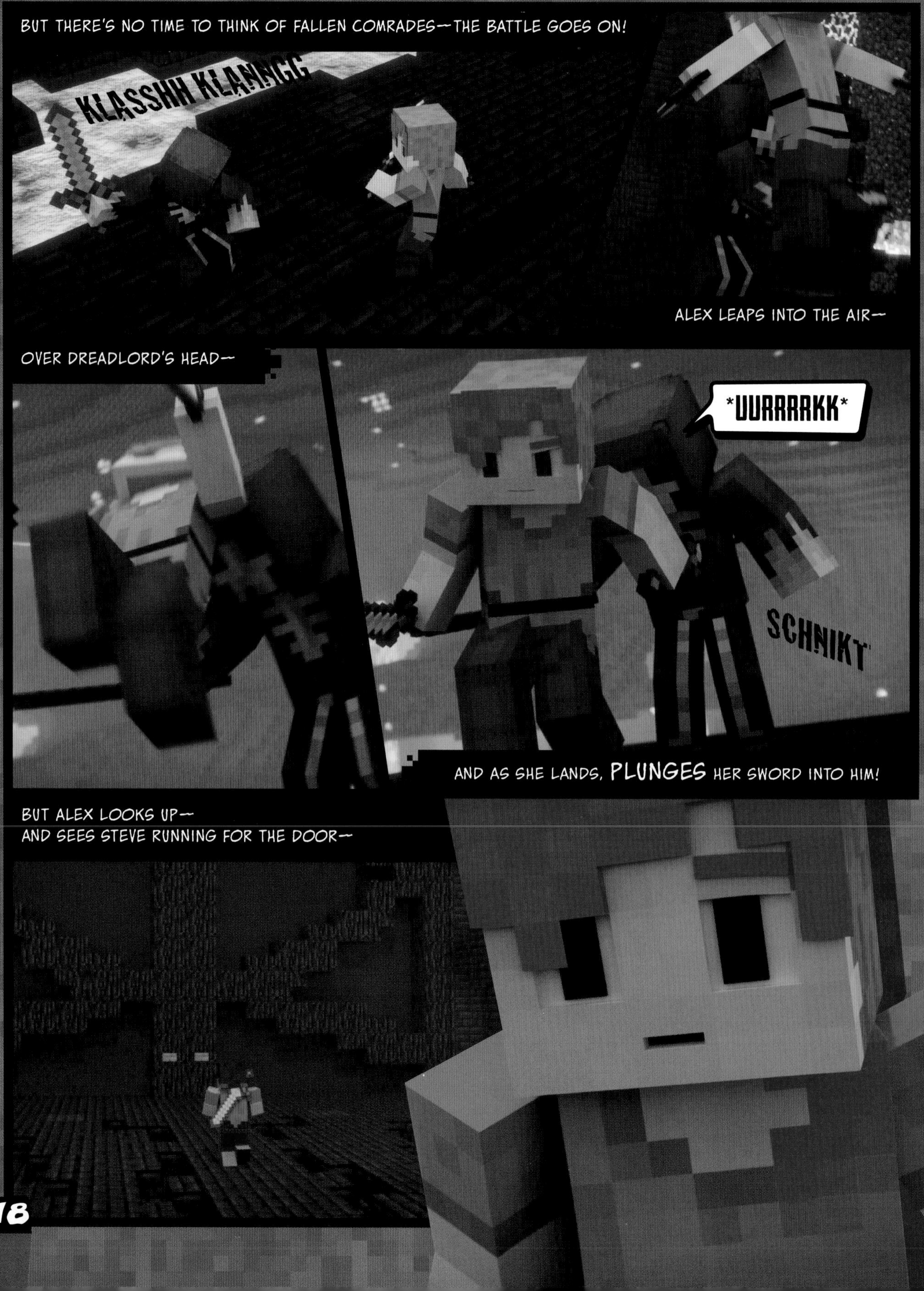
BUT THERE'S NO TIME TO THINK OF FALLEN COMRADES—THE BATTLE GOES ON!
KLASSHH KLANNGG
ALEX LEAPS INTO THE AIR—
OVER DREADLORD'S HEAD—
UURRRRKK
SCHNIKT
AND AS SHE LANDS, PLUNGES HER SWORD INTO HIM!
BUT ALEX LOOKS UP—
AND SEES STEVE RUNNING FOR THE DOOR—

CRRREEEAAAAKK...

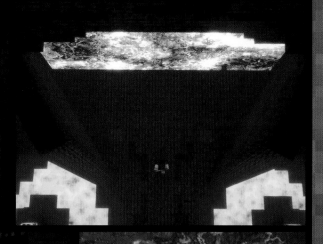

CAUTIOUSLY HE APPROACHES THE SHIMMERING WALL...

AND PLUNGES HIS HAND INTO IT—

THE WALL **GLOWS**—

REFLECTS HIM BACK AT HIMSELF...

BUT IT'S MORE THAN JUST A REFLECTION!

TWO STEVES, BOTH HALF HEROBRINE...

BUT ON THE OTHER SIDE ... IS ANOTHER **ALEX**—HER **DARK REFLECTION!**

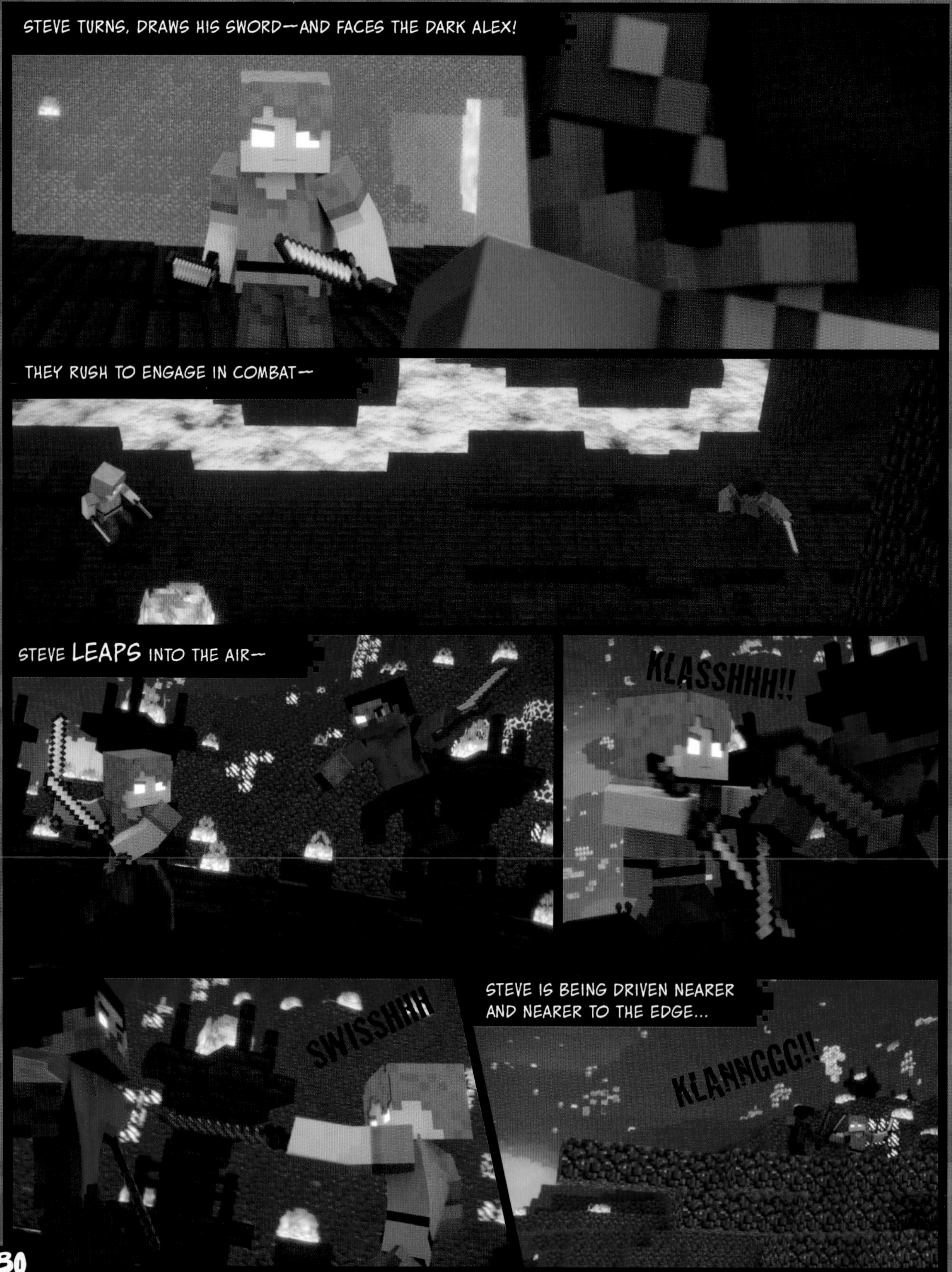
STEVE TURNS, DRAWS HIS SWORD—AND FACES THE DARK ALEX!
THEY RUSH TO ENGAGE IN COMBAT—
STEVE LEAPS INTO THE AIR—
KLASSHHH!!
SWISSHHH
STEVE IS BEING DRIVEN NEARER AND NEARER TO THE EDGE...
KLANNGGG!!

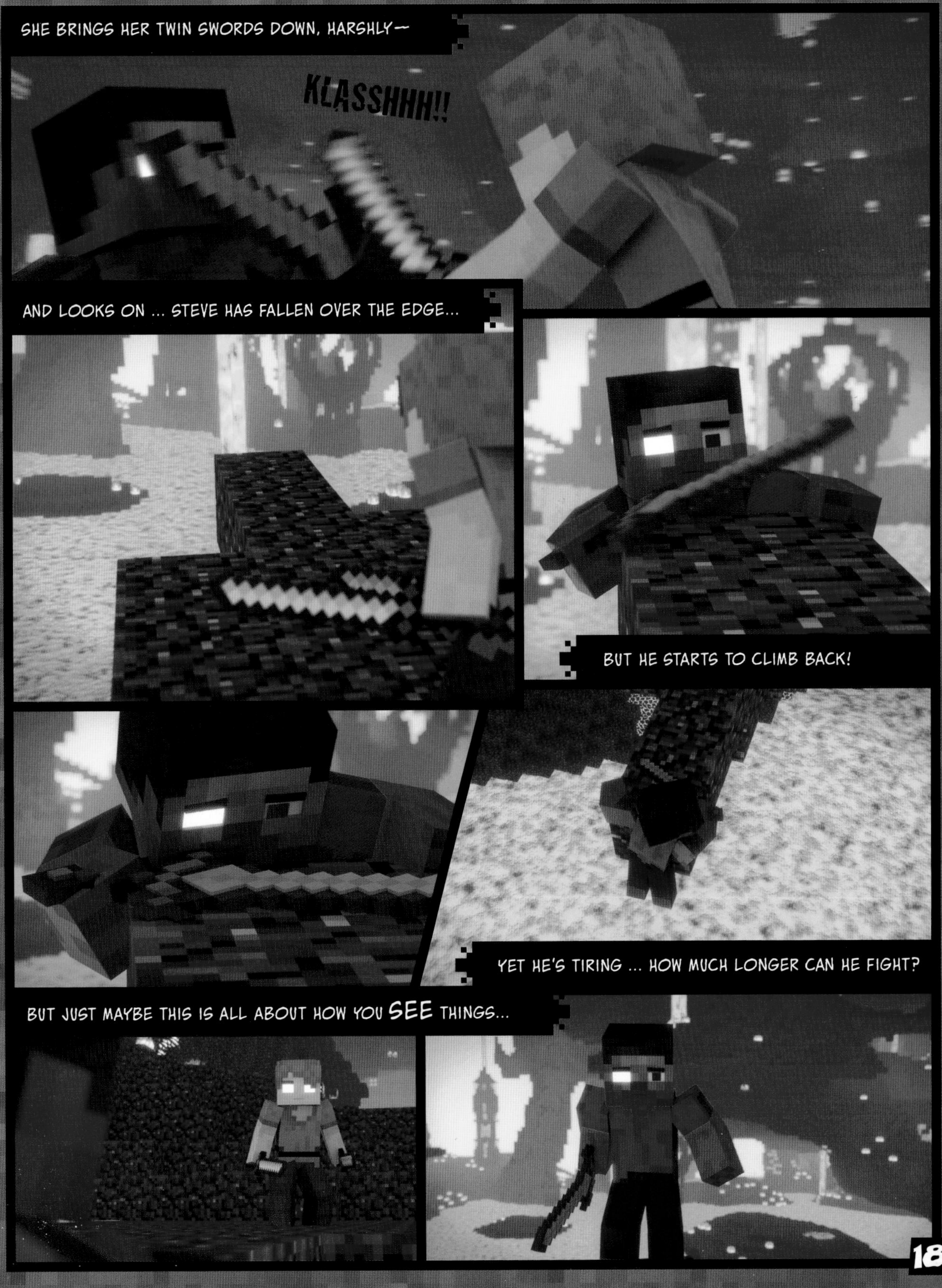
SHE BRINGS HER TWIN SWORDS DOWN, HARSHLY—
KLASSHHH!!
AND LOOKS ON ... STEVE HAS FALLEN OVER THE EDGE...
BUT HE STARTS TO CLIMB BACK!
YET HE'S TIRING ... HOW MUCH LONGER CAN HE FIGHT?
BUT JUST MAYBE THIS IS ALL ABOUT HOW YOU SEE THINGS...

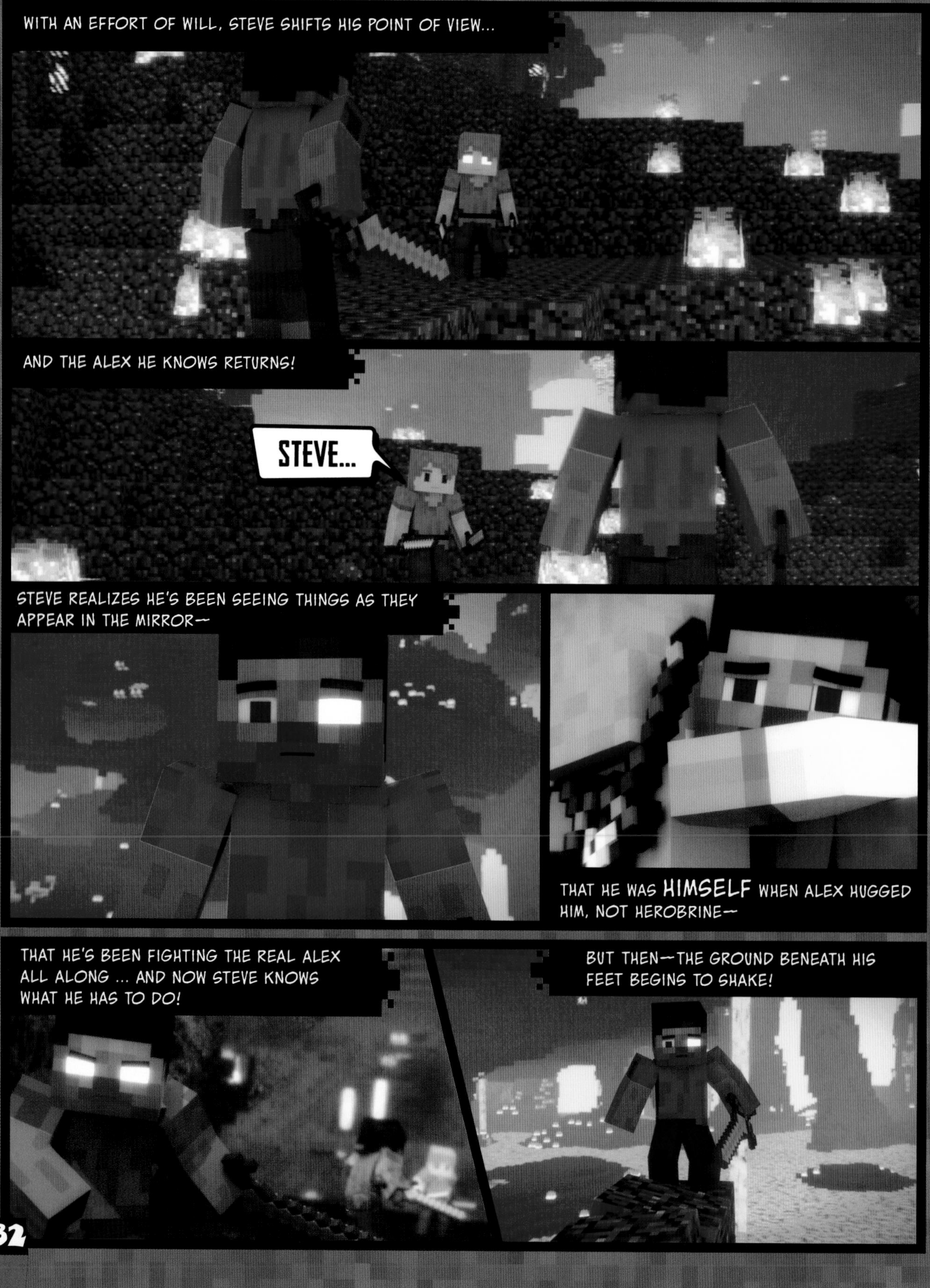
WITH AN EFFORT OF WILL, STEVE SHIFTS HIS POINT OF VIEW...
AND THE ALEX HE KNOWS RETURNS!
STEVE...
STEVE REALIZES HE'S BEEN SEEING THINGS AS THEY APPEAR IN THE MIRROR—
THAT HE WAS HIMSELF WHEN ALEX HUGGED HIM, NOT HEROBRINE—
THAT HE'S BEEN FIGHTING THE REAL ALEX ALL ALONG ... AND NOW STEVE KNOWS WHAT HE HAS TO DO!
BUT THEN—THE GROUND BENEATH HIS FEET BEGINS TO SHAKE!

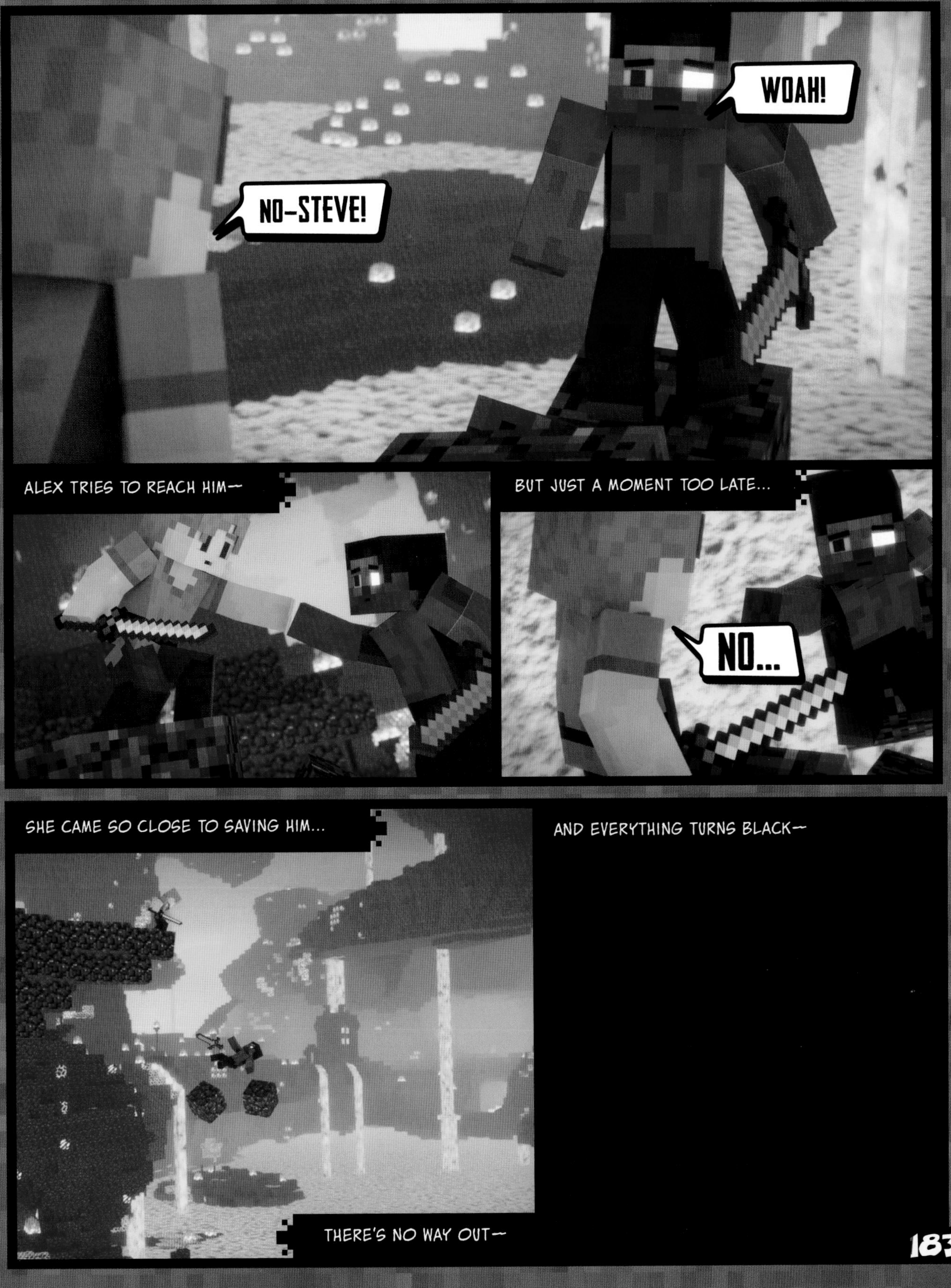
WOAH!
NO-STEVE!
ALEX TRIES TO REACH HIM—
BUT JUST A MOMENT TOO LATE...
NO...
SHE CAME SO CLOSE TO SAVING HIM...
THERE'S NO WAY OUT—
AND EVERYTHING TURNS BLACK—

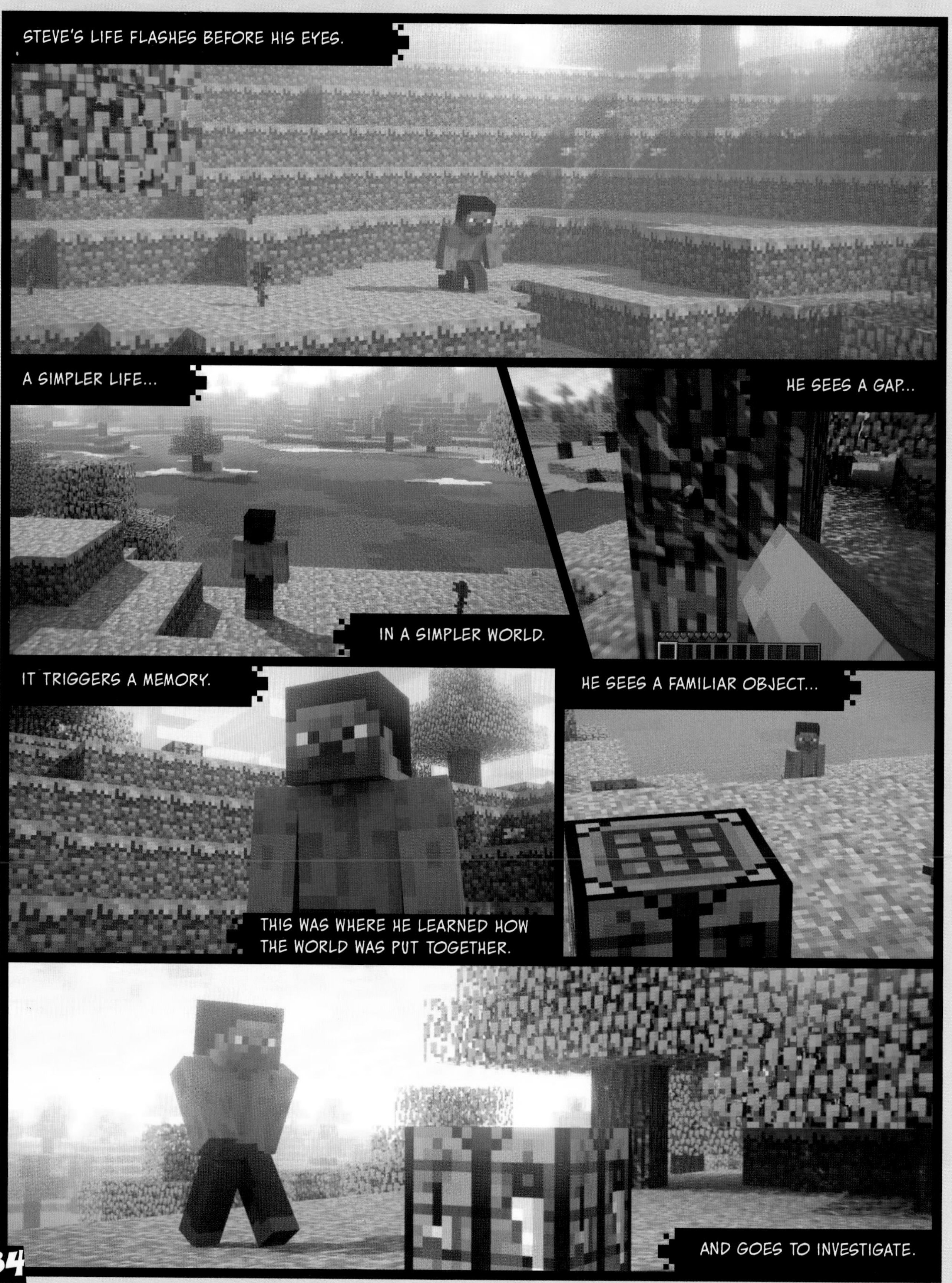
STEVE'S LIFE FLASHES BEFORE HIS EYES.
A SIMPLER LIFE...
IN A SIMPLER WORLD.
HE SEES A GAP...
IT TRIGGERS A MEMORY.
THIS WAS WHERE HE LEARNED HOW THE WORLD WAS PUT TOGETHER.
HE SEES A FAMILIAR OBJECT...
AND GOES TO INVESTIGATE.

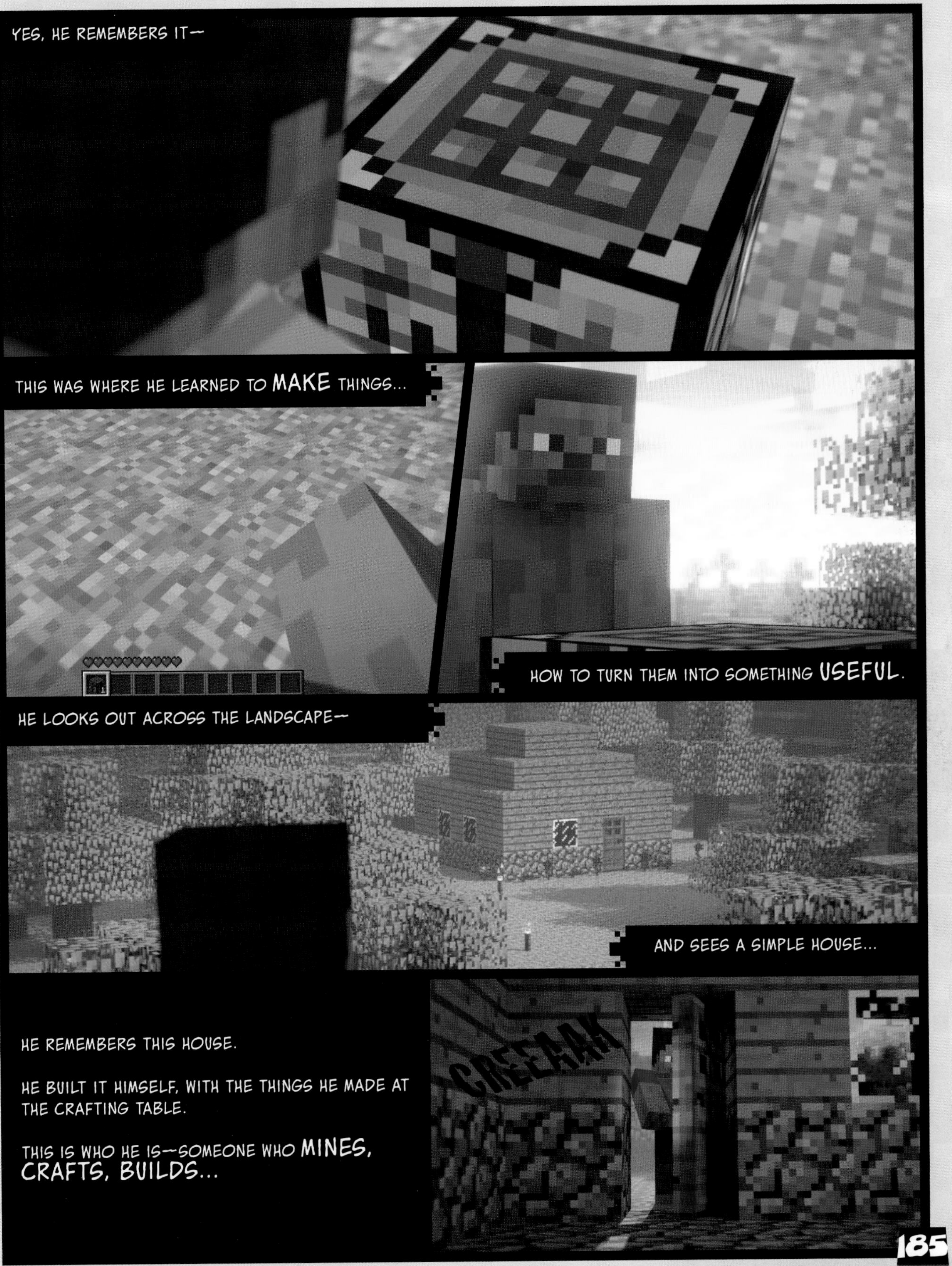
YES, HE REMEMBERS IT—
THIS WAS WHERE HE LEARNED TO MAKE THINGS...
HOW TO TURN THEM INTO SOMETHING USEFUL.
HE LOOKS OUT ACROSS THE LANDSCAPE—
AND SEES A SIMPLE HOUSE...
HE REMEMBERS THIS HOUSE.
HE BUILT IT HIMSELF, WITH THE THINGS HE MADE AT THE CRAFTING TABLE.
THIS IS WHO HE IS—SOMEONE WHO MINES, CRAFTS, BUILDS...
CREEAAK

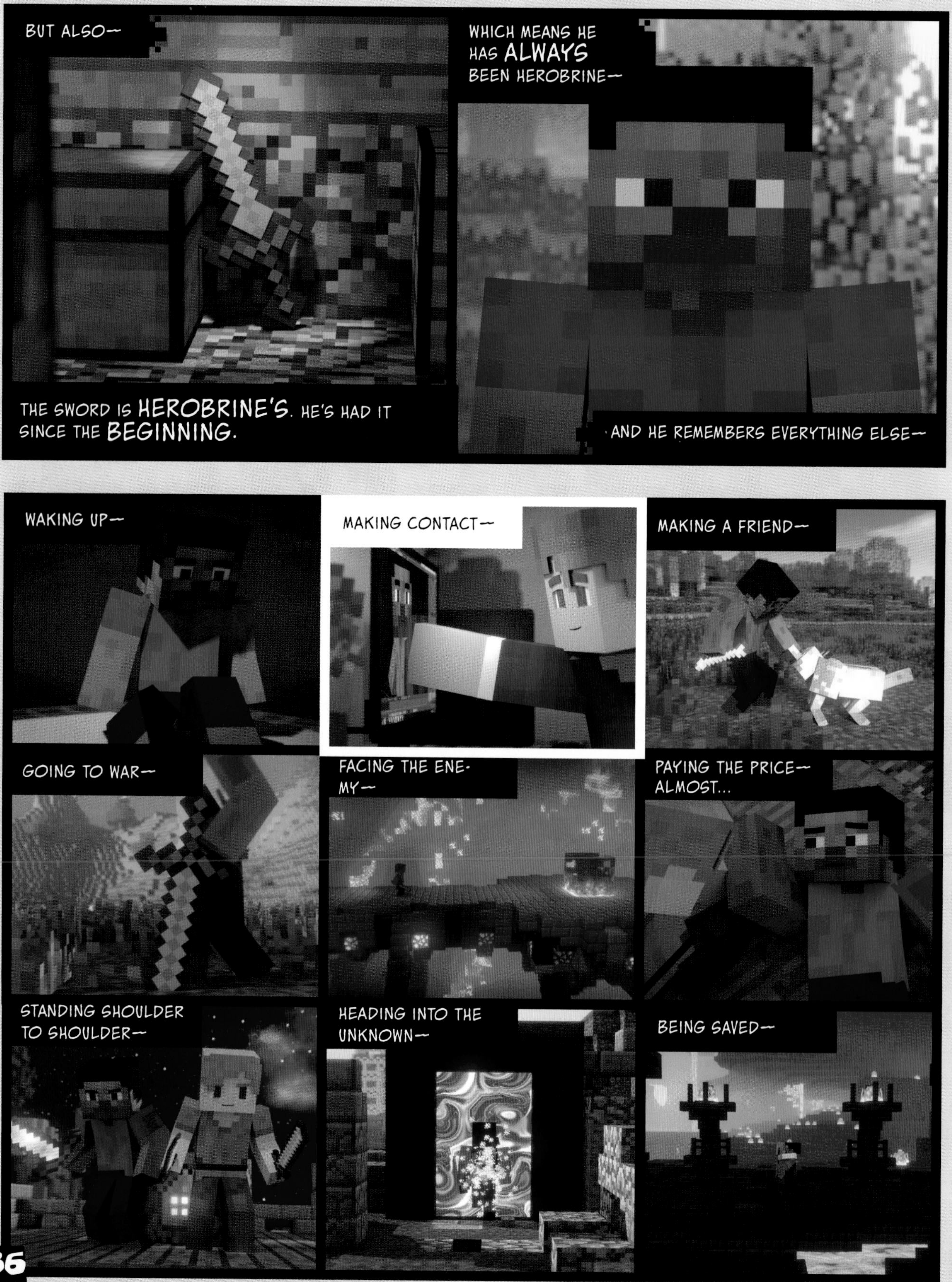

BUT ALSO—
THE SWORD IS HEROBRINE'S. HE'S HAD IT SINCE THE BEGINNING.
WHICH MEANS HE HAS ALWAYS BEEN HEROBRINE—
AND HE REMEMBERS EVERYTHING ELSE—
WAKING UP—
MAKING CONTACT—
MAKING A FRIEND—
GOING TO WAR—
FACING THE ENE-MY—
PAYING THE PRICE—ALMOST...
STANDING SHOULDER TO SHOULDER—
HEADING INTO THE UNKNOWN—
BEING SAVED—

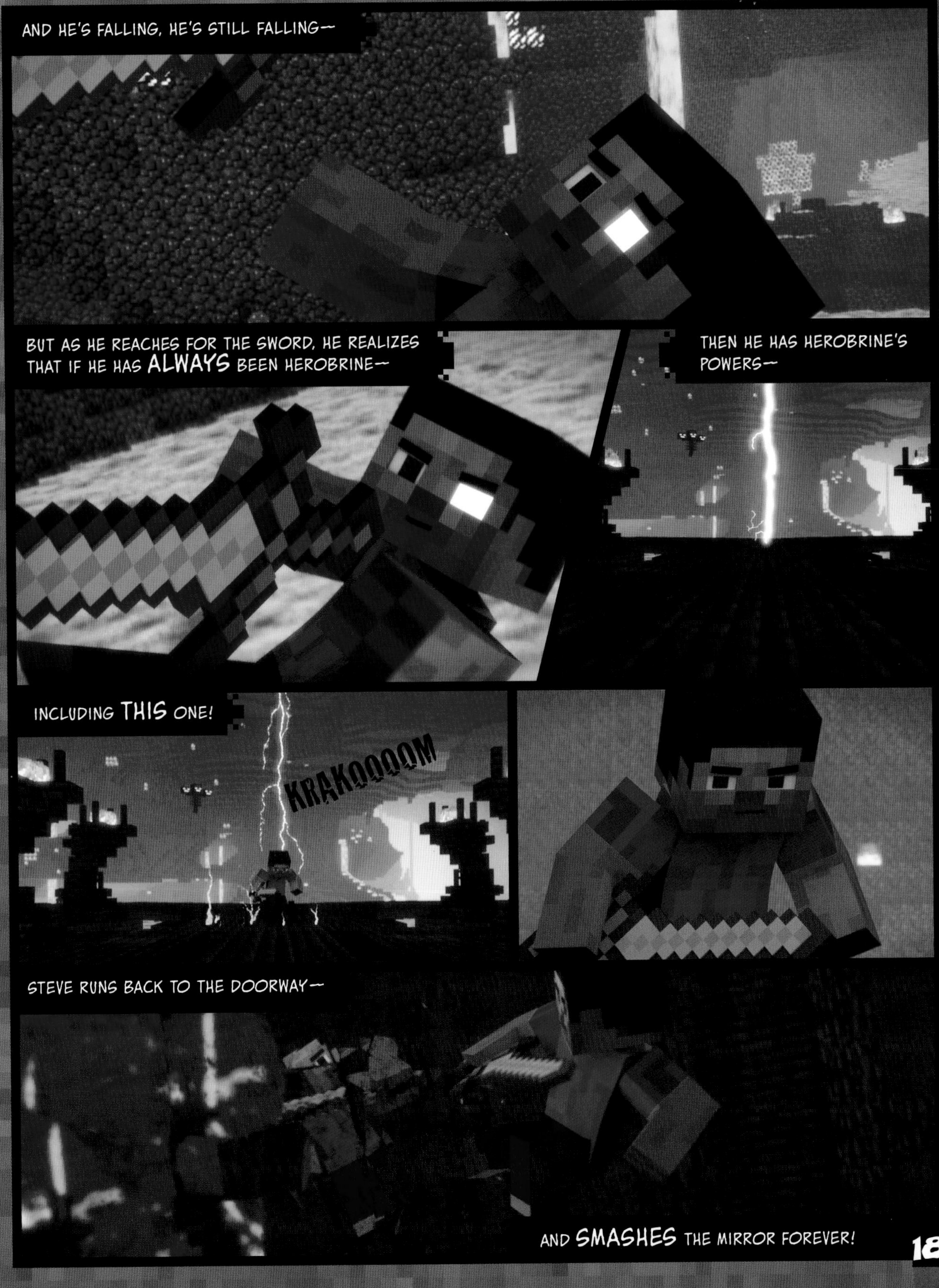
AND HE'S FALLING, HE'S STILL FALLING—
BUT AS HE REACHES FOR THE SWORD, HE REALIZES THAT IF HE HAS ALWAYS BEEN HEROBRINE—
THEN HE HAS HEROBRINE'S POWERS—
INCLUDING THIS ONE!
KRAKOOOOM
STEVE RUNS BACK TO THE DOORWAY—
AND SMASHES THE MIRROR FOREVER!

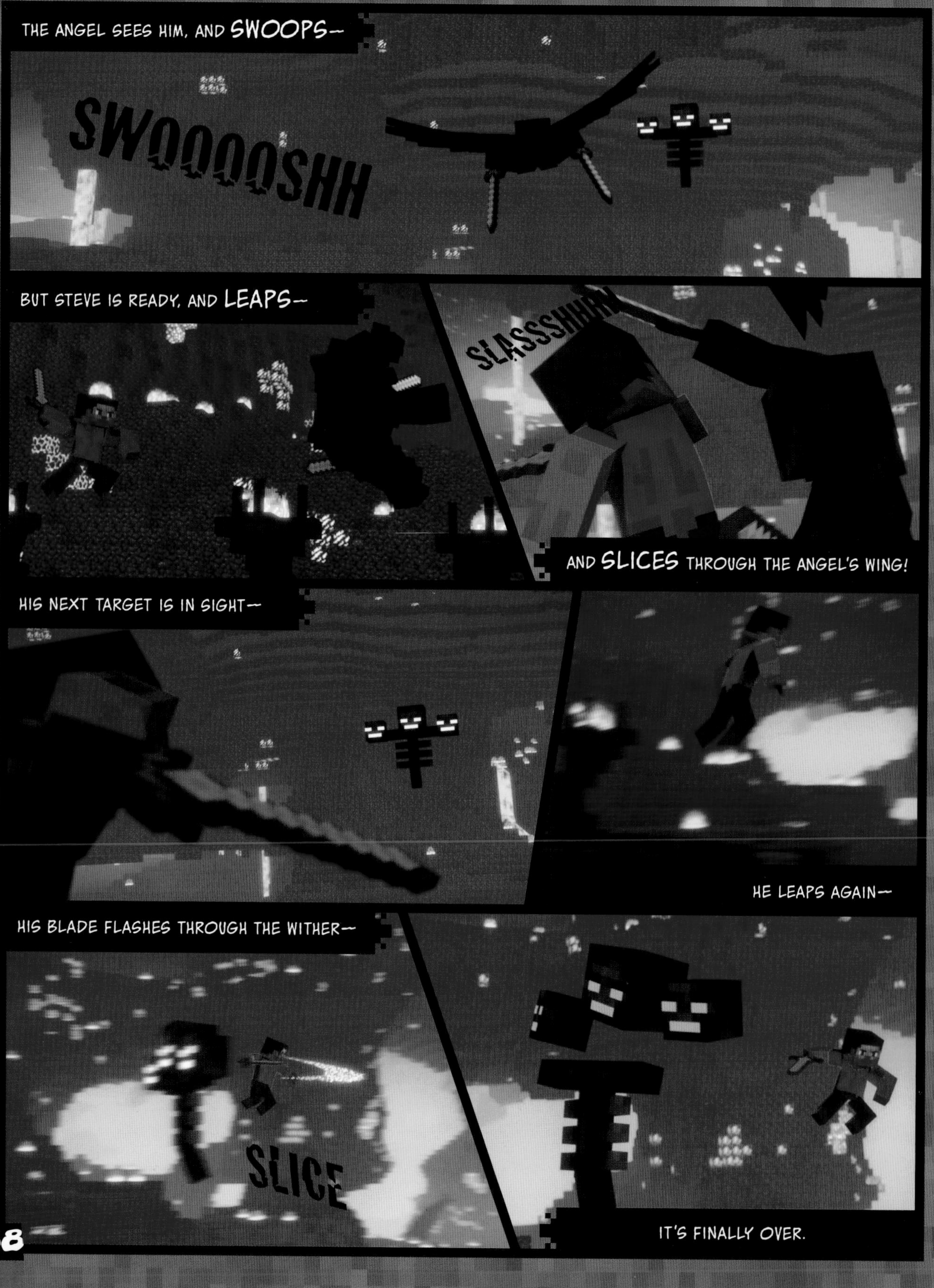
THE ANGEL SEES HIM, AND SWOOPS—
SWOOOOOSHH
BUT STEVE IS READY, AND LEAPS—
SLASSSHHH
AND SLICES THROUGH THE ANGEL'S WING!
HIS NEXT TARGET IS IN SIGHT—
HE LEAPS AGAIN—
HIS BLADE FLASHES THROUGH THE WITHER—
SLICE
IT'S FINALLY OVER.

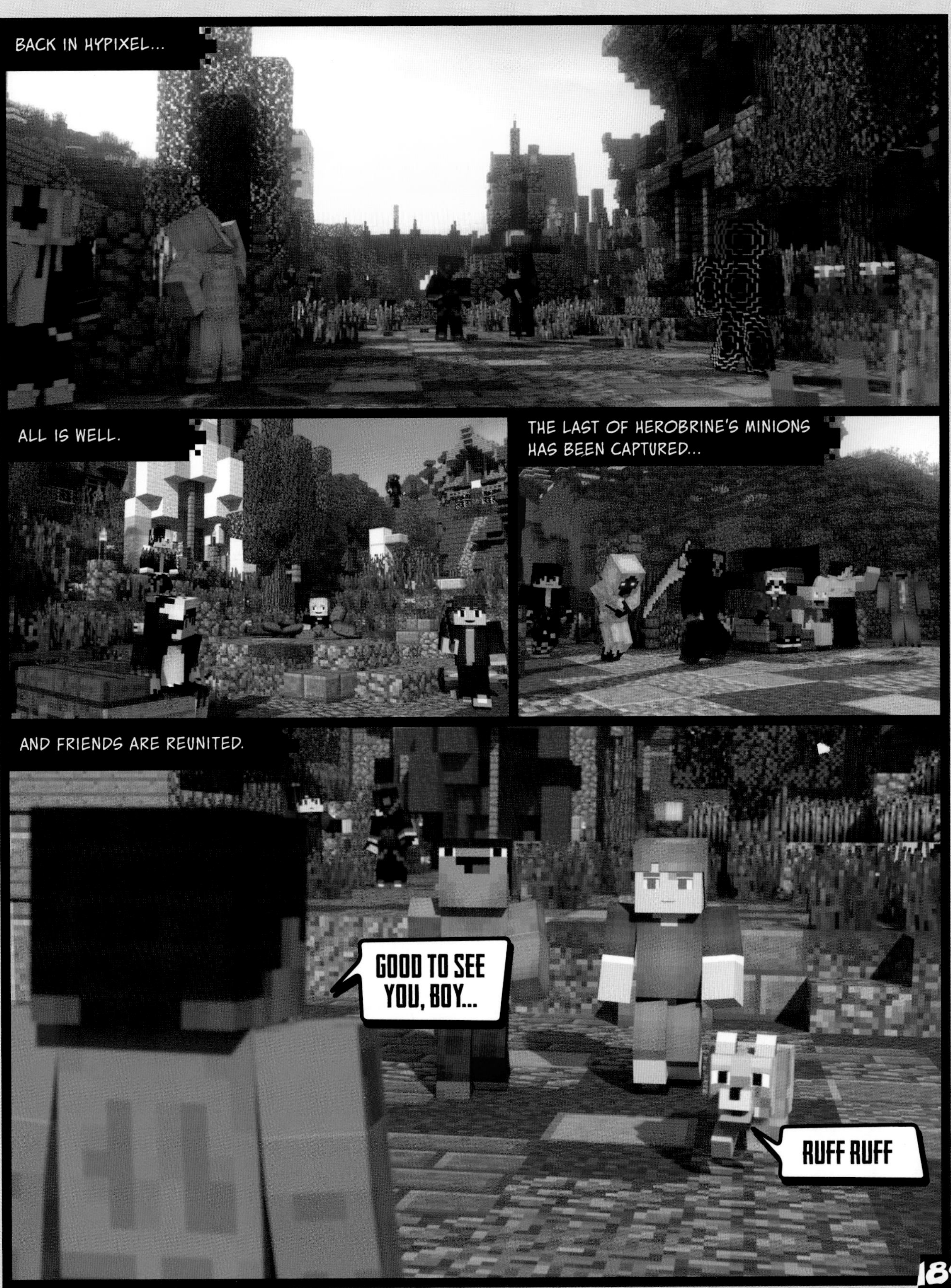
BACK IN HYPIXEL...
ALL IS WELL.
THE LAST OF HEROBRINE'S MINIONS HAS BEEN CAPTURED...
AND FRIENDS ARE REUNITED.
GOOD TO SEE YOU, BOY...
RUFF RUFF

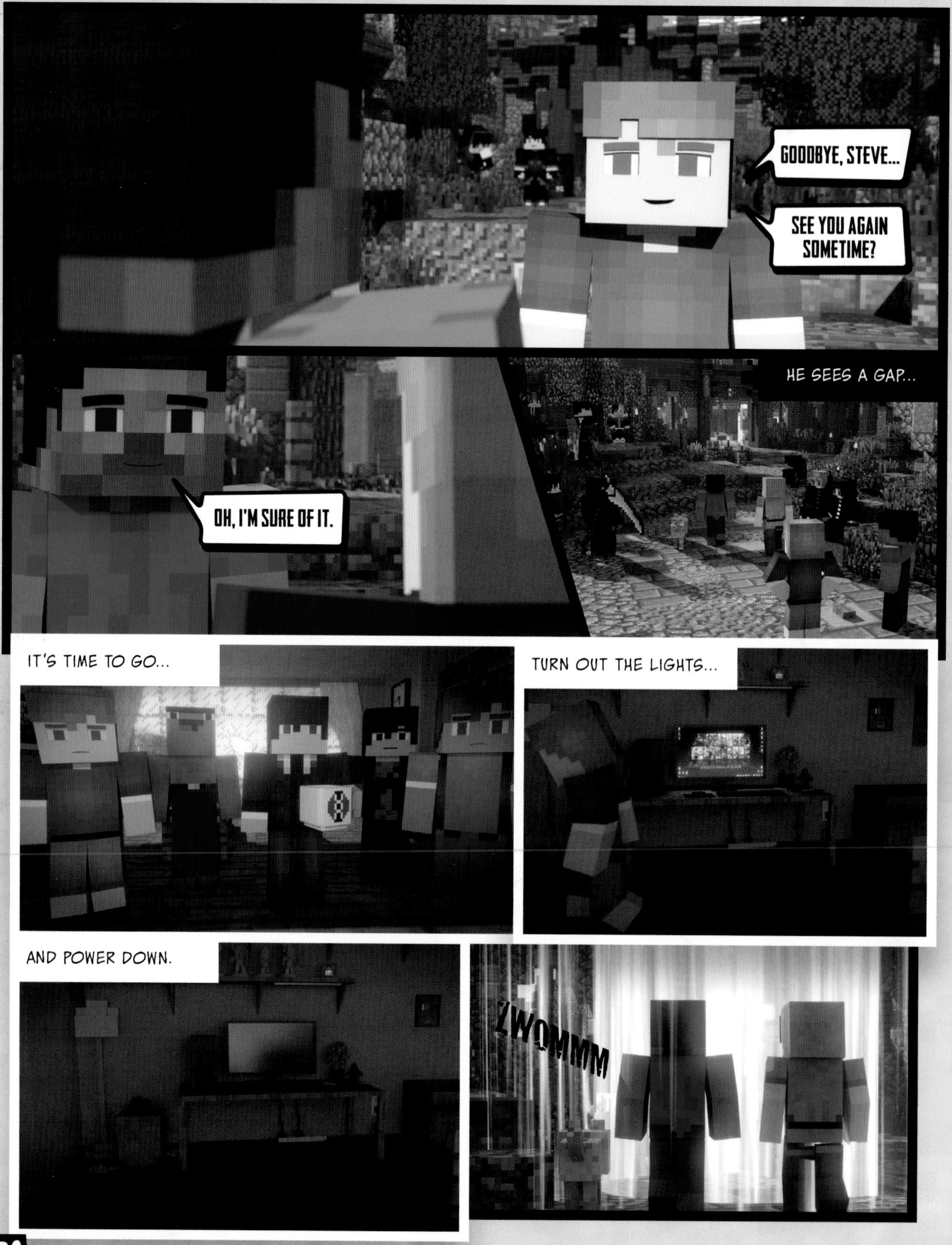
GOODBYE, STEVE...
SEE YOU AGAIN SOMETIME?
OH, I'M SURE OF IT.
HE SEES A GAP...
IT'S TIME TO GO...
TURN OUT THE LIGHTS...
AND POWER DOWN.
ZWOMMM

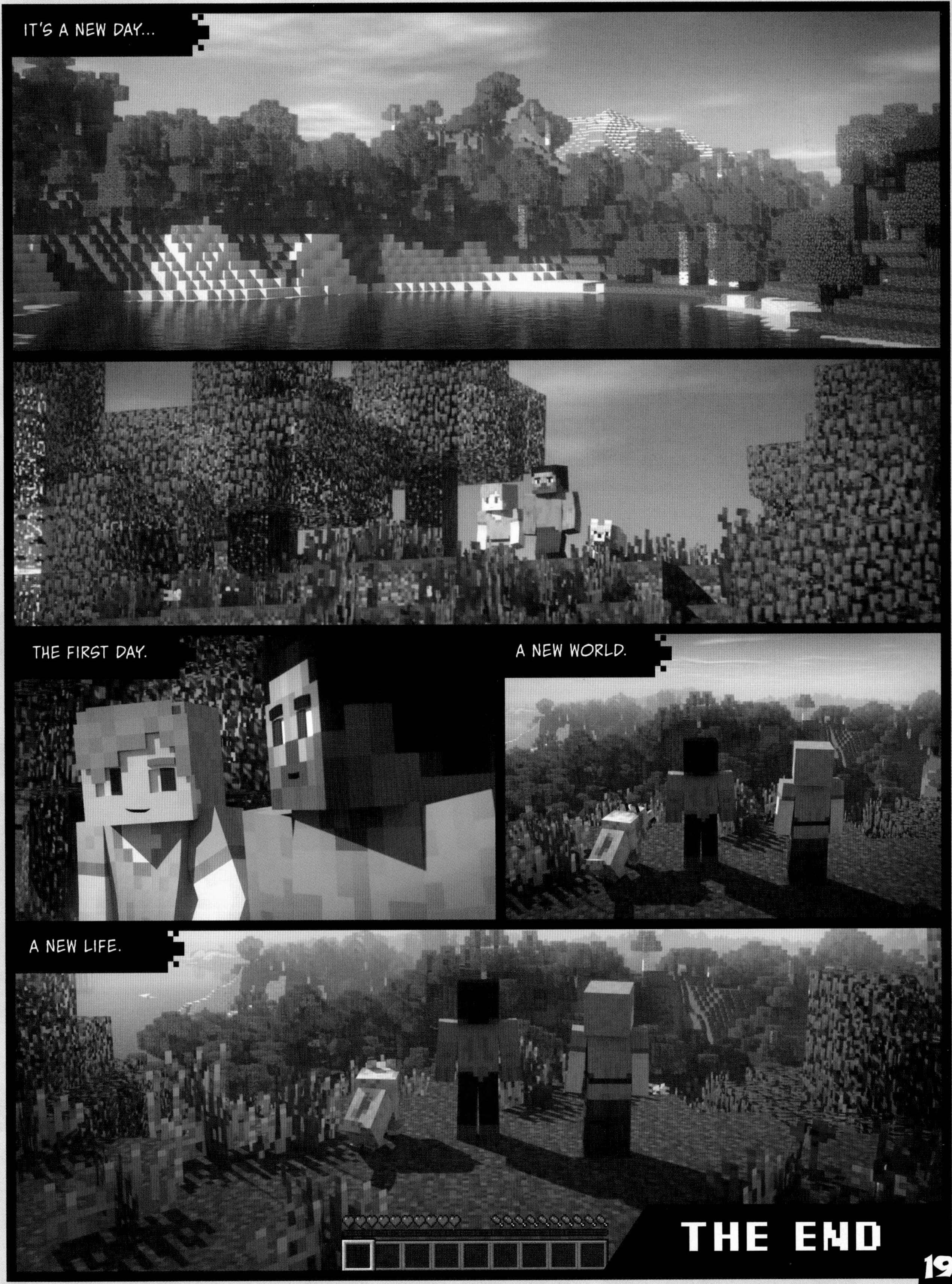
IT'S A NEW DAY...
THE FIRST DAY.
A NEW WORLD.
A NEW LIFE.
THE END